Tara Kane

Also by George Markstein

The Cooler

Tara Kane

George Markstein

STEIN AND DAY/*Publishers*/New York

Without Jacqui Lyons there could be
no Tara. She conducted the orchestra,
directed the scene, and edited the words.
She was the inspiration.

GM

First published in 1978
Copyright © 1978 by Marjacq Scripts Ltd
All rights reserved
Designed by Ed Kaplin
Printed in the United States of America
Stein and Day/*Publishers*/Scarborough House,
Briarcliff Manor, N.Y. 10510

Library of Congress Cataloging in Publication Data

Markstein, George.
Tara Kane.

I. Title.
PZ4.M3478Tar 1978   [PR6063.A644]   823′.9′14
ISBN 0-8128-2474-1   77-91613

To the Captain's Lady
and
Jefferson Randolph Smith
Legends in their own lifetimes

It was the year Queen Victoria celebrated her Diamond Jubilee and William McKinley took the oath as the twenty-fifth President of the United States. Air conditioning was patented, the electron was discovered, and the cause of malaria isolated.

In Europe, Oscar Wilde was imprisoned in Reading Gaol, Toulouse-Lautrec immortalized whores in Paris, and Spain's prime minister was assassinated by an anarchist. In Vienna, Freud was delving into the mysteries of sex. Stalin was sixteen, and Anthony Eden was born. A schoolboy called Adolf Hitler learned the three Rs. Turkey defeated Greece in a thirty-day war.

Across the Pacific, Japan went on the gold standard, and Gauguin painted his island beauties in Tahiti.

It was the year of the Klondike Gold Rush.

It was 1897.

Tara Kane

PROLOGUE

She made a strikingly attractive mourner. Black enhanced Tara Kane; it silhouetted her slim figure and complemented her deep auburn hair. Under the dark veil, tears ran down her pale cheeks, which occasionally she dabbed with a handkerchief. Her generous mouth, which like her large oval green eyes reflected her moods, turned down at the corners. Hers was a private grief she could share with no one and all the sadder for its solitude.

The funeral of her nine-month-old daughter had taken place ten days earlier, and the gravedigger, who was scooping out fresh earth nearby, remembered her clearly. It had been a brief, austere burial with only two people present, the woman in black and the minister. There had been no other mourners. No family. No husband. No one. Afterward, her head bowed, she had walked off alone, and the gravedigger's eyes had followed her as he wondered who the sad, elegant, lone woman might be.

Now she was back, staring at the tiny grave, again alone, lost in her own thoughts.

How forlorn Gabrielle's grave appeared among the other forty thousand tombs in San Francisco's Laurel Hill Cemetery. As inconsequential as the small bunch of flowers she now bent down and placed on the ground that covered the tiny coffin.

For a moment she knelt silent, her eyes blurred with tears, her heart heavy.

Then, gathering her cloak around her, she stood up, and the gravedigger watched her walk off among the pines and oaks and bending willows. After a while he shrugged and went back to his work.

Tara looked back only once. At the gate of the cemetery she stopped, her eyes searching among the rows of graves as she tried to spot for the last time where, in the distance, Gabie lay. But the plot was already hidden from sight.

She sighed. Tomorrow she would be gone, and there would be no one to visit the little grave. She turned, raised her head high, and walked out of the cemetery, her face set with determination.

What she was about to do was the most insane decision of her life, but for her there was no other course.

1

CHAPTER ONE

Tara had hired a hack to take her and her cabin trunk to the ship but, once through the dock gates, movement was impossible.

Across a sea of heads, she could see the *North Fork*, a shabby-looking steamer, smoking from its three stacks and, even from this distance, sadly in need of paint. She looked what she was, a seedy tramp steamer, rusty and battered, more suited for the breaker's yard than a voyage to Alaska.

"Can't go no further," announced the cabbie with finality. He jumped down and started manhandling Tara's trunk. "You'll have to take it from here, miss."

He dumped the trunk on the sidewalk, then held out his hand for the fare.

The gangway of the *North Fork* seemed inaccessible.

"How am I going to manage?" Tara asked the cabbie despairingly.

"That's your problem," he replied, unfeeling. He jumped back into his hack and cracked the whip. Slowly, he edged his way out of the dock, leaving Tara standing. It was hopeless for her to try to move the trunk herself. She couldn't even push it along, let alone carry it. None of the hundreds of jostling, pushing people took the slightest notice of her. "Klondike or Bust" someone had chalked on a warehouse wall, and that seemed to be the goal of all of them.

"Will you help me with my luggage, please?" appealed Tara to a man standing near her. He gave her a blank look.

She came near to panicking. She could visualize herself still trapped in this madhouse when the *North Fork* cast off in three hours' time. The ship sounded its steam whistle imperiously, the shrillness drowning even the hubbub of the dockside.

In the shadow of a warehouse, two men started fighting. One fell, and the other kept kicking him but no one intervened. Nearby, a cart overturned, spilling bags of dried beans on the cobbles. Somebody pushed Tara. She almost fell headlong, but she was too hemmed in actually to go down.

"Whoa!" said a man she was flung against. "Take it easy."

He steadied her and smiled sympathetically. He was a large, muscular man and looked like a sailor.

"Oh please," Tara gasped, "can you get my trunk through to the ship?"

"You sailing on *that*?" He shook his head. "Jesus!"

"I'll pay you five dollars."

She knew she was throwing her money away, but she was so near now that nothing was going to stop her.

"Let's try it," he said, picking up the trunk with a grunt and hoisting it on his shoulder.

It was easier said than done. Progress along the pier was blocked not only by the dense mob but by drays and wagons piled high with mountains of luggage and stores, huge crates and cases, even pens of sheep and horses.

Slowly, the man began to force his way through the crowd. He shoved aside anyone who stood in his path, ignoring kicks and curses. Tara followed and tried not to see the variety of harassed, furious, angry, worried, desperate, tear-stained faces that kept flashing in front of her. People dug her in the ribs, stepped on her feet, kicked her, jostled her. Grimly, she kept a firm hold on her valise and purse and forged on. She had lost sight of the man, but she could still see her trunk moving ahead.

Suddenly people started jostling and pushing in another direction, to the edge of the pier where a body was being hauled out of the water. Tara had a glimpse of a man's white face and rag-doll body, dripping water, being unceremoniously dumped in a wagon.

Then, from behind her, came shouts of protest and howls of rage. The mob started jostling her even harder. She heard the cracking of a whip, and then a wagon began to force its way through, the driver cursing and furiously lashing people who blocked him.

He managed to clear a path, and from the wagon came a new ugly sound, the snapping of angry dogs. Tara saw dozens of dogs chained together, barking and snarling as they were driven through to the ship.

She got behind the wagon and followed it through the crowd to the gangway.

The *North Fork* loomed over the pierhead, already crowds of people lining the rails. They must have got there hours ago, she thought.

At the gangway, the man put her trunk down. "That's it," he said. "The rest is up to you."

"I'm so grateful to you," she said, pressing five dollars into his hand. "Thank you. Thank you so much."

"Going to the Yukon?" he asked, smiling wryly. "Good luck! Hope you survive." And then he was engulfed by the sea of humanity.

Close up, the *North Fork* appeared even more squalid; as she eyed the soot-encrusted steamer and the villainous-looking seamen who blocked the path up the gangway she was filled with dismay. One of them, a red-faced brawny man, kept yelling, "Clear off! Ship's loaded to the scuppers. We're full, damn you." He lashed out with a rope's end. But those at the front of the crowd, who had got this far, continued pushing forward.

"Where's the captain?" Tara yelled to the red-faced seaman, kicking a man who was blocking her path. She forced her way past him, braving his curses.

"What do you want?" snarled the seaman.

"I'm a passenger." She tried to get nearer. "My trunk's over there."

"Nobody comes aboard," the man growled. "Don't you understand English? We're loaded up. No more room."

"You have for me," Tara cried.

She held up the precious ticket for which she had waited for hours on two successive days in a mile-long line of Alaska-bound prospectors all besieging the shipping line for a passage north before the freeze-up. Even then she had been unable to get a ticket for Skagway. She had booked to Dyea as a last resort.

"We're not embarking any more passengers," the man said. "You're too late."

"But I've got my passage," Tara protested incredulously.

"Traveling on your own?" the man leered.

She stared at him perplexed.

"I . . . I'm joining my husband." She almost bit off her tongue. Why should she explain anything?

"Oh sure," he nodded, grinning unpleasantly. "Maybe I can fix you up. For a little extra."

Tara looked at him with distaste. All she wanted was to get on that deck, and it was only a few yards away. If it needed a bribe to shift this ruffian, so be it. She took some money out of her purse.

He laughed. "Come on, sister. Cough up. You'll earn it on board ten times over. You ought to make it easy."

She flushed but, without a word, gave him another twenty dollars. He shrugged.

"OK, I'll get you on board." He turned and shouted to a sailor. "Hey, Rusky, get this dame's junk on board and hurry. She'll pay you extra."

Tara followed him up the long gangway. Each step she took was leading her into a frightening unknown. Yet she felt strangely elated by her achievement so far. Despite all the odds, somehow she'd got a ticket, had made it onto the boat, and very soon she would be on her way.

On deck, passengers and sailors kept pushing past; people were

4

arguing; every inch of space seemed to be occupied. Neighing horses reared and kicked in wooden pens that had been erected as temporary stables. Bales of feed were stacked high. Rows of dog cages were roped to the deck, the animals inside snarling and snapping. Overhead swayed crates and other cargo being hoisted aboard. The sight of the crowd jamming the dockside, a sea of faces staring up, still pushing toward the gangway, all trying to get on this already overcrowded ship, was frightening. If any more people came aboard, the ship would split apart.

"I want to go to my cabin," Tara demanded curtly.

Rusky, who had put down her trunk, scowled. "The captain will fix you up."

Tara bristled. "Where do I find him?"

"Over there." Rusky nodded at a man standing near a lifeboat surveying the confusion with a look of boredom.

"You wait here," Tara ordered.

"Hey, lady," Rusky shouted after her.

She stopped and turned. "Yes?"

He pointed at the trunk. "You owe me."

"Here you are," Tara said and gave him two dollars. He didn't thank her.

She walked up to the captain. He had a walrus mustache, and his eyes were set close together. Unconcerned about the chaos on his ship, the restlessness of the animals wedged tightly together, the pushing and shoving on deck, he leaned against the railing and puffed at his pipe.

"Captain?" Tara asked imperiously.

The man exhaled a cloud of smoke and nodded.

"Yes ma'am, Captain Swain," he said, taking the pipe out of his mouth. "What's the trouble?" he asked lazily, and the familiar way he eyed her made Tara's hackles rise.

"I want to know where my cabin is," she shouted. "I have a reservation."

"Unattached?"

Her eyes blazed. "I beg your pardon?"

"All by yourself?" There was something insulting about his manner. He had seen the wedding ring on her finger. "There'll be a surcharge. One hundred dollars."

"Don't be ridiculous," she exclaimed. "I've paid my passage."

"Ladies on their own," and the way he said "ladies" made it sound an insult, "are a problem. Not easy to fit females into this vessel. We're not built for it. You can see for yourself."

5

"I've already had to bribe one of your men to get on board, and now you . . ."

"My men don't take bribes," Swain cut in, looking her straight in the eye. "And I don't take kindly to accusations against my crew. If you don't like this ship, get off it. I'll have your luggage taken off."

Tara was outraged. "Damn you!" she cried, so fiercely that even he seemed shaken. "If you put me ashore, I'll call the police. I'll have you arrested, the whole lot of you! I'll get the harbor authorities. You won't sail without me, I promise you, Captain Swain. I'll see you never sail again."

He sucked his pipe and then asked, quite mildly, "What's your name?"

"Mrs. Kane."

"Well, Mrs. Kane, there's no need to fly off the handle. Tell you what I'll do. I can see how anxious you are to ship with us, and I guess we can squeeze you in. The only question is, ma'am, do you have the hundred bucks?"

By now she knew she had no choice. She wouldn't be able to get another ship for weeks, not in the middle of the Gold Rush with men fighting for a passage to the Klondike. After what she had been through already, nothing was going to persuade her to get off this ship, not until it landed at Dyea.

"All right, Captain Swain," Tara agreed through gritted teeth. "A hundred dollars." Resentfully, she counted out the money. "Here," she said, almost flinging it at him.

"Welcome aboard, Mrs. Kane," he smiled, stuffing the dollars into his pocket. "I'll have you shown to your quarters."

"I want my own cabin," Tara warned. "I know the ship's over-crowded, but I want a cabin to myself. First class," she added. "I've paid enough."

"First class it is," the Captain said.

She was a little mollified. The man was a crook, the whole ship was a floating thieves' den, the crew racketeers, she had paid through the nose, but at least she would have a place to herself on the long voyage.

Swain ordered a seaman over. "Take this lady and her trunk to Cabin Four," he commanded.

Tara turned and followed the man.

"Hope you have an enjoyable voyage," the Captain called after her.

She did not look around, but she could sense the mockery in his eyes.

The stench in the bowels of the ship was nauseating. As Tara followed the sailor below, her first unexpected whiff of it made her

6

throat tighten, and she pulled out a handkerchief and held it to her nose to stop herself from being sick. Here, on the lower deck, as everywhere else, soiled sawdust and wood shavings were strewn on the floor. They soaked up refuse, pools of urine, and, when seasickness hit the passengers, their vomit. The smell was so overpowering that, for a moment, Tara felt faint.

Everywhere was black with coal dust, a permanent reminder of the *North Fork*'s previous role as a coal carrier. In her hasty conversion for the suddenly profitable Alaska run, she had never been properly cleaned out.

"Here you are, Cabin Four," the seaman said, stopping before a door and unceremoniously kicking it open.

Tara stepped into what she had imagined would be her own cabin. She had visualized a small room with a bunk, maybe a table and chair, a porthole letting in the daylight, perhaps some curtains. Instead it was what had apparently been some kind of storeroom converted into a rough, ready-made dormitory for four people. Some of the wood-work was not painted, and, even in daylight, the only illumination came from two oil lamps swinging from the low ceiling. It was shabby, rough, and cramped, and it stank.

"This can't be right," Tara gasped, as the seaman dragged in her trunk. "I'm traveling first-class. Please get the stewardess."

The sailor straightened up. A broad grin spread across his face. "Stewardess, ma'am? We ain't got such a thing on this tub. And we ain't got first-class either. Unless this is it."

Slowly the reality of what she had got herself into was becoming hideously clear to Tara. He could see her distress.

"You're lucky, ma'am," he told her, trying to sound encouraging. "You got a bunk, and there's only four in here, being all ladies. The men are stacked ten to a cabin half this size. Those that have a cabin. We got three hundred passengers and sleeping berths for only half that. So maybe you got first-class." He closed the door softly, leaving an alarmed Tara looking around her new home.

The other occupants had evidently already moved in. Their clothes were strewn about, and Tara's nostrils made their first acquaintance with a new odor: a clinging, sickly, cheap perfume. The dresses and underwear that lay everywhere were flamboyant and garish, and certainly the three ladies who would be sharing with her did not regard tidiness as a virtue. Considering that they could also have only just arrived, it was amazing how untidy they had already managed to make their quarters.

One bunk did not seem to have been claimed. It was stuck in the corner, a temporary structure, and Tara had difficulty in squeezing through to it.

A thin straw palliasse served as a mattress. There was no pillow, and the single blanket was so revolting that the very thought of it covering her made Tara squirm.

The cramped narrowness of the cabin was oppressive. The dingy light and the cloying odors made Tara decide that, apart from sleeping, she would stay as few hours as possible in here.

From outside, there was laughter, and then the door flew open. The two women who entered the cabin stopped still when they saw Tara.

"What have we here?" asked the taller of the two. She was blonde, in her twenties, her face smothered with thick make-up that was as crude as her ugly features. She wore a low-cut dress out of which bulged gross, flabby breasts. "What the hell are you doing in our cabin?"

Her companion was fat, and her eye shadow and red lipstick did nothing to enhance her piglike sweaty face. The top of her dress was undone, and she carried a half-empty bottle of gin.

"I'll be sharing with you," Tara said, swallowing hard. She could feel herself paling at the very sight of them. "They've given me this cabin."

"Well!" said the blonde. "What do you think of that, Flo?"

Flo looked Tara up and down; then she shook her head.

"You'd better find somewhere else, honey," she hiccuped. "We're full up. There's no room."

Tara was at the end of her tether. "Believe me, I don't want to be here either, but it's just too bad," she said, sitting down on her bunk.

The fat one moved forward. "I wouldn't bother to make myself comfortable, dearie," she said, glaring down at Tara, arms akimbo.

"Yeah," agreed the other. "We don't want anybody else in here."

"Well you'd better complain to the Captain then," Tara suggested coldly. "I'm staying. I won't get in anybody's way, but I'm not moving."

The blonde sneered, then raised her hand. For a moment Tara thought she was going to hit her.

"Wait a minute, Maggie," Flo interjected. "Give the lady a chance." Again the word "lady" sounded like an insult.

Flo pushed Maggie to one side and offered Tara the bottle. "Have a swig, honey," she invited.

Tara recoiled. The idea of drinking from a bottle that had been in Flo's mouth was repellent. She shook her head. "I won't just now, thank you."

Flo nodded, as if that fitted in with her opinion of Tara. "What's your name?" she asked.

8

"Tara Kane."

Flo had spotted the wedding ring. "Married, are you?"

"I'm sailing to join my husband."

Flo sat down on the bunk beside Tara. It creaked under her weight.

"Well, Tara, you got to understand," she explained. "There's seven of us using this cabin."

"Seven!" Tara echoed, horrified. "But there are only four bunks."

Maggie shrieked with laughter.

"Shut up," Flo snapped. She turned back to Tara. "You don't follow. Only me, Maggie, and Belle sleep here, but us and our friends will be using it. Connie, Lola, Pearl, and Frenchy, see? Seven of us."

"But there's hardly enough room for the four of us!" Tara looked around the tiny space.

"Oh sweet Jesus. I tell you she's dumb," Maggie sighed.

Flo ignored her. "I'm trying to explain to you, Tara, nice as can be, that we need this shack for business. Day and night. We got to earn our passage, honey."

Maggie cackled.

"Now take your things and get out of here. Leave us to it." She pinched Tara's arm. "I'm sure a nice lady like you won't have no trouble finding a cozy little corner somewhere in this floating slum."

Tara knew that if she gave up these few feet of space she was lost. "I can see your problem," she said quietly "and I'll do my best to keep out of your, er, hair. But I've got to have somewhere to sleep and this is where I stay."

Flo put her bottle down and studied Tara.

"OK," she said. "But don't say I didn't warn you, *Mrs.* Kane. The girls may not take it kindly. Nothing personal, you understand."

"Oh I don't know," Maggie sneered. "I don't think I like the stuck-up bitch." She mimicked Tara. " 'I don't think I will just now, thank you.' Snobby little prude."

Tara bit her lip. She was not going to allow herself to be provoked. Instead she said with as much dignity as she could muster, "All right, Flo. I think we understand each other. Thank you for making it so clear. I will try to cause you and your friends as little trouble as possible. I shall only be using my bunk at night. To sleep in."

Flo looked at her, amazed. Her previous experiences on the Barbary Coast had taught her that such confrontations usually exploded into hair-pulling, face-scratching fights. But here, in this small cabin, this woman was being punctiliously polite.

She reached for her bottle and took another gulp of gin. Then she stood up.

"Let's go and take a look around, Maggie," she said.

Maggie still couldn't take it in. "The bitch's yellow," she hissed.

To Tara's surprise, Flo turned on her friend. "Just leave it," she said. "She knows the score."

Before they left the cabin, Flo called out, "Be seeing you, *Mrs. Kane.*"

Tara sat staring at the wall feeling utterly miserable. The prospect of long weeks on this ghastly ship had been bad enough, but how was she going to be able to cope with seven whores in a floating brothel the size of a small storeroom?

She sighed. "One day at a time, somehow I'll learn to live with everything."

She went up on deck to get some much-needed fresh air, but the confusion and the noise were as great as ever.

The ship's whistles shrieked, and underneath her feet the engines began to thump. "All visitors ashore," yelled Captain Swain through a megaphone from the bridge, but it was a pointless gesture. No one could have got on or off the boat. The deck was now stacked so high with cargo that even the forward view from the bridge was obscured by the piles of crates and stacks of luggage. The passengers elbowed each other for a space at the rails, all seeking one final glimpse of the shore.

The mooring ropes were released, the engines started to throb faster, and then, suddenly, amid a great cheer, the *North Fork* slowly began to move. A thousand hats and handkerchiefs waved below on the dock, and here on deck people were crying into the wind "Goodbye" and "I'll be back soon," but it was all lost in the noise of sirens, the rumbling chains, the ringing of the engine-room telegraph, the shouts and commands, and the pounding of the engines. Ashore mothers were holding up young children for a last look, and some men had climbed onto poles and cranes and were waving from them.

Gradually the *North Fork* started to edge away from the dockside, from San Francisco, out toward the Golden Gate, toward the ocean, toward Alaska.

Tara stayed for a long time watching the docks and harbor front gradually recede. Other people had moved away from the railings, but she remained, a silent, lone figure, looking back at the shore.

Her elation had gone. Not even the thought that she had started the long journey to find Daniel, that she was actually on her way to him, could ease her melancholy.

Tara's eyes grew misty as she stared into the distance. She opened her purse to look for a handkerchief; she had cried enough.

In her bag was the little compass Daniel had given her. "Think of me, look at the needle," he had said. "It will always point to where I am."

As Tara held it in her hand the tiny needle quivered but, as always, its direction was unerringly straight. Northward. To the Klondike. To Daniel. To the future.

CHAPTER TWO

Terence Oliver Makepeace always described his daughter as a willful romantic, an illogical, headstrong idealist. But the pride and joy with which he gazed at her proved that she was also the most precious person in the world. Dorothy, his wife, had died of pneumonia early in Tara's life, and her memory of her mother was of a very beautiful, golden-haired woman with a porcelain complexion, looking much the same as the miniature mounted in a silver locket her father had given her for a fourteenth birthday present.

Dr. Makepeace, as he called himself, was, in fact, a salesman of patent medicines and the sole representative in the State of Ohio of Dr. Fitzgerald's Kidney Pills. The couple had an English background but had settled in Cleveland long before their only child was born. After her mother's death, Tara grew up in a large, gloomy house, looked after by a kindly but somewhat frightening governess who believed staunchly in discipline. But even at an early age, Tara's forceful personality was clearly established.

When she was twelve, her father sent her to a boarding school where a vain attempt was made to turn her into a prim Victorian miss. When, because of financial pressures, Dr. Makepeace took her away, Tara was delighted, even though the dilapidated new house to which she returned underlined her father's penurious circumstances.

Dr. Makepeace came to rely on Tara completely. He could no longer afford a housekeeper; so she arranged his appointments, cooked for and looked after him, all the time increasingly aware of his dwindling resources and failing health.

In 1894, at an old school-friend's party, Tara had met Daniel. She had been immediately captivated by his warm personality, fieriness, and sense of fun, his good looks. He had danced with her and only her at that party and had made her feel as if she were the only pretty girl there. Daniel was her first beau, and he was everything she had ever desired. He was tall, athletically built, and handsome, with light brown hair and brown eyes that always seemed to laugh. He was also ambitious, but, most important of all, he loved her.

When Dr. Makepeace died later that year, Tara's life began to revolve around Daniel. He took over all the funeral arrangements and helped her dispose of her father's debts. When he proposed to her, she had no hesitation in accepting him.

Daniel was driven by a restlessness to better himself, and they were both idealistic enough to want to realize their dreams. He wanted to give Tara everything: magnificent clothes, a grand house, gifts, jewelry. But his salary as a ledger clerk allowed for none of these things. They decided to move to San Francisco, where he believed better opportunities existed for go-ahead young men. Six months after they had settled in a small apartment in Fulton Street, Gabie had been born, and she and Daniel had thought her the most beautiful baby they had ever seen.

As a mother and wife Tara had felt fulfilled; to love and be loved gave her total happiness. She had believed that her life would continue along that idyllic path. But then the Gold Rush had arrived in San Francisco.

The excitement swept the city like wildfire. Daniel had returned home that fateful evening, his eyes bright, bursting with stories of the gold just waiting to be picked up in the Klondike. He became obsessed by it. He never stopped talking about the prospectors who had struck it rich, and the newspapers served only to fan his enthusiasm.

Tara was bewildered. She had never known Daniel like this before, so completely consumed by an idea. He had hardly been to work since the *Excelsior* had docked, so preoccupied had he been with talking to the new millionaires who had disembarked laden with sackfuls of gold. It had unnerved Tara because she knew, long before he told her, that Daniel was going to join the Klondike Gold Rush.

All that was history. Reality was life aboard the *North Fork*, which grew grimmer with every passing day. The weather was rough, which would have been unpleasant enough on a well-appointed liner; but on this evil-smelling hulk, with the passengers packed like sardines, it was misery. The overloaded *North Fork* had difficulty in riding a storm, and every wave caused her to roll unmercifully.

The ship's facilities were nonexistent. Toilets were buckets, and each odor that hit Tara's nostrils was more offensive than the last. Washing had to be done in tubs of sea water so dirty that Tara soon learned to forgo her personal standards.

Only when she stood on deck and the salt water swept over the rails, dousing the decks and all on them, was there a moment of tangy, freezing freshness. It soaked her, but it was clean and pure after the filth below decks.

She gave up undressing to go to bed because she was too often awakened in the middle of the night by the grunts and giggles from the three other berths where the whores were conducting their business. Bodies intertwined in the dim light, and Tara would long remember the unpleasant sight of Flo's fat belly and her huge melonlike breasts squashing down on some hairy man who was noisily sucking her nipples.

Then she would flee from the cabin, wearily sneaking back when all was quiet. Gradually she resorted to sleeping in her bunk during the day and walking around the deck at night, even though that was also nerve-racking. Time after time Tara was scared by the men who stood in the shadows, silently following her with their eyes. Rough hands would reach for her out of the dark, and she would run for a better-lit part of the ship.

Her experience of the honesty of Captain Swain and his crew made Tara abandon her plan to place her money in the care of the ship's purser. That would be tantamount to throwing it to the fish. She was fast learning the rules of survival on Swain's ship. She considered locking the money in her trunk, but locks weren't sacred aboard the *North Fork*. Finally, she secreted the roll of bills in a little pouch, which she pinned to the inside of her bodice, where it stayed day and night.

Flo, whose sharp eyes missed nothing, noticed the pouch when Tara was changing her dress one day.

"What do you keep in there, the family jewels?" she asked, half joking. Behind the whore's false smile Tara thought she saw a greedy look.

"Nothing," shrugged Tara, "just a couple of trinkets. Not worth a cent, but they bring me good luck."

She could feel herself blushing. She was not a good liar. Flo exchanged a look with Maggie but said nothing more.

Mealtimes on the *North Fork* were among the most disgusting moments of the voyage. The saloon also served as the dining room, even though it could seat only thirty people at one time. There were three hundred to be fed, and Swain had arranged a kind of rough schedule, divided into half a dozen sittings, which still left scores of people to fight for food. Each meal became a succession of quarrels and arguments, often ending in blows.

Even those who succeeded in finding a crate to sit on at one of the rough tables lost their appetites when they saw what was slung in front of them. Stew and hash were the order of the day; whichever it was it tasted and looked foul.

The first time Tara went to eat, the sight of the saloon festooned with carcasses hung from hooks in the ceiling made her want to run. When she sat down, a side of beef kept bumping its fatty skin against her. She rushed out, and for several days could not eat anything.

Then hunger became too much. She felt weak; she had to eat something. She could have bought liquor from the other passengers; there were many people with bottles of whisky to sell, but food was at a premium. She nerved herself to face the ordeal and started lining up for a seat.

Pools of hardened greasy gravy and dried scraps of meat from the previous sittings littered her table. A plate of congealed stew was slung at her, some of it slopping over, but despite her hunger pangs she could not bring herself to eat.

Sitting next to her was a bespectacled man in a crumpled city suit. Behind the glasses, his eyes were blue, very clear and alert. He had two pencils stuck in the pocket of his jacket. He pushed his own plate away, then gave her a sympathetic smile.

"Awful, isn't it?" He had a distinct foreign accent.

Tara nodded.

He appeared to be in his late thirties and had a trim mustache and small sideburns. Tara liked him immediately, especially the laugh-lines around his eyes and mouth.

"I wish I could force it down," she said, shuddering. "I simply can't."

"I don't think we need go hungry," the man said. "Follow me."

On deck, Tara took a deep breath.

"I know," commiserated the man. "I feel like that myself. Now close your eyes."

She studied him for a second, then shut her eyes.

"Open them!" he commanded. He sounded authoritative, but he was grinning when she looked at him.

In his hand were two apples.

"One for you, one for me," he said, holding out one of the green, shiny apples. They were the most beautiful sight Tara had seen in the last four days.

"Oh no, I couldn't," she protested. "You've only got two."

Fruit and fresh water were the two greatest luxuries.

"You're as hungry as I am," he insisted. "Please."

She bit into the hard apple and it tasted delicious. She never would have imagined that an ordinary apple could make such a wonderful treat.

"You're very kind," Tara said. He munched his apple hungrily, but

14

his eyes enjoyed her delight. "Thank you very much, Mr. . . . Mr. . . ."

"Ernst Hart," he announced, gave a little bow, and clicked his heels. Then he went red.

"Forgive me. I still cannot remember that in America one does not do that."

He finished his apple and tossed the core over the side. "You have not told me your name," he said, a little reproachfully.

"Mrs. Kane."

"Oh. You are traveling with your husband?"

She shook her head. "No. I am joining him."

"In the Klondike?" He seemed surprised. "By yourself?"

Tara had to laugh at the way he raised his eyebrows.

"Mr. Hart, this is 1897, not the Middle Ages. Women can look after themselves quite well, you know."

"Really?" he sniffed. Then he smiled. "You must understand. I am from Germany, and there a woman's place is in the kitchen and the nursery. Not on a ship like this."

"Well, that's another thing you'll have to find out about America."

"Why did you not go with your husband? It would have been simpler."

Tara didn't answer. She didn't really want to talk about it. Yet, he seemed genuinely interested, his blue eyes regarding her steadily.

"I . . . I had to look after our baby," she explained falteringly.

He waited, saying nothing.

"She died. She had meningitis." Tara was startled by the matter-of-fact way she had said it. "It was so sudden, after he'd left." She looked up at him. "He doesn't even know."

"I'm sorry," Hart murmured gently. He could see how it affected her; so he changed the subject. "Your husband . . . he has found gold?"

"I haven't heard but, knowing Daniel, I'm sure he's doing well."

"Good." Hart seemed pleased by her confidence. "I hope he becomes a millionaire." He paused. "Tell me. What made him go?"

"What makes any of them go?" asked Tara a little wistfully. He followed her glance. All kinds crowded the decks, clerks in city clothes, roughnecks from the slums, fresh-faced students, graybeards from the forests, cowpokes from ranches, young men with soft hands, hard-bitten adventurers; each one counting the days on the *North Fork* until he would step ashore at Dyea and begin the trail.

"Gold fever," went on Tara.

Hart frowned. "He just left you and the baby?"

"It wasn't like that," Tara said firmly. "He provided for us, and he did what he thought was right. I wouldn't have dreamed of standing in

15

his way. If it hadn't been for the baby, I would have gone with him then." Her lips trembled for a moment, then she pulled herself together.

"Your're very clever, Mr. Hart. You've got me talking about myself. ... I'd like to know what you're doing here. Are you off to make a fortune?"

"No, Mrs. Kane," Hart said. "I'm not interested in gold. I go looking for people."

He saw her puzzled expression.

"I am a photographer. I go to write in pictures, not words. I wish to record this madness for posterity. What Matthew Brady did for your Civil War, I want to do for this Gold Rush, so that people will always be able to see what it was like."

He stopped, a little embarrassed. "It must seem very foolish. Here is everybody out to become a millionaire, and all I want to do is take photographs."

"Not at all," Tara replied "I think it sounds fascinating."

He glanced at her sharply. Then he nodded.

"Yes. I think perhaps you do understand."

"What brought you to America in the first place?"

He waved his hand around the deck. "This. Adventure. The New World. I come from a little German town called Rudesheim. On the Rhine. Have you heard of Rudesheim?"

She shook her head.

"It is wine country. Everything is wine. Hock for Queen Victoria. That is our claim to fame. I am not interested in growing grapes. I am the odd sheep out, you see."

"Odd man out," Tara said.

"Correct. After Heidelberg, I decided to make my profession photography. Two years ago, I took the official photographs of the opening of the Kiel Canal.

"Then I came to America, opened a studio, and took portraits," Hart continued, wrinkling his nose. "Portraits in Milwaukee, Mrs. Kane, are like portraits in Wiesbaden. Solid citizens looking pompous. Boring."

She smiled. In the nicest possible way, he could be a little pompous himself, she thought.

"When I heard of the Gold Rush, I packed my things and here I am."

He pulled out his watch. "Excuse me. I must see that everything is in order."

He had arranged, he explained, to store his equipment in the purser's office.

"I have to pay him twenty dollars a week so that it is safe. It is brigandry, I know, but without my camera, my plates, my chemicals, I am finished. So I check every few hours to make sure it is all there. He knows that if it is stolen he gets no more money. That is my insurance."

They saw a lot of each other after that. They walked together on the deck, and if they found the space they sat together and talked. Somewhere he had secreted a little hoard of food, and he had the knack of producing delicious tidbits for her, like a bar of chocolate or even a piece of cheese. Thanks to these, Tara was able to avoid the revolting food for much of the time.

Hart loved studying people. They would be strolling on the ship, and suddenly he would stop, his eyes focused like a lens on some character he had spotted. When Flo, Maggie, and one of their friends flounced by, Hart looked at them intrigued.

"*That's* what I want to photograph," he said, following the whores with his eyes.

"Surely not," Tara said.

"But they're all part of it," Hart explained. "When I get up there I want to photograph the street girls, the saloons, the gamblers. All of it is a part of history. Then, a hundred years from now, people will look at my pictures, and they'll feel they are there, with us."

Tara knew only of dignified photographers who wore frock coats and stood beside huge cameras carefully arranging groups on special occasions like marriages and christenings. This was something new to her.

"Pictures must be taken where and as things happen," Hart said. "I shall go out to the gold diggings, the brothels, the camps, the trails. My pictures will depict life as it really is."

He stopped. "You think me a donkey?" he asked shyly.

"Ass," corrected Tara gently.

"*Esel* is donkey," he said stubbornly. "No?"

"We say ass." She smiled at him. "And you're not. I hope I'll see your photographs one day."

"Really?" He was genuinely touched. "I will take a picture of you, Tara, in the Klondike. So that people will know there were women like you too."

"First, Ernst, we have to get there," she reminded him.

"What are you going to do when we do arrive?" asked Hart.

"Get to Skagway as quickly as possible."

"Is that where your husband is?"

She nodded. "He's prospecting somewhere around there."

17

Behind his glasses, Hart's eyes opened wide. "But my dear lady, there is no gold at Skagway. To find gold you have to go to the creeks, hundreds of miles to the north."

For a moment Tara was stunned. "I always thought . . ." she began, then stopped. "Are you sure?"

"I've never heard of gold being found anywhere else. But, maybe . . ."

"Well, Skagway's where he made for, and I shall find him," she declared confidently. "Believe me, I will."

"I do believe you, Tara," Hart said. "I can see you love him very much. To come all this way, to put up with this terrible journey . . ." He sighed and stared down at the ocean.

"One day," he said at last, "one day I will find a woman like you. Until then, I suppose, I have my camera. I live for picture taking."

"Of course you will, Ernst," Tara agreed, "and that woman will never want to take your work away from you."

Hart shook his head slightly, then patted Tara's hand. "I hope, dear Tara," he said. "I hope."

CHAPTER THREE

For Tara, the companionship of the German photographer became increasingly important. They would meet every day, almost by unspoken arrangement, and spend hours in each other's company. On the rare occasions when they weathered mealtimes, Hart stood with her in the unruly queues and helped her to get a place at a table.

Then, one morning, Hart seemed to be preoccupied. They stood watching the sea, but he said very little.

"What's the matter, Ernst?" Tara asked.

He glanced around nervously.

"I . . ." He stopped. Skinner, the first mate, was walking past.

"Let's take a walk on the other side," Hart said hurriedly, taking her arm and steering her away. They were in the stern of the ship when they finally stopped.

"Listen, Tara, I wasn't going to tell you this," he blurted out. Then he looked around cautiously once more to make sure no one was within earshot. "I don't want to frighten you."

Tara stiffened.

"What is it?" she asked apprehensively.

He hesitated. Then he said, "Everybody on the ship is in great danger. We may all be blown sky high at any moment."

"What do you mean?"

He lowered his voice. "Last night I couldn't find a place to sleep. Two roughnecks had taken my bunk, and there wasn't an inch of space left in the cabin—you know what it's like. I kept falling over people. There was no room either on deck or inside the saloon. At last I managed to squeeze into one of the cargo holds." Hart paused.

"Go on."

"It was pitch dark. So I struck a match. There was hardly enough room to breathe, but I saw stacks and stacks of wooden cases, a couple of hundred I'd judge. I took a closer look. They are all marked 'Danger—High Explosive.' Tara, we are sitting on hundreds of pounds of dynamite."

Tara stared at him. "My God," she whispered.

"You know what that means. Any time, day or night, the whole ship could explode. There's enough dynamite down there . . ." he gestured. "*Kaput*. Finish. Here," he said reaching into his hip pocket, producing a flask. "Have a sip. It'll warm you up."

Tara drank some. It burned her throat but made her blood move again. Hart took two long swigs.

"Of course, it is very illegal to carry explosives on a passenger ship. If the authorities find out, our Captain Swain will never command anything again. Anyway, somebody must have noticed me climbing into the hold. The next thing I knew, I was dragged out by Skinner and two seamen. Skinner told me the cargo area was off limits to passengers and if they found me in there again—well, he did not go into details."

"What can we do?"

"Nothing. On this ship Swain is the law. Who can we go to? Out here?" He shook his head. "We are trapped."

They both looked out at the ocean, where the occasional appearance of pieces of drift ice heralded the distant northern shores, still days away. A keen wind blew, and it cut Tara's cheeks. The *North Fork* rolled uneasily in the swell, her engines thumping monotonously.

They walked back, past the bridge, on which they could see Swain, wrapped in a heavy coat, his pipe jammed in his mouth, glowering down at them. It was not just the dynamite under their feet that made the *North Fork* a very dangerous ship.

That afternoon, desperate for some sleep, Tara made her way down to the smelly little cabin. Flo and Maggie were already there, with one of their friends, Frenchy, a dark-haired girl with narrow catlike eyes, huge brass earrings, and provocative breasts.

They were all chattering, but when Tara entered they lapsed into silence.

"You haven't met our lodger, have you?" Flo asked Frenchy. "Our Mrs. Kane."

"No. But I heard about you," Frenchy replied, giving Tara a cursory, unfriendly glance.

Involuntarily, Tara yawned. "Excuse me," she apologized. She was determined to remain scrupulously polite. "I'm just so weary."

"Been busy on deck, have you, dearie?" jeered Maggie, and they all giggled. She was herself undressed and began brushing her blonde hair. Frenchy sat on the spare bunk and stretched her arms.

"I guess I'll join the lady and have some shut-eye too," she said, unhooking her bodice. She was bare-breasted and started scratching herself under one armpit.

Tara squeezed through to her bunk, hardly able to believe her luck. It actually looked as if they were all getting ready to sleep.

She took the pins out of her hair, thinking how nice it would be if she could undress completely, have a bath, and curl up on a soft mattress, between clean white sheets, for ten or twelve uninterrupted hours of sleep. But existence on the *North Fork* and a growing awareness of how primitive her new life would be were gradually teaching Tara to look on what she had formerly considered essentials as luxuries.

She was just about to lie down when Frenchy started shouting. "Hey," she screamed at Maggie, "where the hell did you get that?"

"Get what?" demanded Maggie. To Tara's surprise, she was grinning as if the whole thing were a joke.

"*That*, you cow," Frenchy yelled, grabbing at a thin gold chain around Maggie's neck. She tugged, and the chain broke.

"Why, you lousy bitch," Maggie screeched and slapped the dark-haired girl across the face. "You dirty little fuckstress. . . ."

They flew at each other, yelling and screaming. Frenchy grabbed the blonde's hair, and Maggie scrabbled for her face with long, clawing fingers. They were staggering to and fro in the tiny cabin, squealing and cursing, with Frenchy trying to wrestle Maggie down on the floor and Maggie hitting and scratching her. It was the first time Tara had ever seen a no-holds-barred catfight between two whores.

"For God's sake, stop it," Tara yelled. She could not bear the ugly violence, the spitting and swearing, the shrill screams. "Flo, stop them."

Flo gave Tara a contemptuous smile. "Hell no, let them get on with it." She stood, a robe around her, not interfering, stepping out of the way of the two fighting women, her eyes excited.

"If you're so bothered, why don't *you* stop it, Mrs. Kane?" Flo asked, smirking. "You seem pretty good at telling other people what to do."

"All right, I will."

She jumped off her bunk and grabbed the two struggling women, trying to separate them. "Break it up," she appealed. "Stop it."

She found herself in a tangle of arms, legs, and bodies, and suddenly somebody hit her hard. Tara, in blind pain, struck out and her fist caught Maggie's face. The blonde yelled. Tara realized that Flo had also joined in the fight, and now she was struggling against all three women. Somebody kicked her in the stomach, and somebody else knelt on her and was clawing at her bosom. The shrieking had stopped, and the only sound was heavy panting and the occasional curse from one of the prostitutes as a blow came home.

Then, as if by a signal, the fighting stopped. The women got to their feet.

"OK, girls, that's enough," panted Flo. Her robe had been torn off, and her fat body was covered with sweat.

Tara slowly stood up, bruised, sore. She touched her face gingerly. There was a scratch on one cheek, and her lip was bleeding. Her breasts hurt, and her whole body ached.

As Tara crawled onto her bunk, the three other women were drinking from a bottle and giggling. No one would have thought it possible that a few minutes before they had been pulling out each other's hair and clawing one another's eyes. Now and then, one of them stole a glance in Tara's direction, and then they would all burst into their ugly laughter.

"Let's go, Flo," Frenchy said.

"Yeah," Maggie agreed. "Come on. Leave Madame to cry herself to sleep."

When they had gone Tara lay there, her body throbbing. In an effort to soothe her discomfort, she gently rubbed her breasts, which had been the target of clawing nails and punching fists.

Then, as if she had had a sudden electric shock, she sat upright, all pain forgotten. Her pouch had gone. Her money had vanished. She could see the rip in her bodice where the pouch had been torn away. Now she understood what it was all about. Flo had guessed what she kept in it.

They had known that, no matter how much they provoked Tara, she would never fight them. But if they could goad her into trying to break up a brawl, they could grab the pouch. That was what their plan had been. And she had fallen for it.

Wearily, she got up, and searched the floor of the cabin to see if the pouch had dropped somewhere although she knew it was useless. Slowly she dragged herself back to her bunk. Her body hurt so much, and she felt so tired, she could not even think any more. All she wanted was some peace, some quiet. . . .

She closed her eyes, and she was immediately engulfed by an oppressive sleep.

As she stood on the bridge, the ship gave a sudden lurch, and Tara had difficulty keeping her balance.

"Yes, Mrs. Kane?" asked Swain. He was sweeping the horizon through binoculars and did not bother to look at her.

"I've told you already," Tara repeated, incensed. "I have been robbed. All my money's been stolen."

Swain lowered the binoculars. He shouted an order to the helmsman, and the engine room telegraph clanged twice. Then he turned to her. "That is an extremely serious allegation," he said. "Who is supposed to have done this?"

"The women in my cabin."

"They stole it, are you sure?"

"I wouldn't say it if I wasn't," replied Tara.

"Have you any proof?" Swain asked.

"They've got my money," Tara insisted doggedly.

"You do get confused about such things, don't you, Mrs. Kane? I remember you wildly accused one of my men of extortion when you came aboard."

"Captain Swain, I remember very well what happened when I came on board," Tara said.

He cleared his throat. "Mr. Jensen," he shouted, "take over. I have some business to attend to. Come along, Mrs. Kane."

She followed him below to Cabin Four. Flo was in her bunk, and Maggie was arranging her hair.

"Why, Captain Swain, you should really let a lady know you are visiting," simpered Flo, pulling a dirty blanket up to her chin.

Maggie did a slight curtsey. "Do come in, Captain, we are honored," she giggled.

Swain sat down on the one chair. Tara stood by the door, feeling like an outsider.

"Your fellow passenger here is alleging that you ladies stole her money," he announced.

"Mrs. Kane, how could you?" Flo gasped, looking shocked.

"Not just these two," Tara said. "One of their friends as well. She was also here."

"Name?" grunted Swain.

"They call her Frenchy," Tara said.

"Oh, Miss Burdette," Flo minced. "A close friend. Are you accusing us of being thieves, Mrs. Kane?"

"I am," Tara stood her ground firmly. "She is a thief, like you two."

"I'm not taking that from anybody," Maggie snapped. She was sporting a shiner where Tara's fist had connected with her left eye.

"Mrs. Kane, kindly observe the basics of polite behavior," Swain huffed. "This isn't a cathouse, I'll have you know. These ladies are passengers on my ship."

"Yes," Flo said, tossing her head. "She must apologize. Instantly. I don't know where this woman comes from, but I am not used to this kind of talk. Are we, Maggie?"

"I want my one hundred and sixty-five dollars," Tara demanded. "They took it."

"One hundred and sixty-five?" Swain was impressed. He gave the two whores a closer look. "That's a lot of money, ladies. Are you sure you haven't seen it?"

"Of course, Captain," said Flo.

"It was torn from my bodice," Tara said. "I kept it in a pouch, pinned in here."

"Are you saying they attacked you and took it?"

"Not exactly attacked me. They staged a fight, and in the confusion . . ." Tara faltered. It wasn't easy to explain.

"I don't like to say this about another female, but she is telling a pack of lies," Flo interrupted. "The truth is that this woman drinks."

Tara gaped at her.

Swain nodded. "Go on."

"When she is under the influence, she becomes very violent." Flo was relishing it. "It has made life very difficult for us, sharing this cabin, as you can imagine. Last night, she attacked my friend Maggie. You can see what she did to her. It is true there was a struggle. Miss Burdette and I tried to help Maggie to subdue this wild creature. I regret that when she is in drink, she has the strength of three men. We eventually had to use force—something we are not used to. She is trying to get her own back on us now."

"You're damn well right," Maggie said. Flo looked at her disapprovingly.

"I see," Swain said. He gave Tara a cold look. "Well? What do you say to that?"

Tara shrugged her shoulders. "What's the point, Captain? You don't want to believe me."

23

"We are quite prepared to have our things searched, Captain," offered Flo, looking smug. "Please go through everything."

He stood up. "I don't think that will be necessary. I am quite satisfied. I think, Mrs. Kane, you lost your money, and you are trying to put the blame on these two ladies."

"If she ever had any money," Maggie sneered. "One hundred and sixty-five dollars, that's a likely story. The stuck-up sow."

"You've wasted enough of my time, Mrs. Kane," Swain growled. "I have to get back to the bridge. But you listen to me. I'm evicting you from this cabin."

"I paid my passage," Tara cried. "It's my right."

He cut her short. "You got no rights, lady. I make the decisions, and I don't see how you can expect these two ladies to be prepared to share quarters with you any more. They're entitled to comfort and privacy, not wild accusations. You better be careful, Mrs. Kane."

"Where am I supposed to sleep?" Tara was trying hard to stop herself crying tears of rage.

He grinned. "That's your problem now. It's a big ship, and I imagine you'll find a corner to bed down. Anyway, what have you got to worry about? You got no more money to be stolen, have you?"

The three of them joined in mocking laughter while Tara choked back her tears and controlled herself.

"My trunk is in here," she said coldly.

"You can leave it," Swain said.

Tara turned, and as she walked out of the cabin, she slammed the door as hard as she could.

Their laughter was still ringing in her ears as she walked up the companionway to the deck.

"Damn you! Damn you! Damn you," she sobbed. She wasn't sorry for herself, just furious at her impotence.

Hart found her on deck, huddled against one of the horse pens, trying to shelter against the bitter northerly wind.

"Where have you been?" he asked. "I was looking all over. . . ."

He broke off when he saw her swollen lip and the scratch on her cheek. There was a swelling over one eye.

"*Gott im Himmel,* what has happened to you?"

"Oh, Ernst." Tara burst into tears.

Hart put his arms around her and held her tight. "My dear, please don't cry. Tell me what's wrong, please."

"Have you got a handkerchief?" she asked, feeling for one in her pocket. He produced an enormous polka-dotted red piece of cloth.

"Thank you," she sniffled and gave her nose an almighty blow. Then she got a small mirror out of her purse and looked at herself.

"Oh my God," she said.

"Never mind," Hart smiled. "Tell me what has been done to you. You are not the crybaby." He became serious. "What has happened?"

"My money's been stolen," Tara said, "everything I have."

"We must find the thief at once and get it back," Hart declared. "We must find out who did such a thing."

"I know who's got it," Tara sighed wearily. "That's no mystery. I'm afraid, Ernst, I won't get it back."

"We'll see about that," he growled. He looked at her face. "Is that how you were hurt? Who attacked you?"

She told him.

"What do you expect?" she added. "He's in league with those whores. I bet he's getting a rake-off from my money. God, I could . . ."

Hart stood up. "You wait here."

"Where are you going?" Tara asked. At this moment, she was afraid of being alone. "Please stay."

"I shall only get ointment," he said. "Your lip is very swollen. Otherwise, in this wind . . ."

He was back after a few minutes with a small tin. He put some grease on his finger and then gently brushed her lip with it. He rubbed his hands in his big red handkerchief and gave her a little smile. He's a very understanding man, she thought, a real friend.

"Give me your hand," he said.

Hesitatingly, she held out her hand, and he pressed something into it. She opened it, and found he had given her thirty dollars.

"It's not much, but I haven't got a lot left. You know what I have to pay these crooks to keep my equipment. As soon as we get ashore, I'll take some portraits and make money."

"I can't take it," Tara protested, trying to give it back to him.

Hart drew himself up stiffly. "The matter is closed," he said. "There is no question of discussion. It is my pleasure and my privilege as a gentleman, thank you." Even in her misery, Tara had to smile at his stilted manner.

"Also," he added, "you will hurt me very much if you refuse."

"All right, thank you. It's very good of you. As soon as I meet up with Daniel, I will pay you back."

"Of course, Tara."

Tara became one of the homeless, constantly on the hunt, after dark, for some free space to bed down in. The favorite spots were always taken first, and quarrels often ensued when two or three people claimed the same niche. But at least the men, once they had found a place, could lie down and close their eyes. For a woman, sleep remained uneasy throughout the night. People lay down beside her, strange hands groped for her, and she heard their heavy breathing next to her. Once Tara woke up to find a man's looming face a few inches from hers, leering, and his hand moving toward her body. She shot up and ran off, and for the rest of the bitter, freezing night she walked around and around the deck, too frightened to settle down anywhere else.

She lived in the same dress because there was nowhere to change. She felt filthy and uncomfortable; she was ashamed of her appearance—her hair unwashed, her face drawn and tired, her eyes bloodshot from lack of sleep. Even Cabin Four, with its sexual acrobatics, seemed a haven compared to this nomadic existence.

"We must sleep together," Hart said.

She didn't know what to say.

"No, no, no," he protested, and she could swear he reddened, "I do not mean like that. Do you take me to be so dishonorable to take advantage of you?" When he was excited, his accent became more pronounced. "You do not understand. We can keep each other warm, correct? And you will not be molested if you are sleeping with a man."

"Let me think it over," she said. Then she saw she had hurt him by her hesitation. "All right, as long as . . ."

"Don't worry," he assured her.

But that night, she couldn't find Hart. She stepped over recumbent forms on deck, passengers huddled together in companionways, trying to sleep in any sheltered spot they could find. The wind was howling, and Tara had wrapped a scarf around her head to keep out the biting cold. But there was no sign of Hart.

She found him in a corner of the saloon. He was slumped over a table, an empty bottle rolling to and fro in front of him, in rhythm with the movement of the ship. Tara shook his shoulder. "Ernst," she whispered.

He opened one bleary eye and stared up at her, uncomprehending for a moment. He made an effort to pull himself upright.

"Come and sit down, Tara," he invited woozily. "Come and sit here, and tell me the story of your life."

"No," she said. "You stay here. I'll be all right. I'll see you in the morning."

He lurched to his feet. "Nonsense. *Unsinn*. I will go with you. We sleep together, so you are safe." He laughed.

"I'm not tired," Tara lied.

But he insisted on coming on deck with her, she having to support him as they looked for somewhere to sleep. Eventually, in a passageway, Tara managed to find space between two snoring men. She helped Hart lie down, then sat beside him, resting against the bulkhead, thinking.

"Good night, Tara," Hart muttered. "Don't worry, I'll protect you. I'll be right here beside you. Sleep well."

He leaned against her, and, in a moment, he was deep asleep. Once he nuzzled her cheek and then snored again.

Tara sat open-eyed in the darkness, staring into space.

CHAPTER FOUR

They had been at sea nearly three weeks, and, although it was only the middle of September, the weather was growing harsher and the cold more intense. Tara's lips were chapped, her skin felt raw, her ears throbbed.

Sometimes, when she thought of Daniel, he had turned into a vague shadow, and she had difficulty in seeing in her mind's eye the familiar face of the man she loved so dearly.

Then she would bring out the letter he had left her on the day of his departure. That awful morning, when she had awakened to find she was alone in their double, bed, a cold sensation had crept over her, and she had lain for a long while staring at the ceiling.

They had eaten a quiet dinner the night before he left, and afterward they had made love with a passion and intensity Tara had never felt before. Eventually she had drifted off to sleep in his arms, aware only that soon she would be alone, deprived for what seemed an eternity of the man she loved so greatly.

In the morning, on the mantelpiece in Gabie's nursery, she had found the compass and his letter. Now she read yet again the words she knew so well: "Fate cannot keep us apart for long. Think rather that each day which passes from now on is one day nearer our reunion. I love you so very much."

"And I love you," Tara whispered. The compass had become her talisman; it pointed to Daniel, and it would guide her to him.

She remembered when he first told her that he was going to get their pot of gold. He had been so excited at the thought of being rich beyond their wildest dreams. They could buy a house on Nob Hill,

Gabie could have a private nurse, they could take trips to Europe. Yes, the world was going to be their oyster.

Tara had been heartbroken, hardly able to face the thought of separation from Daniel for at least a year. But Daniel had pointed out that to achieve anything in life one had to make sacrifices. Their sacrifice would last only a year, and what rewards that year would bring! Nothing stood in their way. Between them they had sufficient money to finance his trip and for Tara and Gabie to live modestly in San Francisco. It was literally a golden opportunity, and one they could not afford to turn down.

Sadly, Tara had acquiesced. After all, she was the last person to want to stop the man she loved doing what he felt he needed to do.

The owners of the ship had not bargained for the bad weather and rough seas they had started to encounter. The voyage was taking much too long. And so, on the fourth Sunday of the voyage, Tara, like the other passengers, became conscious of a curious silence. The steady, monotonous rhythm with which they had all been living over the past long weeks had gone. The engines had stopped.

People lined the side of the ship as if that would provide an answer. At first it seemed the *North Fork* was lying motionless, but Tara got the impression that she was actually drifting.

Then rumors started spreading among the passengers: The bunkers were empty. They had run out of coal.

Below the bridge, groups of passengers gathered. Swain stood above them, impassive, smoking his pipe. Tara spotted Rusky, the seaman who had carried her trunk aboard. He was taking a door off its hinges.

"What's happened?" she asked him.

"No more coal," he said.

"How could it run out?"

"Maybe they didn't load enough," he shrugged. "Maybe they needed the space."

"That is it, of course," Hart said when she told him. "The owners of this ship wanted to squeeze the last cent out of her. Half those bunkers are crammed with everything except coal."

"Attention," Swain called out through a megaphone. "Attention, all passengers. There's a shortage of fuel, and we will have to burn wood to keep the boilers going. We're going to have to chop up anything and everything that burns."

Bunks, wooden partitions, all the timber was torn out of the ship's insides as slowly, ponderously, the *North Fork* began to move. Chairs and tables followed. Some of the wooden pens on deck were dismantled and the horses tethered to iron rings and capstans, exposed to the lashing elements. The ship's lifeboats came next. Seamen with axes and saws chopped them up and carried them to the boilers while the passengers watched, horrified.

"What happens if we sink?" cried a man.

"We sink," snarled Skinner. "Hurry up with that planking. Number two boiler is low."

The contents of the saloon had been cannibalized, and now cargo was being added to the list. Crates and boxes were thrown to the flames. In front of their eyes, the ship was being stripped.

Two seamen were carrying a big cabin trunk to the passageway leading down to the engine room when a man ran up to them.

"That's my trunk," he yelled. "Where are you going with that?"

The seamen ignored him. The man grabbed one of them. "Put that down," he cried.

Jensen swung the man around. "Shut up. Didn't you hear the captain? It's an emergency. We have to burn everything we can to keep going," he shouted.

"Not my things," the man yelled, struggling to get at the sailors. "You're not burning that."

His fist shot out, and Jensen staggered, his cap rolling on the deck. A whistle blew, and several crew members came running up, led by Skinner. In the confusion, the trunk crashed on deck. Skinner swung a wooden club, and the man fell, his head split.

"Throw him in the scuppers," Skinner panted.

But a group of passengers crowded around now, and Tara saw another man hit Skinner, and then suddenly everyone was fighting. She clung to Hart as sailors piled into the brawl and men rolled around the deck, battling with each other, cursing and swearing. Jensen was on his feet laying about him with a boathook, and two passengers had Skinner up against a bulwark, beating him. Rusky threw a man bodily down a hatch, but more passengers came running to join in.

"They're going to seize the ship," Hart said excitedly.

Suddenly there were several shots, in quick succession. Captain Swain stood on a ladder, a pistol in his hand. Beside him were a couple of his men, also with guns. Men slowly got to their feet, dabbing at bloody noses, or sat down, breathing heavily. Two men lay unconscious, sprawled where they had been knocked to the deck.

"I'll shoot the next man who starts trouble," Swain barked. The

29

pistol circled around the mob. "Have you all gone crazy? I can shoot the lot of you for mutiny, passengers or no passengers, you bloody scum."

The crowd shifted on its feet nervously, looking at each other. Some of them began to back away.

"I'll make you a promise," said Swain. "I'll get you to Dyea. This ship will make it if we have to burn the deck. We'll make it. Nothing is going to stop us. Nothing. Not even a bunch of howling baboons like you."

His eyes roamed around the scowling faces challengingly. "And if one of you raises a finger to one of my men again, he'll never tell the tale."

"We got guns too, Swain," rang out a voice.

"Sure, why don't you bring them out?" jeered the Captain. "Maybe navigate this tub yourself. Shoot the lot of us. You'll never see land again, I guarantee that. And if you do, you'll all get hanged.

"Mr. Jensen," he called out.

Jensen was rubbing his jaw. "Aye, aye, Capt'n."

"Disperse these people," the Captain contemptuously ordered.

He turned to Skinner. "You grab everything that burns in the cabins, tear 'em apart. Baggage, trunks, cases, anything. I don't care if this ship is as empty as an eggshell, but I want those boilers kept fed."

"Yes, sir," the first mate nodded.

"The rest of you," he told the silent passengers, "keep out of our way. You obey orders, or I'll have you."

"He isn't afraid of anybody," Hart said admiringly as Swain stalked away.

"He's a monster," Tara said.

"But look how he tames them." He shook his head. "Nobody argues with him."

"Don't tell me you admire that man," she frowned.

"I admire a man who has the gift of authority. Men are made up of the leaders and the led. Swain is a villain, but he is a leader."

"That sounds very German, Ernst."

"No, Tara," Hart retorted. "It is simply logical."

"Will you still think that when he throws your equipment into the boilers?"

He gulped. "I don't think they'll do that."

"You hope not."

Tara went below to check on her trunk, but when she opened the

30

door of Cabin Four she had a shock. The bunks had been torn out, boarding ripped up; the chair was gone, the table had disappeared, everything wooden had literally vanished. And so had all the luggage, both hers and that of the other women. The cabin was empty.

CHAPTER FIVE

When it appeared, the land looked inhospitable. Tara shivered as she surveyed the mountain-locked inlet of the Lynn Canal, where the ship had anchored for the night. A dull, gloomy sky did not help to make her first sight of Alaska more inviting.

She had expected some kind of port, but there were no piers, no quays, no harbor front, just the beach. She could see, in the gloom, tents and rough wooden shacks, but that was all. A few people moved around, and she thought she could hear dogs barking across the water.

Disembarkation of passengers and cargo was barred until daylight, and Skinner had been going around, inviting people to draw lots for precedence for going ashore when morning came. Tara knew enough about the *North Fork* now to ignore him. Whatever bits of paper he handed out, she was well aware it would be a wild scramble when the time came, and the devil help the hindmost.

"Passage money don't include landing fees," Skinner pointed out, seeing her hesitation. "You want help to get you ashore, you have to pay extra."

"I'll manage," Tara said, and wondered how on earth she would.

"Please yourself." He spat over the side of the ship and moved on.

"If you stay up here, you'll catch your death," Hart said, when he found a half-frozen Tara still standing by the rail, looking at the bleak shore. He took her arm.

"It won't come any nearer by just staring at it," he said. "Come along."

They went below and found the saloon packed with people. The whole atmosphere on the ship had changed, now that they had actually arrived. The tension had gone. Bottles of whisky passed from hand to hand, and everybody was drinking.

"Nobody's going to sleep on this ship tonight," Hart prophesied, and he was right.

Toasts were drunk to the future, to each other, to wealth and success, and to gold. Somebody produced a mouth organ, others started clapping in tempo with the tune, and a woman in laced-up boots began dancing with a gangling, bearded man in the little space they could find.

It went on for hours, the blackness outside forgotten. Tara had no idea what the time was, but midnight had long gone, the wee hours were passing, and the new day, when it came, was being ushered in by a drunken, noisy, smoky revel.

Flo and Maggie were in their element. Flo's lipstick was smeared, her hair awry, and she was shrieking with laughter. Maggie was locked in an embrace with a thickset individual whose right hand was down her cleavage.

Hart produced his flask. "Here you are, my dear. Let us celebrate too. *Prosit.*"

Tara took a gulp, grateful for anything that would warm her up. But she was anxious that he should not get drunk. They had to get off the ship in the morning, in one piece.

The noise was becoming strident. Frenchy danced by herself, holding up her skirt for all the world to see her knickers. Tara looked at Hart. He was watching Frenchy, a curious smile on his face. He took off his steamed-up spectacles, and then he noticed Tara looking at him.

"Yes," he said, "you are right. I am composing a picture. I think to myself, she would make a fantastic photograph like that."

"Is that all?" Tara asked. Frenchy was flaunting herself with abandon, her lips parted, her breasts thrusting. Men vainly reached out to grab her, but she dodged them, laughing.

"What do you mean?" Hart seemed confused. Then he understood. "Oh, I would not dream . . . not a woman like that. . . ."

Tara wanted to laugh at his indignation but kept a straight face. For once, his blue eyes avoided hers as he brought out his flask again.

Suddenly, there was a scuffle. Nobody took much notice, but two men were at each other, and one of them knocked against an oil lamp swinging from a hook in the low ceiling. It all happened so quickly that many people were not even aware of it.

Frenchy screamed; Tara, horrified, saw her skirt on fire, and then the rest of her flared up like a torch. The oil lamp, lying smashed on the wooden floor, sent a stream of burning oil cascading across the sawdust.

Tara looked around for a blanket, a rug, anything to wrap around the pyre that had been the dark-haired whore. But already people were yelling and screaming, and falling over each other as they tried to escape the flames that began to spread.

Hart grabbed Tara and dragged her to the companionway. "Quick," he shouted, but Tara looked back in anguish. She caught a glimpse of Frenchy's agonized face, her whole body engulfed by flames.

Hart hauled Tara up the wooden steps to the deck. There was a wild stampede of people behind them, clawing, fighting, kicking, hitting out to escape from the blazing saloon.

On the deck, Tara slipped on an icy patch, and Hart dragged her up unceremoniously. She heard, vaguely, a bell clanging, and more screams and then smoke began to swirl across the deck.

"You have to get off the ship," Hart yelled at her. "Now, Tara." She stared at him, trying to understand what he was saying.

He pulled her to the rail, shoving aside anyone who came between them, and he held her hands. "Now listen," he said urgently, "get off the ship. You must risk it. Swim ashore. Anything. But get off the ship."

"I can't," she cried, "I can't. . . ."

As she looked at him, he was silhouetted by a reddish glow, and she realized for the first time that the ship itself was on fire now. The flames were spreading rapidly, sweeping up from below, feeding on the wooden deck, the sawdust.

"Don't you understand?" Hart shouted at her. "The *dynamite!* You've got to."

He forced her to face the rail. All she could see was the darkness of the sea and a few lights glowing ashore. The rest was a huge, black void.

"No, Ernst," Tara screamed, "I can't. . . ."

"Don't argue," he yelled at her, shaking her furiously.

Around them, the ship had turned into bedlam, horses desperately kicking out, dogs howling, smoke pouring across the deck, the smell of burning becoming stronger, and the ugly crackling sound of flames growing louder. People were shrieking and trampling on one another. Already there were splashes as men jumped into the water.

"Go," Hart shouted. "It's your only chance."

She stared at him wide-eyed, her legs paralyzed.

Roughly, brutally, Hart took hold of her and lifted her bodily over the *North Fork*'s rail. Disbelieving, she found herself in mid-air, plunging down into the black abyss. She wanted to scream, but her voice would not obey her brain. When she struck the icy water it was as if her breath had been cut off. She was numb with cold and panic. She started thrashing about in blind fear—then all went black. When she came to, she was still in the water, and she heard a thundering,

33

roaring sound followed by a huge flash which lit up the whole sea. She tried to swim, but her legs would not move and she blacked out again.

Tara never knew who it was that saved her. She never saw the boats that set off from the beach to pick up survivors, but for long afterwards she was haunted by the memory of the water around her lit by the blazing ship, on fire from stem to stern, and the terrifying hysterical screams.

The stinging pain of her face being slapped roused her. She opened her eyes, blinking in confusion, her face throbbing, her teeth chattering. Hart, white-faced, muddy, soaking, was kneeling by her side, shaking her.

"Wake up," he was saying anxiously. "Move your legs. You're freezing to death."

She looked around, trying to focus. It was daylight, and she was lying in a freezing pool of water on a beach. She felt icy, as if the blood in her veins had frozen, and she was so stiff she could hardly raise her head. Frantically, Hart was rubbing her hands.

"On your feet," he ordered, putting his arm round her and dragging her upright. "Walk. Keep moving."

Gradually sensation returned. She started hobbling along, supported by Hart. "What happened?" she asked through chattering teeth.

"It's all right, Tara," he said, much more gently, helping her along. "You're ashore. Everything's all right."

"And the ship?"

He shook his head. "There is no ship. It blew up."

"All those people. . . . Still on board. . . . Oh, Ernst!"

"Come along," he urged, holding her tighter.

He was staggering along, trying to help her and dragging his big camera case and his other gear with him.

He saw Tara's look. "A boat came alongside, just before the explosion. I threw everything in. They nearly killed me, but I got away," he explained, embarrassed.

"But the others. . . ."

"It was each man for himself. *Sauve qui peut.* You've got to get some dry clothes," he went on breathlessly. "You'll freeze to death in those."

She was still dazed. "How many were saved?" she asked.

He glanced around the beach. There were some people crouched around fires, trying to get warm after crawling out of the icy waters of the Dyea anchorage. A few dozen surviving men and women.

34

Slowly they moved off. It was bitterly cold, and after all the horror of the night it was deadly quiet. In the distance, here and there, a few pieces of planking, an odd crate, a few bales floated in the cold, gray sea.

As they started trekking toward the little huddle of habitations that was Dyea, they passed some men burying a corpse where it had been found, its sightless eyes staring straight up at the leaden, gloomy sky.

They trudged into the settlement. Dyea! For weeks it had been the name that represented the gateway to the Klondike and the first step to Daniel. She had thought it would be a bustling, lively community. What Tara saw were clusters of tents a quarter of a mile inland and then groups of rickety-looking wooden shacks. The place was littered with rubbish, broken-down carts, abandoned cabins, the ground rutted by wagon wheels. It was dreary and unwelcoming.

In ones and twos, the people who had survived the *North Fork* straggled in the same direction as Tara and Hart, the lucky ones weighed down by packs and other belongings they had managed to salvage. All Tara had left was the purse she had pinned to her dress, with the little compass, thirty dollars of borrowed money, her mother's silver locket on a chain, and the icy, wet clothes she stood in.

They were watched by silent groups of men standing by their tents. Some looked prosperous, but in the main they had the appearance of desperate, miserable paupers.

Dyea had one main thoroughfare, a glorified muddy track, at one end of which stood a rough wooden sign proclaiming: "Trail Street." It was flanked by makeshift, raw timber shacks and led to a frozen river. Beyond that was a narrow canyon that rose toward a pass.

"There's the Chilkoot," Hart said. "That's the route I'll take."

There was one more solidly constructed building on Trail Street. "General Store," read a notice over the entrance. Some pack animals and a couple of horses were tethered outside. On the roof flew a Union Jack.

"Come on," Hart said. He led the way up the wooden steps, Tara wearily dragging herself behind him. Her clothes were freezing on her.

Inside the store there were great piles of food and clothing, blankets, canned goods, bags of flour and beans, sides of bacon. Stacked against the walls were sleds and rolled-up camping equipment, and there were two racks of rifles. But above all, there was an enormous stove in the center of the floor, with the chimney pipe going straight to the roof. It was warm, almost close in the room.

Hart dumped his camera case, and they went over to the stove, holding out their hands, letting the life-giving heat seep into them. An enormously fat man in rubber boots and a checked shirt watched them morosely. Leaning against the counter were two Indians. Their faces were expressionless.

The fat man waddled over and poked the fire in the stove.

"The lady needs some clothes," Hart said. "She's soaked."

"You from the ship?" asked the fat man.

Hart nodded.

"Lucky," grunted the fat man without emotion or interest. He squinted at Tara and Hart. "Lost all your spare gear, have you?"

He went back behind the counter.

"Help yourself," he invited, indicating the store. "Got most things here. Better get some mukluks too."

"Mukluks?"

The fat man allowed himself a ghost of a smile. "Boots. Johnny here will have some."

Johnny was the taller of the two Indians. His weatherbeaten face cracked into the semblance of a smile. It revealed ugly, yellow-stained teeth.

"Five dollars," said Johnny. He held up one finger. "One pair." Then he held up two fingers. "Two pairs, nine dollars." He was used to bargaining. He waited expectantly.

"That's a lot of money," Hart said.

"Don't need to have 'em. Lose your toes instead. Up to you," shrugged the fat man.

A gust of icy air shot through the store as the door opened, and a man, swathed in furs, came in. He pulled back his hood and stamped his feet.

"Twenty pounds of flour," he said, without ceremony. "Twelve pounds of bacon. Twelve pounds of beans. Four pounds of butter. Five pounds dried vegetables. Five pounds of sugar. Three of coffee. Two pounds of salt. One pound of tea. Four cans condensed milk. Two hundred rifle shells."

The fat man started collecting up the items as the stranger rattled them off.

"How much are eggs?"

"Dollar each."

"Fuck that," said the man. He turned and watched Tara while the fat man put some of the goods into a huge sack.

Tara went over to the counter and put down the things she had selected: woolen underwear, a sweater, shirts, trousers, socks, a parka, and mittens.

"Where do I change?" she asked.

The fat man stopped filling the sack. "Change?" He seemed genuinely puzzled.

"I want to put on these things," Tara explained.

"Oh," said the fat man. "Change right here, lady. No extra charge."

The stranger eyed her dispassionately. Johnny and the other Indian picked their teeth in unison. Tara felt herself go red.

"Isn't there somewhere private?" she asked.

"Guess the lady's embarrassed, Thorpe," the stranger said. "Show her some manners."

"OK. OK," said Thorpe. "You go and change behind those sacks. Nobody can see anything. . . ."

Tara grabbed the clothes and went to the corner where cases and sacks stood high. She went behind the stack, which came up to her shoulders. The men were watching openly. Hart had his back to her, picking items off the shelves on the other side of the store.

As quickly as she could, Tara got out of her wet, dirty, torn dress, conscious of the group of men. They were silent, and she knew they were visualizing her undressing. Once she heard the stranger whisper something, and Thorpe erupted with laughter. Her embarrassment caused her to fumble even more with buttons and hooks. She made a bundle of her discarded wet clothes. Wearing rough woolen long johns and no corset felt strange.

She emerged finally, her whole appearance changed. Except for her auburn hair, which hung around her shoulders damply, she looked boyish in the checked shirt, the sweater, the parka trimmed with wolverine around the hood, and the heavy flannel-lined trousers. Johnny had been sent to get some of his handmade boots, and she wore a pair of them now, heavy, watertight, and very comfortable, like overgrown moccasins. They were warm, like the rest of the outfit.

"Fits you perfect," Thorpe said. "Don't it?"

"I like what's underneath better," the stranger said, smiling at her arrogantly.

"How much?" Tara asked coldly.

"Well now," calculated Thorpe. "Pants, long johns, sweater, shirt, anorak—guess twenty dollars will cover it. And you owe Johnny four. Twenty-four dollars."

Tara counted out the dollar bills while Thorpe and the stranger watched with interest.

"Is she your woman?" the stranger asked Hart.

"Yes," Hart said.

She was aggravated until she realized why he had said it. In this land, a woman had to be owned—or she was free game.

"Man ought to pay for his woman," the stranger said, and it was almost a challenge. "Otherwise, somebody might jump his claim."

"Mind your own business," Tara said fiercely, and the man's eyes widened.

"You going up the pass?" he asked. "If you want company to Lake Bennett. . . ."

"She's with me," Hart said emphatically. He blinked nervously through his glasses.

The stranger paid Thorpe and hoisted his bulging sack on his shoulder. "Maybe we'll meet up some time," he said and pushed open the door. For a moment a freezing blast of air shot into the store again. Outside, Tara saw the man's sled and dog team. Then the door slammed to.

Hart was trying on a pair of Johnny's boots, and Thorpe added up his takings on the counter. He seemed pleased.

"You folks need anything else? Guides, dog team, sleds, pack horses, shovels, gold pans, guns?" he asked. "You just come to Thorpe. Cheapest prices in town."

"Is there another store?" asked Hart surprised.

"No," beamed the fat man. "That's why I'm the cheapest. You like them mukluks?"

"Six dollars," rasped Johnny.

"Five dollars," Hart protested indignantly.

"OK. Five dollars," the Indian agreed. "God save the Queen."

"Why does he say that?" asked Tara.

"He's a Chilkat. He thinks it's good for business. He doesn't realize this is United States territory." He chuckled. "Guess the flag fools him."

"Pardon?" said Hart. His capacity for logic was offended.

"I'm not a Yank," Thorpe said as if that explained everything. He put Hart's money in a drawer. "Where you folks making for?"

"Skagway," Tara announced before Hart could say a word. "How far is it?"

"You can do it in a day easy, with a good team. Maybe you need a guide. . . ."

The shorter of the two Indians came forward. "Ten dollars. Good guide," he volunteered. "Me Christian."

"I'll see," Tara said vaguely. She wondered how she was going to travel. There was no railroad. She couldn't afford a sled with a dog team, let alone manage one. She didn't know the route. Well, she would make it there somehow.

"We need a hotel for tonight," Hart said.

"Bailey's is full," Thorpe said as if the name would mean something to them. "Try the Klondike. Beds twenty-five cents a night. Sort of rough, but it's warm and dry. Down the street. No lice either."

Tara's thoughts were already on tomorrow. Somehow tomorrow she would be in Skagway. Tomorrow she would find Daniel and then everything would be right.

The Klondike Lodging House (Prop. Joe Gibbons) was a two-floored wooden building, with a hand-painted sign over the porch announcing that it was both "Clean and Cheap." Its front overlooked Trail Street, and it was right across from the Ritz Bar, a little shack with some bullet holes in its door.

Joe Gibbons evidently did not believe in home comforts. The floors had no covering. The stairs were broken. The toilets were buckets in stalls at the back. The only illumination came from a few kerosene lamps. Downstairs were tables and chairs, and a shabby notice informed guests that this was The Restaurant. The tables were stained, the plates tin, the cutlery bent and broken. The place had never seen a coat of paint.

Some kind of meeting was going on. Gibbons, a man who boasted proudly that he had not had a bath for twenty-one years, presided over it from a table in the center of the room near the big stove, which was surrounded by spittoons. His skin was pockmarked, and he had a bulbous red nose. Spread on the table in front of him were various articles. Tara could see a small cooking stove, pots and pans, a pair of boots, a sleeping bag, some field glasses.

Gibbons hammered on the table with the butt of a pistol.

"OK," he yelled, "what am I bid for this valuable implement?" He held up a small axe. "Sharper than a razor, gents, and hardly used."

Rough-looking men were lolling about on chairs, drinking. "Ten cents," shouted one of them.

"You always was a joker, Snowey," Gibbons complained, and the other men roared. "Now come on, we got to bury Tommy good and decent."

"Twenty-five cents," offered another bearded man.

"Twenty-five cents. Going, going, gone."

Gibbons picked up the boots. "A real bargain these, gents. Waterproof. Tough as hell. Practically new."

"Any blood on them?" called out a voice, and they all laughed.

"You ought to know better," Gibbons grinned. "He wasn't shot in the feet. Fifty cents, anybody? Seventy-five?"

Tara wondered what had happened to the dead man, how he came to be shot, who he was.

Gibbons held up the dead man's sleeping bag. "Kept him dry and snug," he announced. "Clean too. No bugs. Tommy washed."

"Not like you, Joe," one of the men guffawed.

"You're darn right. Don't believe in water. Now what will you give me for this?" Nobody said anything. "Oh come on," shouted Gibbons. "You could even fit a squaw into it."

To Tara's amazement, Hart raised his hand. "One dollar, please."

"Good sleeping bag's worth ten," Gibbons said. They were all looking at Hart and Tara. His German accent had attracted their attention.

"Okay. Going for a dollar once, twice. Sold to the stranger at the back."

"What did you buy that for?" Tara asked.

"You need a sleeping bag," Hart replied matter-of-factly.

"A dead man's sleeping bag?"

"Well, he didn't die in it," Hart reasoned. "But if you don't have one, you're going to die of cold."

"Next time, I'll get my own, if you don't mind."

Gibbons banged the butt of his gun on the table. Gradually, he auctioned off the late Tommy's belongings. Somebody gave fifteen cents for his belt; somebody else bought his sheath knife for ten. His fur hat went for a dollar because two men both fancied it and bid against one another.

When everything had been sold, Gibbons counted the money.

"Well, fellows," he announced jovially, "I don't calculate there's sufficient to bury Tommy, but we got enough to adjourn and drink his health. On the house."

"They even cheat a dead man," Tara remarked bitterly.

"It doesn't matter to him," Hart shrugged. "He's past caring, whoever he was."

Hart went over to Gibbons and asked for two rooms for the night. Gibbons shook his head. "Rooms? I ain't even got two bunks. Place is full up." He peered at them.

"But if you can find space, it is OK by me if you bed down on the floor. For two dollars each," he added quickly.

"The store said twenty-five cents for a bed," Hart protested. "What do you mean, two dollars to sleep on the floor?"

"Take it or leave it," Gibbons grunted.

That night, lying on the hard wooden floorboards in the dead Tommy's sleeping bag, surrounded by strange, snoring men, Tara made a promise to herself. She was going to survive.

Outside, on Trail Street, people were shouting drunkenly. She heard glass smashing. Once there was the sound of shots, which made the men around her stir uneasily, but after a few seconds their snoring continued. Hart was stretched out next to her. Tara glanced at him. He had removed his glasses, and without them he looked much younger. He slept soundly, his equipment piled at his feet.

She stretched out in the sleeping bag. Yes, she decided, I've made a good start. I'm lying in a dead man's sleeping bag, which is something I didn't think I'd ever have to do.

Tomorrow, for the first time in this new world, she would be completely on her own. She would be sad at saying goodbye to Hart, and also a little afraid. Until she found Daniel there would be no one to help, no one to explain things to her, no one to protect her. The prospect made her feel apprehensive, but the challenge excited her too. Once she was in Skagway, she would catch up with Daniel, and then everything would be fine again.

Hart turned over. He was smiling slightly in his sleep, and Tara saw his lips move. He said something in German softly to himself.

"Ich liebe dich," he muttered, *"Ich liebe dich."*

But who it was he loved remained unsaid.

CHAPTER SIX

She could hear singing, hymn singing. A drum was beating in time and someone was shaking a tambourine. A handful of voices croaked about Our Lord in Ages Past. After the drunks of the night, the cursing and shouting of Trail Street, it was the most unexpected cacophony of all.

When Tara emerged from the lodging house, the group was standing in front of the Ritz Bar. The singing had stopped, and a tall, gaunt man with deep-set staring eyes was declaiming to Trail Street at large, periodically stressing his message by thumping a big Bible in his hand. The big drum was strapped to a sad-looking Indian, and beside the tall man stood a buxom woman, her lips a thin, disapproving line. She was the one with the tambourine. Next to her stood another Indian carrying a banner reading: "Bishop Beauchamp's Klondike Crusade."

Their audience consisted of two grinning prospectors, a trapper swaying slightly in an alcoholic haze, and another Indian. And a few feet away was Hart, camera on tripod, cloth over his head and shoulders, photographing the group.

"The moment of salvation has come for you sinners," cried the tall man. Tara could see a clerical collar peeping through his furs. His head was bare, despite the cold, and his silvery gray locks gave him a distinguished appearance. "Spurn the devil, and join in the good work of saving this virgin land for the Lord."

One of the prospectors spat a stream of tobacco juice within a few feet of the Indian with the drum.

"Amen, amen," said the woman with the tambourine, and Tara felt her gimlet eyes fixed on her.

"I have come to guide you to salvation, to bring the word of the Lord to these unfortunate heathen, and to return to them this fine land which is being corrupted and soiled by the men of Babylon and their painted harlots."

Bishop Beauchamp looked around challengingly. The prospectors chewed their tobacco undeterred.

"You miserable pagans," the Bishop cried. "You have joined Satan in pursuit of the evil yellow metal, and all the gold in the world will not save you from the hellfire that is to come. Oh no, my friends, you cannot buy your way out of perdition."

His eyes had swung around to Tara, and he now seemed to be addressing her directly.

"This is no place for a decent woman, among debauched creatures of evil, flaunting themselves like the Jezebels they are. No painted whore will find paradise until she repents."

"Amen," the gimlet-eyed woman intoned. She, too, was staring at Tara.

"Today, at noon, the Crusade will depart for Skagway on the first stage of its great work," the Bishop announced. "Come and join with us, brothers and sisters. Travel with us to that evil den of iniquity where Sodom and Gomorrah are locked in deadly combat with the angels. Come with us and help us to raise the banner of the Lord. Join us as we march on Skagway."

The shivering Indian waved his banner at a signal from the woman, and his colleague banged the drum again.

Tara took a step forward. "I'll go to Skagway with you," she called out.

The Bishop raised both arms to heaven. "Lord," he cried, "I thank thee. A sinner repenteth."

Tara bristled, but she knew her great chance was here. These people would take her to Skagway.

"Come forward, my daughter," invited the Bishop. "Let me shake your hand."

The Indians stared at her impassively. The grim woman seemed unimpressed. "What's your name?" she demanded.

"Tara Kane."

"Are you a papist?" the woman asked fiercely.

"Why should she be a Roman, my love?" the Bishop asked the harridan.

"Tara Kane sounds Irish," the woman muttered.

Tara shook her head.

"Welcome," the Bishop intoned, smiling at her somberly. "The ways of the Lord are indeed mysterious. Perhaps you had to come here to see the light, the way Saint Paul did on the road to Damascus."

"What are you doing in Dyea?" asked the woman. She did not seem utterly convinced that Tara had seen any light.

"I'm joining my husband," Tara said. Deliberately she added, "But a woman traveling on her own in these parts needs Christian company."

"Bless you," the Bishop purred.

"Well, you had better get your things together. Pack them on one of the sleds. We leave at twelve," said the woman, who Tara gathered must be his wife.

"I won't be long," Tara promised.

"One moment," the Bishop's voice was suddenly chilly.

He went up to Tara, and his hard, fanatical eyes stared straight into hers. "You *are* truly seeking to do our work, are you not?"

Tara swallowed. "Of course."

He nodded, apparently satisfied. "Good. But remember, those who take the name of the Lord in vain shall burn eternally in hell's fire. I might add that in my poor capacity, here on earth, I would not show any mercy either."

Hart embraced her in the lodging house.

"I had no idea Mrs. Kane was so religious," he said mischievously. "I could hardly believe what I saw."

Tara lowered her eyes. "I need a ride to Skagway."

"Singing hymns all the way, doubtless," he smiled. "Tara, I'm proud of you."

"Proud!" said Tara. "I'm a little ashamed, I think. They believe they're saving me."

He stood back and studied her, suddenly growing serious.

"Look after yourself Tara," he said. "Take great care. You're a very special woman."

She looked embarrassed.

"I am very envious of Daniel, you know that?"

"Don't be," she said.

He pressed her to him.

Gently she released herself. "His holiness is waiting. I must go soul-saving."

She had never seen him so doleful. "All right," he sighed. *"Hals und Beinbruch."*

"What?"

"Hals und Beinbruch," he repeated. "I wish you a broken neck and a broken leg."

"Ernst!"

"No, no," he said. "As usual, you do not understand me. May nothing happen to you." He reached out and took her hand. "May not a hair be harmed. It is like saying on Christmas Day, 'May this be the most horrid day of your life.' It means, may no day ever be less happy."

"It sounds a bit complicated," Tara said. "But you're very sweet. Good luck on your way north." She kissed him and left him looking after her. He kept looking for a long while.

Three sleds were drawn up on Trail Street, each with a team of dogs. One of the sleds was loaded with wooden crates lassoed securely together.

"We have a precious cargo," the Bishop explained. "Holy Scriptures. Paid for by our benefactor in Skagway. He also built our mission hall."

"He must be a very generous man," Tara remarked.

The Bishop nodded. "Mr. Smith is a very Christian gentleman. There are some pure souls left, even in this wilderness. Now, you will ride with Mrs. Beauchamp," he continued. "Matthew will drive the team."

Doubtfully Tara eyed the small space next to the large woman. Mrs. Beauchamp occupied most of it and, as she eased herself in beside her, Tara felt like a cork being forced into a bottle. Mrs. Beauchamp grunted pointedly to indicate how much she suffered by Tara's intrusion.

Matthew, who turned out to be the Indian who had beaten the drum, stood behind them controlling the four pairs of snapping, growling huskies. Luke, the other Indian, took the rear sled loaded with the crates and the luggage. The Bishop drove the front sled.

"Mush, mush, mush," yelled the Bishop, and Tara held on as the little cavalcade shot off, the huskies yelping excitedly, a whip cracking, and the wind blowing in their faces.

It was a great moment for Tara, and she felt exhilarated. Mrs. Beauchamp sat beside her wrapped in a thick rug, looking as disapproving as ever, but Tara didn't mind; she was happy not to talk. Hart had said the dog sleds could cover thirty miles a day, which meant they would be in Skagway in about three or four hours. Three or four hours, after all these weeks and months. . . .

Mrs. Beauchamp interrupted her thoughts.

"Do you come from a good family, Tara?" she asked.

"My father was a doctor," Tara said coldly.

"Oh!" The Bishop's wife was impressed. "Does your family approve of your traveling in this wild territory?" she questioned, pursing her thin lips.

"Both my parents are dead," Tara said.

"I'm sorry," Mrs. Beauchamp apologized. Then she pressed·on, "Where is your husband? He's not one of these gold prospectors, I trust."

Tara hesitated. She couldn't tell this woman the truth. "He's a Mountie. Up north," she lied.

Mrs. Beauchamp shot her a peculiar look. "But they're not allowed to marry."

"He's an officer," Tara said haughtily, wondering what she was getting herself into.

"Tell me, can you teach Sunday school?"

"Why of course I can," Tara said.

"Good. Mrs. Constantine and I . . ."

"Mrs. Constantine?"

"A delightful lady. Mr. Constantine's wife."

"Oh yes," Tara said vaguely.

"I'd have thought you'd have known. *Inspector* Constantine commands the Mounted Police detachment in Dawson," went on Mrs. Beauchamp importantly. "She and I have a great problem finding helpers. The Indian children are growing up total heathens. Their parents drink," she added, her lips curling with contempt. "Anyway, she and I are looking for somebody to assist us, so when the Crusade reaches Dawson you could—"

"Mrs. Beauchamp," Tara cut in, "I don't want to make a decision right now."

"Oh really? Well, you know best of course, but I must remind you there is little a *decent* woman can do in these parts."

"That rather depends on the woman, doesn't it," Tara said.

45

Mrs. Beauchamp lapsed into a silence frostier than the weather.

The convoy of sleds made good time over the hard, frozen snow, and in the bright sunshine even the cold seemed less harsh. For the first time, Tara saw the real beauty of Alaska, snow-capped mountains and cascading waterfalls.

And then, suddenly, they were in Skagway, heralded by huts and tents and timber buildings. It was a town all right, temporary perhaps, makeshift, rough, but a big sprawl obviously inhabited by thousands of people.

It looked orderly too, the rows of habitations in neat lines, some lots even fenced. The main street was named "Broadway."

Tara stared eagerly at each passerby, hoping to spot Daniel. It was foolish, really, thinking that she would come across him like that, before she had even set foot in this town.

"Are we stopping somewhere soon?" Tara asked. She wanted to get out, start asking directions, find somebody who might know of Daniel.

"We are going to the mission," Mrs. Beauchamp said.

They passed a log building which had an old pair of trousers slung on a line in the front, with the single word "Meals" daubed on the seat in white paint.

"That's the strangest advertisement for a restaurant I have ever seen," Tara exclaimed.

Mrs. Beauchamp grunted. It was obviously an establishment beneath her contempt.

Tara could see the landing stage, with a couple of steamers at anchor. All around her the snow had been churned into brown mud by carts and wagons. There were innumerable tree stumps, standing mutely beside the huts that had been built out of their timber.

Many of the signs were bizarre. "Eggs Fried in Beer, $1.50," read one. Another said simply "Paradise" and underneath, in smaller letters, "Women."

The convoy came to a halt in front of a wooden hut which had "Skagway Mission" painted on it. Some handwritten biblical texts were nailed up outside, like Wanted notices on a sheriff's office.

The little mission hut was completely overshadowed by a big two-floored building next to it, a garish sign identifying it as "The Palace of Forbidden Delights." The three women just walking through the swing doors left little doubt what the forbidden delights might be.

At the door of the mission hut stood a burly man in a black hat with a broad brim, and a thin string tie. His appearance was funereal, and Tara wondered for a moment if he might be the local undertaker.

As the sleds came to a halt, he walked forward, smiling lugubriously.

46

"Welcome to the den of iniquity, your Grace," he solemnly greeted the Bishop, who stepped off his sled and shook his hand. "Welcome in the name of the Congregation."

"You're a sight for sore eyes, Reverend," Beauchamp said, and Tara looked at the man in black, surprised. She thought there was something suspicious about his glittering eyes, his smile, his greeting. He was the last person she would have taken to be a clergyman. And the last person she would have trusted.

Tara and Mrs. Beauchamp unwrapped themselves and got out of the sled. The funereal man gave her a curiously formal greeting.

"A great honor, ma'am," he intoned. "A gracious Christian lady come to beard Babylon. We are all privileged by your presence."

But while he was saying it, he was studying Tara out of the corner of his eye.

"Sister Tara," the Bishop introduced her briefly. "Come to join us in our task."

"Bless you, sister," the man purred, but Tara looked him in the eye, and she sensed they understood one another.

"The Reverend Charles Bowers," explained the Bishop to her. "Our staunch pillar in this sinful bedlam. Converted by the word of the Lord and now an example to all of us. Our strong right hand in our missionary task."

Bowers cast his eyes downward modestly.

"Is all set for the Crusade?" asked the Bishop.

"The town is ripe for salvation," Bowers said. "Posters are up. The flock is waiting to hear the message. I have spread the word that the message of the Lord cometh."

"Good work, Reverend, we must waste no time. Here, Whitehorse, Dawson, Fortymile, Circle City, they need us, there are souls to be saved."

Tara shifted uneasily. There wasn't much daylight left. She wanted to look for Daniel.

"May I unload the holy cargo?" asked Bowers diffidently. "We are starved for the good word."

"Of course, of course." The Bishop rubbed his hands. "Tell me, how is our benefactor?"

"Mr. Smith is well, and anxious for your labors to start," Bowers said. He snapped his fingers, and the two Indians came forward. Matthew and Luke helped them to unload the third sled, piled high with the crates containing Bibles and hymnbooks.

Bowers courteously led the Bishop and his wife into the small mission hall. He looked back at Tara.

47

"Won't you join us, sister," he invited. "I have a pot of tea ready."

"In a moment," Tara said. She was trying to figure out how much longer she would have to play her charade. Perhaps this was the right moment to decamp.

"Don't be long," Bowers urged. "Join us in a little informal prayer of thanksgiving for the safe arrival of the Bishop and his lady."

"I'll come in a minute," Tara said. He hesitated and then went into the mission hut, a little reluctant, she thought, to leave her outside.

Two of the Indians came past her, staggering under the weight of the wooden crate they were carrying. It was marked "Fragile—Bibles." To her surprise, they didn't carry the crate into the mission hall, but went around the side of it and marched straight into a back door of the Palace of Forbidden Delights. Matthew and Luke followed them with another case.

From inside the mission hut came the reedy strains of three people singing a hymn. The Beauchamps and Bowers were evidently getting into their stride. Tara could visualize Mrs. Beauchamp's eyes peering over her hymnbook, wondering what had happened to her.

Forget them, she said to herself. They've got you to Skagway. Now you're here, don't waste time. Find Daniel.

Tara grabbed her sleeping bag, stuffed with her belongings, and marched into the Palace of Forbidden Delights.

The saloon inside was like a barn, with a long bar running the length of the room. There was a painting hanging over the counter of a naked woman lying on a couch, and a piano stood in a corner.

As Tara entered, the bartender, a huge bull-like creature in shirt sleeves, left the counter and walked over to Luke and Matthew, who were warming themselves around a big stove.

The bartender started counting out a wad of dollars, and the Indians' eyes followed each note as he put it down on a table in front of them. As he counted, they nodded in unison imperceptibly. He divided the money into two piles, and Luke and Matthew each pocketed one. Then he shambled back to the bar.

The crates were stacked in front of the bar. Two men began breaking them open. They took out bottle after bottle of whisky and stood them on the bar counter. Each crate contained at least two dozen bottles, but they aroused no curiosity. Evidently, this was a normal delivery.

Around the saloon a few men were lounging about drinking or playing cards. Some saloon girls were leaning against the bar, and two more were sitting alone at tables. As they chatted to one another they

48

looked distinctly bored. On one wall was a poster advertising the Bishop's Crusade.

"Sister Tara," came a soft voice, "join me in a drink of mountain tea."

She turned and saw Bowers standing beside her, grinning. He fitted much better into this setting than in his role as a cleric. His mournful demeanor had miraculously vanished.

"You mean holy water," Tara remarked.

Bowers burst into a roar of laughter and slapped her on the back so hard she nearly lost her balance. He signaled to the bartender. "Two of the best."

"Sorry," Tara said, "I have to get going."

The bartender put two whiskies in front of them.

Bowers raised his glass. She didn't trust him but she liked something about this rogue. He didn't pretend with her.

"Go on," he urged. "Purely medicinal."

She was still chilled from the journey so she sipped the drink, then nearly choked.

Bowers nodded approvingly. "Ninety proof," he said.

"Why Bibles?" Tara asked when she had recovered her breath.

"Bless you, child" he said patronizingly. "Don't you know hooch is illegal in this territory? We look to the good Bishop to bring it in. Unknown to customs, of course. . . . He brings us all kinds of good things, unknowingly. Like you."

"My husband's here," Tara said, reading his thoughts.

"Good," he said. "I approve of the holy state of matrimony. Liddy there is married." He pointed at one of the saloon girls now sitting on the lap of a customer. "So is Stella." Stella was leaning against the bar, her plunging neckline leaving little unrevealed.

Tara put down her glass. "Thanks for the drink," she said.

"Aren't you going to finish it? Sinful to waste God's good rotgut."

She shook her head; then a thought struck her.

"Have you come across Daniel Kane?"

"Never heard of him," Bowers said. He looked at the bull-like bartender, who had been listening to every word. "Have you, Jim?"

Jim shook his head.

"My husband's here," Tara insisted, a little forlornly.

Bowers looked knowing. "Ah. Maybe you ought to try Jeff's Oyster Parlor."

The bartender grinned.

"Oyster Parlor?" Tara repeated, puzzled.

49

"That's when men tell their women they're at a place they're not," Jim put in.

Tara felt they were playing games with her. She walked away.

"Where are you off to, Sister Tara?" Bowers asked.

"The U.S. Marshal," she replied.

Bowers was suddenly very solemn. "The Lord bless and keep you, my child," he said gravely. "Go in Christ."

The laughter that erupted echoed in Tara's ears for a long time.

Marshal Colson's office was not a place likely to inspire anyone with confidence. When she entered, the Marshal had his feet on the desk and was filing his fingernails. His hat was on the back of his head.

"Yeah?" grunted Colson, still filing his nails. He seemed resentful of the intrusion.

Maybe he was just a deputy. "Are you the Marshal?" Tara asked doubtfully.

"Yeah," grunted Colson again.

Tara regarded him with skepticism. He had a scar down his nose, suggesting that at one point in his career somebody had neatly slit his nostril. A gun belt was strapped around his waist with a sheath containing a throwing knife attached near the buckle. Tara thought it a curious weapon for someone charged with upholding public order.

On the desk before him stood a half-empty bottle of whisky and two dirty glasses. For a territory where liquor was illegal, Skagway seemed to be an alcoholic oasis.

Tara cleared her throat. "I'm looking for my husband," she announced, then felt incredibly foolish.

Colson grinned, his broken, stained teeth showing.

"Lost him have you?"

Tara bit her lip.

"He arrived here early in August. On the steamship *Humboldt* from San Francisco. How can I find him?"

The Marshal scratched his stomach. "Hell, I don't know. He'll have moved on, lady, most likely. Nobody stays in Skagway long."

"His name is Daniel Kane," Tara said. "He's about five feet eleven. Brown hair. Hazel eyes. Quite good looking. . . ." She felt slightly embarrassed for saying that.

"And he's prospecting for gold?"

She nodded.

"No gold around these parts, lady." He laughed. "Wish there was. The diggings are way north. Up the Yukon."

Tara thought for a moment. This is where he said he was going, and she hadn't believed Hart when he had said there was no gold mining in Skagway. "I'm sure he's . . ." Then she stopped. She didn't trust this man.

"Strangers come and go. We don't take notice," Colson said.

"Somebody must know. Where is the assay office?"

Colson stared at her. "The what?"

The man is insufferable, thought Tara. "Isn't that what it's called? The place where people register claims? Where do I find it? They'll know him."

"We ain't got no such thing," Colson said. "We don't need it. What do you want an assay office for lady? You got any gold?"

"Well, where do people register their gold strikes?" Tara asked impatiently.

Colson laughed.

"Fortymile, Dawson, all north. I keep telling you. There ain't no gold in Skagway. Leastways, no gold you dig up. Never been any gold. You lost your bearings, lady. Better make for Dawson."

"Dawson—how far's that?"

"Seven hundred miles north. Up the White Pass. Good salmon fishing here. And other sport." He leered crookedly. "They bring their gold here, they don't find it. Sorry."

Daniel had never mentioned going to Dawson; he had always talked of Skagway. It didn't make sense. Maybe Daniel was working a gold strike in secret. If the news spread, somebody might move in on him. With men like Colson running the local law, he couldn't rely on much protection against claim jumpers.

"He could be anywhere there," Colson said, nodding at a map of the whole Yukon area, vast and unpopulated. Next to it were numerous Wanted posters, some issued by the U.S authorities, some by the Canadian Northwest Mounted Police.

"Now if your man was one of those fellows, I'd have spotted him," said Colson. "But unless they're wanted, or dead, or in jail, I don't have nothing to do with anybody."

Tara stood undecided. It was all going wrong. She had only the vaguest idea of the geography of this territory. She thought they found gold all over.

"You all on your own?" asked Colson, interrupting her thoughts.

"I'm all right," Tara said.

"You'll be looking for a place to bed down for the night, I figure."

"I'll find somewhere," Tara said, wishing she was as confident as she hoped she sounded.

"OK," Colson grunted. "Just remember this is a law-abiding town. We got a civic spirit here, and we're proud of it. Strangers are welcome, but we don't want no trouble."

"I've already noticed you're a very religious community," Tara observed frostily.

She picked up her bag and turned to leave.

"Glad to have been of service," Colson called out. "Anything else I can do, just let me know."

He went back to filing his nails.

CHAPTER SEVEN

The Indians called the town Skagus, which meant "Home of the North Wind," and Skagway lived up to its name. In the weak sunshine it had seemed a city in the making, brash, rough, crooked but colorful, lively, young. Now, in the gloom, it was suddenly unfriendly, bare, the wind whistling around corners, the narrow paths at the side of the shacks full of shadows and lurking dangers.

As Tara surveyed the street from outside the Marshal's office, a nagging, unwanted thought began to grow. Supposing something had happened to Daniel? With the law in the hands of a man like Colson, a dozen crimes could probably happen and remain unknown. A fight in a saloon, an argument, a robbery. Anything. Please no, she prayed silently, don't let it be that, but the unease remained.

She started wandering aimlessly in no specific direction, stopping eventually outside a shoplike facade, with "Skagway Intelligencer" spelled out on the glass window. "The Klondike's Biggest Little Paper," boasted the inscription underneath. The current issue was pinned inside the window, together with a notice reading "Office Boy Wanted." The notice was yellow and faded. Evidently office boys were scarce in Skagway. She went into the little shop.

An old man, an ink-smudged apron tied around his bulky girth, was handsetting type behind the counter.

"If you want to place an ad, you're too late. She's going to bed now," he said, glancing at her before returning to his typesetting. "You'll have to wait for next week."

"Is the Editor in?" asked Tara.

He hesitated a moment. Then he wiped his hands on a cloth and shuffled over to the counter.

"I'm the Editor," he said, peering at Tara over the top of his glasses. Also the printer, the reporter, the cashier, the delivery man, the owner, and, for some months now, the office boy. The biggest little paper it might be, but the *Intelligencer* couldn't afford much.

Tara didn't quite know how to begin. The old man sensed her uncertainty. "Well?" he asked. "It's press night, and I haven't got much time. She starts printing in an hour."

"If anything happens in Skagway, you hear about it, don't you?"

The old man nodded. "You could say that," he agreed, with a touch of pride. "All the news that's fit to print," he added, as if he'd coined the phrase. "We don't miss much."

She took the plunge. "Have you heard of a man called Daniel Kane?"

The old man scratched his bristly chin. "Don't recall it. Who is he?"

"I'm his wife. I've just arrived in town."

"Ah, yes. Kane, you said?" He looked at her sympathetically. "Well, Mrs. Kane, he hasn't robbed the bank, that's for sure, because he would have made the lead story, and he hasn't done that. Don't think he's shot anybody, don't think anybody's shot him. We haven't had a good shooting for a couple of months. Nobody's drowned lately, and the only rape we've had has been an Indian girl, and the Indians killed the guy. He was a fur trapper. Mr. Kane ain't a fur trapper?"

She shook her head. The old man was rambling, but at least he was trying to help.

"No, I don't think you need to worry about him having had a . . . misadventure." He picked the word carefully. "We wouldn't miss a thing like that." He paused. "Tried the Marshal's office?"

She nodded.

He squinted at her. Then he leaned across the counter. "Maybe you'd like to place an ad," he suggested tentatively. "Cost you just one dollar. Too late now, but we can give it a prominent position next week. Paper's got a wide readership. Somebody's bound to see it, if he's still around." Suddenly the door burst open, and a man rushed in. He was rosy-faced, kind-looking, fat, and seemed very excited.

"Abe," he panted. "Abe, got a big story for you."

Abe shook his head.

"You're too late. She's gone to bed."

The fat man wasn't discouraged. "Wait till you hear what it is," he gasped, still breathless. "You can't afford to miss it." He paused for effect and took a deep breath. "Serena Bradley's had her throat slit. Thatcher's girl." He stood back triumphantly.

Abe grabbed a pencil and a sheet of paper.

"Hell, the paper's going to be late this week. What happened?"

"They got the man. It's Cal Mason. She was with him upstairs, at the Last Chance. He took out a bowie knife and cut her throat from ear to ear. *And* she was as naked as the day she was born."

"You're kidding," said the Editor, pencil in mid-air.

"I just fitted her. Oak, plain and dignified. Mr. Smith's paying. She was a nice looker. Only five feet two inches, and slim. Medium-sized box. Maybe I ought to fit brass handles."

"Why did Cal do a thing like that?" Abe asked, busy writing.

The man shrugged. "He went crazy, I guess. Maybe she wasn't giving him his money's worth. They're trying him in the morning."

"It'll be in the paper by then," Abe said. "Before she's even planted."

"Don't forget," the jolly man reminded him. "Funeral arrangements by Frederick Grant and Son. One good turn. . . ."

"Sure, sure," Abe said, writing. He finished and then saw Tara still standing there. She had been listening, fascinated.

"Maybe you can help this lady," he said to Grant.

The man turned to Tara for the first time.

"Frederick Grant's the name, mortician, open twenty-four hours a day," he introduced himself, raising his hat.

"She's looking for her husband. Name of Kane, Daniel Kane. You come across him?"

Grant shook his head, looking slightly disappointed. But he took out a little black notebook and turned the pages.

"The only Ks I've had was Kerr last month, you remember, the guy who drank himself to death. And there was a Kennedy in April. No Kane's died in this town."

"And Mr. Grant would know," Abe reassured her.

She left the little newspaper office with a lighter heart. At least he had survived Skagway.

Now her immediate problem was a roof over her head, food, and warmth. There was the Mission Hall, but not even the thought of shelter and a place to rest could persuade her to swallow more doses of the Beauchamps' brand of salvation.

Then Tara stopped. Ahead of her was a sign, roughly painted on boards nailed together, with one word: "Loans." Another notice said, "Cash for any Item."

She tried to think of something on which she could raise a few dollars. She had nothing. No jewelry, no valuables, no . . . Except one thing. The little locket containing her mother's miniature. That was silver. She hated the idea of pawning it. Yet she couldn't walk around Skagway all night. Soon she and Daniel would come back, loaded with gold, and she would redeem it.

She crossed the street and pushed through the swing doors. Waiting their turn patiently in front of a counter with a grill, like a bank teller's window, were half a dozen men, standing silently in line.

The men looked haggard, shabby. This is the other side of the Gold Rush, she thought. One of them clutched a rifle, which he sold for six dollars. The man behind the counter, an unlit cigar in his mouth, a gun belt strapped around him, was called Sam, apparently; they seemed to know him.

The man ahead of Tara just stood, waiting, his hands empty, and she wondered what he had to sell. When it was his turn at the grill he took off his spectacles and handed them to Sam, who gave the man a dollar. Then he added them to a collection of eyeglasses on a rack marked "All one price. . . ." Evidently anybody who needed spectacles in Skagway took pot luck.

"What's this?" asked Sam as she handed the locket across the counter. "This ain't worth a bent dime to me."

"It's sterling silver," Tara pointed out, hating the way he dangled the miniature between his fat, dirty fingers.

Sam ignored her. "You got any gold?"

"No."

"Well, ain't you got something useful? Maybe some tools? A gun? A pair of boots? Ain't you got something a man can use?"

She shook her head. Her face was drawn, pale with fatigue; her stomach was groaning with hunger. She was trying to stop herself shaking.

Sam shifted his unlit cigar. He seemed to feel sorry for her.

"Lady," he said, not unkindly, "it ain't any good to me."

She was too tired, too worn out to say anything. Only her eyes showed her despair.

Sam sniffed. He held up the locket.

"Here, fellows," he called out to the crowd of ragged men who were lounging around, examining the array of pledged goods Honest Sam had on offer. "Anybody want a picture of a lady all in silver?"

No one said a word. The man who had just pawned his glasses stumbled over a spittoon near the stove on his way out.

"I'll tell you what," Sam said, pulling his ear. "I hate to see a little lady in trouble." He examined the locket closely once more. "I'll lend you five dollars on this."

"Can't you make it more?" asked Tara. Five dollars, in this town! With these prices?

"Look, I'm doing you a favor. I'm trying to help you."

"All right," Tara agreed reluctantly.

55

"No deal." It was a soft voice, with a southern drawl, but it had authority. She swung around.

Standing by the door was an immaculately dressed man. He was tall, in his mid-thirties, and across his black vest was looped a heavy gold watch chain hung with charms. Above a well-trimmed mustache he had chiseled features. His eyes were gray, shrewd, alert, curiously piercing but slightly hooded, which made him appear deceptively uninterested.

"Give it back to the lady," he ordered.

"Yes, Boss," Sam said hastily. He thrust the locket at her.

"No," insisted Tara. "I want my money."

"My regrets, ma'am," the man said, shrugging.

She felt her anger rise. "You keep out of it," she cried. "It's none of your business."

The man smiled. "On the contrary, this is my business. I own it."

Tara, tight-lipped, grabbed the locket. "All right then, I'll find somebody else to give me a fair price."

"Not in Skagway," he replied with finality, and his tone was such that she believed him.

"Who are you?" she asked, staring at him with hostility.

"The name is Smith, Jefferson Randolph Smith."

"Mr. Smith, I need that money." To hell with her pride. Five dollars meant a bed for the night.

"May I?" he said. He took the locket out of her hand and looked at the painted miniature. "Very attractive. Is she your kin?"

"My mother."

"I should have guessed," he purred. He turned the locket over, looked at the words inscribed on it. "To Tara." He glanced up at her. "Tara? Is that your name? So tell me Tara, what brings a looker like you to this hole?"

The bland way he appraised her was unnerving.

"I'm here to find my husband," she replied coldly.

Smith's eyes registered surprise.

"Daniel Kane, have you come across him?"

"Should I have?"

Tara felt increasingly uncomfortable. His eyes did not leave her face.

"Well? Can I have my money? she demanded.

He shook his head. "Unfortunately, it's worthless to me." He handed it back, looking her up and down. "But you do have other assets."

She heard somebody snigger. Her blood quickened.

"I'm not for sale."

He raised an eyebrow. "Oh, come now. Everything has its price, and that's a sure thing. Some come just a little more expensive."

She was outraged, and for a moment she had an urge to slap his face. He stood, eyeing her; then he took out a cheroot, bit the end, and lit it.

"We're interested in gold," continued Smith, exhaling a cloud of Havana smoke. But his eyes belied that. "I'll tell you what I'll do. Jefferson Smith never lets a lady go broke. I'll make you an offer."

"For what?" she asked curtly.

"*That's* gold," he said and pointed at her wedding ring.

"I'll give you fifty dollars for it. Now that's a mighty generous offer. That's the going rate for three ounces of gold. But I'll give it to you for that little gew gaw—just to show there's no hard feelings."

Her green eyes narrowed. "No."

"Can you afford not to?" Smith asked.

It was true. She couldn't. If she didn't get some money, what would she do? Become a saloon girl, like the hustlers she had seen in the Palace of Forbidden Delights? Freeze to death? Starve? Fifty dollars could take her a long way. . . .

"Take it or leave it," Smith said carelessly, tipping some ash off his cheroot onto the floorboards.

Tara hesitated, her face flushed. Then slowly she began to twist the ring off her finger. It had never been off her hand since Daniel put it there nearly three years ago when they had exchanged rings. It was difficult to get off. She had to twist and pull before it finally slid from her finger. Then, without a word, she passed the ring over to Smith.

"You see?" he murmured. "Nothing's that permanent."

"What good is it to you?" she asked.

"It's gold, *Mrs.* Kane. Pure gold," he replied mockingly.

He was trying to humiliate her. She sensed his pleasure at depriving her of the symbol of her marriage.

"Pay the lady," Smith ordered Sam. He looked at the ring. He polished it on his vest than examined it admiringly, studying the two names engraved inside. To her fury he started trying it on his fingers. Finally he managed to get it onto the little finger of his left hand.

Sam counted out the money, and as Tara took it she said to Smith tersely, "It's only a loan. I'll get the ring back."

"It'll always be a pleasure to do business with you, Mrs. Kane," Smith replied, inclining his head. "I'm already looking forward to seeing you again."

As she walked out of the store she kept trying to tell herself it was

57

only a ring and that when she found him, Daniel would give her another one, a beautiful unsullied one. But her finger felt naked, and she was aggravated at having had to give in to that scoundrel—surrendering to him the very token of her vow to Daniel, even if there had been no alternative.

Out in the dark, cold night air, snow was lazily falling. Tara shivered. She had to find shelter, a place to sleep and forget.

Next to the little store that sold cigars and tobacco stood the double-fronted wooden façade of the Mondame Hotel. It looked quiet, respectable.

The dingy hallway contained a bell marked "Visitors." Tara's summons, to her surprise, was answered by a meticulously polite Chinese couple. A single room would cost ten dollars for the night. For the comfort of a mattress, a pillow, and privacy, she thought it was cheap at the price.

She was ravenous. She could not recall when she had last eaten a proper meal, and the hunger had been gnawing at her for hours. She sat down to a plate of meat and beans. The meat tasted different from anything she had ever eaten; it was tough and flavorless, but her hunger was such that she wolfed it down in a way that would have shamed her at one time. She gulped the scalding coffee that came with it.

Ten minutes later, there was a knock on the door of the tiny room, and the couple carried in a tub, followed by a copper kettle of steaming water.

The stove in the corner heated the room well, and she felt like Cleopatra as her naked body sank into the tub. When she emerged she knew she could face anything. She put out the lamp and lay curled up in the bed. It was bliss to be alone without fear of intrusion, to feel the sheets, and to be rid of that sleeping bag for just one night. It was only when she touched her finger, her bare finger, and thought of her ring and the man who now had it, that the warmth and comfort felt less secure. She closed her eyes, but the man called Jefferson Smith could not be shut out. He kept bowing mockingly, with a kind of debonair, challenging smile, and she tossed and turned a long time before he disappeared.

When Tara came downstairs in the morning, the hefty figure of the Reverend Bowers rose from a wicker chair to greet her.

"Good morning, Sister Tara. I trust you slept well."

"Yes, thank you," Tara said warily. The last person she had expected to see was this phony cleric.

"Praise be," he said piously. "When your good face was not to be

58

seen, we were afraid that you might have fallen among evil men. We even offered up a short prayer to you."

"Well, it obviously worked," she said brusquely. "Now if you'll excuse me."

"We are very anxious about your welfare," he went on, not stepping aside. "It is so easy for a virtuous young woman to go astray in these parts. May I ask what your plans are?" He beamed encouragingly.

"Yes, I'm leaving for Dawson," said Tara.

He drew his breath.

"That is not a journey for a Christian woman on her own." He shook his head. "I think you should reconsider."

He could see that his clerical act was making no impression on Tara and dropped it suddenly. "You're not being very smart, are you?" he said.

"I'll manage."

She tried to get past him, but he still didn't move.

"Why don't you stick around, Tara? I could fix you up with a good job, believe me."

"Singing hymns?" she asked.

"Aw, you know what I mean. All it needs is a word to the boss: He'll see you're OK."

"I've no doubt the Bishop . . ."

"Who's talking about the Bishop?" he exclaimed. "I mean the boss. Mr. Smith can do anything for a girl. I'll take you to him. He likes to get friendly with the new talent in town. He's taken quite a fancy to you."

"Thank you." Tara put on her mittens and looked Bowers straight in the eye. "You can tell your boss I'm not interested in anything he has to offer."

"Don't be dumb, woman," Bowers said. "You're on your own. You need protection. He'll look after you."

He waved an arm around. "He's paid your bill here, and he'll fix you up in a really nice place."

"I can imagine."

"You don't belong with the holy joes, Tara," he argued, trying to hold his ground. "You're one of us. One of our kind. You'll fit in great. The way you hoodwinked the bish, Jesus, I have to hand it to you. . . ."

Tara drew herself up. "You can give a message to your Mr. Smith." The tone of her voice was deceptively mild.

"Right away," Bowers said eagerly.

"Tell him I'll get my wedding ring back."

59

She stalked out of the hotel, but Bowers was in no way abashed as he watched her go. The boss was right. Here was some stylish new talent. Praise the Lord.

Outside the hotel something important seemed to be happening.

She had no idea what it was, but the excitement was spreading like a brush fire. She saw the Editor of the *Intelligencer* running up the street, puffing and blowing. Then a mob of men appeared, baying and shouting, shaking their fists, completely filling the street, sweeping forward relentlessly. Tara hastily stepped into a doorway as they rolled past her. They were half pushing, half dragging a man. His hands were tied behind his back, and he was being held by both arms. Despite the cold, he wore no jacket, no coat. Periodically somebody kicked him from behind or pushed him, and he would have fallen several times if the two men on each side had not held him up.

The man was terrified. He made no sound and his eyes were glassy. One of the mob threw a bottle, which struck his head, but he merely blinked. Leading the mob was Marshal Colson, carrying a shotgun. He appeared to be enjoying himself. The crowd formed a circle around a tall birch tree, jostling and elbowing each other to get closer. Tara couldn't actually see the tied man any more; he was hidden by the mass surging around him.

She knew this was a lynching. She had imagined it might be something like this—an angry howling mob, a frightened victim, a ghastly bloodlust. The only strange thing was the way the man seemed to accept his fate. Maybe he knew it was all over for him.

She looked around at the screaming, distorted faces. She saw nothing but crazed hate and eager anticipation. Surely the law . . . But of course the law was here. Skagway's law.

The Marshal dragged up a crate. Now he stood on it, and raised his hand to silence the throng.

"Let's have some quiet," he shouted. He waited for the mob's attention. "This ain't a picnic. This here execution is being carried out according to law, sentence of death having been passed by the citizens of this community."

A roar went up from two hundred voices.

Some of the mob parted, and a horse was led into the center. The white-faced man was hoisted on it.

"Cal Mason," called out Colson, turning to the man, who was sitting rigid on the horse, hands still tied behind his back, eyes staring in front of him, "You're going to be hanged for the murder of Serena Bradley. Is there anything you want to say?"

The Marshal didn't wait for him to answer.

"Get the rope up," he ordered. There was a murmur among the crowd. Colson looked furious. "Jesus Christ, where is the goddam rope?" he yelled. "You people don't deserve decent law in this town if you can't even hang somebody efficient like."

"I'll get it," volunteered a young boy and ran off.

Tara could not take her eyes off the face of the man on the horse. She felt sorry for him, no matter what he had done.

"Maybe the Reverend can give him a prayer," called out somebody, and the crowd laughed. Bowers took Colson's place on the wooden crate.

"Friends," he said piously, raising his arms. "Silence. Let us not have levity. This is a solemn moment." He folded his hands in front of him. "Vengeance shall be mine, saith the Lord. Those who live by the sword shall die by it." He paused, apparently trying to think of some other apt scriptural text, but gave up. "Amen, amen," he concluded, stepping off the box.

The boy pushed his way through the throng. Colson raised the coiled rope high above his head. It had already been knotted into a noose.

"There she is," he shouted.

"Come on, come on," chanted the mob.

The rope was swung over a bough of the tree. Tara felt sick. She turned and walked away from the crowd. She had seen enough. Then she stopped.

Marching up the street toward her were six men. They were walking abreast, in step, their faces set. Tara could see the high-necked collars of scarlet tunics under their fur-trimmed jackets, and a broad yellow stripe down the length of their blue breeches. Their bearing was upright, military. The leader's pistol holster was already unbuttoned, and the other five also carried rifles.

The crowd around the tree were too preoccupied to notice them. Colson put the noose around the neck of the wretched man on the horse.

"We've had prayers, so I guess we can get on with it," Colson yelled, raising his hand.

From behind the mob there was a shot. The Mountie sergeant had fired into the air.

"Stop," he shouted.

Behind him, his five men were cradling their rifles.

The mob parted as Colson walked through to face the Mounties.

"Keep out of this, Sarge," he rasped. "You've got no jurisdiction. This is United States territory."

61

"Release that man," said the sergeant. He had lowered his pistol, but he still had his finger on the trigger.

"This is a legal execution," Colson bawled. "You got no right to interfere."

"It's a lynching," said the sergeant tersely. "You've got two minutes to break it up."

"Or else?"

"We'll take him."

The Mounties stood impassively, like statues, unblinking, staring almost through the throng. The crowd stirred restlessly, muttering.

Colson drew himself up and confronted the sergeant.

"I'm warning you. This is none of your business. Get moving."

"Lynching is unlawful anywhere," the sergeant said. "Get that man off the horse."

"He killed a woman," Colson protested. "He's getting what he deserves. Stay out of it."

The sergeant turned to his men.

"Right," he said.

The Mounties advanced, but the crowd closed their ranks. Colson stood in front of them arms akimbo, smiling complacently. The mob at his back, outnumbering the six Mounties fifty to one, gave him confidence.

"You lay a hand on anybody, and you'll . . ." he warned, his hand hovering near his gun.

"You're obstructing the law," the sergeant said quietly. He was very calm, and very determined.

"Run 'em out of town," yelled somebody in the crowd. Others voiced their agreement. From somewhere, a piece of frozen snow was hurled, and hit one of the Mounties in the face. It was followed by a rock.

Tara saw the crowd surge forward, and then she heard an ominous sound, the bolts of the Mounties' rifles being pulled back.

"No goddamn Mountie tells us what to do," Colson yelled, and the mob was vociferous in its agreement. His finger stabbed at the star on his coat. "You see that? I'm the U.S. Marshal, and what I say goes. You got no rights in Skagway."

The Mounties ignored him. Slowly, deliberately they advanced with their guns at the ready. Colson swung around, facing the mob.

"Are we going to take this?" he goaded them. "Are you going to let these red bellies get away with it?"

"Marshal!" called out a commanding voice.

Across the street a man had appeared on a white horse. His face was obscured momentarily by the bright cold sun. Then Tara recognized

Jefferson Smith. He cantered across the street until he was between the Mounties and the mob.

"Gentlemen," Smith declaimed, facing the crowd. "Remember that we are all law-abiding citizens." He was half smiling, a dapper, elegant figure. A man in total control.

"But Jeff . . ." Colson began.

Smith started to edge his horse through the crowd, which parted respectfully for him. He stopped next to Mason. There was complete silence. Leaning over, he lifted the noose from the man's neck. Then he walked his horse to the center of the throng and held up his hand. He was like a general commanding a rabble. His authority was unchallenged. He *does* own the place, Tara thought, as she watched Marshal Colson glowering at him resentfully.

"My friends, we are all proud of the way we run this town, and we must certainly cooperate with the officers here," said Smith.

"This ain't their territory," a man yelled. "Tell them to get back to Dawson."

"On the contrary, any disagreements about territorial boundaries must be decided in a proper court of law," Smith pointed out smoothly. "If these officers feel they have jurisdiction, it is not for us, gentlemen, to argue."

"Hey Soapy, cut the speechifying," shouted somebody from the back, and another man yelled, "You're selling out, Soapy. You're letting the Canucks take over. We got our rights."

A man pushed forward and went up to Smith.

"Throwing your weight around, ain't you," he accused. "Trying to run the town your way. It's you they should arrest."

Smith looked down at him with contempt.

"I'm doing it by the book, Reid. Nice and legal," he retorted. He patted the neck of his beautiful horse, which was getting a little restless. He never took his eyes off the crowd. "If you know what's good for you, you'll agree with me." His teeth flashed in what his friends would call a smile, and his enemies a snarl. Either way, it was dangerous.

"You murdering bastard, Cal," cried out a dark-haired man in the crowd. He had wild eyes, and some of the men around him parted a little to give him room. He tried to push his way nearer to the prisoner. "You're not going to get away like this."

Smith edged his horse forward a little. "He isn't going to get away with anything, Matt," he said. "Take it easy."

"I don't want your smooth talk, I want him strung up," yelled the man. "Serena deserves better than this, and you know it. She was my woman."

"Sure," Smith said. "Nobody's smooth-talking anybody." He was doing just that, thought Tara. "Serena will get the best funeral money can buy, I promise you. So you mourn her decently. Like me. There'll be no lynching."

"You're yellow, Soapy," Matt yelled, and those near him looked around uneasily. "Six red bellies with pop guns, and you turn yellow."

There was stunned silence. Quietly, a dozen tough-looking individuals had moved in and were forming a protective ring around Smith and his horse. Two carried clubs, the rest had guns, and their hands hovered close over them.

"We all know how you felt about her, Matt. Does you credit, boy." Smith looked down at the man mockingly. "Cal's going to get his desserts, never fear."

"You're selling us down the river," Matt cried. Two other tough-looking men, one with an eye patch, appeared suddenly behind Matt.

"Cal took my woman and killed her, and I'll get him, even if your whole gang is there. I'll do it myself, you son of a bitch."

"You'd better get out of town, Thatcher," growled one of the men behind Matt. They had put their arms around his shoulders as if they were all old friends. Then Tara spotted the gun one of them was pressing into his back.

"I'll be waiting, Cal," he called out, and then he was bent double as one of the hoodlums twisted his arm until he winced with pain.

Smith trotted back to Mason. The man was still sitting upright, hands tied.

Smith took the bridle of the horse and led it through the crowd. He stopped in front of the Mounties, who were eyeing him warily. Around Smith, men shifted restlessly.

"Here's your prisoner, Sergeant," Smith said. "He's your responsibility now. Do your duty. Get him out of town if you don't want a riot."

The sergeant looked at Smith with intense dislike. "Don't need you to tell me my job, Smith," he said curtly.

Smith didn't even blink.

"Cut that rope, corporal," the sergeant called.

The corporal, a lanky fair-haired man, cut the rope tying Mason's hands and then helped him down from the horse. The man was stiff and had difficulty moving his arms.

"I'll be around, Cal," Matt called out, still in the grip of Smith's men. The crowd murmured, but Smith raised a hand nonchalantly, and the buzz died down.

"OK, Mason," the sergeant said. "You're in our custody now. Hold out your hands."

The man stretched his wrists out without a word, and a pair of handcuffs snapped shut on them.

"Sergeant," Smith said. "The citizens feel pretty mean about this man. Just remember that. A lot of folks fancied Serena, and some of them might get itchy if you stick around too long." His smile never left his face, and his voice was as smooth as ever.

"You leave that to us, mister," the sergeant said curtly.

"I can't rightly blame Matt here for the way he feels," Smith added, "and I'd hate to see him do something foolish."

"We're hitting the trail to Dawson today. Nothing had better happen to him meantime."

Smith nodded. "Excellent," he said. "The last thing we want is any kind of international incident." He smiled at Colson. "Isn't that right, Marshal?" It was not a question, it was an order.

The sergeant gave a command, and his men formed up around the prisoner. Without a second look at Smith or the sullen crowd, they marched off.

"My compliments to Inspector Constantine," Smith called after them, and there were a few titters among the bystanders. Smith turned his horse around and faced the assembly genially.

"Gentlemen," he shouted, "drinks for everybody. At my place. On the house."

Smith's gang gave a ragged cheer, and the rest joined in. They started drifting down the street in the direction of the saloon. For a moment, Smith sat and watched them. He manipulated them like a puppet master, thought Tara. How disdainful he looks when they aren't watching him.

Slowly Smith urged his white horse forward, and it began to trot lazily up Holly Street. Just as Tara was turning to go, Smith spotted her. He cantered to her side, bowed in the saddle, and took off his hat politely.

"That invitation includes you, Mrs. Kane. I'd be flattered if you'd join us."

Without a word, Tara turned on her heel. Smith rode off. He was smiling.

Back at the Mondame Hotel, Tara got some ink and paper and then, upstairs, locked the door of her room. She had little time, but this must not be botched. She sat down and began writing a letter.

My dear Tara, [she wrote] We are all so delighted that you will be arriving soon, after these many months, and the Constantine household is in quite a tizz at the thought. I am dying to hear all

65

the latest news from home. You have, of course, a long journey ahead of you, and since this is no easy venture for a gentlewoman on her own [Tara was rather pleased with that] your dear brother-in-law insists that as soon as you arrive in Skagway you approach the local post of the Northwest Mounted Police, and ask them if they have a detachment proceeding to Dawson in whose company you might travel. They are *splendid* men[Tara underlined that] and you can *rely* on them absolutely. We would be so relieved to know that you are traveling in safe hands, and have an escort until you join us. We know they will take good care of you. We eagerly await your arrival.

Your loving sister,
Sarah.

P.S. If you see dear Mrs. Beauchamp, give her and the Bishop our kindest regards.

Tara read the letter twice and then back-dated it to June 30, 1897. She thought that, under the circumstances, she had done an admirable job. It nicely interwove truth and fiction, and she felt she had reason to be pleased with her ingenuity. After all, she knew that the commander of the Mounties at Dawson was an Inspector Constantine. She knew he was married. She knew Mrs. Constantine was an acquaintance of Mrs. Beauchamp. So far so good.

What of course she had no way of knowing was whether Mrs. Constantine's first name was Sarah, or if she had a sister at all.

There was only one way to find out.

Outside the police post, four sleds were drawn up with their dog teams. Tara walked in, demure and helpless, introduced herself, and told a startled Sergeant Campbell how grateful she was for their help in getting her up to Dawson. She handed him the letter.

Sergeant Campbell stood by the stove, reading it, a worried look on his face. He read it again. It was well creased and bore the marks of being folded and refolded over many weeks; Tara had spent some time making the notepaper look worn.

"Well," the sergeant said at last, "I just don't know. Nobody told me about this.

"That's just like Sarah," Tara laughed. "She probably forgot. She must have taken it for granted you'd know."

He looked down at the letter in his hand. "We got no orders, and without orders . . ."

66

"Sergeant, you can't just leave me here," Tara gasped. "Why, my brother-in-law would never forgive you!"

It was a very creditable performance, and she could see that her argument had made a direct hit.

Campbell grunted uneasily. Then he went to the door of the hut. "Corporal," he yelled.

The tall fair-haired man came in. "What about this, Lloyd," said the sergeant, handing him the letter. The corporal read it quickly, then glanced at Tara.

"Did you know about this, Sarge?" he asked. Campbell shook his head.

"Maybe we ought to take her with us," he suggested, almost to himself.

"We got the prisoner," the corporal pointed out. "We ain't equipped to carry ladies. Not across the pass."

"I can look after myself," Tara said hastily. "I won't be any burden I promise you. Please don't worry about me."

"Didn't know Mrs. Constantine had a sister," the corporal muttered. "She never mentioned it."

"Well, why should she?" snapped the sergeant.

"Maybe you could telegraph Dawson," Tara suggested. She had already found out that there was no telegraph link.

"Wish we could," the sergeant grunted. "There's no way."

Tara looked suitably disappointed.

Campbell studied the letter again and scratched his chin. "Well now, what on earth do we do with you?"

"You must take me along, Sergeant," Tara insisted. "I haven't seen my sister for years. You've read how excited they all are, so think how angry my brother-in-law will be when you tell him you left me behind," she added almost as an afterthought, well aware of the effect that would have on him. She said a prayer, inwardly, that if heaven couldn't forgive her, Inspector Constantine would.

The two men exchanged glances. "I guess we could fit her on one of the sleds," Campbell muttered. He looked at the corporal. "Yours."

Lloyd didn't seem overenthusiastic. "What about the prisoner?" he asked.

"I'll take him, and we can fit the stores on the other two."

He looked at Tara. "Where is your luggage, Mrs. Kane?"

"I've only a sleeping bag," she said.

"And your clothes?" he went on remorselessly, his eyes taking in her unladylike appearance.

"Everything was stolen."

She was saved by another Mountie coming in.

"All set, Sarge," he announced. "Everything's stowed away and shipshape."

"You'd better check," the sergeant ordered Lloyd. Tara was left alone with him.

"The inspector is a strict disciplinarian," he told her, and her heart started sinking. "He won't tolerate anyone bending regulations. Unauthorized transport of civilians on patrol is bending regulations. Now if you were under arrest or injured . . ."

"Surely just helping me isn't forbidden?" pleaded Tara.

He chewed his lip. Then he made up his mind. "Seeing you're the Inspector's sister-in-law, and that they're expecting you, I guess it'll be all right," he said slowly. "But I depend on you to sort it out with Mr. Constantine if he gets mad at me."

"I'm sure he'll be more than grateful to you, Sergeant," Tara said. So far her plan had worked.

CHAPTER EIGHT

Tara admired the expertise with which the corporal handled his team. He had a short-handled whip with a long, braided sealskin lash that cracked like rifle fire, but he relied far more on his voice. It ordered, threatened, encouraged, persuaded, cajoled, but was always obeyed.

For hours after leaving Skagway they traveled across flat, frozen timberland, following a kind of primitive road, the route of thousands of travelers north. The snow fell steadily. Then the trail grew narrower, the ground more hazardous, the sharp razorlike rocks more menacing.

As the convoy began to ascend the White Pass, the temperature dropped to twenty below zero. This kind of cold was something new; it hurt. Tara felt pain in her nose; inside her nostrils, the tiny hairs froze into sharp little barbs which, as she breathed in the biting air, drew blood.

They were now hundreds of feet up, and the dogs had fallen silent. The effort of pulling thier heavy loads required all their energy, and the Mounties urged them, patiently, reassuringly, along the corkscrew trail, which was dominated by ugly slate cliffs. Below the sheer fall, boulders and rocks were strewn with skeletons and the wreckage of wagons and sleighs that had tried to edge their way along the track and failed. Tara clutched at the sled, pushing away the sickness of fear. Lloyd was whistling silently through his teeth as he drove the team slowly, carefully, in the track of the sergeant's sled.

The precious daylight was fading as they made camp behind some six-foot-high boulders. The dogs were unhitched, cooking gear unpacked, a tent pitched. Two of the men gathered wood and began cutting it up. The dogs were fed first; that was a golden rule. No orders were given; every man knew his task. Their professionalism impressed Tara.

Campbell was setting up the cookstove, and she went over to him. "Is there anything I can do?" she offered. "I'd like to help."

"Shouldn't think you've got much experience of this kind of cooking, ma'am," he replied gruffly, "thanking you all the same."

Inside the tent, the stove was lit, and everyone gathered around it. Outside, the wind shook the canvas, and Tara thought she could hear a wolf howling. Now and then the dogs whined.

One of the men struck a big lump of frozen snow on a branch, which began to melt in the heat of the stove. As the snow dissolved, the water was caught in a pan.

Tara was ravenous. She almost drooled at the aroma of the beans, bacon, corned beef, and potatoes being cooked. The Mounties had supplies of dried sliced potatoes, which they boiled in hot water. And there was steaming coffee. The whole meal was delicious, and when without even asking, the sergeant gave her second helpings, she ate with the same vigor all over again.

The prisoner ate his food listlessly. They had taken off his handcuffs. He was as silent as ever, staring straight into the glow of the little stove. Mason was a strange man, thought Tara. She still had not heard him say a word; almost as if, when he killed that girl, he'd died too.

"It's sort of primitive, Mrs. Kane, you'll have to forgive us," said the sergeant, pouring her more coffee. "We're not used to traveling with ladies."

"I think you've cooked the most delicious meal, Sergeant Campbell."

One of the Mounties laughed. "Bet that's the first time anyone's called rations that," he said.

"How far are we from Skagway?" Tara asked.

"We've covered fifteen miles, today," Campbell said. "It's been easy going. We've been lucky."

He took out a tobacco pouch and started rolling himself a cigarette. "If the weather holds, we'll make the post at Summit Hill in a day or so." He licked the cigarette paper into shape. "If we stay lucky, I reckon we'll reach Lake Bennett in four or five days."

She was thankful for one thing. So far they hadn't asked her any personal questions. Sometimes she thought she saw the lantern-jawed sergeant looking at her thoughtfully, but perhaps it was her imagination, Uneasily, she wondered if he was growing suspicious of her. He had not once asked her about her "sister" or the Constantine family. If he had doubts, he kept them to himself.

Suddenly, outside, there was furious howling and yapping. It was cut short by a sharp yelp, followed by whining.

Hennessy came in, stamping his feet. The sergeant glanced at him questioningly.

"It was only Sawashka," said Hennessy, "trying it on again with Ikkee, the stupid mutt."

The sergeant nodded. "Sawashka won't try that again for a couple of days. He needs a lesson now and then," he explained to Tara as he made room for Hennessy beside the stove, "to show who's top dog. Most important thing you can have out here is a reliable dog team," he added, finishing off his cigarette. "If you're out on your feet, you can't drag your dog team anywhere. But by Christ, they can get you to safety. The dogs are your life. You can't look after them too well. And if you're starving, you can always eat 'em."

"*Eat* the dogs?" Tara made a grimace.

"Tastes mighty good too," the corporal recalled. "Lived on dog for nine days once. Makes prime loin chops. If they get hungry enough, they eat each other. And they'd eat you, if they're famished. That's the way it goes."

"I couldn't," she shuddered. "I'd rather starve."

"Hope you never run out of food," Campbell said quietly. "Eh, Lloyd? With respect, Mrs. Kane, pray that you never have to find out what real hunger does to you out here."

Campbell stretched himself. "I want an early start in the morning," he announced. "I guess we'd all better have some shut-eye." He hesitated and looked at Tara. He cleared his throat. "Normally, Mrs. Kane, we all bed down in the tent—it's the warmest. But seeing you are a lady it would be best if . . . I mean, if you prefer . . ."

"Sergeant Campbell," Tara smiled, amused by his embarrassment. "Why don't we do just that? I've got my sleeping bag, and I'd feel much safer. If that's all right with you?"

"That's dandy, then. You'll have that corner all to yourself, and I'll be right here and . . ." He was obviously relieved.

70

"Don't worry about me, please," Tara said. "I've slept on the floor with a hundred men snoring around me. This will be a luxury."

"You just yell if there's anything you want," pressed Campbell. "And there'll be a sentry on guard all night. You'll be quite safe, I assure you."

"I never doubted it," Tara said.

He turned to the prisoner. "Let's have 'em," he ordered. Obediently Mason held out his arms, and the handcuffs snapped shut again.

"Don't try anything," Campbell warned. "And don't snore."

He turned down the oil lamp, but the red glow from the newly stoked stove continued to illuminate the tent. Tara lay in her sleeping bag, with the sergeant a couple of feet away. His pistol holster was open, the gun was attached to a lanyard around his neck, and she sensed it would take little to wake him up.

Outside she could hear the occasional crunch of the sentry's footsteps on the frozen snow. The moaning wind and the creak of the tent were unfamiliar sounds. The dogs were still apparently resting. Tara turned over and lay listening to the regular, heavy breathing of the others. She did not know why, but she was afraid. Nothing could happen to her in this tent. She was surrounded by the Mounties. The prisoner was handcuffed. But her apprehension kept her awake a long time.

They broke camp early the following morning, determined to cover as much distance as possible. It was a bright, hoary day, crystal clear and as sharp as a diamond.

As the convoy progressed, Tara, for the first time, saw the price the White Pass demanded of those who braved it. They passed exhausted prospectors, moving at a snail's pace, short on supplies, desperately whipping their tired, scrawny, half-starved dog teams.

"Crazy fools," Lloyd muttered. "Greenhorns got no business in this godforsaken country."

A day later, they came across a man sitting by a rock. Strewn round him were sacks of supplies, wooden boxes, mining equipment. He had scrawled in the snow, in big letters, "Outfit for sale—Cheap."

Campbell halted the sled train.

Halfway down the man's face the tears had frozen on his cheeks. But his eyes were still streaming as he sobbed to himself.

The sergeant went over to the man while the other Mounties watched impassively. "What's the matter, partner?" he asked gently.

The man shook his head.

"You can't stay here," said the sergeant. "Not like this. Where are your animals?"

"Dead," said the man.

"Where are you making for?"

The man remained silent.

Campbell studied him. "Want to come with us as far as Summit Hill?" he offered.

"I'm staying. Right here," the man said.

"What the hell are you waiting for? Somebody to buy all this? Out here, on the trail?"

"Leave me," the man said.

Campbell shrugged. "OK. If you change your mind, the post is northeast, up that way . . ."

Campbell returned to the dog train, signaling them to get ready.

"Can't force a man against his will," Lloyd said when he saw Tara's face. "A man's got a right to freeze to death. We offered." They traveled on in silence.

Suddenly, there was a shot. Then another one.

"Keep down," she heard Campbell yell from the sled in front.

The prisoner sagged, face up, halfway out of the sled, and in the middle of his forehead was a neat little hole. A thin trickle of blood was meandering its way across his brow.

"Over there," the sergeant shouted, pointing at a clump of fir trees. He signaled to Hennessy and Russell. "We'll cover you," he yelled.

The two Mounties started edging their way up to the trees.

Tara scrambled out of the sled and flung herself on the ground, just as the corporal began firing into the wood.

Three more shots whizzed past the two Mounties who were racing toward the trees, ducking among rocks and boulders for protection. Campbell fired back from behind the sled that carried their stores.

Tara was totally confused. Everything was happening so fast. All she could do was lie flat on the ground, feeling her heart pounding against the frozen earth.

Two further shots rang out from inside the wood.

"You're surrounded, you don't stand a chance," Campbell yelled. "Come out with your hands up."

They waited, tensely. Then a man emerged, holding his hands high above his head. Hennessy and Russell covered him warily. Lloyd reloaded his rifle.

The man was dark-haired, dressed like a trapper, and a cartridge belt crisscrossed his chest. He seemed vaguely familiar.

As she scrambled to her feet, Tara was shaking. For the first time in her life, she had witnessed men shooting to kill, had seen a man murdered in front of her eyes. It seemed unreal and terribly matter of-fact, and she shuddered at the easiness of it all.

"Is the bastard dead?" the man asked, looking at the slumped body of Mason.

"Dead as he'll ever be. What the hell's going on, Thatcher?"

"I swore I'd get him," Thatcher said with satisfaction. "I trailed you from Skagway. He killed my woman," he added simply.

"I heard she was anybody's woman," the sergeant growled, unfeeling. He had unlocked the dead man's handcuffs, and now he clicked the steel bracelets shut on Thatcher's wrists.

"Save yourself the trouble," the man grunted. "I don't aim to go anywhere."

"You can bet on that," Campbell said, surly.

Before they moved off, they buried Mason. One of the Mounties nailed a rough cross together, and they stuck it on top. "Cal Mason," they carved on it, "Died Sept. 22 1897."

Mason's death had a marked effect on the sergeant. When they next made camp, he remained aloof from the others, talking in curt monosyllables.

The other three Mounties seemed to understand. When Campbell barked out an occasional order, they jumped to it, without talk.

"He's got his hands full," Lloyd whispered to Tara. "Nothing personal, Mrs. Kane. Only he's in a heap of trouble. You don't lose a prisoner, not in the Mounties."

They did not need to tell her when they were passing through Dead Horse Gulch. The snow in it was packed hard, the trail trampled by thousands who had come during this summer and autumn, relentlessly pursuing the route north. The wailing of the sharp wind sounded to Tara like the screams of dying animals and the shrieks of maddened, desperate men who had met their end here.

It was thirty degrees colder than on the coast. She longed desperately for warmth, not only a physical temperature, but something warm for the eye. Her surroundings were dazzlingly white, hard, cold; in the shadows, gray-white; in the cold sun, blue-white; on the peaks in the distance, silver-white; even the steam that rose from the panting dog teams was white.

The final thousand feet to the top of Summit Hill was the worst ordeal Tara had yet had to face. To lighten the dogs' burden, she and Thatcher had to make the climb on foot. It brought home what a luxury it had been, sitting back in a sled, warmly wrapped, being pulled along, holding on tight, sometimes terrified the sled would tip over a narrow edge, or slide down a ravine, but all the time having the comfort of letting others strain and pull and shove.

She staggered and groped her way along, once slipping, and sliding, panic-stricken, twenty feet before Hennessy managed to grab her.

"You can have a rest when we get to the post," the sergeant said, trying to encourage her.

"How much farther is that?" she gasped, speaking with an effort, breathless from the steep climb.

"It's right ahead."

Four hours later, it seemed no nearer.

To Tara the police post at Summit Hill began to assume the image of a distant paradise. It represented warmth, shelter, hot food, a roof over her head, a place where she could rest and ease the awful pain in her limbs. It meant a sanctuary at last. For the Mounties it was the official frontier, the border between United States territory and British Columbia. She looked forward to her first sight of it with growing excitement. But all she saw, as they trudged on, was the same inhospitable landscape. She tried to think of Daniel struggling up this trail, keeping going by sheer will power, gritting his teeth, each step feeling heavier than the last.

Then she saw the sign, half covered by snow. It was primitive and weatherworn. "Border One Mile," it said.

One mile! She bit her chapped lips. Her eyelashes were frosted, her face hurt. She dragged herself along, holding on to the sled the dogs were painfully pulling up the slope, and she tried to work out the distance she covered each time she took a laborious step, but she gave up. She was so tired, so cold, she couldn't think properly.

At last, she saw the sergeant's team halt. Campbell was pointing straight ahead, and waving them on. Tara's heart jumped. She could see a cluster of huts and two poles, flying the Stars and Stripes and the Union Jack side by side. Thin wisps of smoke rose from the cabins. The corporal cracked his whip over the heads of his team, but it was more in triumph than reproof. They had been spotted at the post, and men in furs came out of the huts and waved to them.

For Tara, suddenly they meant more than food and shelter. This was the border. This was the Klondike. This was not the end of the trail, but the beginning.

From a distance, Tara was difficult to recognize as a woman. But once inside the post, she was the center of attention. The NCO in charge, a sergeant called Grayburn, fussed over her like a mother hen. He was a rugged man, with a slight limp, and his mustache was waxed into needle-sharp points. He had a patrol out, and Tara was immediately given a berth in their empty bunkhouse. A tub of steaming water was brought to her and extra blankets put on the bunk. Her sleeping bag was carried in for her, and she found herself being treated like a lady.

Tara wondered how Campbell explained her presence. Would she be subjected to a barrage of questions? Instead, she was invited to join the men for dinner in the mess, a prospect that filled her with apprehension.

She expected it to be a rough and ready affair. But they turned out in their scarlet tunics, buttons flashing, cavalry boots polished like mirrors, and they observed strict protocol. Every man remained on his feet until Tara sat down.

She was thankful she had made some attempt to be presentable. She had soaked in the tub and brushed her hair. She had no change of clothes, but she looked like a woman, and they had seen none for a long while.

As the men took their places with a clatter, she wondered if they were always so correct and formal in the mess. What will happen when they find out I'm here under false pretenses? she thought. But the looks they gave her were just curious, and, she sensed, appreciative of female company.

Tara studied the dozen men sitting around the table and noticed how alike they were: each large and powerful in build, six-footers to an inch, and, except for the sergeants, none over thirty. They were tough men, these troopers of the NWMP's Yukon Division. They sat ramrod straight, collars buttoned high, each on his best behavior, Grayburn sitting on her right and Campbell on her left.

The mess hall was built of crude logs and dominated by two enormous stoves, with chimney pipes to the timbered roof. There was a blazing wood fire as well, and over the mantelpiece hung a huge framed picture of Queen Victoria. On the opposite wall was a photograph of an elderly man.

Grayburn followed Tara's glance. "That's Sir Frank White," he explained. "The Minister of the Interior. The trail's named after him."

"I had imagined it was called the White Pass because of all the snow and ice," she said.

"Well," Grayburn said, "I guess it's really Skookum Jim's Trail. He opened it up. Better maybe if he'd never scouted it. Might be a few around now who aren't any more."

The food was coarse but good. There was corned beef hash, caribou steak, pancakes, beans, and fried potatoes, served all together. In this climate she was constantly hungry, wolfing down enormous helpings of food she would never have touched a few months ago.

Then came the moment that she had been dreading.

"You lost your husband, Mrs. Kane?" Grayburn asked sympathetically. She was aware that Campbell, on her other side, was listening intently.

For a moment, Tara did not know what to say. "Lost?" She gasped.

"I notice that you don't wear your wedding ring," the sergeant said.

Tara tried to collect her thoughts. "Oh, that." She dismissed it lightly, hoping it was convincing. "I wear it on a chain around my neck, sergeant, where it's closest to me." She smiled at him charmingly.

"Oh, of course," he said hastily.

Tara waited tensely for the next question. Where was her husband? What was she doing on her own? If she had to answer things like that, her whole story about being Constantine's sister-in-law would collapse like a house of cards.

She changed the subject.

"Tell me, Sergeant Campbell, you remember that man Smith in Skagway, does he rule the place?"

"Soapy?" He smiled grimly. "He's town boss all right. You didn't have a run-in with him, did you?"

She decided to keep quiet about that, but the name he had used puzzled her.

"Soapy?"

Grayburn twirled his waxed moustache. "Yeah, Soapy," he snorted. "Biggest bunko man in the Territory." Again he noticed her confused expression. "Con man, Mrs. Kane. Trickster."

"But why Soapy?"

"Some place in Colorado he sold shaving soap for five dollars a piece to anyone who believed his story that there was a twenty-dollar bill hidden under the wrapper. Made a small fortune out of the suckers."

So the elegant man who lorded it over Skagway with his smooth manner and soft drawl was just a cheap crook.

"Guess he knows how to fool 'em," Campbell said. "He even laid a telegraph wire that only ran for six miles and got people to pay five bucks to send ten words anywhere in America."

"And when they found out?"

He shrugged. "Mrs. Kane, folks have two rules about Soapy Smith. One, they don't argue with him. Two, they keep their eyes in the back of their heads when he's around."

Every time she felt her bare finger, her anger rose.

And yet . . .

For some reason, she was curiously intrigued by him.

They rested for twenty-four hours at Summit Hill, and Tara discovered that the border post was the end of the line of many a man's gold rush. As would-be prospectors came along the trail to cross into British Columbia, the Mounties checked each man's supplies. If he didn't have 1,150 pounds of food, he was turned back.

She heard men protesting furiously that they had come this far and nobody was going to stop them now, but the Mounties were firm. Unless they had at least three month's supplies, they could not go on.

Sled dogs and pack horses were also examined, and if an animal looked unfit that too meant return to United States territory.

Tara wondered if Daniel had passed this test. Maybe he had not had enough supplies. Maybe his dog team was on its last legs. She dearly wanted to ask if they remembered him, but that would have opened up the whole Pandora's box.

She stood and looked at the lone figure of a prospector leading his limping horse back down the trail and thought of how many fortune hunter's dreams must have come to a halt right here at Summit Hill.

Next morning, Campbell and his group prepared to set off once more. Tara was eager to get on; although she needed the rest, the hours had begun to drag. They still had a vast distance to cover, and the sooner they continued the trek the better.

Soon the huts of the frontier post receded, and even the two flags, straining on their seventy-foot poles against the lanyards, looked like little toys in the distance, and Summit Hill had gone.

Then the blizzard struck.

The Mounties, driving their teams, became strange, mute, frost-encrusted forms. The dogs' fur turned white, the sleds were thick with icy snow, and if a man held a gun in his bare hand his flesh froze to the metal. The howling sleet and wind made the convoy look like phantoms. To protect them from frostbite their faces had to be completely covered. Tara realized that without goggles she would have gone blind. As it was, they kept frosting up, and she was actually unable to see most of the time. She raised her gloved hand and tried to brush the lenses clear, but in a few moments everything was blurred again.

They were down to covering maybe a few yards an hour. At intervals the wind was so violent, and the flurries of snow so thick, that they all seemed to be motionless, straining against an invisible wall. Then the pressure would ease, and they would drag themselves forward again.

Much of the time Tara kept her eyes shut behind the opaque frosted goggles. Despite the fury of the wind, she found herself nodding off once or twice. It was her first brush with the lure of the white death: the curious desire to fall asleep in the middle of the wilderness, to allow oneself to be lulled into oblivion. Lloyd, who was driving her sled, saw her head nod and shook her shoulder roughly. People in blizzards who went to sleep rarely woke up again.

After a few hours, the weather changed gradually. Tara was able to uncover her face and breath properly once more. The dogs perked up and started moving faster. Now there was total silence. It enveloped them like a stifling blanket and frightened her. She wondered if she had become deaf. A group of caribou appeared in the distance. Up in the sky some geese passed in a ragged V, but they made no sound. After the raucous wind it was eerie.

Three hours later they made camp. No one talked. They were too exhausted.

CHAPTER NINE

Before the Gold Rush, Lake Bennett had been one of the loveliest places in the Territory, as if nature were trying to prove that the Yukon was not merely a cruel, savage, icy wilderness.

Now the lake was encircled by hundreds of tents, large and small, some brand new, some ripped and torn by the storms they had endured. There were dog tents, army tents, tiny lean-tos, huge marquees; there were tent brothels, tent barber shops, canvas saloons, tented cafes. The snow-covered lakeside echoed with the whine of saws, the crashing of trees, the blows of axes, the hammering of nails, shouts of men warning of falling timber.

For now Lake Bennett, gateway to the Yukon River, was one giant boatyard. Everyone here was working overtime to build boats ready to go up the river when the ice thawed: boats that would have to be sailed, rowed, dragged, poled through some of the most treacherous waters known to men.

After the loneliness of the White Pass, Tara found the sight of this swarming, noisy canvas township cheering. Campbell thought otherwise. He looked around the stacks of felled timber, the boats littered about, bottom up, in every stage of construction, the refuse dumps, the array of tents, and he scowled. "They're tearing the heart out of the place. Those trees took centuries to grow. Centuries. Now look at 'em."

The Mounties pitched tents by the shore. Tara looked across the lake, now frozen solid. The river reached beyond, a white highway. Along that river was their route to Dawson.

"But it's frozen," she exclaimed, dismayed. "How can we?"

"We travel on the ice. How else?"

"Then why don't all these people do the same?"

"The foolhardy ones do, but it's easier in a boat, even though it means waiting for the thaw. We ain't got the time, and we don't need to carry so many stores."

Tara suspected that Daniel was one of the foolhardy ones.

"Some of these sourdoughs are building themselves coffins and don't know it," Lloyd said disparagingly. "They might as well try shooting the rapids in a soap crate."

Campbell's face betrayed his distaste at what he saw around him.

"You don't like prospectors, do you?" Tara observed.

"They don't belong here," he replied. "They don't fit. They tear the guts out of the place, and they don't put anything back. You wait till the gold runs out. They'll disappear. And all they'll have left behind them will be those." He gestured to the tree stumps.

"And when the railroad comes?" asked Tara.

"Won't make any difference. Oh, sure, communications will be easier. We'll have that telegraph wire at last. But nature will win. There'll never be cities, highways, big ports in this territory."

"Never?"

"Well, I don't want to see it, and I won't be here if it does happen," Campbell said with finality.

They stayed two days at Lake Bennett, resting the teams for the journey ahead. Slipping away from them whenever she could, Tara spent her time seeking any scrap of information, any clue that could help track down Daniel, even though she was sure he would have moved on by now. Nevertheless, she went from tent to tent, sawpit to sawpit, asking questions.

There had been hundreds of Daniels here, men with beards, young men whose names nobody knew, who hadn't talked about themselves to anyone, and who had left as anonymously as they had arrived. Tara sensed that the men resented her questions. They were too busy felling and sawing, building boats and rafts. They worked furiously all day long, counting the weeks to the thaw. They had no patience for anyone who interrupted them, and they often turned their backs on Tara and continued working without replying.

Tara remained calm, for she knew that the odds against any of these men recalling him were enormous.

When she returned to the Mounties' tents, Hennessy came running up and said, "What happened to you, ma'am? The sergeant is just about to send out a search detail."

"I was only looking around," Tara protested when she saw how angry Campbell was.

"You got no business wandering off like that," he snapped. "We're responsible for your safety."

"Sergeant, I can look after myself," Tara replied firmly.

"Maybe you can, maybe you can't, but from now on you stay close to us," he said. He paused. "What were you looking for anyway?"

"I wasn't looking for anything."

"No?" Campbell did not seem convinced, but he said no more. And it left Tara uneasy. Was he only concerned for her safety?

The evening of the second day, Tara came across Thatcher standing on the shore looking out across the lake.

Near Thatcher hovered a Mountie, keeping an eye on the handcuffed prisoner. The man was an enigma to Tara. He was morose. He traveled in his sled, did as he was told. Only sometimes, when they camped and he sat in a tent with them, did he show any interest and then only in her. He would stare at her, but he never spoke.

Thatcher glanced at the Mountie. "Listen," he whispered. "You know they're going to hang me. Help me get away." His eyes bored into her.

"No," Tara said.

"Why not? You're on the run too. I saw you."

"Saw me where?" she frowned.

"In Skagway," he said.

"I . . ." she began. Then a voice interrupted them.

"Mrs. Kane," Campbell said, "may I see you for a moment?"

He took her arm and led her away from Thatcher. He looked disapproving. "What did he want?" the sergeant asked tersely.

"Nothing," Tara replied.

"I'm sorry, ma'am, but I must ask you not to consort with the prisoner," he said stiffly. "I cannot allow that."

"I wasn't consorting," Tara retorted.

"Talking to the prisoner is forbidden. If it happens again, he will be kept in the strictest confinement at all times."

"I'm sorry, Sergeant. It won't happen again."

Tara was troubled. She was convinced he did not trust her. He seemed to make a special point of watching her.

80

Why had she lied to him about Thatcher? The man was thinking of escaping and had sought her help. She should have reported that, she knew she should have.

Now Tara felt even more guilty when Campbell looked across the glow of the stove at her. Increasingly she dreaded the reckoning that lay ahead. Even the marvelous sensation of using a frozen river as a highway did not ease her anxiety.

Isolated graves, bunched in twos and threes, were the herald of the White Horse Rapids, to which the frozen river had led them.

Tara gazed down on a curtain of raging torrent where the waters never froze. They cascaded and thundered, white crests rising four feet high, a swift current of water spiked with jagged reefs and sharp rock teeth lurking treacherously to rip the bottom off any craft. The walls rose sheer on either side of the foaming crest. There were invisible dangers too, like whirlpools that could trap the unwary and keep them spinning helplessly until they were sucked under or shattered against the rocks.

"We're going the long way round," Campbell announced. "I'm not shooting that with a woman."

"That'll cost us two or three extra days," Lloyd pointed out. "It adds six miles, and you know how lousy that trail is. I vote we go down the rapids."

"The regulations say no women," Campbell said emphatically, "and I'm not breaking any more."

"The trail might be too tough for her," Hennessy suggested.

"Listen, if she's strong enough to get this far, she can tackle the long way. Let's go."

It took them two and a half days to manhandle the sleds along the cliffs overlooking the rapids, and Tara began to understand why men would rather risk a sudden, quick death in the surging waters than the backbreaking, slow, slippery portage on dry land.

The sleds had to be dragged, pushed, and, at one point, even carried along narrow paths, through tiny rock passages, up and down slippery trails, sometimes balanced precariously over a glacial boulder, sometimes a few inches from a plunge to death. The dog teams, unhitched, had to be led step by step.

As if to mock those who, like them, took the slow way, they passed messages tacked to tree trunks, or stuck on broken oars: '

"Boat Cora and Meda safely shot the White Horse Rapids loaded with 4,000 pounds."

81

Or, "Gudmund Jenson, GG Tripp, Tom, Mike went through all right."

But there were other, grimmer reminders too.

"Three Unknown men, drowned below the White Bluff," said a wooden marker.

Tara's body ached, muscles she never knew she had hurt, her shoulders felt as if a leaden weight had been tied to them, and the sheer strain of dragging herself along the trail, helping to carry some of the load, was so exhausting that all she wanted was to drop down, sink to her knees, rest.

They stopped briefly at a mount of rocks. On it a primitive cross had four words only:

"He never made it."

Who was the man who had never made it? Daniel must have come along this route. At the foot of the cliffs on the other side, she could see more graves—tiny crosses, one or two wooden posts—all of them men for whom this was the end of the Gold Rush.

Hennessy came to join her. "Guess I owe you an apology, ma'am," he said.

Tara looked at him. "What on earth for?"

"Well," he said scratching his head. "I said this might be too tough for you. You proved me wrong. You can handle yourself OK."

He could have said nothing that pleased her more. He said it grudgingly, she knew that, but they had all been watching her, and she was aware she had passed the test.

"Maybe we could even have done the rapids with you," he said, slightly embarrassed.

"Why, thank you," Tara said. Somehow all the aches and bruises were a little easier to bear.

They were camped for the night near Lake Laberge when Tara saw an opportune moment to talk with Campbell. Increasingly she felt she had to confess something.

"Thatcher's asked me to help him escape," she said quietly.

He stopped chopping logs and straightened up. "That's right," he said.

She raised her eyebrows. "You knew?"

"Of course," he said. "Why else would he have talked to you?" He went back to chopping the wood.

"He didn't tell me how. Just asked me to help, and I said no."

"Only one thing puzzles me," said Campbell, not looking at her.

"Yes?"

"Why you didn't tell me before."

"I don't know," Tara admitted. "Maybe . . . maybe I was feeling sorry for him."

Campbell gathered up the chopped wood. "Now you're not?"

She felt awkward. "I've been thinking about it. Since Lake Bennett. I think I owe it to you. To tell you."

"I appreciate that," Campbell said. "Even if I did know all along." He gave her a curious sort of smile and walked off to the tent. Tara stared after him, wondering what else he knew.

"How many more days to Dawson?" she asked him later that evening. She was warming herself over the fire, and he handed her a mug of coffee.

"Couple of weeks, maybe," the sergeant said, noncommittally.

She sipped the coffee. Campbell remained taciturn. He volunteered nothing.

"Sergeant," said Tara.

"Yes?"

"What's Inspector Constantine like?" It was out before she realized what she had said.

He looked at her blandly. "Your brother-in-law? Why, don't you know?"

Inwardly she winced. "Not—not really. I don't know him very well."

"Hmm," Campbell said, and threw another piece of wood into the flames. "I guess he'll have a lot of questions to ask you."

Of course he knew the truth. He was saying as much.

"You think so?" Tara tried to make it sound casual.

He nodded. "Guess so."

He leaned forward. "You haven't talked much about your husband, Mrs. Kane." He rubbed his nose. "What he's doing. Where he is."

"It's a long story." Her voice was low.

Campbell stood up. "None of my business anyway, Mrs. Kane. You tell the inspector."

"You know I could never have made this journey by myself," Tara said. "Without your help, I don't know what I'd have done. I'll tell him that."

He gave a curt nod. "Better turn in now," he said. "I'll check the guard." And he left Tara to her thoughts and misgivings.

The subject of Inspector Constantine was not raised again, but Tara was increasingly troubled by her subterfuge.

Some days later, a few miles before Fort Selkirk, they met another Mountie patrol. Campbell conferred with the man in charge, Campbell doing most of the talking, the officer glancing across at her. She caught an occasional word from where she was sitting in the sled, "sister," "letter," "expecting her." The officer walked toward her, and she knew that it meant trouble and more lies.

He was a handsome man, dark with a neatly trimmed mustache and brown eyes. She saw the rank insignia on his collar. An inspector. She steeled herself.

He saluted her. "I hear you're on your way to Dawson to meet with your brother-in-law." His American accent was unexpected. Most of the Mounties she had met so far had been British.

"Isn't that a surprise," he went on, cocking his head to one side. "You know, you don't look anything like your sister."

"We're quite different," murmured Tara and consoled her conscience with the fact that she was telling the truth.

"It's amazing. I never would have believed you're Alice's sister if I hadn't been told."

Alice! And she had signed the letter Sarah. Thank goodness Campbell had given it back to her. If this man saw it . . .

"Anyway, I'm sorry you're in for a disappointment," he said. "Your sister's at Fort Constantine. In married quarters. Didn't she tell you?"

Tara had never heard of the place.

"Isn't that near Dawson?" she asked simply, avoiding his question.

"Not exactly. It's across the river from Fortymile. The empire's most northerly outpost."

"Oh." She wasn't sure what to say.

"Mrs. Kane, isn't it? What's your husband's first name? Maybe I've already met him."

"Daniel," Tara said, "Daniel Kane."

"No." He shook his head. "Means nothing to me."

"Pity. I hoped you might have come across him."

"Well, Mrs. Kane. It's too cold to stand around here gossiping, isn't it? Guess Mr. Constantine will have lots to talk about with you."

He smiled broadly. "I leave you in Sergeant Campbell's good hands, meantime." He saluted again.

"Thank you." Tara's heart was pounding.

The inspector walked back to his teams, and Campbell started up the convoy to Fort Selkirk.

"Guess Zac knows your sister right well," Lloyd said genially.

"Zac?"

"Inspector Wood. Great Guy. Great-grandson of President Taylor. He's a real trouble shooter. Nothing escapes Mr. Wood."

Tara had the uneasy feeling that Lloyd was only too right, and she wondered whether the inspector had told Campbell that she was an impostor.

Fort Selkirk was a windswept, barren hole, and not the least depressing thing about it was the local store, presided over by a surly miser who priced a can of condensed milk at two dollars and everything up pro rata.

Tara ate in the saloon with Campbell and the other Mounties. They had freed Thatcher's hands, but Hennessy and Russell sat on either side of him. The customers went on drinking, gambling, snoring, shouting, taking no notice of the lawmen, their prisoner, or the woman who had entered with them.

Sawdust covered the floorboards, and there were spittoons stationed at strategic points. Incredible, thought Tara, how much spitting these rough men did.

"No kicking regarding the quality or quantity of meals will be allowed," read a notice on the wooden wall. "Assaults on the cook are strictly prohibited."

There were other house rules, clearly laid down:

"Guests are forbidden to spit on the ceiling. Quarrelsome or boisterous persons, also those who shoot off without provocation, guns on the premises, will not be allowed to remain in the house."

"Dogs are not allowed in bunks. Two or more persons must sleep in one bed when asked to do so by management."

"All guests are requested to arise at six a.m. This is because the sheets are needed for tablecloths."

"All the comforts of home," Lloyd said, seeing Tara studying her surroundings.

"But it's warm," she said. "At least it's warm."

The highlight of the evening was the two eggs they all got with their thick rashers of bacon, their beans, and their bread. Two eggs each, sunny side up.

"Curly likes to keep on the right side of the law," Campbell chuckled.

"Guess he's got a bad conscience about something."

Tara swallowed hard.

Curly came over, rubbing his hands, his bald head shining like a mirror in the glow of the oil lamps.

"Everything satisfactory," he beamed. "Everybody ready for seconds?"

He was very anxious to keep them happy.

"That old squaw thief came out here as a missionary," Campbell remarked when they'd finished eating.

"I don't believe it," Tara laughed.

"He found selling illicit liquor a mite more profitable."

She thought of Bishop Beauchamp and the phony Reverend Bowers. Campbell must have read her mind.

"Yeah, something happens to Bible thumpers here," he agreed.

Three days out of Fort Selkirk they were in the tent when unexpectedly the flap was pulled aside and an apparition stood there, looking down at them.

The face was coarse, the body enormous, swathed in a blanketlike fur jacket with a hood drawn over the head. Huge mittens gave an indication of the size of the hands. Around its neck was a primitive necklace.

"Hello, Kate," Campbell said as if he had been anticipating the visitor.

Tara was dumbfounded. She could not believe this was a woman. The he-woman pushed her way in between two of the Mounties and slumped herself down by the stove. She grunted something and warmed her massive hands. She had a crude, sexless face, with a flat nose, thick lips, and furrowed skin that looked like tough leather.

"Granite Kate," Campbell said to Tara by way of an introduction. He evidently knew her well. So apparently did the other Mounties. They simply went on eating.

"Got any grub?" rasped a hard, dry voice.

Hennessy reached over and dished out some of the eternal bacon and beans, which he gave her. Kate pulled out a broad-bladed knife from her belt and started scooping the food up, eating noisily, slurping like a pig at a trough.

This could not be a woman, Tara thought, not the way she looked and talked. She reeked of fish and stale meat.

"Where are you heading for?" asked Campbell.

Kate smacked her lips. "Don't know yet."

She stared at Tara. "Who's she?"

"The lady's traveling to Dawson," Campbell said. "What are you doing here?"

"Saw your fire. Thought you might have room for me."

For a few minutes no one spoke.

"We don't want you around," Campbell said. He said it quietly, without heat.

"You might be going my way," she rumbled. "No reason why we shouldn't team up."

"You're not wanted," Campbell repeated.

"Hey, you," Kate said, ignoring him. She leaned forward and jabbed her finger into Tara's knee. "Who are you?"

"She's none of your business," Campbell warned. "Let her be."

Kate spat into the empty tin plate, and Tara winced.

"Her kind don't fit," grumbled the monster.

"They can't all be like you, thank God," Lloyd said, and the others laughed.

"Rot your balls," Kate said, without rancor.

Campbell stood up. "OK, Kate, that's enough. Time to get moving. Take your team and move."

She looked up at him, yellow teeth bared in a crooked grin.

"Dogs haven't been fed. And they're tired. Can't travel now."

"You're not sleeping in here. You smell too high."

"Don't shit yourself," Kate said pleasantly. "I'll hole up somewhere."

She grunted as she heaved herself up and shuffled to the flap of the tent. Then she disappeared outside.

Tara stared after her in wonderment.

Campbell noticed her expression.

"Yeah, some woman," he said. "She's always been around these parts, traveling round the Klondike, in all weather, at all times."

"She's enormous," Tara exclaimed.

"She can handle a dog team better than any of us," Lloyd said. "She's a crack shot, she can follow a trail in a sixty mile-an-hour blizzard, climb a rock face like a goat, and she fights like a heavyweight."

Tara detected a note of respect.

"But you don't want her around?" she asked.

"Kate knows the score," Campbell said. "She's trouble. She tastes liquor and there's a riot. She's mean. She knows why nobody wants her."

"Traps furs. Shoots animals. Trades with the Indians. She gets by. She's a Yukon woman."

"One thing you can bet on. A man's got to be mighty hard up to touch Granite Kate," snorted Hennessy. Then he saw Campbell's face. "Begging your pardon, ma'am."

"Is she really a woman?" Tara asked.

"Guess so," grinned Lloyd. "Trouble is, nobody's dared go close enough to find out for sure."

They all guffawed.

Granite Kate reappeared next morning at breakfast. Unbidden she sat at the fire and cooked her own food. If a Mountie got in her way, she elbowed him aside. She ate her food in her horrible fashion, grunting to herself. It didn't seem to bother her that she was a very unwelcome guest.

Daylight had not improved Kate's appearance. She seemed even bigger. Her footsteps left great imprints in the snow, like the tracks of some huge beast. The one person she seemed to have an affinity with was Thatcher. Outside, she crouched beside him, feeding him scraps of her own food. When the sentry ordered her away, she spat at him and mouthed obscenities.

"Keep away," Campbell warned her, but she just snarled at him.

"You wouldn't keep a dog chained like this, you son of a bitch. I hope your guts rot in hell."

Two of the sleds had broken runners, and Campbell decided to camp for a further twenty-four hours while they were fixed. He had been driving all of them hard, and they were grateful for the rest.

Granite Kate showed no signs of moving on. She helped herself to their supplies, used the fire, warmed herself in the tent at the stove, taking full advantage of the Mounties' presence for as long as she could.

"You're a lousy scavenger," Campbell complained. "I ought to kick you out of here."

Kate spat into the snow.

That night, Tara was awakened by a shot. All around, the sleepy Mounties tumbled and fell over each other as they rushed out. She could hear the dogs yapping wildly. Tara scrambled to the flap of the tent.

She saw a sled drawn up, with a dog team harnessed, ready to move off. Next to it, the knife in her hand, stood Granite Kate, her teeth bared savagely, facing the Mounties. She looked like a wild animal at bay.

Hennessy and Russell were holding the prisoner. He was still handcuffed, but the chain that had kept him captive was broken and trailing behind him.

"What the hell are you playing at, Kate?" Campbell demanded angrily.

"You got no right," she yelled. "You got no right to chain up a man like a dog. Man don't belong in chains and cages. You're a lousy bunch of redbellies, who got no call dragging a man like he's an animal."

She was beside herself with rage.

"And I'm telling you for the last time, you got no right to interfere with the law," shouted the sergeant. "We've been mighty patient with you, but you keep away from now on, you understand. If I see you round here again, I'll put *you* in a cage."

Kate stuck her knife back in her belt, all the while mouthing words Tara coouldn't hear. Then, without further ado, she turned to her sled, picked up the whip, and cracked it over her dog team. Swiftly they started off, disappearing into the darkness.

"You won't get another break like that," Hennessy said, bundling Thatcher away.

"What happened?" Tara asked when Lloyd and Campbell came back to the tent.

"The sentry spotted her," Campbell said. "She'd thought he wasn't looking and went and woke the prisoner. She'd sawn through the chain before he realized what was going on. So he fired a shot and yelled."

"And you just let her go?"

"You can't hold Kate, any more than you can jail a bear. Oh sure, she'll turn up again, somewhere, any place between here and the ice cap. Could be she'll kill somebody, and then we'll have to shoot her."

"*Shoot* her?"

"Well you can't see Kate letting herself get arrested, can you? If she went on the run, she'd never give in. She'd keep running until she dropped, or somebody put a bullet in her."

"You make her sound like a wild animal."

"Maybe, but she belongs," said Campbell. "She belongs the way the moose does, and the caribou, and the grizzly. That's why she gets on with the Indians. She's part of the Klondike, not like all the johnny-come-latelies. If Kate found a ton of gold, she wouldn't care a sou. That's something I respect."

Campbell, she realized, would feel a great loss if anything ever happened to the extraordinary creature.

"Tell me." Tara hesitated. "Her necklace. What were those strange things around her neck?"

"Teeth. Animals' teeth."

"But some of them were very small."

"Yes," said Campbell. "Those were the human ones."

Tara, as the days passed, was coming to terms with the bitter climate, or so she thought until one evening Campbell stared at her face. She knew her complexion was unflattering, but she had never seen the sergeant look at her like that.

"How long have you had that?" he asked. They were sitting in the tent, and she had taken her mittens off. Tentatively, she touched her face. Her fingers felt her chapped lips, her nose.

"What's the matter?" she faltered. "What's wrong . . ."

Campbell suddenly got up, and before she knew what was happening his face was on hers, and she felt the warmth of his lips on her left cheek.

Instinctively she tensed, and yet it was a completely dispassionate kiss. She could swear his rough mouth was sucking her cheek.

He held her in a firm clasp while it lasted, and then he released her. It had been an impersonal, clinical embrace.

"Sergeant!" exclaimed Tara, blushing.

"Yukon first aid, Mrs. Kane," he said. "The quicker it's done the better."

"First aid!" she repeated, her green eyes wide.

"For frostbite. Primitive but mighty effective."

"Me!" she didn't want to believe it. "I've got frostbite? Where?" She felt her face again.

"That mark, on your cheek there," he said. "You had a touch. It's got to be sucked out before it's too late. Just rub it." He saw her panic.

"It's OK, Mrs. Kane. You'll be all right. It just nipped you. But you got to be careful. Keep your face warm. Wrap a shawl round it, or something."

A shiver went through her. She had heard about frostbite, how it turned into gangrene, and prospectors were left without their feet, their legs. . . .

"Here, take it easy," Campbell said gently. "You got nothing to worry about. Everybody gets a nip like that out here. You just have to do something about it, that's all."

She gave him a wan smile. "Thank you," she said. She touched her cheek again. She could feel the spot now. She started rubbing it with her fingertips.

"You just have to remember about it. Keep yourself covered. And have an eye open for it. It doesn't hurt, you see, not till it's too late. Sometimes folks don't know they got it even. That's when it's a killer."

It added a new dimension to her fear of the Klondike. She was recognizing the visible hazards, but this unseen menace was a new horror. She pulled her parka closer around her. Yes, she thought, you still have a lot to learn about this country.

The last night before Dawson, Tara found herself alone in the tent with Campbell.

"Sergeant Campbell . . ." she said. Now the moment had come, she was terribly unsure of herself.

"Anything bothering you, Mrs. Kane?"

He wasn't making it any easier.

"Thank you for the way you . . . you've looked after me. You and the corporal, and everybody.

"The men enjoyed your company," he said gravely.

"I could never have made the journey on my own. Not without you."

Campbell nodded, like a man who knows something is a fact.

Tara decided to take the plunge. "I think I owe you an explanation."

For the first time, he glanced at her. "Why don't you save it, Mrs. Kane? Until you reach Dawson."

"No," insisted Tara. "I have been thinking, and—"

"It doesn't matter now," Campbell said quietly.

"But I don't want you to get into trouble," she burst out.

He gave her a little smile. "I appreciate that, Mrs. Kane, but it's a little too late. I'm sure it'll sort itself out."

But he got to his feet. "I want to take a look at the dogs. I thought Ikkee was limping."

He stoked the stove first and then put on his fur jacket.

Tara looked at him pleadingly. "Please," she said. "It won't take a minute. You see, the truth is—"

"The truth is that we've nearly reached journey's end, Mrs. Kane." He fastened his jacket. "And tomorrow there'll be a little reception committee for you in Dawson, I'd guess."

She frowned. "For me?"

"Sure." His blue eyes stared right into hers. "Inspector Wood sent a courier ahead to Mr. Constantine telling him his sister-in-law was on her way. I figure Mr. Constantine must be mighty excited. Probably counting the hours until you arrive." He left the tent, leaving Tara to her fear of tomorrow.

CHAPTER TEN

Only two years before, Dawson had been a wilderness, at the junction of the Yukon and Klondike rivers, a pasture for moose, unclaimed by men. Now it was noisier, rougher, crazier than any place Tara had ever seen. It never slept; thousands were making fortunes, going bankrupt, gambling, cheating, drinking, and womanizing twenty-four hours a day.

A square foot of floor space in a log cabin cost $200. Ten-cent cigars sold for $2.00. The favors of a dance-hall girl fetched $100.00 and upwards a night; even a drunken embrace from one of the raddled hags of Paradise Alley cost $20.00.

It was a town full of muck and dirt, smelly with garbage and uncollected filth, crowded with people who did not wash or shave. In this ant heap, the ants were too busy to pay attention to the grandeur

91

of the scenery around them. There was little time for beauty in Dawson.

Saloons, gambling dens, and bordellos sprouted like toadstools, and what happened in them was nobody else's business. Bartenders earned $600 a month, as much for their skill in breaking up fights as in pouring drinks.

Deep in the heart of Yukon Territory, Dawson had turned itself into an American frontier town on Canadian soil. Nine out of ten men there were Americans, drawn by the gold, and the Stars and Stripes flew defiantly in the main street.

Gold was the common tongue. The Chinese who ran the laundry, the little Russian who sewed trousers and coats, the German boot repairer, the greenhorn from Florida, the Englishman from London, the dandified French gambler, they all spoke each other's language: the value of gold. A man who didn't have gold was worth less than a sled dog. Much less.

The handful of Mounties maintained a presence, headquartered in a log cabin, and acted as a reminder when they walked down the teeming streets, that somewhere beyond this wild isolated town there was a government.

Presiding over all this was a blunt, impatient, sardonic looking man, with high cheekbones, a hook nose, and a Vandyke beard. He described himself as "Chief Magistrate," "Commander in Chief," "Home Secretary," and "Foreign Minister." On paper, he was commander of the Yukon Detachment.

His name was Charles Constantine.

A Union Jack hung limply outside the police cabin. As Campbell's patrol drew up in front of the ramshackle headquarters of the Dawson Unit, Tara steeled herself for her first confrontation with the Inspector. She had gone over the meeting a dozen times in her mind, trying to anticipate how he would react to her story; one thing was obvious, the bluff was over.

The Mounties unhitched their teams and marched their prisoner off. Thatcher, handcuffed, shuffled along giving Tara a mean look as he went.

"Come along, Mrs. Kane," the sergeant said, "let's go."

Inside the cabin Campbell indicated a wooden chair. "You wait here," he ordered, and she knew now what it felt like to be a lawbreaker. Guilt tightened her stomach, and she looked appealingly at the sergeant. But he turned his back on her, knocked on a door marked "Commanding Officer," and waited.

92

"Enter," came a voice from within, and Campbell went inside. Tara leaned forward, hoping to catch a glimpse of the Inspector, but the sergeant shut the door too quickly.

A stern Queen Victoria glowered down on her from the wall. She recognized the picture; the same one had hung at the police post on Summit Hill.

She wished there was a mirror somewhere so that she could at least try to make herself more presentable. She couldn't remember when she had last looked at her face. It made her feel even more insecure.

The outer office, in which she was sitting, was Spartan, a battered safe in a corner, a dozen rifles chained on a rack, Wanted notices, and a map of the Yukon district on the wall, a faded photograph of a row of policemen, arms folded, hanging from a nail. Tara saw it all, and yet took little in. She was too nervous.

On top of the safe lay an ancient thumbed copy of the *Illustrated London News*. She started turning the pages of the magazine, skimming the captions under the drawings. Captain Dreyfus languishing in his cell on Devil's Island. Boers in the Transvaal signing the Orange Free State Treaty. The Shah of Persia being assassinated. Sun-helmeted troops in the Sudan. It was like looking at pictures from another planet.

Then Campbell emerged. He closed the door, his eyes avoiding her.

"This way, Mrs. Kane," he said flatly.

He didn't usher her into Constantine's office. Unexpectedly, he indicated for her to follow him.

She stood up and walked with him out of the headquarters building, around to the back, to a wooden hut. Now she noticed Campbell had a bunch of keys. He unlocked the door.

"In here," he said, and stood aside to let her pass.

She found herself facing four cells. Thatcher sat on a bunk in one of them, his head in his hands. He looked up through the bars, puzzled, when he saw Tara.

Campbell held one of the cell doors open.

Tara stared at him.

"In . . . in there?" she faltered.

"I'm acting under orders," he said awkwardly.

She stepped into the bare cell with its bunk and one stool. She shivered and turned to Campbell, but he had already slammed the door and was locking it.

"You're not leaving me here?"

"I'll bring you some blankets," he said, and then she heard the door of the hut closing and the key turning.

She sank onto the stool in disbelief. She was in jail. Surely they couldn't do this to her? Without even talking to her?

Apart from the bunk and the stool, there was a single pail in the corner of the cell. It was the source, she realized, of the evil smell that pervaded the air.

How long was she going to have to endure this? She felt chilled to the marrow and she was trembling a little, but whether it was the damp cold of the cell, or just fright, she couldn't tell.

Then she heard the door of the lock-up open. An officer in a red tunic appeared and unlocked the cell. His sharply pointed beard was neatly trimmed, and he wore riding boots, polished to a mirror finish.

He entered the cell and stood in front of her. He didn't have to tell her he was Constantine.

Tara looked up at him from the stool.

His eyes were unfriendly, and he studied her coldly.

Tara braced herself. "Am I under arrest?" she asked.

He held out his hand. "The letter, please." For a moment, she didn't understand. Then panic returned.

"The letter . . ." she mumbled.

"From my wife. Your sister." There was no smile.

She had kept the scrap of paper since Skagway, and now she nervously pulled it out. In all these weeks, it really had become worn and wrinkled.

He took it and glanced over the writing, then tore it up. He said nothing.

From his tunic, Constantine took a folded piece of paper and handed it over to her.

"The bill, madam," he said frigidly. "I will take American dollars if you do not have Canadian currency. I have made out a receipt."

"What bill?" Tara asked, dully.

"You owe the Government for transportation and food and shelter. Shall we say, five dollars a day. I reckon two hundred dollars will pay for the facilities you have obtained by false pretenses and forgery."

"I didn't . . ." she began, but it was pointless. "I haven't got the money," said Tara, in a low voice.

"Of course not. That is why you are in here, madam. Obtaining goods and services from the taxpayer by deception is a serious criminal offense."

He sounded like a judge passing sentence. She wondered what would happen if she burst into tears. Her bottom lip started to tremble.

"I hope, madam, you will control yourself and not resort to

94

anything theatrical, like fainting or crying," cut in the Inspector, stonily. "It would make no impression on me."

"I'm terribly sorry," Tara said, contritely. "For everything."

"I find that, invariably, people are sorry after they've been caught. That never impresses me very much either."

"I only fibbed to get them to bring me to Dawson," Tara pleaded. "I was stuck in Skagway. So I told a story hoping—"

"A *lie*, madam."

She lowered her head.

"I don't make a habit of it. Please believe me, I feel very bad about it."

He looked unconvinced. "It's very easy to say that."

"But how else can I say it?" she asked. "I've told you how sorry I am. Do I have to go down on my knees?"

He walked over slowly to the bunk by the wall and sat on it. Everything was polished about him, she noticed, his boots, the brass buttons, the Sam Brown belt. Constantine put the finger tips of his hands together and studied her.

"All right," he said, "what the devil made you embark on your charade anyway?"

She told him, then waited anxiously for his reaction. It came like a cold shower.

"Frankly, Mrs. Kane," he said, "my opinion is that you've come a long way on a wild goose chase. You know how big the Yukon is? The size of France. Much of it uncharted. Your husband could be anywhere."

"I'll find him," Tara insisted.

"Women like you are a menace in this territory. They're not wanted here. Footloose, roaming around, unattached, without funds, nobody looking after them—they cause trouble. I'm a policeman, Mrs. Kane. I don't want trouble."

He looked around the cell. "People who give me trouble land in here. I don't imagine you enjoy it."

"And exactly how long am I supposed to be in here?" asked Tara.

"That depends."

"I have a friend here," she said, noticing his hesitation. "I'm sure he'll vouch for me. He's a German photographer. I traveled with him on the ship . . ."

"Then you're in for another disappointment. Mr. Hart has already left. He's going around the gold creeks, taking photographs. He may be gone for months. So you see, you're friendless. You'd better return home."

Tara shrugged. "I'm sorry. I'm staying. My mind is made up."

"So is mine," he said without heat. "I'd give a man who cheated the Government thirty days' hard labor. Since you won't remove yourself from Dawson, thirty days' hard labor it shall be."

She looked disbelieving.

"I don't have adequate facilities for female lawbreakers," he went on, "but wrongdoing has to be punished. It will be very hard labor."

He got up and walked to the door of the cell, then paused.

"You didn't really think you'd get away with it, did you, Mrs. Kane?" he asked. He slammed the door shut and locked it.

"What are you in here for?" Thatcher yelled from his cell.

"Oh shut up," Tara said.

An hour later, Campbell re-appeared. "OK, Mrs. Kane, on your way," he said.

For a moment she had a wild hope. "Are you letting me go?" she asked.

He shook his head.

"What's happening to me?"

"Come along," he said, and took her arm. Again he avoided her eyes.

He towered above her as they marched through the town, she carrying her sleeping bag, trying to keep up with his long strides. Dawson's main street was well trodden, so there was no deep snow, but Tara slipped and nearly fell a couple of times on the frozen mud underfoot.

Bystanders paused in the street and stared at them. She wished he would slow down a little, or at least offer to carry her sleeping bag.

"Where are we going?" Tara panted.

"Mrs. Miles's place," he said curtly.

"What sort of place is that?"

"You'll find out," he said, not slackening his pace.

"Sergeant," she puffed. "You know I hated deceiving you."

"It doesn't matter now," Campbell retorted.

"But I want to apologize," she said breathlessly.

He slowed down and turned to her. "It doesn't matter," he repeated.

Tara was of a mind to tell him that she thought he was being unfair, but then she had not been fair when she had coaxed him in Skagway. She hitched up the sleeping bag, which seemed to be growing heavier by the yard. Campbell made no move to help her, and she knew her punishment had already begun.

"We're nearly there," Campbell said a little while later. They were outside the Ward Hough General Merchandising Company, and a man in a fur hat waved at Campbell.

"Hi, Andrew," he called out. "Back in town?" He looked curiously at Tara. "What's she done?"

Tara wanted the ground to open up. She hated being a public spectacle.

"I'll see you, Ward," Campbell said briefly; but he did not stop.

He took her elbow, steering her across the street to a wooden, two-storied house. Its front was neatly painted, something which made it stand out in the neighborhood. Ice-laden steps led up to the porch. There was a "No Vacancies" sign on the front door. Well, thought Tara looking up at it, at least there aren't any bars at the windows.

"In you go," Campbell ordered, and followed her inside.

She thankfully dropped her sleeping bag, glad to get rid of its weight.

The hallway had an unusual smell which, at first, Tara couldn't place. It was not unpleasant, just different. Then she realized what it was. Here it smelled clean. A crude Indian rug covered the floor. There was no sawdust, no spittoons, no cigarette burns on the staircase. This was the first home she had been in since San Francisco.

"Mrs. Miles," called out Campbell.

A severe-faced woman emerged from the kitchen in the rear, and Tara's heart sank. She was in her late fifties, with every steel-gray hair in place. Her starched apron creaked as she walked. She was the personification of a prison matron. She nodded briefly to Campbell and appraised Tara caustically.

"Hello, Linda," Campbell said. "Can I have a word with you? In private."

A door with a shiny brass knob closed behind them, but not before Tara heard Campbell saying, "Mr. Constantine sent this letter . . ."

By the stairs there was a large wooden chest, and Tara went over and sat down on it. A cheap framed reproduction of "The Stag at Bay" stared down at her. The walls were covered with dowdy paper, but after all the bare wooden planks and logs she had seen over the last months it seemed almost elegant.

When the door opened, Mrs. Miles came out with the Inspector's letter in her hand, followed by Campbell.

"Mrs. Kane," she said briskly.

Tara stood up, feeling like a prisoner on report. Mrs. Miles pursed her lips.

Campbell shifted uneasily.

97

"Can I leave her in your charge, then?" he asked.

"I don't know yet," grumbled Mrs. Miles, examining Tara like a prize cow at a dairy show. "I don't know if I want her."

"Mr. Constantine would be most obliged," pressed Campbell.

"Charles Constantine won't have to put up with her," snapped Mrs. Miles. She frowned at Tara. "You know what this says?" she asked, indicating the letter.

"I can probably guess," Tara murmured.

"Mr. Constantine has asked me to work you like a skivvy for thirty days. Now I need a domestic—"

"Indeed," interjected Tara.

"—but she has to be honest, decent, and respectable" went on Mrs. Miles, ignoring her. "Can you truthfully say you're all of those things and that you're not lazy or work-shy?"

Campbell was watching Tara, his face expressionless.

"I'll work for my board and keep because I need a roof over my head. However, I would like to make it clear, Mrs. Miles, that I am not a trained domestic."

"By the time I'm finished, you will be," Mrs. Miles assured Tara grimly. "And if you don't like it, you'd better take it up with the law now."

Tara bit back what she wanted to say, but her eyes smoldered defiantly.

Mrs. Miles stuffed the letter into her apron pocket and turned to Campbell. "Well, Mr. Constantine knows better than to send me a Paradise Alley hustler. But if she's no good, he gets her back and be sure you tell him that. I only hope I'm not making a mistake."

"We appreciate that," Campbell said.

Mrs. Miles produced a sour smile. "You ought to. It's lucky for you I happen to need some help."

Campbell nodded at Tara and beat a hasty retreat.

"Now, you and I have to get a few things straight," said Mrs. Miles, leading her through to the kitchen. Tara sat on a stool in front of a big wooden table on which Mrs. Miles was punishing some dough. A huge kitchen range gave off some very comforting warmth. On it two saucepans were bubbling and simmering, emitting a very pleasant aroma.

"I have certain rules, and these you will obey," Mrs. Miles announced. "This is a respectable rooming house. You don't socialize with the lodgers. You don't go out in the evening without my permission. You are not allowed visitors. You don't whistle nor do you sing. You take a bath on Sundays, and you make sure your nails are always clean and your hair tidy."

She pounded the dough ferociously.

"You will get up at six every morning, and you will help me with the housework. I expect you to make up the fires and the range, wash up, scrub the floors, clean the rooms, do the laundry, polish the brass, black the grates, and keep the place generally tidy."

"Is that all?" Tara asked.

Mrs. Miles shot a piercing look at her, but Tara kept her face quite straight.

"And I'll have no lip from you," Mrs. Miles warned. "I do the cooking. Sometimes the lodgers need a little patching and sewing done, and we will divide that between us. At all times I shall expect you to be willing and cheerful."

"Of course," Tara concurred, her lips twitching.

"In return, you will have your lodging and full board."

"Oh, that is kind," Tara said. But her feeble attempt at irony was lost on Mrs. Miles.

She frowned and went on, "The parlor is only used on Sundays. It is not to be occupied during the week, but it must be dusted every day."

She punched the dough. "Any questions?"

"Yes," Tara said. "What are the wages?"

Mrs. Miles stared at her astonished.

"*Wages?*" she exploded. "Now look here, young woman, you're getting board and lodging free. Do you know how much food costs in this place? It's going to cost me money to feed you. And I could get seven dollars a week for your room."

Constantine had it well worked out, Tara thought. You get food and lodging in jail but no pay.

Mrs. Miles returned to savaging the dough.

"Believe me, Mrs. Kane," she huffed, "if you don't want to do it, or if honest work is too hard for you, tackle Mr. Constantine. I've run this place by myself before, and I can do it again, any day."

She wiped her hands on a cloth. Tara sympathized with the battered dough. She knew exactly how it felt.

"Come along, I'll show you your quarters."

Although it wasn't a cell, it was the smallest room Tara had ever seen. The ceiling was so low she had to stoop, and she could virtually span it by holding out her arms. She was amazed at how much furniture fit into such a small space. There was a bed, covered with a wafer-thin mattress, a small dresser, and a minute wardrobe designed for a doll's house. One corner of the room housed a small stove. She would have to get rid of the only picture, a print of a sickly-looking, pouting boy blowing bubbles while a kitten gazed up at him admiringly. On the dresser stood a washbowl and jug.

Surprisingly, Tara liked it. At long last she would have privacy. The small window actually had a tiny chintz curtain. There were plenty of blankets, and, as everywhere else in the house, it was clean and neat.

"Wood for the stove is in the back yard," Mrs. Miles said grimly. "Chop the logs yourself. In this house we don't rely on men."

"I think I'll be very comfortable," Tara said, and she meant it.

"I don't want any mess in here. It's got to be kept spotless. If you need anything, tell me," Mrs. Miles added gruffly as if she was ashamed of sounding too nice. "Get yourself settled in, and then we'll have a cup of tea. I won't expect you to do much today, but tomorrow morning you start at six sharp, understand?"

Tara dragged her sleeping bag upstairs, then sat on the bed and tried to collect her thoughts. This was not how she planned it. She had come thousands of miles, spent months traveling here, and now she was the very thing she would never have been in San Francisco—a domestic servant.

She took out the little compass. The needle quivered and kept pointing to—where, she wondered. In San Francisco it had pointed this way. In the Pacific, it had remained, as always, unwavering. High up on the Pass, it had kept pointing. Always farther, always to the beyond.

Tara went over to the window and looked out at the street below. This was where she had to begin her search, among the saloons, the stores, the dance halls. Here, somewhere, she would find news of Daniel.

"That's right, isn't it?" she whispered to the compass, balancing it in the palm of her hand. "I'll find him, won't I?"

She had made up her mind to get on with Mrs. Miles. Despite her pomposity, in a curious way Tara rather liked her. How on earth had she come to be in this wild, rough, crazy town running a boarding house as primly as if it were in Boston? And who were the lodgers? She had not seen any of them, yet the sign had said "No Vacancies."

"Tara!" came a shout up the stairs.

It was the first time Mrs. Miles had used her Christian name. Was it also the first crack in the ice? Or merely rubbing it in that she was now a servant, and servants were addressed that way?

In the kitchen, she found Mrs. Miles surrounded by steaming pots and pans, preparing her major event, the evening meal.

"They're hungry men, they work hard, and there's got to be plenty for them," she said, lifting saucepan lids, adding a pinch of salt here, stirring there. "I give them good value, and they know it. Decent home cooking is worth something in this town."

There were five boarders, Tara discovered as she sipped a big mug of tea, none of them gold prospectors.

"I won't have any temporaries," snorted Mrs. Miles. Mrs. Miles divided would-be lodgers into two categories: temporaries, for whom she had no time, and permanents—traders and businessmen who made their bonanza supplying the Gold Rush.

"We serve supper at six sharp, and I don't wait for anybody who's late," she said firmly. "Breakfast must be ready by seven in the morning."

Obviously the place was run by the clock.

"This is a respectable house, and I expect everyone to stick to the rules." She tasted the soup. "I won't allow anyone in shirtsleeves at the table. And you'll have to wear a dress, understand? I can't have you looking like that." She eyed Tara's trousers disapprovingly.

"They're the only repectable things I've got," Tara said. "I lost my clothes . . ."

"I don't call a female in trousers respectable. I'll have to find you a dress," Mrs. Miles said. "Come along."

She made sure nothing was going to boil over and then marched Tara up the stairs. From a cupboard she produced some underwear, black lisle stockings, a pair of clogs, and a gray woolen dress with a high collar.

"There," she said, "these ought to fit you. They belonged to the last girl, but they'll do."

Tara dearly wanted to know who the last girl was and what had happened to her. Did Mrs. Miles acquire her also from the ranks of errant ladies who had fallen foul of the law?

"Here's your apron." She gave her a big white, starched square. "When you serve at the table, of course, I'll expect you to wear this," and she handed Tara a little pinafore.

Mrs. Miles returned to the steamy depths of her kitchen again, leaving Tara to change. She took a quick look at herself in the tiny mirror in her bedroom. The dress was shapeless, and the drab gray material did nothing for her coloring. As for the high neckline, its propriety would have won the approval of John Knox himself.

Yet Tara had had so little chance of varying her wardrobe and was so sick of the outfit she had worn since Dyea that any change of clothes was welcome, even this somber frock.

When she re-entered the kitchen Mrs. Miles looked up. "That's much better," she nodded. She slammed down a saucepan lid. "You don't use scent, do you?"

Good God, thought Tara. Does she really think I trekked bottles of perfume up here?

"Regrettably, I can't afford to," she replied, her voice hard.

"Good. I cannot abide it, and it will not be used in this house. Soap and water is good enough."

And starch, added Tara silently, plenty of starch. Maybe she bathes in the stuff.

From the parlor that couldn't be used on weekdays came the chimes of a grandfather clock. It was the first time she had heard one in this new world, and it gave her a momentary pang. That sound belonged to memories of San Francisco and her father's house in Cleveland.

Mrs. Miles interrupted her thoughts.

"All you need do tonight is serve the supper and then clean up," she said, as if announcing a national holiday. "You'll eat in the kitchen, *after* we've finished in the dining room."

"You mean, I have the left-overs?" Tara exclaimed indignantly.

"They'll be plenty for everyone, and that includes you. When I need you I shall ring the bell. When we leave, you clear the table and do the dishes. Breakfast must be laid before seven tomorrow morning, but whether you do it tonight or in the morning, I leave to you. First thing when you get up you must get the range going, light the fire in the dining room, and start boiling the water."

For a rebellious moment Tara considered telling Mrs. Miles to look for another slave, because she'd got the wrong woman. Then she decided no. There was nothing else for her. In a way, it was even a challenge. She would prove to the dragon that she could cope.

She got her first glimpse of the boarders that evening when she carried the huge soup tureen into the dining room. It was very heavy, and she was terrified that she would drop it before she could put it down on the mat in front of Mrs. Miles.

The five men in the room all looked at her. Mrs. Miles was presiding at the head of the table, the lodgers arranged on either side of her. Two of them, tall, thin men with identical side whiskers, were alike even down to their neckties. These were the Bartlett brothers, who lived in fear of the railroad coming to wipe out their successful freight-haulage business. Opposite them sat Harry Robbins, the man Dawson knew as "Doc" although he was no physician; he was the town's dentist and offered bargain rates—two dollars for pulling one tooth, only three dollars for two. Eugene Brock, a pince-nez balanced on his nose, was a storekeeper who had sniffed riches early in the day, set up a general store in the main street, and now, so it was rumored, had a tea chest full of gold nuggets. Then there was Joe Lamore, sawmill owner, who had turned timber into his own kind of gold mine.

"This is the new maid," said Mrs. Miles primly, as she ladled out the soup.

Tara carefully distributed the overflowing soup plates to each man, knowing their eyes were studying her. The Bartlett brothers said nothing, but Robbins muttered, "Thank you."

"What's your name?" the storekeeper asked as she placed the soup in front of him.

"Her name is Tara," a frosty Mrs. Miles interjected quickly, not giving Tara a chance to speak. Her tone indicated that there would be no other questions on the subject.

"I'll ring when we are ready," Mrs. Miles said. By her glass was a small silver bell. Its summons would become a familiar sound to Tara's ears.

The remainder of the dinner was an unending succession of carrying in hot plates, taking out dirty dishes, and being totally ignored by everybody. Mrs. Miles had cooked a gargantuan amount of food, providing bowls full of beans and sauerkraut and mashed potatoes to go with huge steaks.

At one point she pushed open the door and caught the tail end of a conversation.

". . . this place would become another Skagway if we let that man get away with it," the dentist was saying.

"That's the truth," Brock agreed. "I tell you now, Soapy Smith is beginning to take over Dawson. Already he owns four of the saloons, did you know that?"

Tara wanted to listen. Instead she had to collect the plates, making as little noise as possible.

"So what's the law doing about it?" asked one of the Bartletts. "This is Canadian territory. We don't need to allow Yankee hoodlums in here . . ."

"But ninety per cent of the people in Dawson are American citizens," Lamore pointed out. "Anyway, what can a handful of Mounties do? They're outnumbered two hundred to one."

"They should have hanged Soapy Smith years ago," commented Robbins, but Tara missed the rest of it because she had to bring in the apple pie.

In the kitchen, the words echoed in Tara's ears. Soapy Smith! Here in Dawson? The bell rang, and she rushed into the dining room empty-handed.

"Tara, where's the apple pie?" admonished Mrs. Miles. "And don't forget the cream." That was Mrs. Miles's pretentious term for condensed milk.

Tara dispensed the helpings of pie, all the time listening to Brock, in the middle of telling the others about "Soapy's girl ... The one who ran away from Skagway. I don't blame her either, wanting to escape from that louse.

"What happened?" asked the second Bartlett brother. "I haven't heard."

"Well," Brock began, enjoying being the bearer of scandal, "seems this saloon hustler," he caught Mrs. Miles's eye, "this, er, play for pay girl is Soapy's new fancy, and she ..."

"Tara," commanded Mrs. Miles in a loud voice. "The cream! We are waiting."

"Yes, Mrs. Miles." Tara's ears were burning. She would have given anything to hear the rest. She had an uneasy feeling they were talking about her, that this was the saloon version of her escapade.

She rushed back with the job of condensed milk just as Brock was coming to the end.

"... so she tricked the Mounties and they fell for it. Would you credit it? But, of course, when she got here, Constantine put her under arrest."

"No kidding?" said the dentist, helping himself to cream. "Where is she now?"

"Oh, I guess they got her locked up somewhere," Lamore said.

"Maybe Soapy will come chasing after her," Robbins said. "If she's his girl, he won't let go. You know his reputation. Once he owns something ..."

As Tara fled to the kitchen she heard Mrs. Miles say, "Gentlemen, that rogue and his hussies are hardly suitable topics over the dinner table. That sort of talk belongs to the barroom. Like him and his women."

Shaking, Tara poured herself some black coffee, wishing there was something stronger around. Smith's saloon hustler, indeed!

Tara was up first thing in the morning, doing all the chores Mrs. Miles had listed. After the lodgers left, the hard work started. She began by scrubbing the hallway on her hands and knees.

"*Are* you one of Soapy's women?" Mrs. Miles suddenly asked. Until now she had shown little interest in Tara or her background. She appeared to accept her presence without curiosity, and Tara had been left wondering what Constantine had actually written in his note.

She looked up, pushing away a stray strand of hair. Mrs. Miles stood in the doorway of the dining room looking down at her.

"Am I *what*, Mrs. Miles?" she asked, keeping her voice level.

"I asked you if you were anything to do with Soapy Smith and his crowd."

Tara tossed the floorcloth into the pail next to her and stood up.

"No," she said indignantly. "I'm not. What on earth makes you ask a thing like that?"

Tara knew only too well, but she was determined not to let on.

"Hmmm," sniffed Mrs. Miles. "Never mind, but I'll tell you straight, I wouldn't have one under my roof. I don't want anything to do with that kind of female."

"I see," Tara said.

"Not that I pay attention to saloon gossip," Mrs. Miles went on, "but I want to know the truth. Tell me, where is Mr. Kane? Or should I ask, is there a Mr. Kane?"

Tara controlled herself.

"After all, a married woman wears a wedding ring," added Mrs. Miles, her eyes fixed pointedly on Tara's left hand. Tara was becoming used to that accusing look.

"Very well," she replied, holding her temper in check. "Since you're so curious, there is a Mr. Kane, and I don't wear a wedding ring because I had to pawn it." Mrs. Miles's eyes opened wide. "Yes, pawn it. I was starving, and I had nothing else to sell."

"Oh." Her tone clearly indicated that she disapproved of any woman who would part with the symbol of her matrimony.

"I had no choice," Tara said. "Do you know what it's like to be destitute? Alone, in a place like Skagway?"

Mrs. Miles softened a little. "I'm sure you had a rough time—but what were you doing in Skagway?"

Tara told her story again. If she expected sympathy, she had come to the wrong person. Mrs. Miles shook her head. "You're a very foolhardy young woman, and you've got yourself into a right mess. How on earth do you expect to find him here?"

"I will," Tara replied firmly, her chin set stubbornly.

Mrs. Miles contemplated her with disapproval.

"Do you know what it takes for a female to survive on her own in these parts? Look at yourself. You're soft. Saw it the moment I laid eyes on you. If you had to cut off a frostbitten toe, skin a dog and cook him, shoot a crazed Indian, you'd go to pieces. If I were you, I wouldn't go on. You're not up to it."

That riled Tara. Too many people were telling her what she was not up to. "Don't worry, Mrs. Miles, I'll make out." She added, "You managed all right, didn't you?"

Mrs. Miles grunted. "That was different. I had no choice." She paused. "I was left with a broken wagon and a few supplies when my husband died, in '95. I couldn't have turned back if I'd wanted to. . . . I buried him and that took my last money. Anyway, there was nothing to go back for. What would I do? Live with my memories in an attic? That wasn't for me." She sighed. "I looked round Dawson and saw the way the men were being exploited, paying the earth for a lice-infested berth, eating food you wouldn't feed a pig. There wasn't a roof under which a God-fearing soul could lodge. So I said right, Linda Miles, this is your chance."

She had got hold of a stove, baked bread, and sold it for fifty cents a loaf until she had earned herself three hundred dollars. Then she opened an eating place, under canvas, and served good, wholesome, cheap meals. When she had piled up enough capital, she opened her lodging house.

"This is where I've made my stake, and it's mine, every board and every nail of it," she said fiercely. "I'm my own mistress, I'm not beholden to anybody, and I know how to look after myself. Which is more than you can do."

"I've got this far," Tara said but not boastfully. She was gaining a lot of respect for Mrs. Miles. Dour and formidable she might be, but Tara found herself admiring the starched lady.

"You have, but on other people's backs." Mrs. Miles said it without rancor, more like a mother putting a daughter straight. "You haven't stood on your own feet, have you? Anyway, all this talk won't get the housework done," she growled, turning to go. "You'd better finish here and then clean the rooms."

"Mrs. Miles," Tara said, "I need some time off."

"Time off!" Mrs. Miles boomed. "You haven't even started working properly and you want time off?"

"I've got to start getting around and look for Daniel. I'm sure I'll locate him, but I've got to ask around, go to the Mines Registry, inquire in the town, check if anyone knows his whereabouts. . . ."

"You mean wander round Dawson by yourself, talking to strangers, going into saloons, all on your own." Mrs. Miles was appalled.

"Yes, Stand on my own feet."

"You don't know what Dawson is like. It's out of the question. You are in my charge, and I will not . . ."

"I'll be all right," Tara said. "Anyway, that's the reason I'm here. I won't find Daniel by sitting in this house."

Mrs. Miles studied her hands, then looked at Tara sternly.

"Very well," she said ponderously. "You can have an hour now and then. During the day. But it's out of the question in the evening. After dark I will not have you roaming about, understand? Also, you are not to go into any bars, saloons, or dance halls. Nor will you talk to strange men in the street."

All those things, thought Tara, were exactly what she might have to do. All she said was, "Of course, Mrs. Miles."

"And you ask my permission every time you leave the house."

"I will."

"Get on with your work then."

After their conversation Mrs. Miles seemed to think more kindly of her. Tara even got the feeling that perhaps she liked her. She put a woven Indian blanket on her bed. She smiled at her occasionally, a rare thing for Mrs. Miles to do. She told her she could borrow a book if she wanted something to read; a rather limited offer, since Mrs. Miles's library consisted of only the Holy Bible, *Uncle Tom's Cabin*, *Lamb's Tales from Shakespeare*, and Mrs. Beeton.

And when she fell into bed, dog-tired, bones weary, hands rough after sixteen hours' work, Tara knew she was proving herself capable, a quality Mrs. Miles respected.

CHAPTER ELEVEN

Although she saw them every day when she served at the table, Tara found out more about the lodgers as she tidied and dusted their rooms.

At the table, Joe Lamore was a prim little man. Tara didn't like the way he eyed her across the dining room, but he always behaved perfectly. Mrs. Miles's forbidding presence probably guaranteed that. The other side of the sawmill owner was revealed in his room. On a chair by his bed was a stack of old *La Vie Parisiennes*, all well thumbed; clearly Mr. Lamore enjoyed looking at the pictures of busty ladies in decolletage. Tara wondered where he got his supply from.

Mr. Lamore also drank. In a medicine cabinet he kept his whisky, expensive Scotch, not cheap rotgut, and a glass he washed himself in the basin. He was something of a dandy too; some two dozen silk cravats hung in the closet.

The identical Bartlett brothers occupied two adjoining, identical rooms. There was even a framed, signed picture of a woman on each of their dressers, one dedicated to "My dear Willy" and the other to "My dear Wally" and both signed "Yours affectionately." The women were different, but looked pretty much the same. The Bartletts were preoccupied by the threat of the railroad. There were maps in their rooms with the proposed railroad drawn in, and clippings on the subject from old newspapers. They often sat composing long letters to Ottawa and Washington, which they sent down to Skagway in batches, hoping they would be delivered months later in the corridors of power.

Mr. Brock, the storekeeper, was an affable gentleman. He loved his old carpet slippers, and he had a rack of pipes from which he carefully selected one every day. "Don't dust 'em, don't touch 'em, don't do anything with 'em," he instructed Tara. Next to the rack was a huge china jar, always full of tobacco, and when Tara came into the room in the morning, there was usually a thick fog still in the air, proof that Mr. Brock had puffed away late into the night.

Mostly, the men went out after supper. Tara visualized Mr. Brock poring over the ledgers in his store, adding up long columns of figures. The Bartletts too were hardworking men, and the lights burned late in the wooden office they had downtown.

Sometimes somebody would rush to the house in the evenings for "Doc" Robbins. He would pick up his undentistlike black bag, and follow the caller into the night to patch up the latest casualty in some brawl. He liked extracting bullets much more than teeth, and next day he would regale his fellow lodgers with details of his latest impromptu operation, until Mrs. Miles's disapproving eye caught him.

Lamore, Tara guessed, was the dark horse among the five. When he went off into the night, she was sure he headed straight for the fleshy attractions of Front Street—maybe even the disreputable Paradise Alley. He was a vain man. In front of his mirror stood bottles of pomade, oils, and scent. For a sawmill owner he had remarkably smooth hands and manicured fingernails.

If any of the lodgers ever came home drunk, they were very circumspect about it. Once or twice, Tara, in her bedroom, thought she heard footsteps on the stairs in the early hours, but the lodgers knew better than to wake Mrs. Miles. In the morning, Tara, as she served breakfast, would wonder which was the gadabout. But if there was one with a hangover, he managed to conceal it.

If she was curious about them, the lodgers were even more curious about her. Mrs. Miles's introduction had been a very curt one, and during the first few weeks, they limited themselves to saying "Good morning" or "Good evening" politely. Had Mrs. Miles not been around, Lamore might have been more adventurous, Tara knew.

Then, one day, Robbins met her on the stairs and asked, "Any word yet from your husband?"

Tara looked at him astonished. She had no idea he knew about Daniel. "Not yet," she replied, "but I'm sure I'll find him."

"That's right," said Robbins. "Don't be discouraged. I'm keeping my ears open too."

Tara asked Mrs. Miles about it.

Mrs. Miles shrugged it off. "Don't pin any hopes on it. I told them you were searching for your man, just in case they came across his name. Timber people and haulage contractors and storekeepers and such like hear a lot, and you never know . . . but don't rely on it."

"I won't," Tara said. "But thank you. I appreciate it."

"It's nothing," retorted Mrs. Miles, turning surly. But Tara was happy Mrs. Miles seemed to care. She wanted to help, and that was a nice feeling.

The lodgers, in their own ways, knew all the kinds of women Dawson spawned, and Tara didn't fit into any of the molds. She was attractive, but she was not a good-time girl. She worked hard, from morning till night, she often looked tired and worn out, but she remained something of a mystery woman. She was married, but she wore no wedding ring. She kept to herself, and when sometimes she went into town, they all wondered where she went off to. She was shy, yet she had the manner of a woman who could look after herself. She didn't have much of a wardrobe, but she always made an effort to look her best.

Lamore took the plunge. "Oh, Mrs., er, Tara," he said, and then cleared his throat.

"Anything I can do, Mr. Lamore?" Tara had changed the sheets on his bed, given him fresh water in his jug, dusted everything.

"Yes," he said, and she caught a sniff of the pomade. "I was wondering if, er, well, if I could show you around sometime. The sights of Dawson, so to speak . . ." He laughed weakly.

"I'd like that very much," Tara said politely, thinking there was nothing she would like less than an assignation with Mr. Lamore, "but there is so much work here, and I never have any time. . . ."

"Surely you can make some," he urged.

"I don't think so, Mr. Lamore," sighed Tara. Luckily, at that moment, Mrs. Miles came in from the shed at the back of the house.

"Maybe sometime," Lamore said and fled.

"What did he want?" Mrs. Miles seemed to have a sixth sense.

"Oh, nothing," Tara said, "nothing at all."

The first passerby Tara stopped to ask the way to the Government Claims Office grinned at her.

"Struck it rich, honey?"

"Wish I had," Tara said. "Is it far from here?"

"Second on the left," he said, "you can't miss it."

Tara thanked him and hurried on. When she turned the corner, she knew what he had meant. There was a crowd of fifty or sixty men gathered in front of a building flying the Union Jack from a flagpole over the door.

Tara saw a small notice which read "Government of British Columbia, Mining Recorder, Dawson Division." Underneath it informed her that business hours were "Ten a.m. to noon. Two p.m. to four p.m. Closed for lunch noon to two p.m. Jas. R. Pinkus, Recorder."

Some of the men were hammering on the door and stamping their feet impatiently.

"He should have been back from grub ten minutes ago, the lazy bastard," complained a man standing next to her. "Keeps us goddamn freezing."

She had told Mrs. Miles she was slipping out only for an hour, and that was thirty minutes ago. She would suffer for it if she were late.

Then the door opened and there was a rush inside. Somebody was stemming the torrent very effectively, because most of them surged out again and, scowling, started forming a line.

An undersized, ferret-faced man appeared at the doorway and yelled, "One at a time, or I shut for the day. This is a government office, not a bear garden."

He slammed the door, and then, tamely, the first man went inside and the rest stood and waited. Tara went to the end of the line. She marveled at the authority the small, slightly built man had over the prospectors, any of which could easily have picked up Mr. Pinkus by the scruff of his neck with one hand.

"Ah, but he's a mighty important fellow, is our Recorder," explained the man ahead of her. "Nobody starts arguing with Pinkus. If he doesn't give you your piece of paper, your claim's worthless, anyone can jump it. He's a real son of a bitch too."

The first prospector came out of the building, and the next one in line went in. At this rate, Tara thought, it's going to take well over an hour before I'm anywhere near getting inside.

"I don't want to file a claim," Tara said. "Only check something. Do you think they'd let me slip in ahead of them?"

"You must be kidding," he said, astonished at the ignorance of her question.

"Is it always so crowded?" she asked, concerned at the slow progress she was making.

"This is nothing." The man was clutching a small bag and Tara wondered if he had some nuggets in it. "I've seen five hundred men standing here. Last week, the Mounties had to move in."

"They all found gold? Like these men?" It seemed hard to believe that so many men were striking it rich every day.

"Jesus, no," guffawed the man. "They're staking claims just to be on the safe side. They got holes in the ground mostly. They rush to register a claim and all they ever find is gravel and sand."

"What about you?" She nodded at the bag he was holding.

He smiled enigmatically.

"I can't wait," she said. "Is there any way . . ."

"You got five bucks to spare?" asked the man.

"Just about."

"Okay, honey, if you go round the side and knock on the little hatch there and hand Pinkus your five dollars, you can jump the line."

"I can?" she queried dubiously.

"That's the way Pinkus operates."

She looked at the crowd in front of her.

"What about them?"

He shrugged.

"Five bucks is a lot of dough for a fellow who's broke. It's cheaper to wait in line."

At the side of the building she found the wooden hatch. Tara banged on it and waited.

After a few moments the hatch cover shot back, revealing the sharp sparrowlike features of Pinkus.

"Yes?" he snapped.

Tara help up a five-dollar coin.

"I want to check on a claim," she said. "Now, please."

A skeletal hand shot out and grabbed the money. "All right," Pinkus said. There was the jangling of keys, and then a door beside the hatch opened. Tara stepped into a small room lined with files. Through an open door she could see the front room with a counter, protected by a wire grating. Beyond it was the face of a man who was obviously waiting for Pinkus to go back. Two pairs of scales stood on the counter, next to some chemicals and retorts.

"Well?" demanded Pinkus.

"I want to find out if you have a claim registered in the name of Daniel Kane," Tara explained.

"What's the location?"

"I don't know. Somewhere in this district."

"When did he get his certificate?"

"His . . . ?"

"His free miner's certificate," Pinkus said testily.

"Within the last eight or nine weeks, I should imagine," Tara guessed. "He came here from Skagway."

"Most of them do," sniffed Pinkus. "Wait here. I'll see what I can find."

He went into the front office, shutting the door.

Tara read the detailed list of charges on the wall ("For every free miner's certificate . . . $5. For recording any claim . . . $2.50. For recording any abandonment . . . $2.50"), then the densely printed copy of the Mining Acts of 1890, 1892, and 1895, laying down the laws of gold prospecting.

Pinkus finally returned, holding open in front of him an enormous bound ledger, each page filled with entries in the same spidery handwriting. He put it down on the table and pored over it. Then a finger stabbed on an entry.

"Yes," he said. "The system never fails."

Tara rushed to his side.

"Where?" she gasped excitedly. "Where?"

"The search fee is two-fifty," Pinkus intoned.

Her hand trembled uncontrollably as she got out the money and threw it on the table.

"What does it say? Show me."

Mr. Pinkus raised the ledger and read from the entry.

"September 29, 1897. Daniel Kane was issued with a Free Miner's certificate on payment of the statutory fee of two dollars and fifty cents, and a copy of the said certificate is duly filed with me in my authority as the District Mining Recorder acting on behalf of the Chief Gold Commissioner of the Government of British Columbia."

"Let me see," Tara begged excitedly.

"Here." Pinkus pointed at the small entry.

Tara read it, but the lines swam in front of her eyes. "Where is he?" she exclaimed. "Where is the claim?"

Pinkus shut the ledger. "That'll be in the Claims Register, and it costs another two-fifty."

She paid him, and he disappeared once more. When he came back, he shook his head. "There is no claim."

She stared at him, bewildered.

"He has not filed one."

She licked her lips. "I don't understand."

"All that has happened is he applied for and was issued with a certificate entitling him to prospect for gold within the jurisdiction of this territory. A Free Miner's Certificate. That is all."

She steadied herself by holding onto the table.

"I thought . . . I thought it meant . . ."

"No, ma'am," Pinkus said. "It is all under the relevant paragraph of Section Twenty-two." His tone indicated that no one could ask for a more lucid explanation.

"But where is he? There must be an address?" It was as if somebody had snatched it all from her just as it was in her grasp.

"No such particulars are listed or required until, and unless, a claim is staked. Then it has to be done within fifteen days of discovery. Naturally, once that is registered and all the formalities have been completed, including the positioning of the requisite marker posts on the site, I will have a record of the exact location and layout of the said claim."

"You mean you have no idea where is is?"

"Ma'am, to this date I have issued thousands of these certificates. Every prospector in the Yukon has one. Most of them I never see again. They never come back unless they think they've struck gold."

"There must be some way to find him."

"Not from my records," Pinkus said firmly.

It was all Tara could do not to burst into tears. He had been here, in this very building only a few weeks ago. And now he had vanished again.

"You are at perfect liberty to search the records again at a future date in case there are any new registrations," she heard Pinkus say. He could see the impact the news had made on her. "For payment of the requisite search fee, of course."

Overwhelmed by disappointment, she walked into the street with unseeing eyes, oblivious to the shouts of a driver as she nearly stumbled in front of his wagon.

All right, Tara said to herself, quickening her pace. At least you know he came to Dawson. The little compass needle spoke true. Now you must pick up his trail from here. Somebody must have come across him, it's not that long ago. He could even have teamed up with somebody here.

"I am finding him," she reassured herself.

"You are late, Tara," Mrs. Miles called out when she returned to the house. "You've been gone an hour and fifteen minutes," she went on as she came into the hall, wiping her hands on her apron. "When I say an hour—"

She stopped when she saw Tara's face.

"What happened?" she asked. "Did you find out something?"

"Yes, oh yes," Tara said, her eyes bright. Increasingly her disappointment was being swept away by the knowledge that Daniel had been close to her such a short time ago. "They've got his name listed at the Claims Office. Mrs. Miles, Daniel has been in Dawson."

"Well, where is he now?"

"I don't know yet. But he was here on September 29th. He took out a Miner's Certificate—just a few weeks ago. Isn't it wonderful?"

"But where is he now? Where is his claim located?" persisted Mrs. Miles, ever practical.

"I'm not sure, but if he's still around I'll find him, and if he's moved on, I'll follow him. I don't care where," said Tara, breathless.

"Do you know how big this territory is? Supposing he's gone north?"

"I'll find him." Her conviction gave her strength. "Maybe he's even in Dawson still."

"Hmmm," Mrs. Miles grunted skeptically. "Anyway, you'd better take your things off and give me a hand with dinner."

Tara was in a world of her own as she started up the stairs. First she would scour the town, in case he was still around. Then she would try the gold fields, all of them.

"Let me know if you need more time off to look for him," Mrs. Miles said.

Tara turned and looked at her.

"Thank you," she said gratefully.

Mrs. Miles cleared her throat. "And you may call me Linda," she added, quickly disappearing into the kitchen as if embarrassed by her momentary lapse.

CHAPTER TWELVE

The Monte Carlo Saloon was packed. Tara stood blinking, trying to adjust herself to the smoke-laden atmosphere and the deafening noise. She could hear a piano being hammered, glasses smashing, the clicking of roulette wheels, men shouting for drinks, laughter at one table, a violent argument at another. All about her, there were men with their arms around girls, girls sitting on men's laps, people jostling one another to get served at the enormous bar, men slumped at tables, their heads in their hands.

At the back of the huge room was a stage, hung with red velvet drapes and beside it a pianist, a languid character with a straw boater who played his tinny music with eyes shut, lost in his own world. Occasionally he reached out for a drink on the top of the piano.

Every inch of space was crowded, except for the center of the floor, where drunken men and women were dancing, some swinging each other around to the tune of a waltz no one could recognize, others just swaying in rhythm, clutching one another, all of them periodically colliding. They were all trying to dance to the accompaniment of a small group of musicians on the stage, two violinists and a banjo player, who most of the time ignored the pianist.

The music was drowned by a group of men drunkenly singing:

Casey would waltz with the strawberry blonde,
And the band played on—
He'd glide 'cross the floor with the girl he adored
And the band played on. . . .

They stamped the rhythm out, and it was to this tempo that the dancers moved while the tiny band tried desperately to make itself heard.

Tara had come here to ask about Daniel. Every man's path crossed the Monte Carlo, she gathered, and here somebody could well have heard of him. She mustered up her courage and decided to begin her inquiries at the bar.

"Let's have a whirl," said a man's voice. He grabbed her and, without waiting for her reply, steered her to the dance floor. He had not shaved for several days, and his check-patterned lumberjack's shirt hadn't been washed for longer. Tara tried to pull away, but he pressed something into her palm. She opened her hand; he had given her a little triangular piece of ivory with a number on it.

"What's this supposed to be," began Tara.

"Well, you're not doing it for free, are you, honey?" The man was surprised. "That's your token, Buck a dance, right?"

Tara stared at the triangle.

The quartet started up again, and this time there seemed to be some agreement between the pianist and the musicians on the stage as they performed the semblance of a polka.

Tara's partner swung her around the floor, pressing her close to him. She got a couple of strong whiffs of rotgut and stale breath. He grinned at her delightedly, then stepped on her foot heavily. She could not help grimacing with pain.

"Gee," he said, holding her tighter, "I'm sorry. Guess I'm clumsy as hell."

Suddenly Tara felt as if she had been struck by a giant; only the lumberjack's firm grip kept her on her feet. She looked around to see what had hit her. A gigantic woman was bear-hugging a young man whose head reached only to her massive bosom and who looked as if he were suffocating as they danced. She must weigh at least three hundred pounds, Tara calculated, repelled by the sight of the sweat pouring down her face, making rivulets along her three chins. Her shoulders were enormous, and she had arms like thick columns. She wore a huge sequined dress, which covered her body like a tarpaulin. Every time she breathed, the sequins glittered. Tara, fascinated, saw one of the rivulets of sweat meander down into the cleavage between her massive breasts. Her mouth was a huge gash of violent red lipstick. The most disconcerting thing of all was her eye. She had only one, and it glared at Tara bloodshot and furious. Where the other eye should have been was an empty socket.

"Watch your big feet," the woman snarled at Tara.

The lumberjack pulled Tara around, away from the monster.

"Phew," he said. "The last girl that bumped into the Grizzly Bear lost her scalp. I'd rather tangle with an elephant."

"She looks pretty fierce," Tara said, still mesmerized. The she-mountain was half squeezing her partner to death a couple of feet away.

"Fierce? Not been around long, have you? How do you think she lost her blinker?"

Tara shook her head.

"Buffalo Liz gouged it out with her nails over at Sam Bonnifield's place. The Grizzly broke three of her ribs and stomped her face in."

Tara shuddered.

The lumberjack smiled at the recollection. "Yes sir, that was some fight."

The music stopped, and Tara made to get away from him. He put another ivory token into her hand.

"No," said Tara, "I'm sorry . . ."

He looked concerned. "Did I hurt your feet?" he asked.

"I think I need a rest," Tara said.

"Sure." He was full of solicitude. "I'll get us some bubbly."

He dragged her toward the bar, pushing people aside. How the devil do I get rid of him, Tara wondered.

The lumberjack thumped the counter.

"Hey, Pierre, pint of fizz."

Even above all the noise his loud voice was heard by the bartender. He produced a bottle and two glasses. "Thirty bucks."

The lumberjack felt in his shirt pocket and brought out a thick wad of money. Thirty dollars for one bottle of champagne, thought Tara. She wished she had money like that.

The lumberjack must have seen the expression on her face because he said grandiosely, "Nothing's too good for any little lady I go with. And you've made two bucks, honey, haven't you?"

"Two bucks?"

"Don't they tell you nothing? You get two bucks commission on every bottle of fizz the customers buy. Hasn't Soapy told you?"

She stared at him. "Soapy Smith? Jefferson Smith?"

"Who else?"

He pushed a glass into her hands and raised his. "Here's mud in your eye."

"What's Soapy Smith got to do with it?" Tara asked.

"Christ, where have you been?" asked the lumberjack, amazed. "He owns the joint. Aren't you one of his girls?"

Tara put the glass down. "I'm sorry. You've made a mistake."

"What the hell do you mean?"

"I've got nothing to do with this place or Soapy Smith."

"So what the hell are you here for?" he asked angrily. "You pick up a fellow and . . ."

"I think it's the other way around, isn't it?"

He drank down his champagne in one gulp. "What's your name anyway?" he asked.

Mrs. Kane," said Tara.

"Mrs.," repeated the lumberjack. "Christ. No woman's a Mrs. here. You'd better learn that for starters." He wiped his mouth with the back of his hand.

The music started up again, a quick ragtime beat.

"Come on," he said. "You owe me this one."

"Here you are." Tara handed him back his token.

The lumberjack looked at it, and his eyes grew mean.

"I don't want that goddamn lousy thing. I want the dance I paid for."

He threw the little ivory triangle into a nearby spittoon.

"Please . . ." Tara began.

"You're dancing with me if I have to drag you out there," he snarled.

117

There was a sudden roar from the dance floor. The one-eyed woman mountain was slugging it out with another big, hefty whore. They stood hitting one another like heavyweight boxers while the crowd egged them on, cheering, clapping, and whistling.

"Jeez, it's the Oregon Mare," Tara's partner shouted enthusiastically. He seemed to have forgotten all about the dance, and Tara breathed a sigh of relief.

Now the women had their claws in each other's hair and were struggling like two crazed wrestlers. Suddenly they both lost their balance, and the Monte Carlo shook from floor to ceiling as they crashed onto the wooden boards. They rolled over, tree-trunk-like thighs revealed in the confusion of clothes and flesh, tearing at their opponent's hair, slamming their hamlike fists into each other's faces.

Two men joined in the fighting, and then the dance floor erupted into a seething mass of brawlers. The dancers began pairing off against each other, so that couple was fighting couple, the women scratching and clawing one another while the men concentrated on smashing each other's jaws and noses.

"Jeez, what a great fight," said the lumberjack excitedly. He looked at Tara invitingly. "Let's join in, kid, eh?"

"No, thank you," Tara said emphatically.

Through the haze, at the other end of the saloon, the swing doors were shouldered open and two men in scarlet appeared. They forced their way into the center of the brawling mass and started picking up the combatants by the scruff of their necks and banging their heads together.

"Goddamn spoilsports," snorted the lumberjack.

The two Mounties sauntered around the saloon, eyeing everyone. They were outnumbered a hundred to one, but they turned their backs disdainfully, almost daring someone to raise a hand against them. Their walk was slow, deliberate, their stare challenging. They said nothing.

They came toward the bar and Tara recognized Inspector Constantine. She tried to hide behind the lumberjack. Then Constantine spotted her. He ambled over, his cold eyes boring relentlessly into her all the while.

"So, Mrs.. Kane," he said dryly. "This is where you spend your time."

"I'm only here because I'm looking for my husband," Tara mumbled, flushing. "I've never been here before."

His glance took in the lumberjack, the bottle of champagne, and

118

the two glasses. "I can see that," he said curtly, tapping his booted foot on the floor. "You disappoint me, Mrs. Kane."

"Perhaps you shouldn't jump to conclusions quite so quickly."

The bartender, the drunks, the whores, the gamblers were all watching her.

"When a woman is found in this place," remarked Constantine, looking around, "in this company, at this time of night, I can only draw one conclusion, ma'am."

He signaled to the constable, and they walked on, continuing their circuit of the saloon. As soon as they had left a buzz of conversation went up, the shouting and the noise beginning again.

The lumberjack looked at her curiously.

"What was that all about?" he asked.

Tara ignored him and turned to the bartender who was collecting their glasses and wiping the counter.

"Excuse me," she said.

"What's your pleasure?" grunted Pierre, taken aback. Few people in the Monte Carlo ever said "excuse me."

"I'm looking for somebody. . . ." began Tara.

"Isn't everybody?"

"A man called Kane. Daniel Kane. He was in Dawson a few weeks ago. Do you remember him?"

"Kane?" He shook his head. "Walked out on you, has he?"

"Did he come in here?" she pressed. "Perhaps he got talking to somebody.

"Wait a moment."

Pierre went to the back of the bar. Under the picture of a naked woman reclining on a sofa stood the cash register and the scales that were used to weigh gold. Pierre opened the till and took out a small pile of notes. He thumbed through them.

Tara's heart jumped as he came back to her, holding one of the pieces of paper.

"Yeah," said Pierre. "I remember the guy. Sure I do. He owes us forty-five bucks." He spat with great accuracy into a spittoon behind the bar. "If you find Mr. Daniel Kane, tell him we want our dough."

She looked at the paper in his hand.

"What's that?" she asked, trying to check her excitement.

"His marker. He was going to get the cash and gave us an IOU."

"Let me see," she said, reaching for the note. It was Dan's all right. It was his handwriting, his signature. "What's it for?"

"What do you think? Booze. Women. What's a guy come in here

119

for? He said he'd be back, and that's the last we saw of him. I sure would like to catch up with him. . . ."

Booze and gambling perhaps, but not these floozies, not Daniel.

"When was this?" Tara asked.

"Four, five weeks ago." He looked at her closely. "What's he to you, anyway?"

"He's my husband," Tara replied quietly.

"Oh is he? Well then, in that case, lady, you'd better pay his debt," he said coldly, his eyes hostile. "The boss doesn't like welshers. If you're the next of kin, it's your obligation, I guess. Your man shouldn't go around cheating people."

"He doesn't cheat," Tara protested indignantly.

"Mort," Pierre yelled. A stocky man dressed in black detached himself from two girls at the corner of the bar and came over.

"You got a problem, Pierre?" he asked, his eyes examining Tara.

"Got a marker here for forty-five bucks. The guy ran out on us. Now his wife's showed up. She don't want to pay."

Mort nodded. "We got pretty strict house rules, lady, and the boss don't make exceptions. Seeing as we can't get hold of your husband, you'd better pay up.

"You tell Mr. Smith he can say that to my face," Tara retorted.

"He ain't around," Mort said.

"Then I'd better tell him when he does get here," she replied.

He looked at her dubiously. "You a friend of his? Haven't seen you before."

"Why don't you ask him," Tara said haughtily.

"You know the boss?" Mort repeated warily.

"Yes," Tara said. "I know him quite well."

She loathed invoking his name.

"Well, in that case . . ." said Mort, who Tara guessed was the Monte Carlo's resident thug. "We'd better leave it for the moment." He exchanged a look with Pierre.

"Exactly," concurred Tara, thanking God Smith was in Skagway.

The lumberjack pushed his way forward and clutched Tara's arm. "Hey, you," he interrupted. "You trying to ditch me? Let's go."

Tara jerked her arm away. "Not now," she said.

"Listen, I don't buy a woman fizz, spend dough on her so that she can walk out on me," snarled the lumberjack.

To Tara's surprise Mort intervened. "The lady says to go away," he said quietly.

"Who the hell . . ." began the lumberjack.

"The lady don't want you," he cut in, drawing his jacket a little to one side and revealing the butt of a pistol.

The lumberjack was clenching and unclenching his fists, but the sight of the gun calmed him.

"What makes her so different, anyway?" he demanded.

"She's a friend of the boss," said Mort.

"*She* is?" the lumberjack grinned. "That's not what she told me."

"I don't care what she said to you, fellow," Mort said. "She don't want to know, and we don't want any more trouble tonight. So move."

The lumberjack gave Tara an evil look and shuffled off muttering.

So Soapy Smith doesn't just run Skagway, thought Tara. In this joint, too, his word was law.

"I have to go," Tara said.

Mort smirked at her. "The boss will be pleased to hear you're in town," he said. "He's arriving in a couple of days. I'll tell him you're here."

He winked. "Guess everything will be taken care of for you, eh?" he whispered conspiratorially.

"Good night," Tara said.

She turned and pushed her way around the dance floor, past the gamblers and out into the cold air of Front Street. Under no circumstances did she want to meet Soapy Smith, not until it was on her own terms.

Next morning, after the boarders had left, Mrs. Miles came into the kitchen. Her mouth was thin with displeasure.

"Mr. Constantine brought some very disturbing news about you," she said severely.

"If you're referring to the Monte Carlo Saloon, I was there asking about my husband, hoping to find somebody who would know his whereabouts."

"That's not the story I heard. I was told you were drinking there, consorting with highly disreputable characters, and getting involved in a drunken brawl, like a cheap, common slut."

"That's a lie," snapped Tara.

"My information comes, of course, from Mr. Constantine. He saw you," said Mrs. Miles disdainfully.

"Well, then he knows it's a lie," Tara persisted.

"I'm not going to argue," grated Mrs. Miles. "The kind of woman who behaves like that has no place under my roof."

121

"You don't want to believe me, which is your business of course," Tara said scornfully. "However, let me tell you something. Nothing, nobody is going to stop me doing what I have come to do. Not you, not Inspector Constantine. I shall go wherever I must, talk to whomever I think might help, and if you don't like it, that's too bad. I'll make my own way, no matter what."

"A woman has her reputation to think of."

"To hell with my reputation. I want to find my husband," Tara shouted. "I love him. He's the only thing that matters to me in this whole world. And if you don't understand that, I'll get my things."

Mrs. Miles retreated slightly. This was a Tara she hadn't seen before, determined, tough, and very proud. Perhaps the submissive way she had acted so far concealed a different woman. Somewhere in her there was a volcano, just waiting to erupt.

Mrs. Miles cleared her throat.

"No need to talk like that," she said in an aggrieved tone. "I am only concerned for your welfare. Things can happen here you wouldn't believe. A female on her own is easy game. You have no idea what can happen to a woman who is by herself."

"I have a shrewd suspicion."

Mrs. Miles turned to go.

"Mrs. Miles," Tara said, stopping her, "if you see Inspector Constantine in the next few days, could you kindly tell him that if he has anything to say about me, would he please say it to my face and not go carrying tales. I can manage without him interfering. He wouldn't listen to me. Maybe one day he will."

"I don't think I'll say anything of the sort to him," Mrs. Miles said. She looked Tara straight in the eye. "And you'd better remember you're serving a sentence. You're my charge for thirty days and they aren't over yet."

CHAPTER THIRTEEN

Sunday was the one day the respectable citizens of Dawson, and there weren't many of them, strolled along the duckboards of the main street. Most of the saloons had their shutters up, briefly, for the Sabbath. Once the evening came they were back in business but, for a few hours on a Sunday afternoon, it was their siesta time.

"Sacred Concert—Admission Free" proclaimed a notice outside the Monte Carlo, and Tara hesitated. She felt a wry curiosity at the ludicrous idea of anything sacred happening behind the facade of Soapy Smith's establishment.

Inside the saloon the roulette wheels were still, and the bar deserted. Up on the stage, in front of a primitive backcloth, the dance girls were performing a series of tableaux to a captivated all-male audience. Tara could hardly believe what she saw.

A couple of saloon girls stood impersonating what Tara gathered were Roman soldiers. They clutched homemade spears and pasteboard shields while a woman at the piano tinkled out some kind of hymn tune.

On the center of the stage a redhead was draping herself suggestively around an enormous wooden cross. She wore pink tights and a white tunic, cut low, exposing one shoulder and her breast. Slowly she gyrated around the cross, executing what she obviously considered artistic poses. She managed to twist and grind her way around the cross so that, gradually, she exposed more and more of her bosom as the tunic slipped.

The audience applauded her efforts and allowed itself a few less than sacred whistles. A curtain fell and then, almost immediately, parted again. It was the finale. Six girls had formed a kind of pyramid, balancing the redhead up on high while the pianist beat out dramatic chords. The redhead raised her hands, a beatific expression on her face, the saintliness somewhat spoiled by the fact that she was chewing tobacco.

It was the Monte Carlo's version of the Resurrection.

Tara turned to go, just as Mort the bouncer came around shaking a box. "Silver collection," he announced, buttonholing members of the audience. "For good causes." All of which, Tara figured, would turn out to be Mr. Smith. She walked out of the saloon.

"And how is Mrs. Kane doing?" asked a voice at her elbow. Campbell was strolling past but had stopped when she came out. She was pleased to see him. A familiar face, a man she felt she owed a lot to one way or another.

"I'm being very law-abiding as you can see," said Tara. "How are you, Sergeant?"

"Not sergeant any more," he said, pointing at his sleeve. The three chevrons had gone. "You're talking to a constable now."

"What happened?" she asked, dismayed.

They walked along the street.

"Got busted," he sighed resignedly. "The inspector took 'em away."

"Because of me?" It must be her fault. "Oh, I *am* sorry." It must have taken him years to get those stripes.

"No, not entirely." He gave her a little smile. "I'll get 'em back one day. I'll bring in some guy single-handed or something, and he'll forget all about it."

He kicked an empty can off the wooden planking.

"It's been a lousy deal all round. Thatcher strung himself up in his cell. Constantine was up all night writing the report. He likes things tidy. Maybe it saved us a lot of hassle, but he doesn't see it that way. And he's worried about jurisdiction. Maybe I should have left the other guy in Skagway."

"But you couldn't let him be lynched," Tara said.

"When you bend regulations, you either come out smelling like a rose, or you pay. I paid." He shrugged.

"And I didn't help."

"How are you surviving Mrs. Miles?" he inquired.

"Surviving," Tara groaned.

"Then you haven't found your husband yet?" he asked.

"I know he's been in Dawson. I found his name at the Claims Office, and now I'm looking around the town to see if anyone knows where he is."

"You just stay out of trouble, Tara," he said. It was the first time he had used her name. "Don't bite off more than you can chew."

"What do you mean?"

"Be careful who you mix with. It's your business, but I'd hate to see you in real trouble. Find your husband, then get out."

"That's all I'm trying to do, Sergeant Campbell. . . ."

"Name's Andrew," he said. "Sure, I know. Just watch yourself."

"What exactly are you trying to say?" She looked at him questioningly.

He stared her straight in the eye. "Got to check on a couple of things," was all he said, turning to go.

"You'll let me know if you come across my husband?"

Campbell nodded.

She watched the red-jacketed figure stroll off.

In her search for a clue to Daniel's whereabouts, Tara learned that in Dawson people lost their identity.

"Daniel Kane?" they asked. "What's his name?"

At first she was at a loss for words. Then she began to understand: Phantom Archibald. Waterfront Brown. Billy the Horse. Deep Hole Johnson. Limejuice Jim. Two-step Louie. Arizona Charlie. These were the names men were known by. That was what they called each other, and that was what their friends put on their tombstones when they were buried.

"I'd like to help you, honey," the dance-hall caller told her. He went by the name of Hamgrease Jimmy. "But who calls himself Daniel Kane?" He shook his head. "Doesn't he have a moniker? What do his pals call him?"

Clambake Dalton also tried to be helpful.

"He'd get a name, see, and it'll stick with him. Maybe he's good at cards? Maybe they call him Blackjack Dan? Faro Kane?" Tara shook her head. "Two-spot Kane? Frisco Dan?"

Even Tara had to admit that his description could fit one of a thousand men. And she didn't even know what he looked like now. Was his hair long or had he kept it short? Did he have sideburns? Had he grown a beard? In the past Daniel had shaved religiously, but in the Klondike he had probably grown a beard to protect his face from the cold. She couldn't guess what he would weigh. He could have grown thinner from a shortage of food or fatter on a bean and potato diet. But relentlessly she pursued her quest.

Dawson, she discovered, was full of weird characters, all drawn there by their craving for gold. With some, she wondered what made them think they were cut out for such adventure, like the curious little person everyone in town called the Evaporated Kid. He was only four feet ten inches, so small, they jeered, that he looked like a bottle with hips, and when he stood beside Sparerib Joe, who was nearly seven feet tall, the two were straight out of Barnum and Bailey.

Life in the bars, the dance halls, and the saloons went on twenty-four hours a day. At six in the morning, when Tara was still rubbing the sleep out of her eyes as she lit Mrs. Miles's fires and served breakfast, the Monte Carlo, the Golden Nugget, the Dominion, and all the other dens were only just closing their doors.

One place that acted as a clearing house for information, and charged one dollar to post notices on a board, was the A.C. Store in the center of town.

Tara noticed such an appeal, in spidery handwriting, which read:

Lost! On November 27 at about 11 p.m. a gold sack between Old Man Buck's Cabin and the small boarding house selling lemonade. Any person finding same will do a very great favor for aged miner who must get out. A liberal reward will be paid by inquiring at Ferry Beer Saloon at Lousetown Bridge.

A couple of roughnecks read it over Tara's shoulders and guffawed. They shambled off, still laughing about the old fool.

Poor man, thought Tara, what an optimist.

Mostly the others were about lost animals, a stolen rifle of "great sentimental value to the owner, having killed six men with it," an offer to sell a silver-decorated saddle with silver spurs for ten dollars, "a bargain offer at any price."

Later that afternoon a new notice went up on the board of the A.C. Store:

Daniel Kane of San Francisco. Will anyone who knows the whereabouts of Daniel Kane, believed to be prospecting in the Dawson area, please communicate urgently with his wife. A reward will be given. Contact Mrs. Tara Kane care of Mrs. Miles's Boarding House, Third Street, Dawson.

"This came for you," Mrs. Miles said a couple of days later. She handed Tara a letter.

Tara dried her hands on her apron and looked at the envelope. "Mrs. Tara Kane," it read, and in the top left-hand corner the word "Private."

She didn't recognize the handwriting. She ripped open the envelope as Mrs. Miles stood watching, making no attempt to hide her curiosity. She waited for Tara to say something.

It was a very short note:

Dear Mrs. Kane,
I may be in possession of some information which could be of interest to you. I look forward to the pleasure of your company tonight at supper. I will call for you at six o'clock.
Yours most sincerely,
Jefferson R. Smith

Tara stared at the note.

"What is it?" Mrs. Miles asked. She craned her neck to try and get a look at it.

Tara's head was in a whirl. "Who brought this?" she asked.

"A very unsavory character," Mrs. Miles said disapprovingly. She was getting impatient. "Who's it from?"

For a moment, Tara was tempted to tell her to mind her own business. Then she handed the note over. Mrs. Miles read it, her face gradually clouding over.

"Well, that's out of the question," she decreed at last. "You know what sort of man he is. You can't go out with him."

"If he's got information about Daniel . . ."

126

"The man's a blackguard, and it's probably just a lie," exploded Mrs. Miles. "He wants to entice you. Good heavens, Tara, you couldn't even think of accepting."

"I must, Linda. I'd have supper with the devil if he'd lead me to my husband. Anyway, why else should he bother? He knows something."

"Sit down," Mrs. Miles said in a conciliatory tone. She sat opposite Tara. "Look, my dear, I do understand. But Mr. Soapy Smith does nothing for anyone except himself. Why should he help you? Use your head. If this man asks a woman for supper, it's only for one reason, and you know what that is. . . . A man like him always wants what he doesn't have. He wants to add you to his scalps, and he's using your husband as an excuse."

"Well, I don't agree with you." Then she noticed Mrs. Miles's pained expression. "Linda, I appreciate your concern. I'll be careful, I promise you. But you can't expect me to refuse. Would you? In my position?"

"I wouldn't dream of having anything to do with a scoundrel like him," declared Mrs. Miles. "Never."

Tara stood up. "I'm sorry. I must go tonight. Will you give me the time off?" Then she added gently, "Don't forget, Linda, I've served my thirty days."

Mrs. Miles waved her away. "Please yourself," she said coldly. "You're over twenty-one. I had hoped you'd seen and heard enough to take heed. You can go for all I care, but don't say you weren't warned."

"Trust me, Linda. I know what I'm doing."

In her room she looked at herself in the mirror. "Just remember one thing, Tara Kane," she said to her reflection. "Don't trust him an inch. Just think of the humiliation he caused you. The way he mocked you. The wedding ring he took from you. The lesson you owe him."

She read the letter again. He's an arrogant beast, she thought, so damn sure of himself he calmly announces he's picking me up at six, not even asking if I'm free, not even considering I might refuse.

The grandfather clock downstairs was striking six o'clock when Mrs. Miles banged on Tara's door.

"He's come for you," she called out in a gruff tone. Tara could hear her thumping down the stairs again, not waiting for her reply. She took one last look in the mirror. Her face was pale, so she pinched her cheeks to heighten her color and decided she was reasonably pleased with her appearance, considering that she had only one dress and no jewelry.

She put on her coat and went down the stairs to the hall. It was empty.

Mrs. Miles, busy in the kitchen, did not look up when Tara appeared. If she had, she would have seen a Tara who had made herself into a woman the lodging house hadn't yet discovered. She looked almost elegant, her luxuriant dark auburn hair swept up and carefully arranged. Here was no housemaid who spent most of her hours surrounded by dirty pots and pans. Here was a young woman who did not need jewelry or perfume or furs to make her beautiful. Her natural loveliness was more than sufficient.

"Linda," Tara said, "where is he?"

"Outside. He's not coming into my house," spat Mrs. Miles, and those were her last words. She did not reply when Tara said goodnight, adding, for conciliation's sake, "I won't be late."

As Tara emerged from the house, he came toward her and raised his broad-brimmed hat.

"What a pleasure to see you again," he drawled. He looked at her from under his hooded eyelids and smiled. "May I?" he inquired, bowing slightly and offering her his arm.

She looked at his ungloved hand. There on the little finger was her wedding ring.

"I must be back soon," Tara said coldly, ignoring his proffered arm. "I hope we're not going far."

"Hardly," he said. "I promise to bring you back safe and sound and completely intact." He glanced at her mockingly.

They began walking down the street toward the center of Dawson. A group of men standing outside the Dominion stared at them openly. Tara had a shrewd idea what they were thinking: Soapy Smith and his latest woman.

"Tell me, Tara, how do you like Dawson?" Smith asked. He said her name casually, as if he'd known her for years.

"It's hell. I loathe it."

He laughed.

His smooth, unruffled manner was insufferable. Wanting to say something to jar his smugness, she added, "And I think you're the devil behind it."

"At least hell's warm," he said. "And it's entertaining. So is the devil, I trust. Heaven would be so drab, don't you think? Think of those boring do-gooders playing harps all day."

In truth Tara was not sure whether she would like heaven, knowing some of the people she might find there, but she wasn't going to give him the satisfaction of agreeing.

"Where are we going, Mr. Smith?" she asked, hoping her question sounded like a shower of cold water.

"Oh, a little place I have," he murmured. "I hope you like it."

It was called the Regina Café. Tara had noticed the four-story building, the biggest in Dawson, under construction, without realizing what it would become.

When she stepped inside, she was amazed. She was looking down an elegant hallway, at the end of which was a mahogany reception desk. The floor was covered from wall to wall with deep red Brussels carpet. Hanging from the ornate ceiling were glass chandeliers. The wood-paneled walls were decorated with gold leaf. There wasn't a bare floorboard in sight; no sawdust, no stains, and, as yet, no spittoons. The place smelled of fresh paint, and carpenters' tools were lying around.

"When the whole thing opens it will be Dawson's finest hotel," Smith said, looking around proudly. "Fifteen rooms, all steam-heated. Yes, sir. Turkish baths. All lit by electric light. I'll get the power from a ship on the river. Class, that's what it's going to have."

This was a new angle on Smith's operations. She associated him with rackets—confidence tricks, cheap saloons, tawdry establishments, and whores. This was different. Smith was well aware that she was impressed, and she knew this was exactly what he had intended.

"This will be the lobby," Smith said, guiding her around. "Over there I'll have an orchestra playing chamber music. The furniture is being shipped from San Francisco. This way," he added nonchalantly, leading her to the stairs.

"What's up there?" Tara demanded suspiciously.

"Dear lady," he smiled. "We're going to have supper." He looked straight into her eyes. "What did you expect?"

"The dining room's downstairs, isn't it?"

"It's not ready yet," he explained, his eyes mocking her. "Nor are any of the bedrooms," he added.

Tara was furious with herself for blushing.

He took her along a corridor and opened a door. Inside she saw a table laid for two. On it were candles in tall holders, already lit. Apart from these the room was dark. At her place was a small silver vase with wild flowers in it. Bone china plates were laid on a snow-white tablecloth. The silver cutlery and cut crystal glasses shone and sparkled. All this luxury seemed strangely out of place in Dawson.

Smith went to the corner of the room and tugged at a bell rope. For a hotel still under construction, the amenities were already functioning very smoothly.

He came back to the table and took the chair opposite her, his gold watch chain twinkling in the subdued lighting. More than anything she was aware of her wedding ring on his finger. She stared at it wistfully. If only she were looking at the twin ring on Daniel's finger.

There was a soft tap at the door, and a little Chinese entered. He handed Tara a printed menu.

"I hope you're hungry," Smith said. "And if there's something else you'd prefer . . ."

She couldn't believe such fare existed in these parts. She hadn't seen such a list of delicacies since her honeymoon.

There was *Consommé à la jardinière*; Rock point oysters; broiled Caribou chops *aux champignons*; Saratoga chips; followed by pears and peaches; chocolate *gâteau*; Stilton cheese and coffee. And to drink, apart from the wines cooling in the bucket on a side table, there was Chateau LaTour 1878, a thirty-nine-year-old port, and Napoleon Brandy.

Tara marveled. Maybe the meat was just dressed up in a fancy name, but oysters, fresh vegetables, and fruit hadn't passed her lips since San Francisco.

"I shouldn't admit this, but I'm using you." He paused, his eyes teasing her. "The chef's on trial tonight. I've imported him from the Palace Hotel in Frisco, and he has the highest recommendations. Now we're going to find out if he lives up to them."

He nodded to the Chinese, who padded silently out of the room.

Smith played the perfect host. He filled their glasses and then silently raised his, looking across at her. She was beginning to find his smooth attentiveness disconcerting.

When she took her first taste of the food, Smith watched her reaction closely.

"What do you think?" he inquired.

"Delicious," Tara said and meant it.

Smith kept her wine glass filled, not too much, but continuously replenished. The mere fact that he could produce such luxuries so far from civilization earned her grudging respect for his ingenuity. Nonetheless, she had the feeling she was being manipulated, that he was fitting the strings to pull later.

"You said you had some information about my husband," she said, breaking a long and oddly intimate silence.

"There's plenty of time to talk about that," he protested, pouring her some Hermitage.

"No," Tara said firmly. "This is not a social occasion, Mr. Smith. That's why I'm here."

He took a sip of wine and regarded her thoughtfully, a little smile hovering.

"I guess you've heard the most terrible stories about this scoundrel Soapy Smith. How he runs all the rackets. How he owns dives and saloons. How he takes advantage of people. What a rogue he is. Correct?"

You believe you're playing a really disarming game, don't you, thought Tara. Aloud, she said, "Why should I listen to stories about you, Mr. Smith? I've seen you in action. I know how you operate."

Now he was smiling broadly. "Sure. I'm a businessman. An entrepreneur."

Tara pushed her plate away. "Businessman? Selling people ten-cent bars of soap for five dollars? Rigging up fake telegraph lines? Fixing roulette wheels? You call that doing business?"

Smith shook his head, a little sorrowfully.

"You really don't understand, do you? I'm a kind of educator. I teach people lessons they badly need. Hell, I put them wise, don't you see? Show them how easy it is for a sucker to be parted from his dough. I figure that's more a public service than some folks realize. There's many a guy walking around watching his money after a course of instruction from me. Now doesn't that appeal to you?"

Tara glared at him. "No. It so happens I'm honest, Mr. Smith."

He leaned back and looked at her cynically. "My, that's quite a statement, coming from you."

She felt her face burn.

"I reckon you haven't much cause to preach me sermons. I got to hand it to you though. You got the nerve of Old Nick." He wiped his mouth with his napkin. "Maybe that's why I decided you and I had to get to know each other better. Any dame who takes Mounties for a ride the way you did, and gets away with it, who has the nerve to tell my men she's my girl, well, she certainly merits closer acquaintance."

Tara's green eyes blazed. "How dare you . . ."

He grinned at her. "Well ain't it the truth? Didn't you spin a load of lies to the territory's finest so you could travel up here? Didn't you con your way into my saloon, using my name?"

"No, no," Tara said, and she hoped she didn't look as guilty as she felt. "They—they jumped to conclusions, that's all."

"Of course," he chuckled. "Just so. Don't look so worried, honey. I admire you. You're a good-looking woman all right, but you got talent as well. Real talent. I got a feeling you and I sort of fit."

"Mr. Smith," Tara said, an edge to her voice, "I don't."

He got up and walked over to her, pulling out a silver cigar case from which he took a long cheroot. He bit the end off, then lit it from the nearest candle.

"One day you will, I promise you," he said very softly, looking down at her. "One day you'll care a hell of a lot."

Tara looked away. "You flatter yourself," she snapped. Then she turned her head, and faced him boldly. "Now, what have you heard about my husband?"

"Ah." He blew out a cloud of smoke. Then he began pacing around. "Your husband," he repeated, as if reminding himself. He continued pacing. "Tell me," he said, from behind her chair so that she could not see him, "what would you say if I told you your husband is dead?"

She gripped the edge of the table. She tried to stop her growing panic. "I . . . I wouldn't believe you." Her voice was low.

Now she could see his face. His expression was bland.

"Really?"

Tara collected her wits. "I *don't* believe you," she declared, more firmly.

He shrugged his shoulders. "Well, maybe you're right. Could be. Then again . . . would you care for a little brandy?" he asked politely.

Tara shook her head. She could only think: He knows something.

"Tell me what you've heard about Daniel," Tara pressed.

He poured himself a generous measure in one of the two balloon glasses on the table.

"There's a rumor that a man called Daniel Kane from Frisco is prospecting around Fortymile."

Smith went back to his seat opposite her. "I'll take you there if you like."

She studied him suspiciously. Was this the confidence trickster at work?

"I can help you look for him if you'd like me to." He held up the brandy glass to the candlelight, gazing deep into the amber liquid. "A votre santé, Tara." He paused. "Don't think the only reason I'm offering to go to Fortymile is to see if I can locate your missing husband," he continued with a hint of a sneer. "I happen to have business interests there, and they require my presence. Since I'm going anyway, you're welcome to trek along."

Tara was about to speak when the door burst open.

Framed in the doorway was a stunning-looking woman. She wore a silver-fox jacket over a figure-hugging black gown, her dark hair piled on top of a good-looking, hard face with generous lips. Perhaps the most startling thing about her was the belt encircling her slim waist. It was made entirely of gold nuggets; some even hung from it. There was a fortune there, and Tara gaped at it.

132

"So," the woman said, walking slowly over to Tara and looking her up and down. Tara caught a whiff of scent.

"Miss Cad Wilson," Smith said lazily, "Mrs. Tara Kane."

"I heard she was your new filly," Cad said insultingly, looking at Tara but addressing him.

Tara stiffened.

"You know better than to believe everything you hear, Cad," retorted Smith, his tone mocking. "And now that you've met Mrs. Kane, I'm sure you have other matters to attend to."

Cad's glance swept the table. "Trying to make an impression?" she jeered. "My, my. Just take a look at this." She picked up an empty bottle. "Champagne, wine, candles. You *are* trying hard, Soapy."

"I don't like you calling me that, Cad," Smith said.

They stared at each other angrily, the atmosphere between them full of unspoken threats. These two were old sparring partners, and this was not the first time she had confronted Smith in such a situation.

Cad smiled menacingly and turned to Tara, who was rooted in her chair.

"Let me give you some advice, honey. You don't belong in Dawson. If I were you I'd get out, and that's good advice."

"Cad, it's time you were getting back to work," Smith said.

Cad darted a look at him. Then she leaned forward, picked up his brandy glass, and poured what was left of the liquor onto the white table cloth.

"Sweet dreams," she smiled, her eyes sharp knives ripping through Tara. At the door she stopped and blew a kiss to Smith. Then she swept out, leaving the door wide open behind her and her perfume in the air.

Smith got up and closed the door and then replenished his brandy glass. "Well," he said, ignoring the interruption, "What do you say? Are you coming to Fortymile?"

"Just you and me?"

"Can you think of a better combination?"

"Why should I trust you?" Tara demanded. "I'd like to know exactly what you've heard about my husband."

"There's not much more to tell," he replied, unruffled. "It's kind of third hand, anyway, but it sounds like Daniel Kane all right. From Frisco. Rumor has it he's a pretty sharp poker player too."

It sounded as if it could be Daniel.

"And how did you . . ."

"I sort of kept a few ears open," Smith said airily. "I got interested in him."

"Why?" she asked sharply.

"Because he owes me money and because . . ." he paused, "and because I am interested in you. So I put the word out. Just another public service, Tara."

"I'm sure," she said drily. "Anyway I'd like to think it over."

"You don't have much time. I'll be leaving tomorrow morning."

Tara stood up. "If I decide to join you, I'll be ready by then. Now I think it's time for me to go." She picked up her purse and then walked over to face him. "By the way," she said, as if a thought had just struck her, "I'd like my wedding ring back please."

"Ah," he sighed. He looked down at the gold band on his finger, breathed on it and polished it against his vest. Tara wanted to hit him.

"Despite what you might have heard, I'm a man of principle, and one of my strongest is never to mix business with pleasure. I've had a delightful evening, and I'd hate to spoil it by discussing sordid money matters. You're talking about a deal we made, and, as my pappy always used to say, a deal is a deal. Remember Tara, you're at perfect liberty to reclaim it at any time, but right now I guess the price is a little too steep for you."

He opened the door for her.

"I could pay you by installments, say two-fifty a week," she suggested.

Smith's eyes twinkled. "One hundred and fifteen dollars paid off at . . ."

"One hundred and fifteen dollars!" exclaimed Tara. "You only advanced me fifty. What's the rest? Interest?"

Smith felt in his pocket and pulled out a piece of paper. "The balance is made up by this," he said, unfolding Daniel's IOU. "Plus a surcharge for late payment."

"Of all the low, rotten—"

"Now, now, Tara, business is business."

"One day," Tara said through gritted teeth, "you *will* give it back, and it might be sooner than you think."

He made an elegant gesture with his hand, then pocketed the IOU.

"That, Tara, is the day I'm waiting for. And until then, since the sight of it aggravates you so much, I'll keep it in a safe place." He removed the ring from his finger and ostentatiously put it in his vest pocket.

Smith insisted on walking her back to Third Street, past his empire of Front Street dives.

Tara had noticed three men following them. To begin with she was uncertain, but now she looked over her shoulder again. Smith noticed her glance.

"Relax," he said. "They're deputies." He was wearing his arrogant smile.

"Your gang, you mean?"

He shrugged. "Somebody has to keep law and order." He took her arm as they came to a big frozen puddle. "It's a citizen's duty. Hell, businessmen like me have investments, and they have to protect them."

They were crossing the street in front of the Alaska Palace when the swing doors were swept open and a man was flung into the slush by two bouncers who stood and watched while he painfully scrambled to his feet.

"Don't come back," yelled one of them, as they turned their backs on him and went into the saloon.

The man stood in front of the saloon and shook his fist. It was an impotent gesture, thought Tara; nobody inside saw him. Then he shuffled off.

"Another of your educational establishments?" she remarked.

He nodded approvingly. "Giving a student a well-deserved lesson."

They turned into Third Street and walked on in silence for a while, the three discreet shadows still following them.

As they approached Mrs. Miles's house, Smith said, "Tara, be careful. About Cad. Don't take any chances if she's around."

"Your lady friend?" said Tara coldly. "I really don't think we've much in common. I wouldn't worry about it."

"I know Cad," Smith said. "She can be dangerous."

"I'm sure," Tara smiled coldly. "And I'm sure you have a very good relationship."

He didn't rise. "Just be careful," he repeated.

They were outside Mrs. Miles's house. "Good night then, Mr. Smith. I'll think about Fortymile," Tara said, pulling out her key.

He stood in front of her and shook his head. "You know something, Tara? You're the first woman I've ever spent an evening with who at the end of it still called me Mr. Smith."

"You forget," Tara reminded him, "that ours is strictly a business acquaintance." She smiled at him, matching his mockery. "And, Mr. Smith, maybe I have the same principles as you. Never mix business with pleasure."

She turned her back on him and opened the front door.

He raised his broad-brimmed hat and bowed courteously. But she was already gone.

That night, her dreams were as confused as she was, but one of them she would remember always.

She was walking up to a camp fire, and even though she was some distance away she could see a man sitting by it. When he looked up she realized it was Daniel, and the look of delight on his face and the way he called her name were thrilling. They started running toward each other, and just as she was about to feel his arms around her she woke up, tears running down her cheeks, and he had vanished.

She lay in the darkness, looking at the ceiling, remembering the dream. Perhaps it was some kind of premonition, a pointer to what she should do. She knew she would risk anything, even traveling alone in Soapy Smith's dubious company, if Daniel were at the end of the trail.

She got up and packed her few belongings, then sat down and wrote a note.

Dear Linda, (it read) "By the time you see this I will have left to go to Fortymile where, I am told, Daniel now is. I know you will be very angry when you discover that I have gone and probably think I'm rash and thoughtless, but I'm sure you will agree that I cannot neglect this opportunity. Please try to understand. I am most grateful to you for taking me into your house and when I am reunited with my husband I hope to see you again and to thank you in person. Meanwhile, please do not think too badly of me or my hasty departure. My sincerest best wishes, Tara Kane.

She picked up her sleeping bag and tiptoed downstairs. She left the note on the kitchen table, where Mrs. Miles was bound to find it later that morning.

CHAPTER FOURTEEN

They spoke little on the journey north. When they camped, Smith prepared the food, made sure she was comfortable, but virtually ignored her. He was polite, correct, and just a little superior. All of which made him intensely annoying to Tara. Perhaps it was his self-confidence, the cool assurance with which he handled the sled, the dogs, herself. I thoroughly dislike him, she said to herself and then wondered why she kept repeating it.

"That's Alaska over there," Smith said, pointing into the distance with his whip. "It's United States territory. And *that's* where we'll look for your husband."

Unlike Dawson, Fortymile did not even pretend to be civilized. What passed as the street was also the sewer. Gambling had no such refinement as roulette wheels or green baize tables; a wooden crate and a pack of greasy cards was all. Whisky was a rare luxury; the shacks that served as saloons sold hootchinoo at fifty cents a shot. It was a vile brew, concocted from molasses, sugar, dried fruit, fermented with sourdough, flavored with anything handy, distilled in empty coal oil cans and served hot.

Night life was equally raw. The local whores made Dawson's saloon girls seem like duchesses; in Fortymile nobody looked at a woman's face. They paid her a couple of dollars and took her for ten minutes into some dark corner.

As Smith's dog team approached the township, Tara was confronted by the sight of a body swinging to and fro on a primitive gallows. The face wore a stiff grimace, frozen rigid in the cold, and there was a piece of paper pinned to the corpse's shirt. "THIEF," it proclaimed in capital letters.

"They don't waste much time here," Smith remarked.

This bleak and windswept settlement had established itself at the junction of two frozen rivers, the Yukon and the Fortymile. In the middle of the Fortymile River was a small island. It looked rocky and unfriendly. She thought she could see some huts and a spiral of smoke. To her surprise, Smith guided the dog team across the frozen river toward the island. She could now see the huts clearly and a group of men watching them, one or two of them waving.

Smith snapped his long whip hard over the team of huskies. The sled glided off the frozen river and onto the shale beach of the island. The men ran over to them as Smith unwrapped Tara and helped her out of the sled. Eagerly she scanned their faces. They were bearded, some had shoulder-length hair, and they wore a strange variety of clothes, furs, skins, Indian anoraks. One of them, yes, he could be Daniel. He had his build, the color of his beard could be his, maybe.
. . . Her heart beat faster as he came closer. She started toward him, then stopped. No, those weren't Daniel's eyes; he wasn't Daniel. As he came nearer, Tara wondered how she could have been so mistaken.

Then Smith was at her side, holding her arm. She tried to cover her disappointment. For some reason she was embarrassed at his witnessing her blunder.

"Greetings, General, welcome to Paradise," a white-haired man cried out, sweeping off his cap and bowing low. Much to Tara's amazement, he took her hand and kissed it. "Dear madam, at last," he declaimed. "It has been far too long. We have awaited your arrival eagerly."

Tara was perplexed. She turned to Smith questioningly.

137

"My friends," he called out, "this lady has come from Dawson. Mrs. Tara Kane, all the way from Frisco. Mrs. Kane is looking for her husband. Daniel Kane. Somebody here knows Daniel Kane."

"Daniel Kane, did you say?" asked a man behind Tara. She swung around. He was a tall man in a scout's hat and buckskin jacket, wearing army boots. He had a goatee beard and a military bearing. "Sure, I know him."

"You know Daniel Kane?" Tara stammered.

"Allow me to introduce myself. Colonel Lee, ma'am, at your service," he said, snapping smartly into a military salute. "Late Sixth U.S. Cavalry."

"You know my husband?"

"Indeed, ma'am," the Colonel assured her. He looked around the crowd. "Maybe . . ." He hesitated. "Maybe we can talk privately. . . ."

"Of course," Tara agreed eagerly.

"This way, ma'am," the colonel said politely. He walked her a little way out of earshot. "That's better. We don't want to be overheard by the enlisted men."

"What about my husband, Colonel?" asked Tara.

"Ah yes, a fine man. You his lady?" He looked at her approvingly. "Just what I figured. I knew he'd married a real good-looking bride."

"Please tell me where he is," she pressed, trying not to sound rude.

"You know he saved my life?" he said.

Tara looked at him, startled. "No. When was this?"

"Typical," nodded the colonel. "So modest. Doesn't even tell his lady he saved my life."

"I haven't heard from Dan . . ." Tara began.

"I know," the colonel said, concerned. "Communications are terrible. Told the general so. Half the couriers don't get through. Not fair on the wives. What a hell of a place this is."

"*Please*," she begged, "tell me about him."

"Well," the colonel said, pulling his goatee. "We were cut off. Surrounded by the varmints. Only me and Dan left. And by jimminy, you know what he did? Slipped out of the rocks, killed six of the savages, got through to the fort, and brought the relief column just as I was down to my last two shells. Custer was a fool, but with men like me and Dan, he would have survived," he declared.

"What are you talking about?" she stuttered. "That's not my husband. That's not Daniel Kane."

"Sure it is," the Colonel insisted. "Lt. Daniel Kane, B Troop, 6th Cavalry." His face clouded over. "Hey, wait a moment. Lord you're right. He never did get married. Come to think of it he got killed in

138

'89. In New Mexico." He looked sad. "That's not your Daniel Kane, is it, ma'am?"

"No," Tara said, "it isn't." She didn't know whether to cry with rage or pity, she felt so let down.

"My apologies, ma'am. I must have got mixed up, I guess." Colonel Lee gave her another salute and ambled off slowly.

Smith appeared at her side and looked at her inquiringly.

"Any luck?" he asked.

"Luck?" Tara said bitterly. "He's crazy. He's still with General Custer."

Smith shook his head sorrowfully. "That's what happens sometimes in the Klondike," he said. "It gets too much for some people. What a disappointment for you."

She faced him.

"You mean, *that's* all there is? *He* was the information you had for me? We came all this way for *him?*"

Her eyes were smoldering.

"Have faith, Sister Tara," Smith said reproachfully. "Of course not. There's quite a little colony here. Men from all over the diggings. They've been everywhere. You simply have to keep asking. They'll know, don't worry."

"Are you telling me Daniel isn't here at all?"

"I said I had information about him. I didn't say I could hand him to you on a plate. After all, Tara, you wouldn't expect me to do it all for you, would you?"

He had that arrogant, mocking look again.

"I think—" began Tara angrily.

"And I think you ought to have a word with the fellow in that hut over there," Smith cut her short. "Wouldn't surprise me if he knows something."

Tara looked uncertainly in the direction of a small mud hut.

"Maybe I ought to warn you that he's a squaw man," Smith drawled. "Has an Indian spouse. That's his shack. Why don't you go and ask him?"

Tara slowly walked toward it, certain that Smith was laughing at her.

She had to double over to enter through the low door. Inside, the hut was dark, and a pungent, sickening stench assailed her nose; it was a mixture of rancid fat, human sweat, and unwashed bodies. In the darkness, Tara could vaguely make out a man sitting on the floor, smoking a long pipe. He said, without preliminaries, "Sit down. You're the lady who's looking for her husband."

139

"Yes," Tara said cautiously. "I don't know if you can help . . ."

Slowly, as her eyes adjusted to the gloom, she became aware of an Indian woman with a leathery face and vacant black eyes. She sat on the floor too, at the back of the hut. There were no chairs.

"That's my squaw," said the man. "She's the reason I'm stuck on this godforsaken island. She's a Chilkoot princess, and they're after my scalp."

Tara prepared herself for another yarn.

"I took her from them. They sent a war party after me, and we had to hole up for three weeks, hiding. Ate our dog team to keep alive. If ever they catch us . . ."

"I'm sorry," said Tara, briskly. "Now about . . ."

"Could start an Indian rising in the whole Territory," he continued as if she hadn't spoken. "They nearly burned Circle City because they thought we were hiding out there." He glanced at the impassive woman. "Thought of selling her, but you don't sell a princess, do you? Anyways, she ain't much good in the bag."

What was the matter with these people? Why couldn't they just tell her what she wanted to know?

"Have you come across my husband?" she asked directly.

"Yeah," he said. "Sort of remembered the name. Kane. Like Abel. Young gold prospector, ain't he?"

She nodded, warily.

"Saw him along the Throndiuck. He was camping there."

"When?"

He shrugged. "Year ago."

"Can't have been that long ago. He only left San Francisco last July."

"Well," said the man, "maybe it was less. Maybe it was last month."

"Which was it, for heaven's sake? It can't be both." Tara did not bother to mask her impatience. She wanted to get out of this hole, away from these smelly people.

The man cackled. "Why not? Sometimes it feels like I married the princess here twenty years ago. But it was only Spring. Just after the thaw."

"This man you think was my husband. What did he say? What did he look like?"

"Don't know."

"But you *saw* him." She was clenching her fists in agitation.

"I think I saw," said the man. "Then again, maybe I didn't."

"Look," Tara said. The claustrophobia was closing in on her.

140

"Would you remember a little better if I helped your memory?" She held out a dollar.

"Sure." He took the money and stuffed it in his pocket.

"Well?"

"Well, I'll tell you. He had struck it rich. He made a real killing." She held her breath.

"Guess he's worth a hundred thousand if he's worth a cent."

"And?"

In the gloom he looked puzzled. "What else?"

"Was he well? Did he look well?"

"Sure."

Something was wrong. She knew it. She could not believe he was speaking the truth.

"Describe him to me," she said.

"Well," he began hesitantly. "He's tall, I guess. Six feet. Maybe more." Tara thought he was studying her face for a clue. "Yeah, that's right. Very tall."

"What about his scar?" she asked.

"Oh, that's right. Yeah, he's got a scar all right."

"On his right cheek?"

"Wonder how he got it. Big, ain't it? Knife fight or something?"

Tara glowered at him. "You liar. You rotten miserable liar. You've never laid eyes on him. You've probably never even heard of him."

The Indian woman's eyes didn't flicker.

"What's the matter?" complained the man. "What the hell do you expect for a buck?"

"Oh God," Tara cried, turning and rushing from the hut.

Outside she stood taking deep gulps of fresh air, trying to collect herself. It was crazy. The whole place was crazy. Everybody was telling unbelievable stories. What kind of people were these?

Smith walked among them slapping men on the back, nodding earnestly as they talked at length, laughing at their stories. They greeted him like an old friend. The white-haired man insisted on calling him "General," but the others addressed him as "Governor" and "Senator."

"I want to talk to you," said Tara grimly, going over to Smith.

"Later," he replied.

"Now," persisted Tara.

He shrugged.

"I don't think there is any point in going on with this charade, Mr. Smith."

141

"Really?" He smiled. "Pity. They're having a squaw dance tonight, I was hoping you'd stay for it."

"I think not," she retorted frigidly.

"I know you haven't seen any females, but actually they have a squaw in each hut, most of them. They don't come out often. Some have more than one. You'd make a big hit, Tara. But if you'd rather not . . ."

"Shall we go?" she asked curtly.

They walked toward the sled.

"You didn't really think I'd find out anything about my husband here, did you?" She faced him accusingly.

"Who knows? People like these hear a lot, they see a lot, who can tell?" He looked at her. "Never does any harm to talk a little bushwa, Tara." He helped her into the sled. "That's Indian," he added. "Bushwa means moose bull. I like talking moose bull."

"They're nothing but a load of idiots. They're all mad." She exploded, "I don't know who's the biggest liar. Them or you."

Smith smiled. "Must be them. This place is called Liars' Island."

By the time the sled drew up outside the one ramshackle building in Fortymile which passed for a hotel, Tara's anger was at boiling point.

"We'll be staying here tonight," Smith said, ignoring her hostility. Silence had hung over their journey back across the frozen river. He moved to the side of the sled to help her alight.

"Take your damn hands off me," Tara said.

Her eyes swept over the dilapidated front of the seedy, uninviting hotel. "Looks delightful," she said scathingly. "I suppose you own this too. Another of your rackets?"

Smith burst out laughing. "Oh, Tara, you should just see yourself when you get indignant."

"I'm glad you find it all so amusing, Mr. Smith, bringing me all this way just to have a good laugh at me."

"And worth every mile of it."

Two passersby stopped and stared at them; the woman, chest heaving, angry, fists clenched; the man, amused, mocking, eyebrows raised.

"So there's nowhere else to look for him?" she inquired. Her sudden smile was lethal.

Smith shook his head.

"I suppose you think you're very smart. Some joke, hoodwinking me into coming to this godforsaken place on a wild-goose chase. Using me as a cheap form of entertainment."

"Come on, Tara."

She stepped closer to him. Smith saw her lift her hand to slap his face, but he adeptly grabbed her wrist. He caught her other hand and, holding her arms above her head, he started to dance her around the sled, humming a lively tune, whirling her effortlessly in a parody of a polka. The bystanders laughed.

Tara tried to kick Smith, but he held her at arm's length and continued to whisk her about, humming and grinning broadly.

"Stop it," she cried, helplessly. The crowd gave a small cheer.

"Why Tara, you're marvelously light on your feet. I had no idea you danced so well. Hope you'll save me every dance from now on."

He was laughing at her openly now.

She choked as he whirled her around once more, picking her up so that she was suspended in mid-air, her feet kicking out at him.

As abruptly as he had grabbed her, he put her down on the ground, forcing her hands behind her back as he kissed her hard on the lips.

It was the final humiliation. The men cat-called, whistled, and applauded. Smith turned and bowed.

"Come on," he said, grabbing her hand. He half pulled, half dragged her into the shabby building, up the rickety, narrow staircase to the landing. He kicked open the door at the top, dragged her across a small, barely furnished room and threw her down on the bed. It almost knocked the breath out of her.

"Now you stay there," he said mildly. "You stay there until I get back."

She got off the bed and stood, panting.

"How dare you," she gasped.

"Dare?" he looked at her amused. "I dare anything, Tara, believe me."

Smith looked at his watch. "High time I did my collection. Part of my public duties here include running the post office. An onerous task, but I do it for the sake of the community. Every month I have to collect the takings. The only reason I came here today, Tara."

"That's very public-spirited of you," she said.

"Tomorrow we return to Dawson," he continued. "While I'm out, do not leave this room. Understand?"

"Yes, Mr. Smith. Certainly, Mr. Smith. Anything you say, Mr. Smith."

"Yes," he said calculatingly. "I like it. I like it a lot. When you get mad, you're really very attractive." He put on his gloves. "Now make sure you don't misbehave. At least not until I return."

Her head was pounding, her heart beating wildly both from physical exertion and raging temper.

"*Au revoir*," Smith said, lifting his hat. Then he went out, gently closing the door. Tara flung herself on the bed, shoulders heaving, crying with the disappointment and injustice of it all.

"Oh, Daniel, if only you were here," she sobbed. "If only I could find you. I want you. I need you."

Above everything, she felt so miserably alone and abandoned. From the moment Smith had mentioned Fortymile, she had talked herself into believing she would find Daniel here, that her search would be over, that once again they would be together. Linda Miles had been right. There was no sign of Daniel, and she hated herself for being such a gullible fool. Smith had played a cruel hoax on her; to cap it all, she had been publicly humiliated by him.

Gradually, her tears subsided. She had to accept that she was no further forward with her search than she had been six weeks previously. That was the hardest part.

She sat up, drying her tear-streaked cheeks with the palms of her hands. She fished in her pocket for a handkerchief and blew her nose. Still sniffing, she got up from the bed and went over to the washstand, poured out some water in the bowl, and bathed her eyes. As she looked at herself in the mirror, she became aware for the first time of the room she was in. It was like the town outside, joyless, shabby, ill-kept. It was scantily furnished, and dominated by a huge double bed.

Her lips tightened. Now she knew what was in Smith's scheming mind. His things were neatly arranged on the chest of drawers. A shaving brush, a stick of soap, a razor. This must be his usual pied-a-terre on his visits to Fortymile.

There was something else on the chest—a woman's hairbrush. Tara drew a long, dark hair from it. A woman's hair, which could well have come from the head of Cad Wilson. Disdainfully, she let it drop on the floor. There was a closet too. Inside hung male clothing, obviously Smith's. And there was a woman's robe on a hanger. Tara's lip curled. How convenient. She could picture Smith producing it with a flourish as "something comfortable to slip into."

Fury engulfed her. The dirty, smarmy crook.

"All right, Mr. Soapy Smith," she said, walking around the room. "You want to play games, we'll play games."

The window overlooked the unpaved, rutted thoroughfare that passed as Fortymile's main street. Tara went over and tried to open it. It was frozen shut. She smashed the glass. A gust of freezing air blew into the room, but she was too preoccupied to notice.

First she took the shaving mug, the beaver-bristle brush, the stick of soap and threw them out of the window. The razor quickly followed. She took a fur jacket from the closet and flung it out of the window. It landed in the mud below. The first missiles Tara threw attracted little attention. But now a man in the street stared and pointed.

"You son of a bitch," Tara said with feeling, launching Smith's trousers and shirts into space. Under the window a little group had now gathered, fascinated by the barrage landing around them. They started picking up anything that took their fancy.

Tara was breathing fast from her handiwork. She spotted the woman's hairbrush. "As for you," she snapped, hurling it so far that it landed on the opposite side of the street.

There was a fur hat, and that went sailing forth, quickly followed by a necktie. Next came the silk robe. She flung it out into space, and it billowed like a silk parachute as it floated down to earth, draping itself across a wagon hitched to a post. The crowd recognized it as a woman's wrap and cheered. It cheered again when Tara next appeared at the window with a pair of shoes she had found at the back of the closet.

She paused. She was running out of missiles. Then she spotted a leather Gladstone bag on the other side of the bed. She rushed over and opened it. There were papers inside, a box of Havana cheroots, underwear, and a silver hip flask. Tara bombarded the street with them, item by item. As the hip flask descended in a neat arc, a man spotted it and made a dash for it. The cheroots scattered all over the mud as the lid of the wooden box opened. Finally, the Gladstone bag, with J R S embossed on the calf hide, went out of the window.

The crowd below had grown to thirty or forty people, and they were loving it all.

"Hey, lady," somebody yelled up at Tara, "are you going to throw Soapy out too?"

She waved, but she was not finished yet. She turned and stood surveying the room. He would find his little love nest pretty bare when he came back. Nothing to wash with, no underwear, no clothes to change into, no cheroots, no bag, nothing.

Tara nodded with satisfaction. Maybe this was going to be one time when that smug smile would be wiped off his face.

She went over to the bed and looked under it. Yes, there it was, the chamber pot. Triumphantly she carried it to the window. Then grandly she flung it to the crowd below.

The sight of Soapy Smith's chamber pot sailing into Fortymile's main street was heralded with a burst of whistles, applause, and laughter. Tara grinned. That was the most satisfying of all. They were laughing at Soapy Smith. The king of the Klondike, the ruler of a hundred rackets, would never be respected quite as much again.

Still she wasn't through. The water jug went crashing, the washbasin following. An oil lamp went out. She picked up a small bedside table and managed, with effort, to heave that out. The clothes hangers followed, then the bedding.

"If you want to make love, you'll be mighty cold," chortled Tara. "Believe me, Mr. Smith."

Suddenly she spotted Smith walking purposefully up the main street toward the hotel. It was the first time Tara had seen him in a hurry, not suave and collected as usual.

He strode through a barrage of cheers and catcalls. It was sweet music to Tara's ears. Never before, she was ready to bet, had a crowd jeered Soapy Smith. But every man must lose some dignity when his long johns make an unexpected appearance in public.

Tara looked around wildly. She had to keep him out. She rushed to the door and locked it. She noticed a framed verse hanging on the wall, and "Nothing's as Bad as It Appears To Be," tastefully embroidered, went flying out of the window too, just missing Smith's head as he stormed into the hotel.

She heard him thundering up the stairs. He rattled the door handle.

"Let me in, Tara," he yelled, "god damn it, open this door." She wished she had something in her hand to throw at him, but all the best missiles were already lying in the street.

She could hear him crashing against the door. She smiled complacently. She was not afraid, just enormously amused. For the first time since she had met this arrogant joker she had got the better of him. She had made him look like a fool.

Suddenly, with a splintering of wood, the door gave way. Smith stood there, red-faced and breathing heavily from the effort.

"What the hell . . ." began Smith, looking wildly around the room. He was neither smooth nor arrogant, just angry and bewildered. It was lovely.

"Excuse me," Tara said serenely and tried to push past him.

He grabbed her arm viciously.

"You're not going anywhere," he said. "What the hell do you think you're doing?"

"Leaving," Tara explained matter-of-factly. She tried to pull her arm away but it was locked in his grip. He was hurting her, and she knew that was exactly what he wanted to do.

"Mr. Smith," Tara cooed, "there are a lot of people outside. If you don't let me pass, I shall scream. I'm sure they'd come upstairs . . ."

His hooded eyes were blazing. "I don't care," he snarled. "I want an explanation!"

Tara's smile was almost benign. "It was just a well-deserved lesson, Mr. Smith. In your own tradition, I think you'll agree."

"And what exactly are you trying to teach me?"

"I would have thought you could have guessed. Obviously, I'll have to spell it out. Firstly, to pay you back for using me and my trust for your own personal amusement and ends. I could plainly see what you had in mind. Secondly, for making a spectacle of me. Now you'll be able to appreciate just how humiliating that can be. I call that a public-spirited service, don't you?"

"You're talking hogwash," he replied. "The trouble with you is that you've got a one-horse mind. I suppose you hoped I was going to seduce you." He was regaining his smugness. "Well, you flatter yourself, Mrs. Kane. There is another room in this hotel."

"You're on your own, Mr. Smith."

He let go her arm and stood, almost sneering at her.

"Tell me," he said quietly. "Just how do you expect to get back to Dawson?"

"I'll make my own way," Tara replied. "I'll do it by myself."

He laughed. "The journey . . ."

"I'll manage," she cut in. She looked around the bare, empty room. "In any event, I guess you'll have your hands full clearing up."

She pushed past him, leaving him looking surprised.

"God damn it," she heard him calling after her, "you're no lady."

And then he started laughing uproariously.

Tara came out into the street to find the crowd still standing around. They parted, almost reverently, to let her through. After all, she had given them a good free show. A pair of drunken miners brawling, a couple of whores hair-pulling, an Indian being beaten up, which was about the measure of excitement in the main street, was nothing compared to the woman who had made a mug of Soapy Smith. They eyed her with interest. She did not look particularly tough. This was no hard-bitten Jezebel from the saloons of Dawson, and yet she had managed to do what no one else dared to do. There were ugly rumors of what happened to characters who crossed Smith.

A little murmur ran through the crowd: would Smith come out after her? Tara wondered that herself. She didn't look back at the hotel but walked slowly, deliberately, not showing how nervous she really was.

She had reached the edge of the crowd when she heard footsteps behind her and a man calling out, "Hey, lady, just a moment."

She turned. He was a young man in a stiff collar and a neat necktie. He wore a business suit under his anorak.

"Pardon me, lady," he said, breathlessly. He had been running after her. "I'm Hitchcock of the *Nugget*. What was that all about at the hotel?"

She shook her head.

"I don't want to talk about it, excuse me," she said.

"You can't do that," he complained. "It's a great story. Not every day Soapy Smith's long johns go flying down the main street. What's your name?"

"It doesn't matter."

Her mind was not really on him. She wished she could clear her thoughts, work out what she was going to do now, how she would get back to Dawson.

"If only that damn German photographer had been there," said the reporter sorrowfully. Then he laughed. "I can still see that chamber pot . . ."

"What photographer?" Tara asked.

"Herr Hart. He loves that kind of stuff. A tree trunk fell on a man yesterday, and he took plate after plate. He's crazy about shooting things as they happen."

"Is he here? In Fortymile?" she demanded, her excitement rising.

"Sure," replied Hitchcock. "He's set up just behind the general store. Taking portraits of all the beauties in town, beards, warts and all."

She rushed off. Hart, here in Fortymile. She couldn't believe her luck. A familiar face at last.

She found the tent next to a stable. "Your picture taken for five dollars," read the notice hanging from it. Three men were standing patiently, hunched in their furs, waiting their turn. They were morose, hard-bitten characters, and Tara wondered why on earth they wanted their portraits taken. She was so keen to see Hart she wanted to push ahead of them and burst inside. But their gloomy, unfriendly faces made her think again. Anyway, it would be more of a surprise for Hart when she suddenly appeared in front of him, the next in line.

Tara joined the little queue. The flap of the tent parted, and a man emerged from his sitting. The man at the head of the line went in. Two more turns, thought Tara impatiently, I wish he'd hurry up. Actually, Hart's expertise was such that each sitting only took five minutes. Finally, only Tara was standing outside the tent.

The third man left and then Hart's head popped out of the tent, looking around for the next customer. When he saw Tara his eyes opened wide.

"Tara," he gasped. He rushed out and hugged her. "Oh, Tara, how wonderful." He kissed her on both cheeks and then he took her hand. "Quickly, come inside. It's too cold out here."

There was little room inside. The camera stood on its tripod in front of a chair. A blanket, which also served as a backcloth, was strung across the tent, dividing it in half.

"Dear Tara," said Hart, "how good to see you again."

He looked no different, she thought, despite his wanderings. And his excitement at her unexpected appearance was quite touching.

"Ernst," Tara said, "how have you been?"

He raised his hands. "Fantastic. You would never believe it. I have hundreds of photos. *Hundreds.* What an exhibition I will make." Then he stopped. "But I want to hear about you. Have you found Daniel yet?"

She shook her head. "He's around somewhere, I know he is," she said. "I found no trace of him in Skagway, but I know he went on to Dawson. Now I'm not sure where he is." She bit her lip, trying to hide her despondency.

"I'm sure you'll find him, Tara. Of course you will," he said reassuringly, and she could have hugged him. Everybody cast doubts, everybody kept telling her how impossible it was, how little chance she had. Except for Hart. Only he truly believed as she did.

"Ernst," Tara said, taking his hand. "You have no idea how happy I am to find you."

"I want to hear all about it," he said sympathetically, her low spirits patently obvious to him. "What are you doing in Fortymile, anyway? How did you get here?"

So she told him what had happened since they had parted company in Dyea. Hart was an attentive and understanding listener. When she described the scene at the hotel, he laughed.

After she had finished, Hart got up.

"I shall take you back to Dawson," he said firmly, in his officious, Germanic way.

"Can you manage it? Have you got the room?" She looked anxiously around the crowded tent, littered with boxes, crates of chemicals, stacks of photographic plates, clothes.

"I've always got room for you, Tara," Hart said. "All we have to do is pick up some extra supplies. I have finished my work here anyway, so there is no problem, no problem at all."

149

There was one thing Tara had to do before she left Fortymile. She had to confirm that Daniel had not been here.

"There is no point, my dear. . . ." Hart said.

"Why?"

"Because I have already asked." He smiled. "You see, dear Tara, although I thought by now you might have found your husband, I have always inquired wherever I have stopped, for if I had found him I might also have met up with you again." He took off his glasses and started polishing them vigorously to hide his sudden shyness. "If nothing else," he continued, "It would have given me great happiness to photograph you both, reunited."

Tara was touched. She had had no idea that during his travels he had been trying to help her.

"Oh, Ernst," she said, "you *are* kind. I'm really grateful. You're a true friend."

For a moment he stood, looking down at her. Then he said briskly, "Come along. We will go and get some supplies, and tomorrow we will pack up and leave for Dawson. Is that all right?"

"Yes," Tara said.

"You sure?"

"Yes," she nodded. "There's nothing more in Fortymile for me."

But before she left the town, she went to the District Claims Office and checked for herself. Hart had been right. There was no record of a gold prospector called Daniel Kane.

Tara did leave a record of her own visit to Fortymile, however. From the *Klondike Nugget*, 2 December 1897:

LIVELY ALTERCATION

by Our Own Correspondent

Fortymile: A lively altercation was witnessed by citizens of Fortymile in the main street. The participants were a respected businessman well known in this territory, Mr. Jefferson R. Smith, and a married lady, a Mrs. Kane.

It appears that an argument had developed between the parties which led to heated words resulting in a crowd gathering. They were entertained by a spirited confrontation between the principals, much to the amusement of the spectators.

One bystander said afterwards that it was a good thing the lady did not have a gun, because she was apparently so furious that Mr. Smith might have sustained serious harm.

CHAPTER FIFTEEN

Tara's forebodings about facing Mrs. Miles grew hourly. It was one thing to walk out, quite another to return and admit she had been on a fool's errand. She was not even sure if she still had a roof over her head; perhaps all that awaited her was a door slammed in her face.

When they arrived in Dawson, she and Hart parted company. He looked a little crestfallen at losing her so soon, but Tara promised to come and see him when he had set up shop. He planned to rent a shack in the center of town and start taking portraits. In his spare time, he could process the stack of undeveloped plates he had taken out on the trail.

"Oh. It's you," was Mrs. Miles' greeting. "Alone, are you?" she said grimly. "No husband, eh? I can guess."

"I'd like to explain—" began Tara, but Mrs. Miles cut her short.

"Not greatly interested in hearing. I told you what would happen if you hitched up with that scoundrel. Well, you wouldn't listen, would you? Now look at you."

"Linda, I know you must be angry, and hurt. I appreciate it, really I do," Tara said, her eyes cast down. "I know what you must think of me for rushing off like that—but you know why I did it. Please understand."

"Well, don't just stand there. You'd better come in." She closed the door behind Tara and faced her, her expression a study of disapproval.

"It was a wild-goose chase, wasn't it?"

Tara nodded.

"And now you got nowhere to stay?" Mrs. Miles went on relentlessly. "Sorry you walked out, eh?" She sniffed. "Well, I'll take you back for the time being. As a servant girl. I'll pay you five dollars a week, and you get your keep and lodging. That's all. Don't expect the favors you got before." Tara wondered what they had been. "You can do what you like. Outside of my own four walls, you're on your own."

"I want you to know—" Tara said, but Mrs. Miles interrupted.

"I took you under my care. I looked after you as if you were my own kin. And you say thank you by going off with *that* man without even telling me. You have disappointed me. I'm very distressed."

She turned away.

"Linda, it wasn't like that," protested Tara. "He never . . . Look, if you'll only listen to what really happened. Please, Linda."

151

"I'll be obliged if you don't address me in such familiar terms from now on," Mrs. Miles said.

"Very well, Mrs. Miles." Tara swallowed hard.

Mrs. Miles shot her a quick glance. "You do agree, don't you, that trust is the most important . . ."

"Please!" Tara cried. "Please don't lecture me. I got my just reward in Fortymile. I paid for the way I behaved."

Mrs. Miles's manner softened imperceptibly.

"Very well," she nodded, "just do your work, and we won't talk about it again. As long as we both know where we stand."

After that, Tara scrubbed and washed and polished and cleaned like a Trojan. In a way she was glad she had so many chores piled on her; at least it gave her little time to brood over the way Smith had treated her. The lodgers, meanwhile, were pleased to see her back, but in Mrs. Miles's frigid presence they had to keep their curiosity about her reappearance to themselves.

A few days later, as Tara was cleaning the stairs, Mrs. Miles raised the subject once more.

"I was appalled when I found your note and then heard that you'd gone off with him," she said.

"Well, you needn't be appalled any more," Tara replied. "I didn't stay with him." She went back to her work. "You know, Mrs. Miles," she said, not looking up, "I sometimes think you forget why I am here. I'm not interested in anything or anyone except finding my husband. You all seem to think I'm on the make, a fortune hunter, an easy woman."

Mrs. Miles opened her mouth and shut it again.

"I've got one object and one object only in my life now. I'll do what I have to do, I'll go where I have to go, but do me one little kindness. Believe me. Help me. Don't treat me like a saloon hussy who's only out to roll some sucker for his nuggets."

Mrs. Miles stood for a few seconds, regarding Tara's back. Then, without another word, she returned to her domain, the kitchen.

The first free moment Tara had, she decided to go and see Hart. He had set up a temporary studio and had pinned up a big canvas banner announcing "Ernst Hart, Photographer." He was enjoying considerable success taking his five-dollar portraits, developing and printing, getting enough money together to go out again and shoot the pictures he really wanted to have—the Gold Rush at its rawest. He was in his darkroom when she opened the door of the shack.

"Come behind the curtain. Do not turn on the lamp. Make sure there's no light," he shouted.

152

She groped her way in. It was pitch black and his hand came out of the darkness and guided her to a crate.

"Sit here, Tara. I'm just developing some plates. We can talk but there mustn't be any light."

It was a curious sensation, sitting in the darkness, listening to Hart moving around, the splash of water, the tinkling of glass plates in the basin, almost as if she were blind.

"Any news, Tara?" Hart asked. "How did the old dragon take it?"

"What do you think?" she replied into the void. "No. Just sermons because I went away with Smith."

"You mustn't take any notice of that," came his voice.

"It's easy for you to say," Tara said. "It's different for a woman. Everybody takes it for granted because I traveled with a man I'm his woman. After all, I came back with you, and nobody's gossiped about that."

There was a pause. She could hear him washing some plates.

"Well, the man *was* Soapy Smith," she finally heard him say.

"So what?" remarked Tara.

There was a laugh in the dark.

"They say he is a formidable man with the ladies. He collects them like butterflies. They say he knows exactly how to get a woman. A real Don Juan."

"Indeed."

There was a slight hesitation in the dark. Then Hart asked, "Didn't you find him so, Tara?"

For some reason she was glad he could not see her face. "No, Ernst," she replied, and her voice was firm. "Not in the least. I thought he was a crooked, lying, deceitful blackguard."

She heard him chuckle.

"Why do you laugh?" she asked sharply.

"Nothing, nothing. Only you sounded so emphatic, it was funny. Like you were trying to convince yourself. I must definitely ask him if I can photograph him for posterity. Jefferson Smith, King of the Klondike. He sounds extraordinary."

Hart struck a match and lit a hurricane lamp.

Now she could see a little. The light was still low, but Hart stood in front of her, wearing a white gown, like a surgeon.

"I am sorry it is so primitive," he apologized. "On the Chilkoot the wind once blew half my tent away, the light came in, and ten days' work was ruined. At least Brady only had to duck bullets and shells."

He started to take off his coat.

"Come, *Liebchen*, I'm thirsty. I will buy you a drink."

153

Tara shook her head. "I don't think so, Ernst," she said. "Thank you."

He sat down opposite her.

"Tara, what's the matter?"

"It's just sometimes it feels like I'm chasing a phantom," she sighed. "Every time I think I'm getting close, he's gone again, or has never been there in the first place."

"I told you," said Hart. "You must keep looking."

"But where? How? How many Liars' Islands are there?"

He nodded. "Isn't that a fantastic place?" he said enthusiastically. "I took a whole portrait gallery there. They are all rogues, vagabonds, people who have given up, misfits, all gathered on that one little island. The faces! The expressions! Fabulous."

"Not for me," said Tara sadly. "Just a bunch of fools. And they'd tell you anything for money. That's what I thought of your island. It was the bitterest disappointment I could have had . . . after all Smith had said. I really thought he'd picked up something."

"We definitely need a drink," Hart said. He grabbed Tara's arm. "I will have no discussion. We both need a drink. You see what happens when one is too sober? So let us have something to make us unsober."

They walked up Front Street, Hart cracking his little jokes and singing a strange German student song to Tara.

"You're very cheerful, Ernst."

"With you I am always happy," he said, pressing her arm a little tighter.

They arrived at the Monte Carlo. It was the last place she wanted to go, but despite her protestations he pushed open the swing doors, and they entered the inferno, Hart holding Tara's hand firmly.

The humidity of the place made Hart's glasses steam up, and for a moment or two he stood, blinking owlishly, trying to see. Then he polished them and replaced them on his nose. He said something to Tara, but the noise was so great she couldn't understand it.

"What?" she yelled at him.

"You stay here," he shouted. "I'll get us some drinks." He left her pressed in a corner and began battling his way to the bar.

Suddenly Mort the bouncer was beside her. "Hey," he said, "I'll get you a table."

She was taken aback by his unexpected consideration.

"It's all right," she said. "I'm with somebody."

"OK," he said, "where is he?"

"At the bar."

"We can't have you getting pushed around like this, Mrs. Kane,"

154

Mort said, full of solicitude for her but quite unconcerned about Hart. She found herself being propelled across the room. Near the gambling area, three men were sitting around a small table, a bottle of whisky between them.

"Sorry, fellows," said Mort. "Mr. Smith's guest."

"I'm not—" began Tara, but nobody heard her. The three men, tough, hard-bitten characters, stood up meekly and shuffled off.

"Thank you," Tara said. She disliked getting the red-carpet treatment befitting one of Soapy's women, but it was good to rest her feet.

She could see Hart looking for her, two glasses in his hands. She waved to him, and he managed eventually to get through to her.

"A table no less," he said. "How did you manage that? They're standing on top of each other over there."

"Influence," said Tara.

"Soapy?"

"Yes, damn him."

She looked around uneasily. Why did Hart have to come to this saloon? She didn't know what she would do if Smith showed up, suave, haughty, drawling his words, his soft Southern accent belying his toughness.

"Ernst, let's have our drink and go," she pleaded.

"Nonsense. This is only my third," he said. "*Prosit.*"

"Your third?"

"Ah." He did his impersonation of being ashamed. "You have seen through me. Yes. I had two at the bar. While I was waiting. I knew you wouldn't mind."

Mort appeared with a bottle of champagne. He put it down with two glasses.

"Compliments of the house."

"I don't want it," Tara said.

"Boss's orders. You get a bottle of champagne every time you come in here."

"Please, take it away," she commanded.

"No, no, no. *Mensch*, what are you doing?" interjected Hart, beaming a little woozily at Mort. "Tell the boss he is very kind and the lady accepts."

Mort gave him a cool look, then said to Tara, "If there's anything you want, just say so."

But Tara's eyes had spotted something else. A few tables beyond them sat Cad Wilson, playing cards, gold nuggets heaped at her elbow. All the other players at her table were women.

155

"Just look at that," Tara whispered to Hart.

He blinked his eyes. His head was lolling slightly. He was helping himself to the champagne, and Tara knew he was getting drunker by the minute.

"Beautiful, beautiful," he burped. "Lovely ladies."

They sat in a circle, Cad beautifully made up, wearing a stunning off-the-shoulder gown with a deep cleavage. Opposite, sweat running down her face, was the Grizzly Bear. Next to her was a slim, cool, elegant girl. She looked young and demure enough to be in a convent school. Blanche Lamont was only nineteen, but she had three times that number of lovers and her savings were the talk of the saloons.

Looking across at Cad with a cold grin was a blonde woman, sharp-featured, attractive in a cruel, hard fashion. Her teeth shone, reflecting small dancing spotlights on Cad's face. Tara saw she had a diamond, an enormous diamond fixed between her two front teeth. Diamond Tooth Gertie was one of the toughest of Dawson's whores, as tough as the diamond she bared when she drew back her lips in that vixenish grin. The fingers that held her cards were long, sharp talons.

Except for the Grizzly Bear, with her elephantine proportions and that awful eyeless cavity, they were all attractive, sensual, and lustful.

Crowded around the table were a group of spectators, watching every move the saloon queens made as they played out their hands. Cad put a long, thin cheroot in her mouth and then snapped her fingers. Three matches were offered. Idly she lit her cheroot from one and ignored the others.

Cad made her play and the others threw in their cards. The men behind her murmured, and Cad acknowledged her success contentedly, scooping up the pot from the middle of the table. There were two gold nuggets in the pile, as well as dollar bills and coins.

Tara studied Cad more than the others. The woman was beautiful and had style, no doubt about that. She held herself regally, magnificently playing her part as queen of the Monte Carlo. Tara could imagine her effect on men. She also remembered how vicious Cad's eyes had been when they'd cut through her in the hotel room.

Gertie said something across the table, her diamond sparkling. Cad looked around through the smoke and haze, and her eyes bored straight into Tara's.

Cad sat rock still for a moment and then beckoned to Pierre, who was just setting down some drinks from a tray. In the din, Tara couldn't hear what she said, but the faces around the table were enough of an indication. These weren't women. These were cobras. Her heart pounded as she watched Pierre weave his way through the press of people to her table.

156

"Miss Wilson sends her compliments," he said, "and she suggests that you come over and play a little poker."

Tara swallowed. "Please tell Miss Wilson I'm just leaving," she replied.

"Miss Wilson won't like that," Pierre pointed out. "When she invites somebody to play, they play."

"Explain to her I'm very tired," Tara said.

Pierre shrugged and began to make his way back to the women's table.

Tara turned to Hart. He was slumped across the table, his head on his arms, snoring. She shook him.

"Ernst!"

Hart opened one eye and gave her a foolish smile.

"*Du bist so schon*," he murmured and went back to sleep again.

"Mrs. Kane!" a voice shouted. It was so clear and so loud it cut right through the babble. Cad Wilson was on her feet, hands on her hips, glaring at Tara.

"What's the matter, Mrs. Kane? You afraid?"

Gradually the din in the saloon subsided. All eyes were on Tara.

Slowly she got to her feet.

"Afraid of what, Miss Wilson?" she asked.

"I'm challenging you, challenging you to go for broke. Or maybe you can't afford it."

She glanced around, enjoying the tension she had caused. Everybody was waiting breathlessly. This might turn out to be one of the best Saturday nights Dawson had yet seen: Soapy's two women having it out.

"I don't wish to take up your challenge," Tara said. It was a mistake. Cad threw back her head and laughed derisively.

"Didn't know you were yellow, Mrs. Kane," she goaded. "Pity. Figured you were a real woman, but I guess we all make mistakes. Or has Jeff told you to keep out of my way? Frightened his little Miss Innocent might get mussed up?"

Tara wanted the floor to open. She glanced at Hart, who was blissfully unaware, and knew that she would get no assistance from that quarter. She swept her chair to one side and walked over to the round table. People parted to let her through. As Tara stopped in front of Cad, every eye was on them.

"Let me put you right, Miss Wilson," Tara said, her voice trembling with anger. "It is *I* who do not wish to accept your challenge because *I* have no desire to descend to your level."

An audible gasp went around the saloon.

"Ladies, ladies," Mort said, suddenly appearing, his hands raised.

157

"Let's not say something somebody might be sorry for. Let's not have any trouble."

"Shut up," Cad said, without looking at him. He shrank back.

"You bitch!" Cad spat.

Tara felt her stomach turn.

Cad slowly came around the table and stopped in front of Tara. She stood, her hands on her hips, her mouth a straight line of hatred as she eyed Tara up and down.

The pianist on the other side of the saloon began frantically hammering away on his keyboard, but the crowd around the women ignored him.

"Kick her out, Cad," bawled Gertie. "Boot her fanny into the street."

The crowd started moving back from the table.

"I've got no argument with you, Miss Wilson," Tara said very quietly, turning to leave.

"But I have with you, and one way or another we're going to settle it now," shouted Cad, grabbing Tara's arm.

"Let go of me," Tara cried, trying to wrestle her arm free.

"Only when I'm good and ready," hissed Cad.

"This is . . ." began Tara. She was about to say "ridiculous," then she saw the sea of faces around her.

They would never let her go. If she turned and ran, they would force her back. This was the floor show. She heard a voice call, "Three to one on Cad," and another, "I'll take the other one. Two to one."

And then Cad lunged at her. Tara backed away, bumping into a table laden with glasses. The crowd jeered and chorused "chicken."

Tara's temper broke, and she slapped Cad across the face. In a moment they were locked together, their hands in each other's hair, swaying to keep their balance, breathing heavily, struggling, clawing, their faces close to each other, both masks of venom. Tara got her hands around Cad's throat and pushed her away with Herculean strength.

Cad came at her again, diving unexpectedly, pulling Tara down on the floor. They rolled over and over, scratching and mauling each other. There was a heavy clunk as the clasp of Cad's nugget belt gave way and it fell off her waist. She managed to straddle Tara and with the palm of her hand forced her head back, cackling and laughing hysterically all the time. Tears of pain streamed down Tara's face, but with an almighty effort she freed her legs and stabbed her knee in Cad's spine. Cad rolled off, moaning, and Tara got hastily to her feet.

The crowd cheered and applauded. Cad pulled back her lips in a

158

ferocious snarl and hit out. Her fist caught Tara's left eye, and Tara lashed back, again striking Cad's face. Then they were locked together again; Cad punched Tara in the stomach, and she sank to her knees. As Cad prepared to kick her in the face Tara doubled over and sank her teeth into her ankle. Cad emitted a high-pitched yowl and hopped up and down, clasping her leg. Dizzily, Tara got up again. The whole room was reeling, like a gaudy carousel turning at full speed. She could taste the salty flavor of blood in her mouth.

They were squaring up for another onslaught when they were divided by the person of Jefferson Smith.

"Well!" he said laconically, looking from Cad to Tara, a smile hovering around his lips. "This is a fine way for two ladies to behave."

"Let them get on with it, Soapy," yelled the audience. "They're just warming up. Don't be a spoilsport, Jeff."

"Drinks on the house, for everybody, at the bar," he shouted. He put his right arm around Cad's waist and his left around Tara's.

They were too dazed to take in what was happening. Cad, under her smeared make-up, had a swollen chin where Tara had cuffed her, her beautiful dress was torn and soaked with sweat, and there was a small trickle of blood from her nose.

Tara appeared to have come out the worst. She had a bruise which was rapidly turning into a black eye, and her mouth was bleeding.

Cad limped as Smith escorted them to a table, and they both sat silently for a minute, while Smith stood arrogantly appraising them.

"Nobody puts on free shows in my place," he drawled. "If I want to promote prize fights, I'll ship in Corbett and Fitzgerald." He took out a cheroot and lit it. "You two ladies are costing me a lot of booze."

He looked accusingly at them and then at the bar, by now four deep with customers consoling themselves with his free liquor.

"Now what the hell was that about?" he asked, pulling up another chair and sitting down facing them.

"We got into an argument. It was nothing," Cad said.

"Nothing?" laughed Smith. He was enjoying himself. "In that case I'd like to see what you'd do to each other if you had something to fight about."

Tara was hardly listening. She was aware only of her throbbing left eye and the pain in her stomach where Cad had punched her. She knew she looked awful.

Cad tossed her tangled hair. "It was a little disagreement, that's all," she insisted.

"Mort's story's different," he said. "He came running and said you'd called out Mrs. Kane. Challenged her to settle things. What things?"

159

"Jeff, he's got it all wrong," sighed Cad.

"Well, you get this straight, sweetheart." Cad winced as he took hold of her chin. "I don't mind females having a little hair pulling over me, does a man's ego good to have a woman fight for him, but don't do it in seventy-dollar dresses I paid for." He let go of her chin and flicked some torn braid. "And don't do it in my saloon, either—it takes up good drinking time."

He turned to Tara. "Are you all right?" he asked, and Tara could feel Cad's resentment at his concern. Then he smiled mockingly. "I thought you were a lady, Mrs. Kane. Didn't think I'd ever live to see the day you got yourself involved in a barroom brawl."

Tara stood up. Her pride was more important than the pain she felt. Across the tables she could see Hart, in the corner, still slumped asleep.

"Good night," Tara said to no one in particular, with as much dignity as she could muster. Her dress had been ripped and she was holding parts of it together. She could feel her left eye closing up. Cad's whole fury had been behind that punch.

"Hey," called out Smith as she walked off. He got up and followed her. "I'll see you get safely home."

"That won't be necessary," Tara replied coldly. "I already have an escort."

"Yes, sir, I can sure see that. Looking after you right properly and keeping you out of mischief too. Where is your Sir Galahad?"

They had reached Hart's table. The photographer stared up at them woozily. Then he took in Tara's appearance.

"*Mein Gott,* what has happened to you? Your face. Your dress. You look as if . . . you have been in a fight."

"That's very observant, sir," Smith said, "because the lady has." He gave Hart a withering look. "She got into a hassle, and I guess there wasn't anybody around to look after her."

Hart looked at Smith dully.

"Ernst, this is the fellow I told you about, the great Soapy Smith. He's always around when one goes slumming."

Smith puffed at his cigar and then, through a haze of blue smoke, he grinned. "Why, if I didn't know you so well, I'd say that was downright unkind." His teeth flashed at her. "A stranger might think you didn't like me, but I know that could never be."

Hart stood up a little unsteadily.

"Mr. Smith," he said.

"Yes?" Smith's hooded eyes looked at Hart cautiously.

"Mr. Smith, I am a photographer. I would be much obliged if you would let me take your picture. I am photographing the Klondike, the people, the Gold Rush. I hear so much about you. You are a very important person. Please sit for a portrait. I will do it for nothing, to have your picture in my collection."

How contemptible, thought Tara. After all she had told Hart about this man, all he could do was fawn.

"My dear sir," replied Smith, basking in Hart's words, "it will be my pleasure. I'll give you a signed copy if you like, Tara." He turned and smiled at her.

"Don't bother," she retorted. She looked at Hart. "Ernst, you've gone down in my estimation. Good night."

"No, wait," said Hart, "I will escort you back."

But Tara left them both standing. As she walked out she heard Smith call over to a waiter, "Another bottle for the gentleman."

The cold evening air of Front Street was a welcome relief. Her pace was a little slow. The confrontation with Cad had taken its toll, and Tara felt disgusted by the whole affair. Brawling with a whore in a saloon like a harbor-front slut! She was appalled at herself.

Tara heard footsteps crunching behind her and then Smith's voice, "Whoa, Tara, slow down."

She walked faster, ignoring him, but he caught up and walked alongside her.

"I told you to be careful about Cad," he said. "She can be mighty deadly."

Tara looked straight ahead.

"Nice fellow, your photographer friend," he went on, striding to keep up. "Does as he's told."

Smith chattered on, seemingly oblivious to the fact that she had not replied once.

"By jingo, you know you look even more attractive than usual. What kind of man was that husband of yours to leave you on your own?" He shook his head in mock amazement. "A man who neglects a woman like you . . ."

She refused to rise to his bait.

Outside Mrs. Miles's house, Smith swept off his hat. She had her back to him and was unlocking the door. "Good night Mrs. Kane. Sleep well. Don't forget, put a steak on that shiner," he called after her as she slammed the door on him.

The next morning Tara hauled herself out of bed and went over to the mirror. As Smith had predicted, she was sporting a shiner. Gingerly she dabbed her eye with cold water, wondering how she was going to explain it to Mrs. Miles. Mrs. Miles, however, kept to her promise and firmly resisted the almost overpowering temptation to ask Tara what had happened.

Obviously the lodgers were given similar instructions, for when Tara went in with the breakfast, no one said a word; they just stared at her with unconcealed curiosity. Harry Robbins peered at her particularly closely—from professional interest, Tara supposed.

The subject was not mentioned at all that day, but in the evening Joe Lamore returned, apparently having heard a full account of the previous night's confrontation. Lamore treated the rest of the lodgers and Mrs. Miles to a vivid account over the dinner table. At least Tara was pretty sure he had, because Mrs. Miles seemed even frostier than she had been after Tara had returned from Fortymile.

When she had finished for the evening and was on the way to her room, Lamore's door flew open.

"Mrs. Kane!" he whispered urgently.

She turned and looked at him. "Anything you want, Mr. Lamore?"

"Yes, yes," he chuckled, rubbing his hands. "Why don't you come in for a little drink, or perhaps I could take you out for one, to the Monte Carlo."

"I suppose you're trying to tell me that you've heard what happened last night," she said.

"Sure. Got to hand it to you, I take off my hat to any woman who can hold her own with Cad Wilson," he burbled enthusiastically. "Anyway, I'd like to get to know you better. Got a feeling you and I could have a lot of fun." He gave her a conspiratorial wink.

"That's very hospitable of you, Mr. Lamore," Tara said, coolly assessing him, "but, as you know, Mrs. Miles doesn't like me to socialize with the lodgers. Thank you for your offer, but I rarely drink and I've no desire to go into the Monte Carlo ever again in my life."

"I was only trying to be friendly," Lamore grumbled. "No need to act like I'm propositioning you."

"Oh, I didn't mean to sound ungrateful. I'd just hate you to get the wrong impression of me. Good night."

The following day, while Mrs. Miles was out and Tara was alone in the house, she heard someone knocking at the front door. Rushing from the back yard, where she had been chopping up some logs, she paused to glance at her bruised face in the hall mirror, dreading the idea of seeing anyone.

There was another peremptory knock as Tara opened the door. To her astonishment, there stood Cad Wilson, wrapped in a magnificent fur cape with a hood, self-composed, beautifully made up, as usual.

She wore sealskin gloves and was carrying a bag of Indian worked leather. She showed no trace, no hint of the alley-cat brawl of two nights before.

Tara was even more conscious of the way she herself looked, with her black eye, her shining face, and her drab dress.

"Good morning, Mrs. Kane. Aren't you going to invite me in?" Cad asked. She stepped into the hall, and Tara slowly closed the door.

"Yes?"

"Can we talk somewhere?" asked Cad, looking around the hall.

"What about?" Tara demanded, holding her ground. What on earth could they have to say to one another?

"It concerns you, Mrs. Kane," Cad said pleasantly. "I think you'll be interested in what I have to say."

"If Soapy Smith has insisted that you come to apologize for the other night, don't bother. I've no time for you or him," she declared.

"Mrs. Kane, please don't think I'd demean myself," Cad sneered. "As far as I'm concerned you got what you deserved. I've only come here because I've found out something about your husband, so I thought I'd pass it on. If you don't want to listen, it's of no consequence to me."

"All right," Tara agreed warily, "you'd better come in here."

She opened the door of the sacred parlor and Cad went in. Tara could imagine Mrs. Miles's face if she found out the room had not only been used during the week, but used to entertain a woman of Cad Wilson's reputation.

"Sit down," Tara said.

"Thank you," murmured Cad. She was very polite. "I have something I want to show you."

She opened her handbag and gave Tara a wrapped object.

"What is it?" Tara asked cautiously.

"Why don't you take a look?"

Cad sat waiting expectantly, a smile hovering around her lips. Tara looked at her mystified, and then began unwrapping the piece of cloth.

It was a man's silver watch. Tara stared at it in disbelief. She recognized it. She knew it very well.

To Terence Oliver Makepeace
On our tenth wedding anniversary,

read the familiar inscription inside the lid. It was her father's watch, which Tara had given to Daniel. There were the words she had added

163

in San Francisco: "To my most darling husband Daniel, with eternal love from his devoted wife Tara Kane 1897." Tara's hand shook slightly. "Where did you get this?" she whispered.

Cad smiled. "You know it?"

"Of course," Tara looked anxiously at her. "Where . . ."

"Your husband sold it," Cad said. "He needed money for supplies. I understand he's teamed up with a man called Jake Gore. They've got a digging."

"Where?" gasped Tara.

"Oh, a hundred miles from here."

Tara was overcome. She looked at the watch, happiness, delight, surprise all mingling in a rush. The irony of it, that this whore should be the one to lead her to Daniel.

"Tell me where he is, exactly, please," she pressed.

"Well," began Cad. "It's a tough journey. Your husband's shacked up in Hell's Kitchen."

She waited for Tara's reaction. All Tara said was, "How do I get there?"

Cad shook her head. "It won't be easy. You'll have to travel northwest to the Tatonduic River. It's rough country, and when you get near Mount Deville you branch off, here." She produced a hand-drawn map. "It's mostly unexplored territory, but this will help you find it."

"What is it, then? A town?"

"A hole. The end of the line. Guess there's nothing a man won't do for gold," she added cuttingly.

"How did you come by this?" asked Tara.

"Jake's brother bought it from your husband, then he had bad luck at faro at the Monte Carlo. So he paid his debt with it. I saw the name and asked him how he came by it. He told me about Jake and your man."

"They're partners?"

"Guess so. Grubstaking each other. Well?"

"There's just one thing I don't understand," said Tara, slowly turning the watch over in her hands. "Since you hate me so much, why are you trying to help me?"

Cad got up. "Listen, Mrs. Kane. I don't want you around Jeff. Is that clear enough? He's my property. We belong to one another."

Tara stared at her. "Believe me, Miss Wilson, you're welcome to him. If I never see him again, I'll be happy. You're a fool if you think I'm even interested in him."

164

"I'm not arguing, I'm telling you," declared Cad. "Find your own man and get out of the Territory. You know where he is now. Take him and get out."

"That's the only thing I want to do," Tara said fervently.

Cad drew on her gloves. "Then get on and do it."

Outside, Cad turned and looked Tara up and down, a fashionable, well-dressed woman inspecting the domestic in her working clothes, face smudged, hair awry.

"For the life of me I don't know what the hell Jeff sees in you. Men are crazy," she said and walked off.

Tara slammed the door after her, then rushed to her room. She sat on the bed and pressed the watch to her cheek. He had held this in *his* hand. Something that had been a part of him all these months was now leading her to him at last. She was so excited that she did not even let the thought that Daniel had needed to sell it, the one thing he had promised to cherish all his life, bother her.

She put it on the dresser, next to the little compass. At last a tangible clue to Daniel's whereabouts, only a hundred miles from Dawson. Two or three days' journey, and she would be with him. Hell's Kitchen, she mused. It could not be all that bad, not if Daniel was there.

Her requirements were simple, she decided. She needed a sled, a dog team, supplies, a gun, and a proper map. All that on fifteen dollars. She decided that she could probably do without the gun, after all. She did not even know how to use one. But the rest were essential.

Of course, she knew people who would probably be willing to help her. There was Soapy Smith for one. But he would charge a heavy price, a price she could not afford in cash and one she was unwilling to supply in kind.

That left Ernst Hart and the lodgers.

She was sure she could get a sled and team from the Bartlett brothers; weren't they in the haulage business? Then Mr. Brock, if she asked him nicely and paid a small deposit with the security of full compensation when she met up with Daniel, would be bound to advance her sufficient supplies for the journey. As for a map of the route, who better to approach than Hart? After his behavior the other night he could hardly refuse.

Twenty-four identical Jefferson Smiths with self-satisfied smiles were hanging from a clothesline to dry when Tara entered Hart's studio.

To begin with, Hart was extremely wary of Cad's motives. Even after Tara had shown him the watch and explained what Cad had told her, he seemed unconvinced. It was even less easy to assure him she was capable of finding Daniel in such a hole as Hell's Kitchen.

He pulled out a map of the Yukon and graphically described the terrain she would have to cover. It was practically unexplored, no place for a woman on her own. In the interests of a comprehensive photographic record of the Klondike, he would accompany her and photograph this uncharted territory for posterity.

"No," cut in Tara.

"I'm worried about you. A woman alone on such a journey. It could be highly dangerous. You will not be safe."

"Don't be silly," she scoffed. She felt like adding that she had handled herself pretty well in a barroom fight, but thought better of it.

"I have a better idea," Hart proposed. "You stay in Dawson and I will go and find Daniel. I will tell him you are here and he will come to you. That will be a much safer arrangement."

Tara laughed. She couldn't help it. "Oh, Ernst," she said, seeing his puzzled look. "Sometimes you just don't understand. Do you really think I'm going to wait a day longer than I have to? Do you imagine that, having found him, I'm going to sit back and wait for him to come to me? Do you really believe that?"

"That is what you should do, but I also know you are a stubborn *Frauenzimmer*," Hart said.

"A what?"

"An obstinate lady," he translated, refolding the map. "I think you are very unwise, but I know no one can stop you. When do you plan to leave?"

"Well, if you really want to come ..."

"Of course," Hart said. "You don't think I would let you go alone. I must be with you to protect you and to keep you out of trouble."

"Like the other night?"

For a moment he looked shamefaced. "*Ach!* That was the other night. When will you be ready?"

"Tomorrow."

"All right. We will leave in the morning and go and find your Daniel. I will close the shop and prepare my equipment for the journey. There will be room enough on my sled for you too."

"It's all right. I've hired my own team."

Hart looked at her sharply and then grinned.

"My, my, Tara. You are becoming quite the independent lady of the Klondike." He paused. "I am very happy for you," he went on a

166

little wistfully. "I have said before, dear Tara, your Daniel is a very lucky man, to have married a woman who is so devoted to him. And now tell me how you are going to explain all this to your formidable Mrs. Miles?"

"I've already told her," replied Tara, getting up to leave.

"Are you sure you've made the right decision?" Hart asked.

Tara smiled at him. "Of course. Is there any other? Anyway, with the watch and the compass, and you to guide me, I'm well prepared for anything."

When she left Tara felt in better spirits. She would never have admitted it to anyone, but she had been frightened of doing the journey alone and, although she hadn't gone to Hart with the remotest intention of asking him to accompany her, she was relieved that he had volunteered. He was a true friend.

CHAPTER SIXTEEN

Early the following morning Tara trudged with the Bartlett brothers to their depot, where she picked up the sled and team. From there she went to Brock's store and collected her supplies. Then, with a certain amount of trepidation, she drove the sled to Hart's shack. He was already waiting, wearing his little German hat with the beaver brush, his sled piled high with equipment.

Hart watched Tara approaching, a broad grin on his face.

"I should have had my camera ready," he said, tugging at the straps that held down her supplies. " 'Maiden expedition of a Yukon lady' is what the caption would be. Sure you have everything?"

Tara nodded.

"Well, Mrs. Tara Kane," Hart said, going over to his sled and picking up the reins, "let's get going and find your husband."

The hundreds of miles she had traveled in other people's sleds, watching them handle their dog teams, listening to their calls, had not been wasted. For the first few miles she was frightened, but then—she didn't quite know when it happened—she realized the dogs were traveling the way she wanted, obeying her. It was a wonderful feeling of independence, no longer having to rely on anyone, to be her own mistress.

They were circling Lousetown, on the trail north, when she noticed a horseman following them from the direction of Dawson. He was galloping furiously, and Tara tightened her lips when she recognized him. Jefferson Smith was gaining on them.

167

"Let's go faster," she called out to Hart, cracking the whip over her team. He looked around and saw the rider. Smith waved a hand at them.

"I think he wants us to stop," said Hart and, to her annoyance, he slowed down his team. Smith pulled up alongside them, his horse breathing steam from its nostrils. He sat in the saddle easily and looked down at Tara.

"There's a rumor you're leaving us, Mrs. Kane," he said.

Tara stared straight ahead. Smith's horse pawed the frozen ground.

"Story I hear is that you're taking her north," Smith said, turning to Hart.

Hart nodded. "Did you like the portraits, Mr. Smith?" he asked eagerly. "I left them at the Monte Carlo last thing."

Smith edged his horse closer to Tara. "You're not going," he said to her.

She turned her head up to him, eyes cold. "Who says?"

"No question," declared Smith. "It's no place a woman can go."

She stared straight through him.

"You're not expecting *him* to look after you?" asked Smith, baring his white teeth. He did not even deign to look at Hart, who was watching with his nervous blink. Smith bent low in the saddle, his face within inches of hers. "Hardly very capable, is he?"

Tara glowered at him, then looked away.

Hart cleared his throat. "Mr. Smith," he called out.

"Yes?" said Smith, but his eyes remained on Tara.

"You need have no worries about Mrs. Kane, I promise you," said Hart. "She will be well protected."

Smith laughed. "By you?"

He made it sound ridiculous. He moved his horse nearer to Hart, and now he spoke to him tersely, his eyes hard, no smile on his face.

"Listen, mister," he said, menacingly. "You look after her well. You make sure every hair on her head is safe. Because, I'm telling you fair and square, if anything happens to her—" His hand reached out and grabbed Hart by his coat collar. "If anything happens to her I'm going to hold you responsible. She gets harmed and I deal with you, personally."

They stared into each other's eyes, and Hart was afraid, Tara could see he was. She had never seen Smith like this. For the first time Tara realized that what Cad Wilson had said was true, he actually cared what happened to her.

Smith released Hart. The very gesture was contemptuous. He turned the horse to Tara. "Since you won't change your mind you'd

168

better have this." He reached into his coat. She saw the glint of something metallic. "Here. Take it."

It was a stubby pistol, a tiny .22 Derringer, beautifully made, with an engraved mother-of-pearl handle.

"If anyone gets too close for comfort, use it," he said. He flashed a mean look at Hart. Then, without a word, he swung his horse around and galloped off.

Hart stared after him. There was a slight flush on his face. "You know, Tara, maybe one day I'll have the pleasure of photographing the mighty Mr. Smith hanging from the gallows," he said, and there was real animosity in his voice.

Tara looked at the pistol she was holding. It fitted into her hand perfectly. Then she noticed the inscription along the squat barrel: "A Sure Thing from JRS."

"What are we waiting for, Ernst?" she said, putting the pistol in her bag, next to her goggles, the compass, and the watch.

It was as if she had communicated her sense of urgency to the dogs. They streaked through the snow, often moving ahead of Hart's sled. She felt as she had never felt before, free, completely in control of her destiny, no longer beholden to somebody else. She almost resented having to travel in partnership with Hart.

Hart had been observing this new, assured Tara. When they camped she automatically knew what to do. She set up the stove while he collected firewood. She stuck a lump of frozen snow on a branch in front of it, catching the melting drips of water in a pan as she had seen the Mounties do. She made sure that her dogs were fed. She was handling herself like a woman of the Klondike.

Once she looked up and saw Hart watching her. "Why are you staring at me?" she asked.

"Because you've changed," he said. "You're not the shivering, timid, frightened orphan I met on the ship."

"What am I now, then?"

"You're a woman who can look after herself," he said, a little grudgingly. "You're different. You'll survive. No matter what happens, *you'll* survive."

She was pleased because she knew he was speaking the truth. She had changed, without even being aware of it. On the ship she had felt so lost and appalled by the conditions she had been subjected to, but now she never questioned the primitive life of the Yukon. She had learned to make the best of anything and everything, to come to terms with her new existence. Every day was one more day she had survived, and a day closer to being with Daniel.

As they got ready to bed down for the night, Tara said, "I'll take the first watch, if you like."

He was startled.

"Out here, somebody had better stay awake the whole time, don't you think?" she asked. "I'll take two hours and then I'll wake you."

"Is that what the Mounties taught you?"

"We could do worse, Ernst."

She went to the corner of the tent and picked up his rifle.

"Can you handle that?" he asked incredulously.

"Of course," she replied, as if she'd used a rifle every day of her life. "Good night."

Outside, Tara crouched in front of the fire Hart had built near the dogs. She sat, wrapped up, the rifle across her lap, smiling at the memory of Hart's amazed look. He had had that look when she told him in Dawson that she had already hired herself a dog team.

What he did not know was that her sense of independence was greater than the reality. Could she ever bring herself to point the rifle at a human being and pull the trigger? She hoped she would never have to find out.

Tara gazed up at the sky. It was a clear, sharp night and the bright stars twinkled; somewhere beyond the frozen snow ahead was Daniel.

She got up and fed the flames of the fire with more logs, then walked around the perimeter of the tiny camp, partly to keep herself awake and partly to stay warm. Despite the cold, the silence, the empty void, she did not feel afraid. At last the vast emptiness of the Territory did not threaten her. Now she was part of it.

Two uneventful hours later she slipped into the tent and shook Hart for his watch. Before she went to sleep, she thought with a little feeling of triumph, no, I'm not afraid any more.

She wondered if Daniel would notice the change in her.

Tara stirred uneasily. She opened her eyes and then sat up, stifling a scream. A man was standing over her, a hideous grin on his face and a pistol in his hand.

"Howdy," he said genially.

He was a mean-looking character, with shoulder-length hair, a flat animal-like nose, close-set eyes, and earrings. He stuck his pistol in his embroidered Indian belt and reached down.

"Get up," he commanded, hauling her to her feet.

Tara pulled her arm from his grasp and stepped back. "Who—who are you?" she stuttered, terrified. "Where's Ernst?"

170

"You're his woman, are you?" said the man. "Well, that's a waste for sure."

He pushed her against the wall of the tent. Stupefied with fear, she watched wide-eyed as his ugly face came nearer, his mouth seeking hers. His tongue was trying to prise her lips apart. Tara turned her head from side to side in a feverish effort to escape his repulsive embrace. He was forced to relax his hold momentarily, and she lashed out with her hand. Although the blow was a wild one, her nails left a welt down his cheek. She spat on her hand and then wiped it across her mouth, trying to expunge the contamination.

The man grinned malevolently and dragged her from the tent. "Look what I found, boys," he announced triumphantly, propelling Tara forward as they emerged.

Two other men stood by the sleds. They both had rifles. Hart was lying motionless by his sled, and Tara was sure he was dead. His glasses lay on the ground beside him.

"Ernst!" she cried, rushing toward him. The men laughed as she knelt by him and took his head in her hands.

"Oh, Ernst!" she cried again as she pressed her face against his. His eyes flickered, and he groaned. She put her hand behind his shoulders and helped him to sit up.

"*Gott, mein Kopf,*" moaned Hart. He reached up and felt it. She gently replaced his glasses on his nose. Then, for the first time, awareness came back to him.

"Tara," he gasped. "Are you all right?"

The three men were standing around laughing. The other two were as forbidding as their companion with the earrings. One had a black eyepatch and was dressed like a trapper. Tara recognized Hart's rifle in his hands. The other had a red beard and an ugly brutish face.

"What do you want from us?" she demanded.

The three grinned at her. "You'd never guess," said the one with earrings, and his two side-kicks snorted.

"I'm sorry, Tara," Hart apologized, grimacing with pain as he spoke. "They crept up on me. I heard the dogs growling, and then I just—I suppose somebody hit me."

"Don't worry," Tara reassured him with a bravado she did not feel. She rose to her feet. "Help him," she said, surprised at her own self-possession. "Take him to the tent."

"He's OK," said the man with the eyepatch. "Nothing wrong with him. Hank never hits 'em too hard."

"'Cept when he wants to," grinned the redbeard, and they laughed.

Hank was the one with the earrings. He grabbed her chin and

171

turned her head toward him. "She and me fancy each other," he said. "Ain't that right, sweetheart?"

"Keep away from me," she spat, kicking out at him, and he jumped back in mock fear.

"Save it," ordered the man with the eyepatch. He seemed to have some kind of authority. "Plenty of time for that, Hank." He went over to Hart, who was sitting shivering and white-faced. "Where are you making for?" he asked.

Hart stared at him vacantly.

"I asked where are you going, mister?" repeated the eyepatched man.

"I . . ." Hart stammered, "we're . . ." He stopped.

"Where?" he demanded, hitting Hart in the mouth.

"We're going north," Tara said. Hart's lip was bleeding.

"Got any gold?" the man asked Tara. He seemed to have decided she was the one that mattered.

Tara shook her head.

"She's lying, Duke," Hank said.

"You wouldn't do that, would you?" said Duke. The eyepatch made his face macabre.

"We have no gold," insisted Tara.

"So what's on the sled? Supplies?"

"Equipment," replied Tara.

"Equipment!" repeated Duke. "What kind of equipment?"

"Mr. Hart is a photographer," she explained.

They stared at her disbelieving. Then Hank went over to Hart's sled and pulled back the tarpaulin covering the cases and boxes. He started trying to open them.

"Careful!" shouted Hart. The sight of Hank manhandling his belongings brought him back to life. "That's my camera."

Hank looked into the big black case. "Jesus, look at this."

He started pulling out the camera, but Hart yelled, "Get your hands off that. I'll kill you if you damage it." He was shaking with rage.

"You want to try, mister?" invited Hank.

Hart swallowed. "You tell your friend to leave my things alone, you understand?" he said vehemently, turning to the others.

"OK, OK," Duke said going over to the sled. "No need for anyone to get heated." He picked up a box of plates. "You taking pictures *out here?*"

"Yes," replied Hart, slightly calmer.

"And what about her?" he asked, nodding at Tara.

"My assistant," Hart replied.

172

Duke scratched his head. "How much money you got?"

"Ninety dollars," Hart said, reaching into his pocket.

"We'll have that," Hank said. Hart meekly passed the money over.

"What kind of pictures do you take?" Duke asked, still looking through Hart's equipment.

"I take portraits of famous people," he said. "Important people."

"We should get our pictures made. What do you say, boys?" Duke cackled.

"You're kidding," Hank said contemptuously. He had been dividing out the money and now handed the other two their shares. "I ain't posing for no birdy. How about you, Shorty?"

Redbeard looked interested. "It's up to Duke," he shrugged. "I never had my picture taken, 'cept that lousy mug shot they put on the Wanted poster. But I don't see why not. All those Yankee badmen got their pictures took, why not us?"

"You're crazy, both of you," spat Hank. "Who the hell wants his picture took?"

"Shut up!" ordered Duke. He turned to Hart. "OK, mister. You willing to picture me and the boys?"

"You'll have your own portfolio. I'll do you in a group and then individually," Hart said eagerly, getting to his feet, his headache completely forgotten. "When it's daylight," he added. Tara wondered if this display of enthusiasm was genuine, or merely an attempt to get them out of a tight spot.

"We got a little hideaway," Duke said. "We'll take you. The rest of the boys there will want to have their pictures took too. Understand?" His tone allowed no argument.

"What about her? Who gets her?" demanded Shorty without even looking in Tara's direction. She could have been a bag of flour.

"Gentlemen . . ." began Hart, his voice high-pitched with emotion.

"Gentlemen!" mocked Hank. "Get the dude. Gentlemen! Shit!" He spat into the fire.

"I need her," pleaded Hart. "I need her for my work. Without her I cannot operate. Photography is a . . . is a very complicated business. I need my assistant."

"You come too," decided Duke.

Tara knew neither she nor Hart had any choice in the matter.

"Yeah, you can have her afterward," chortled Shorty.

"No!" said Hart.

"What did you say?" Hank asked, grabbing him by the collar.

"I said," croaked Hart, frightened and yet more determined than Tara had yet seen him, "you don't touch her."

Hank hit him low and Hart's knees buckled as he sank to the

ground, clutching his stomach. He was as white as the surrounding snow and then he was sick, vomit spewing uncontrollably from his mouth.

"She and me are going to have a little fun, 'cause the lady's all hot for me, ain't you sweetheart?" said Hank.

"Who says she's yours?" growled Shorty.

Hank swung around. "I do."

"My ass you do."

Shorty and Hank stood poised, hands hovering dangerously near their guns.

"Jesus, fellows, keep your hair on," intervened Duke. "There's plenty for all of us. Keep her till later. A nice dame like that don't grow on trees, so cut it out."

Shorty was the first to lower his hands.

Hart was still retching.

"OK, OK," Hank grudgingly agreed, "we share her. But she ain't anyone's property. So we all keep off her till we're back." He strolled over to Tara. "It'll be my turn first, sweetheart," he promised, "when we get home. You'll like that, won't you?"

Tara was petrified. She wondered wildly how she could escape, but her dogs weren't hitched up and even if she could reach Duke's sled, she knew they would kill her and probably Hart too.

"Yeah, you got something to look forward to," added Shorty, and they both laughed.

Hart stood up groggily. "Where are you taking us?" he spluttered.

"Mister, you ask too many questions," Duke said coldly. "Get hitched up. Move."

Little was said once they were on the trail. Duke had a sled, with a pack of dogs as villainous as the trio. Hank and Shorty trekked along on snowshoes beside Tara and Hart, who were driving their own sleds, the whole time keeping their rifles pointing at her and Hart.

The landscape provided no clue to where they were going. It was more barren, more deserted than any terrain she had seen so far. They followed no trodden paths, saw no trails, came across no signs of people, not even a rough cross or a broken sled buried in the snow.

Hourly the terrain became rougher and rockier. In the distance, Tara could see great mountains, so high that the summits were obscured by frozen mist. She scoured the horizon for some sign of a camp, huts, smoke, people, but there was nothing.

Eventually they halted, and Hank and Shorty walked over to them. Duke, with his rifle cradled in his arm, stood watching. A great uneasiness swept through Tara. Then, from behind, Hank covered her eyes, and she felt his coarse hands tie the blindfold securely. She

174

struggled feebly, but Hank's voice said, "Relax, sweetheart. I ain't going to harm you, just some things nobody sees."

"I can't drive the team like this," Tara objected.

"That's OK," Duke said. "Hank'll take over. You can ride like a lady."

She could hear Hart protesting, "My glasses. I need my glasses," and then Shorty: "You don't need nothing, mister. I'll keep them for you. Hope that little bandage ain't too tight."

She sat on the sled listening to the cracking of the whips and the panting of the dogs as they started moving again. She had no idea how long they traveled nor in what direction. The ground was hard and bumpy, and judging by the echoes the teams were being guided through a narrow passage.

Then a shot rang out, and she struggled to tear off the blindfold.

"It's OK," called out Hank. "Nothing to worry about."

Three more quick shots followed, fired from just behind. This must be the hideaway at last.

"Are we there?" Tara asked, trying again to uncover her eyes.

"Keep that on," warned Hank.

Then, after a few minutes, she heard voices.

"Whoa there," Hank shouted, and the sled pulled to a halt.

"Brought you a present," she heard Duke say.

"You can look now," Hank said, roughly pulling the scarf off.

She blinked, her eyes unaccustomed to the sudden brightness. Hart was peering around in his short-sighted fashion.

"My glasses," he demanded, holding out his hand.

Shorty hesitated for a moment, then gave them to him.

The sleds had pulled up in a clearing, surrounded on all sides by high cliffs. There were a few tents and two rough wooden shacks.

Duke was talking to a tall man wearing, to Tara's surprise, the scarlet jacket of a Mountie. When she looked more closely she saw that it was soiled, most of the brass buttons were missing, and there was a hole, edged by a stain, where the Mountie's heart had once been. Strings of Indian beads festooned his neck, and he sported two pistols, in double holsters slung from a cartridge belt, with a third pistol stuck in the waistband of his trousers.

"How much do you want for her?" the man asked Duke as they slowly walked toward her.

Duke shook his head. "She's not for sale. She belongs to us, Blue. Me and the boys found her, so she's ours."

"We'll see," Blue said ominously, his face distorted by an ugly sneer.

For a moment they stood, Blue calculatingly assessing Tara, Duke watching him. She kept staring straight ahead, doing her best to ignore them, trying to conceal the raw fear she felt in the pit of her stomach.

"Where is this?" she asked. "Where am I?"

"Does it matter?" retorted Blue. He grinned. "Let's say you've fallen among thieves."

Tara looked around the group. Shorty, Hank, Duke, Hart a few feet away, eyes wide with anxiety, Blue and, in the background, three strange men, smiling inanely.

"I never would have guessed," she remarked with as much disdain as she could muster. "What do you call it?"

"Paradise," smiled Blue. " 'Least that's my name for it. Some call it Hells's Kitchen."

Tara stared at him. "Hell's Kitchen," she repeated slowly. She glanced at Hart, who was as shaken as she was. "I am Daniel Kane's wife. From San Francisco."

"So?" asked Blue. It meant nothing to him.

"Where's Jake Gore, his partner?"

"You know Jake, eh?" said Blue. "Fancy that."

He turned to one of the grinning chorus, "A friend of yours, Jake?"

Jake was a sallow-faced man with long black hair tied at the nape of his neck. He had a curious kind of shoulder holster under his left armpit, but instead of a gun it held a knife sheath. He wore a gold ring on every finger.

Tara stared at him incredulously. This was Daniel's partner? She could not believe it. How could he have joined forces with such a man?

"I'm looking for Daniel Kane. I'm his wife," she mumbled, her eyes searching his sinister face for some clue as to what had made Daniel trust him.

Jake turned to Blue. "I think she and me got some private business," he said.

Hank suddenly pushed forward. "You ain't doing any claim jumping while I'm around," he threatened. "She's ours, and nobody else's got any business with her."

"We got business," said Jake very softly.

"And I'm telling you she's our property," warned Hank, his hand automatically going toward his gun.

Blue and the others were watching them, interested spectators, but nobody intervened.

"You sure?" asked Jake.

"Try me."

Jake shrugged and turned as if to walk away. Then, with the speed

176

of a rattlesnake, he whirled around and threw something. Hank sank to his knees, Jake's knife protruding from his chest. He tried to speak, clawed for his gun, but death came too quickly. He slumped forward and lay still. It had happened so fast, Tara had not even seen the blade fly through the air, but there was no doubt that Hank was dead. She could not deny that she was pleased.

Slowly Jake walked up to Hank's lifeless body, turned it over with his foot, and drew out the knife, wiping the blood-coated blade on his dirty leather jacket. It left a thick smear, and Tara saw that there were several such brown streaks. Then he slid the knife back in his shoulder holster.

"Sorry," he said amiably to Duke and Shorty, who stood motionless. "Guess you're a partner short."

"One moment, please!" shouted Hart, carefully side-stepping Hank's body. "I would like to take a picture. Now," he went on, not allowing any protest, "this gentleman," he indicated Jake, "standing over there, with that, er, gentleman"—he meant the body.

"What for?" Jake growled.

"To photograph you. Here on the spot. As it happened."

"Just me and him?" asked Jake.

"Yes. We must hurry before the light is gone."

Hart's cold-bloodedness shook Tara. He unloaded his sled, set up his camera, posed Jake Gore by Hank's body, disappeared under his blanket, and exposed the first plate. Then he emerged to change Jake's pose slightly and took another picture.

Other men from the encampment had gathered around, standing silent, watching. When Hart had finished they all applauded and cheered.

"You're OK, mister," said Blue, slapping Hart on the back so hard he nearly lost his spectacles.

"Where's my picture?" demanded Jake impatiently.

"In a day or two," promised Hart. "Now, gentlemen, I am available for anyone who wishes to have their portraits taken. My name is Ernst Hart, photographer to the crowned heads of Europe, including His Majesty Kaiser Wilhelm. Official photographer to the Imperial German Navy and the Casino at Baden Baden. Only five dollars a print. Put your names down now."

There was a rush, headed by Blue. Hart had his notebook out and was busy scribbling down names. Hank's corpse stiffened in the snow, ignored by all.

Jake Gore went up to Tara, who was standing by, pale and numb from what she had seen.

"Come on, let's talk," he said, leading her to a tepee.

Inside there was no furniture, except for a bearskin rug which covered the frozen ground. Jake picked up an earthenware bottle and indicated for Tara to sit down.

"Rotgut?" he invited, holding out the bottle.

She shook her head.

He took a deep swig and then looked at her. "So, you're his wife?"

She nodded. "I . . ." she began.

"Who told you he was here?"

"Cad Wilson," replied Tara. She reached in her bag and brought out the watch.

He looked at it, then again at her.

"Yeah, that's right. That's his."

"She told me to ask for you and that you'd take me to him."

"Sure."

"Where is he?" she asked.

"Camped a few miles from here. At the claim."

"Can we leave now?"

He shook his head. "Weather don't look good. Tomorrow."

"Please," begged Tara. "I'd like to leave straight away."

"Tomorrow," he insisted. "I ain't moving tonight."

"If you tell me how to get there, I'll—"

"I told you," his voice was mean, "we'll leave tomorrow."

Tara checked her impatience. He was the only person who could lead her to Daniel, and he was getting angry.

"How is he?" she asked, trying to lighten the hostile atmosphere that had sprung up. "Well?"

"Sure," Jake said.

"When did you two team up? How did you meet?"

"We sort of bumped into each other," he said. She waited for more but he just sat drinking from the bottle.

"Cad Wilson told me that Dan sold this to your brother," Tara said, putting the watch back in her bag. "Why? Was he broke?"

"Needed supplies, I guess. Arne's always got dough. We share, see? Share and share alike." Jake leered. "You're a mighty good-looking woman," he said, appraising her over the top of the bottle. "Mighty good-looking."

His dark eyes kept undressing her, and it unnerved her. What could have brought Dan and this evil man together, she wondered again.

"Have you been partners long?" she inquired, trying to change the subject.

"Long enough," he said.

178

"Have you found any gold?"

"We ain't rich yet," he said, and snorted.

"Has Dan been up here a long time? she asked.

"Christ, you're going to see him tomorrow," he said sharply. "Ask him. Don't keep pestering me. He'll tell you."

"I'm sorry, Mr. Gore," she apologized, "but I haven't seen my husband for such a long while. . . ."

"Sure, sure," he said. "He says the same about you."

"Does he talk of me?" Her voice was eager.

Jake shrugged. "Sometimes."

"And he's in good health?"

"Never been better."

Tara got up.

"Why don't you sleep here tonight," Jake suggested. "Then we can leave first thing."

"It's all right," she said hurriedly, edging her way to the flap of the tepee. "I've got my own things."

He got up and stood in front of her.

"Why don't you relax?" he said. "You're my partner's woman, ain't you? I'm not going to mess around with my partner's wife, am I?"

He grinned. It was his eyes that told her he was lying.

"Of course not," Tara's voice was slightly high-pitched. "I never thought . . ."

"So what are you frightened about?"

"Frightened? Who said I was frightened?" Tara laughed in an attempt to reassure him. "Mr. Hart will be looking for me. I know you'll understand."

Jake took her hand and started caressing it, all the while grinning down at her. Tara felt her flesh creep, but she dared not move. She knew his hands could just as easily tear her apart.

"First thing in the morning, Mrs. Kane."

She gently freed her hand. "Until then, Mr. Gore," she said, her heart pounding as she left the tepee.

Once outside, Tara stood shaking. She had to find Hart, but there was no sign of him. The camp was completely deserted; even Hank's corpse had been taken away. From the direction of a cave in the rock she could hear men shouting; so, with her heart in her mouth, she went toward it, praying that Hart would be there.

The interior of the cave was illuminated by a roaring log fire and oil lamps hanging from the walls. The place was packed; obviously this was Hell's Kitchen's night time haunt. Hart, oblivious to everything except his problems, was adjusting his camera on its tripod. Tara

179

gingerly edged her way through to him, trying to attract as little attention as possible. He was cursing under his breath.

"Hold these," he said without ceremony, thrusting some plates at her. He was focusing his camera on a ring of outlaws. In the center of the ring were two savage dogs, straining to get at one another, barely restrained by their owners. The men were yelling for the fun to start.

Hart shook his head doubtfully. "The light's terrible in here," he complained. "It will be very difficult."

"Ernst," said Tara urgently, "I'm meeting Daniel in the morning . . ."

He waved her to be silent. "Damn," he cursed, "I don't think anything's going to come out."

There was a roar, and the two men released their respective dogs. They flew at one another, merging into one wild mass, growls turning to yelps as they tore at fur and flesh.

"Tear his gizzard out, Flash," Blue yelled. "Go for him, you bastard."

"Quick, another plate," Hart ordered, snapping his fingers. She gave him one, her eyes mesmerized by the savagery in front of her. The bigger animal, a black brute, had torn off the ear of his brown opponent, and the floor of the cave was splattered with blood and pieces of fur. The dogs' rage had blinded them to everything except the desire to destroy one another. Even pain and loss of blood didn't deter them.

Tara winced as the brown mongrel locked its jaws on the black husky's nose and ripped it off. There was no yelp, just the scrabble of paws on the earth floor, strangled growls, panting. Blood was spurting, and both animals' heads were dyed scarlet. The men were stamping their feet with excitement, shouting bets, jeering, cheering.

"Get him, damn you," howled a man next to Tara. "That's it, boy, that's it," he yelled approvingly as the husky ripped a piece of flesh from the mongrel's hindquarters. "Kill him! Kill him!"

The mongrel gave a sudden, almost human scream. The husky had locked its teeth into his throat and was shaking him like a rag doll. The blood was dripping in a steady stream from where the husky's nose had been. The mongrel could hardly see, blinded by the blood that was pouring from the stump that was all that was left of his ear. Now the husky had him helpless and began dragging him all over the cave, streaking a trail of gore in his wake. Then the mongrel went limp and Tara, shocked and sickened, realized he was dead. But still the maddened husky kept shaking the body, showering drops of blood over the spectators.

Suddenly he keeled over, the mongrel still clenched in his teeth, and around him grew a steadily widening pool of blood. He gave a shudder and died. Only then could they see that the mongrel, with the strength of desperation, had bitten deep into the husky's stomach, so deep that blood and intestines were spewing out.

All around Tara arguments began. There were cries of protest; somebody said it was a draw and that all bets were off. Others protested that Flash had lasted longer than the mongrel and was, therefore, technically, the winner.

"You ain't going to welsh, are you Fenton?" cried one man. Immediately everybody parted, leaving him to face another tall, muscular man. "Just because your mutt got a licking?"

Tara, studying their hate-twisted faces, their bloodshot eyes, their venomous lips, their hands ready to draw guns, knives, anything, thought they looked exactly like their dead dogs.

"Dolly can settle it with Prince tomorrow," interrupted Blue. He looked at the two men like a referee appealing to two contestants. "What d'you say? Your bitch against his critter."

"Double stakes?" challenged Dolly's owner.

"Suits me," Fenton snarled. "He'll rip her to pieces."

The audience drifted off, arguing, while Hart began disassembling his equipment and Tara waited restlessly to speak with him.

"Pretty good, wasn't it," Blue said. "You get some good pictures there?"

"I don't think I have anything," Hart grumbled. "This light is too dim. Can you do the next fight in the open? In daylight? It will make it easier to photograph. They move so fast, you see. . . ."

"Maybe so," Blue said, disappointed. "But that was a good show you didn't get."

"I know," Hart agreed, sorrowfully, to Blue's retreating back.

They were left alone, Tara pacing around the cave, her stomach still churning at what she had seen and inexplicably angry with Hart. It was not just because he had stood coldly photographing that hideous spectacle; after all, he had never made a secret of his reason for being in the Yukon and this was all part of the life. What had aggravated her was his lack of reaction to her news that she had located Daniel. She knew that she was being childish; he had been busy and probably hadn't heard. Nonetheless, it rankled.

"Where's Daniel?" he suddenly asked, packing away his camera.

She turned and faced him. "I started to tell you but you were too busy with . . . with that horrible fight."

"I was trying to take exposures under very bad conditions. It's no good talking to me when I am photographing. You do not gossip with a painter when he is doing a portrait, do you?"

"Gossip!" Tara exploded. "Ernst, I was telling you I have found Daniel."

"Good," he said. "I am pleased. How is he?"

"I'm joining him in the morning. He's camped a few miles away. He's got a claim."

"That is wonderful," he said, but he didn't sound very enthusiastic. "I am so happy for you. You deserve it." He didn't look at her; it was as if he were trying to hide something. "I know what you think. I am a cold-blooded fish, yes? Here you are all excited, and I am only interested in taking pictures of dogs tearing one another to pieces. But you see, that is my mission out here. Don't forget, Brady didn't help the wounded or bury the dead. He stood on the battlefield photographing them. It was his job, and this is mine. These men are part of it. . . ."

He stood up and looked at her. Tara noticed that he appeared very sad. "You do not hate me?" he asked quietly.

"Ernst, what on earth makes you ask such a silly question? Of course I don't hate you. How could I? I could never have got this far without your friendship and help."

She kissed him lightly on the cheek.

"I have to get some sleep," she said. "We start at dawn."

"*We?*"

"Jake Gore and I." She found it impossible to refer to him as Daniel's partner. She could never bring herself to think of him as that.

"The . . . the man with the knife?"

She nodded.

Hart regarded her gravely. "He is a very bad man," he said.

"He knows where Daniel is." She shrugged. "He's taking me to him. That's all that matters."

"Wait until I can come with you," Hart urged. "I will only spend two or three days here taking photographs and then we can go together."

"Oh, Ernst," Tara said. "You don't think I could wait *days* before I see him, do you? You can't know what you're asking."

"No, perhaps I do not. It is much safer, that is all. I think even Daniel would want that." He sighed. "You are always impetuous, Tara. Your trouble is you won't change your mind."

182

CHAPTER SEVENTEEN

It was not only the sounds of revelry and drunkenness that kept Tara awake that night. It was the thought that, at this moment, somewhere, not many miles away, was Daniel, unaware that by this time tomorrow they would be together again. And it filled her with a strange combination of excitement and apprehension. Excitement at seeing him in just a few hours, being in his arms, kissing him; apprehension at what he might have become. Was he still going to be the same man she had married? Had he been scarred by the ordeals he had endured over the past few months? Had she been chasing an illusion, an ideal that survived only as a glorious memory?

And what about her? Was she still the woman he had loved, needed, and cherished? Would he recognize her new-found independence and dislike her for it?

She turned over nervously, her eyes staring into the darkness, her mind racing like an overwound clock.

Her biggest worry was how she was going to tell him about Gabie. How was he going to react when he heard that his darling daughter was dead? She knew that he would guess almost immediately that something terrible must have happened for her to have come to the Klondike; would his eyes be full of love, compassion, understanding? Or would they be hard, accusing, leaving unsaid a suspicion that it need not have happened, that it was her fault? That first look would either confirm their love or destroy it.

She consoled herself with the knowledge that in the small hours of the morning everything looked gloomy. It was a time to feel guilty, insufficient, morbid. Tomorrow, when she was on her way, it would all be different.

From outside came the sound of raucous voices. She strained to hear whether Hart's was among them. Earlier he had gone out to talk with the men, and she could picture him drinking with them, his eyes behind their glasses watching, observing, noting faces, types, characters. Then there was a burst of raw laughter, and someone stumbled against the tent. Tara clutched the Derringer for reassurance inside her sleeping bag. She hoped it was, as Smith had inscribed it, a sure thing.

Are you going to tell Daniel how Smith has helped you, asked a little inner voice.

"Helped me!" she exclaimed under her breath. "Good God, I must be tired. Fortymile? Dawson? He hasn't helped me, he's helped himself . . . except for the gun. Yes, he's helped me with that."

What about the dinner party, the way he looks at you, persisted her inner voice. So what, she thought. He's used me, he's used me all along. But never again. Never, never again.

Toward dawn exhaustion overtook her and, for a little while, she slept, but not long. Soon it was time.

Hart was snoring in his sleeping bag. She packed away her few things, put the gun in her pocket, and hitched up her team. Before she left she went over to the recumbent form of Hart.

"Ernst!" she whispered, shaking him gently. "I'm off now." She could smell the rotgut on his breath. "Goodbye," Tara said, and he answered her with a snore. She would have liked to say farewell to him, but she couldn't wait. She knew he would be lying there for hours.

Jake was waiting beside his sled, which was hitched to a mangy dog team.

"Good team you got there," he remarked enviously.

"I'm ready."

"You follow my sled," was all he said. There was no blindfold this time.

They traveled through a narrow ravine, obviously the only path into the hide-out, then back down the bumpy trail. Finally, they emerged onto open ground, snow-covered and frozen as far as the eye could see.

She wanted to ask how far they were going, how long it would take, but Jake's sled kept too far ahead. All the time she surveyed the landscape, hoping for some sign of their destination, but white emptiness stretched for miles on all sides.

After a couple of hours, Tara drew even with Jake, but he didn't look around at her. The sleds were moving at a good speed, the dogs panting, the wind biting into her face.

"Jake!" she shouted at him. "Slow down."

He reined in his team and stopped. Tara halted hers and walked over to him.

"I thought you were in a hurry to get there," he said.

"How much further is it?" she asked.

"Few miles," he replied.

"We'll be there before dark?"

He looked up at the sky. "Maybe have to camp," he said. "Weather might turn mean."

"I want to get there tonight," she insisted firmly.

"Sure," he said. "If the weather holds."

They started again, Jake once more leading. Tara did not like the idea of spending a night alone with this man. So far, he had behaved correctly toward her, and he had said he wouldn't mess around with his partner's woman, but she still felt uneasy. The image of his knife protruding from Hank's body was something she would never be able to forget.

They had not seen another living soul, which puzzled Tara. If they were approaching gold country, where were the hoards of prospectors always drawn to the neighborhood of a claim like bees to a honey pot?

Ahead of her, Jake pulled up beside some rocks. When she came alongside, he said, "We'll make camp here."

He didn't consult her. It was an order. Not daring to cross him, she started to unpack her supplies.

"Get some wood," he said, handing her a small axe and pointing at a clump of trees.

He unhitched both their dog teams and busied himself setting up the tent. Tara walked to the trees and began chopping at a low bough.

By the time she had enough wood, she was panting, the sweat trickling down her body under the heavy clothes. But she wasn't sure if she was sweating from her exertions or from the sheer fear she felt at the thought of being alone with this man for the whole night.

They cooked beans and bacon and sat in the tent, eating in silence. He scarcely looked at her.

"Couldn't we still get there tonight?" she asked.

"Don't want to be caught in a blizzard out in the bush," he said. "Weather's brewing up." He grinned. "Sorry you got to spend another night away from him. Gets kinda lonesome, don't it?"

"Why didn't you tell me it was this far?"

"Didn't tell you nothing," he growled. "Maybe far to you. Only a few miles to me."

From the sack containing his supplies, he pulled out the earthenware bottle, uncorked it, and took a deep swig.

"Aaah," he spluttered, wiping his mouth with the back of his hand. "That's how a woman ought to be, warming a man's body."

Tara paled. She could just imagine him drinking the whole bottle and then setting on her like an animal.

"I'll check on the dogs," he said suddenly, lumbering out of the tent. She felt in her pocket and pulled out the Derringer. Then she took some blankets and wrapped herself up in them, holding the gun under the blankets.

Jake said nothing when he returned. He flung himself down, again swigging from his bottle.

I must stay awake, Tara kept telling herself. But she had hardly slept the night before, and the hours of trekking in the snow had taken their toll.

Across the tent, Jake was nursing the bottle and staring at her.

"You go to sleep," he said. "I'll keep watch. Nothing to worry about. I got company." He raised the bottle.

"You need to rest too. Why don't you have a nap, and I'll stay awake?"

He shook his head.

"I ain't going to deliver you to Dan all worn out and tired. You gotta have your beauty sleep. Guess tomorrow night he won't give you much time for shut-eye, eh? No, you save your strength, honey, 'cos you're going to need it."

He cackled to himself and took another drink.

"Want some?" he asked, thrusting the bottle in her direction.

"No, thank you," Tara replied.

The look he gave her was almost belligerent. "You ain't a Sunday school teacher or nothing, are you?"

"No, I'm just not thirsty."

He guffawed.

"You don't have to be thirsty to drink rotgut."

After another swig he lapsed into a morose silence, all the while staring at her.

Tara tried to close her eyes to avoid his gaze. But when she lowered her lids, tiredness befogged her. She forced her eyes open again. She had to stay awake. She had to.

"What's the matter?" he asked. His speech was slurred. "Can't sleep? Maybe you're lonesome." He leaned forward. "Maybe you need company?"

Under the blanket, her hand tightened around the pistol.

"No, I'm fine," Tara said. "Listen!" What's that noise?"

For a moment they sat in silence, then he shook his head.

"No," Tara insisted. "I'm sure I heard something. Don't you think you ought to take a look?"

"No, sister," he said. "If there's anything out there it can come in here. I'm prepared." His hand went to his shoulder holster and Tara's heart beat faster as he drew out the knife. "With this baby, nothing can happen. It's a great equalizer, honey. Feel it." He held out the blade to her, his hand weaving slightly. "Feel it," he commanded.

Tara extracted her left hand from inside the blanket, her right hand still grasping the gun. Nervously she touched the blade with her fingertips.

"It's very sharp," she commented, her voice quivering.

He raised the blade to his lips and kissed it. "She's my sweetheart," he cooed. "Nobody argues with her."

To Tara's relief he stuck the knife back in his holster.

"So you see, you're quite safe. Nobody'll bother you. Not with sweetheart here."

"Oh, I know I'm in good hands," said Tara. "My husband will really appreciate the way you're looking after me."

"Sure he will."

Tara screwed up her eyes. She felt desperately tired; her weariness was almost like a physical pain.

"Go ahead," he said. "You sleep."

"No, no. I'm OK. Tell me, where do you come from, Jake?" She hoped she sounded suitably conversational.

"Why do you want to know?" he asked, suspiciously.

"You're Dan's partner, aren't you?" she said. "Of course I want to know all about you. If you're a friend of my husband's I naturally—"

"I'm not," he cut in. "I'm his partner, not his friend. Grubstaking a guy doesn't mean you're his pal. We just got the same ideas, that's all."

"What ideas?"

"To get rich quick," he grinned. "That makes guys great partners."

"You share everything fifty-fifty?"

"More or less," he yawned.

"You take a nap," encouraged Tara.

He grunted and immediately closed his eyes. Tara, lying opposite him, studied his ugly, coarse-featured face. Then, her eyes fluttered and, without realizing it, her head fell forward and she was asleep.

She awoke with a start. Jake was wide awake, staring at her.

"What time is it?" gasped Tara.

He shrugged. "What's bothering you?" he asked. "You look as if you trod on a skunk."

"Nothing," Tara said. "I just woke with a jolt, that's all."

"You afraid of me?" he asked. He didn't seem drunk any longer. He spoke softly.

"Afraid? Of you? Of course not, I've told you before. How could I be afraid of my husband's partner?"

He said nothing.

"Maybe we ought to start off again. It's time to leave, isn't it?"

"Maybe," he said.

She waited for him to make the first move, because she didn't want him to see the little gun when she unwrapped the blanket.

187

"Stop jittering yourself," sneered Jake. "You just said there ain't nothing to be scared of."

He turned his back on her and put his head outside the tent. "Yeah," he said, "guess we might as well get going. Weather's cleared."

There had been no storm, not even a flurry of snow. Jake had been looking for an excuse to break the journey. Why had he not taken advantage of it? She felt almost lighthearted with relief as he gathered his various belongings.

When he wasn't looking she loosened the blanket and put the Derringer back in her pocket. She was still terribly tired. She had not had a restful sleep; it had been full of tensions and weird images. She felt unrefreshed, jumpy, her eyes hot and prickly. She yawned.

Jake looked at her. "We can stay here some more," he offered. "You can sleep plenty."

"Of course not," Tara said. "I want to get going."

"I'll hitch up the teams," he said, and went outside.

She felt better. She was excited. This was really the day. She was going to see Daniel again. After all these long months of looking, searching, asking, she was definitely going to be with him, at last. She went out of the tent to where Jake was loading the sleds.

"Jake," she asked, "How much farther?"

"Couple of hours," he answered. "Not much more."

"You mean it?"

"Sure," he said. "You're going to be on top of him in no time." He fastened a strap. "You'll be loving and kissing all you want soon."

She was too thrilled to resent his familiarity.

"Thank God," she muttered to herself.

She looked up at the blue sky. It was going to be a beautiful day.

Four hours later Tara saw, in the distance, what looked like a frozen lake, partly encircled by some haggard pine trees. Pitched by the edge of the solid expanse of water was a tent. It was a long way ahead, and from this distance it looked like a black dot, but there was no doubt about it; somebody was camped there.

Her excitement grew and she lashed away at the dogs, urging them to go faster.

"Is that it?" she yelled, as she drew level with Jake's sled.

Jake nodded.

Tara felt a sense of triumph, of thankfulness. She had found him. Here, miles from anywhere, somewhere in the Klondike, she had managed to find Daniel.

Her whip cracked furiously as she urged the dogs to pull faster and faster. She had overtaken Jake, and now she was forging ahead, her heart beating with joy.

"Come on, come *on*," Tara shouted at her dogs, all the time her eyes fixed on the tent. She wondered if Daniel had spotted the two sleds, if he was trying to make out who Jake's companion was. From so far away she couldn't see anybody, but perhaps he could see them.

As she drew nearer, she could see the snow heaped against one side of the tent, where winds and blizzards had drifted it. There was still no sign of life. She imagined Daniel might be in the tent, cooking himself a meal, maybe studying a map, maybe thinking of . . .

She brought her sled to a halt, a few yards from the tent. Without a thought for anything except that this was finally the moment she would see Daniel at last, she rushed forward, tumbling and sliding through the snow in her eagerness.

"Daniel! Daniel, I'm here!" she called out, her cheeks flushed with excitement, her eyes shining as she pulled aside the tent flap. The tent was empty.

For a moment she stood stunned. She could see enough to know that this was certainly somebody's quarters. Some clothes were lying about, there was a canvas sheet spread on the floor, there were cooking utensils, mining tools, a parka.

She stood puzzled, looking around her then, slowly, Tara turned and went outside. Jake's sled stood beside hers.

"Where is he?" demanded Tara. "Where's Daniel?"

"Around," he said.

"Where is he?" she shouted.

"This way," Jake said.

She followed him around to the back of the tent. Tara's troubled mind took in one frightening fact. There were no footprints. No one had walked around here for days.

"There he is," announced Jake and stepped aside so that she could see.

A few feet in front of her was a little mound. Stuck on the top of it were two pieces of wood, tied together into a cross.

Tara stood, staring with disbelief, the blood draining from her face. "No," she whispered, "no."

"That's him," Jake said. "Say howdy."

Her whole body felt numb. She was so shocked she was not even crying. She just gazed at the grave, shaking her head.

This could not be. She would not accept it. Daniel buried here in the frozen ground, alone, abandoned? No, never.

"That's how I got his watch, see," Jake said. "He never was a willing giver."

His voice brought her back to reality. She turned and looked at him, her face a mask of horror.

"That's not Daniel," she choked. "I don't know what your game is, but that's not my husband."

He grinned. "Please yourself. But I guess you're a widow woman now."

"You're lying," she screamed.

"Don't worry, sweetheart," he smiled, "you ain't going to be lonesome."

He reached out and grabbed her.

"No!" she shrieked, clawing at his face. He swung a fist and, suddenly, the whole world turned upside down, stars flashed in her head, the earth spun, she could feel herself falling, then, for a moment, everything went black.

When she came around a few seconds later, she was on the ground, his full weight on top of her. He was tearing at her clothes, ripping them, groping between her legs, forcing his hand down the front of her trousers, thrusting deeper.

"Take your hands off me," Tara sobbed, but no sound came from her throat. Her voice was paralyzed. She tried again, and it emerged as a frantic croak, "Leave me alone."

"Says who? I want you," he panted, bringing his mouth down on hers, his tongue stabbing at her closed lips like a greedy serpent. His right hand cupped her uncovered breast and fondled her nipple. She tried to turn and twist to protect herself, but his body was full on her. His strength was enormous.

Tara lashed out, so he hit her again, splitting her lips. She could feel his hairy body on her exposed flesh, his growing pleasure as his hand traveled across her naked stomach. He was slobbering, saliva dripping from his mouth as he began unbuttoning himself, his sheer weight keeping her writhing body pinned to the thawing ground. With his other hand he took hold of her chin.

"Quit fighting, bitch!" he snarled, his eyes glittering. "I'm going to fuck you, then I'm going to kill you, just like I told Cad."

Her throat was filled with bile as he plunged his hand between her bared thighs, forcing her legs apart. Her arms thrashed at him but he ignored her feeble blows.

Jake was so preoccupied he didn't notice her pulling the gun from her pocket. She rammed the stocky muzzle into his left ear and, without hesitation, squeezed the trigger.

Jake went rigid, his eyes opening wide, as the fat, chunky missile embedded itself in his brain. Then his body went limp. Tara passed out.

It was only minutes later, but it might have been another day, another week, another month when her eyes fluttered open. Where his head lay felt hot and sticky.

"Oh God!" she screamed from under Jake. He was amazingly heavy and sprawled right across her, making it almost impossible for her to move. With all her strength, she pushed him over on his back. His sightless eyes stared up at the graying sky.

Tara gagged at the thought of what she done. She couldn't quite believe that Jake was dead. The only proof was the blood oozing in a slow but steady stream from his ear.

She stared down at him. She didn't want to cry, but tears rolled down her cheeks. She sat sobbing like a child, the salt tears stinging as they flowed into her cut lips.

She was alone, with a dozen dogs, a dead man, and a grave for company. She did not know where she was; she had no idea in what direction they had traveled. The harnessed dogs were sitting quietly, momentarily silent; the tent billowed soundlessly in a cold wind whispering across the snow.

There was the grave, the anonymous lonely mound with the primitive cross. It was not Daniel's grave, a voice in her head insisted. She could face anything but that, because if it was Daniel . . .

Like a sleepwalker, she got slowly to her feet. This could not be the end, she thought. This could not be all that was left of Daniel.

"Daniel," she cried.

All remained silent.

"Daniel!" she screamed again.

She had to know who was in the grave. She had to know or she would go crazy. She grabbed a pickaxe from the tent, her mind so demented she was not even aware of its weight. She ran to the grave and with the strength of a lunatic started hacking away. She kept at it, a woman possessed, panting, crying, moaning.

She didn't even notice how the wind began to blow, with icy blasts sweeping across the tent, the corpse, and the woman madly hacking away at the rock-hard soil.

The frozen outer layer began to crack. Now she could see the outline of a body. she fell to her knees, and with her bare hands she started clawing away at the last blanket of frozen earth. She could recognize the chest of a man, the shoulders.

Desperately she began to remove the earth that covered the dead man's head. Her hands were bleeding, scratched, torn, her nails were broken, but she didn't know or care. She had to see his face. She was

191

almost hysterical, mouthing prayers, pleas, as she brushed away the last veil of soil.

She was looking on the hard-set face of a middle-aged man. His eyes were frozen shut, as if he were sleeping—sleeping with a hole through his heart. He had been murdered.

But he was not Daniel Kane.

"Aaaah!" she screamed, jumping to her feet, her eyes wild.

"He's not dead! He's not dead!" she yelled to the vast emptiness surrounding her.

"He lied! He lied!" she shrieked, laughing hysterically.

She stood half nude in the raging wind, snow, swirling around her, buffeted by a freezing gale, and she laughed.

It was the laughter of relief, of happiness, of hysteria.

Gradually her elation receded, and she became aware of the howling wind, the swirling snow, the frenzied yapping of the dogs. Her teeth began to chatter. She was freezing cold. She was half naked, her coat, shirt, and underclothes torn. She recalled what the Mounties had told her: once you start freezing, you're finished and, surrounded by all this death, knowing Daniel was still alive, she was filled with a tremendous desire to survive.

For the next few minutes she rushed around, getting together some wood, lighting the stove in the deserted tent, preparing coffee to warm herself. Her hands were shaking and caked with dried blood as she clasped the mug, enjoying the warmth of the liquid scalding the back of her throat. As she drank she looked around the tent.

There were some stores, canned food, sugar, and a few tools. A spade, some pans for washing gold dust, and clothes. A pair of snowshoes, a parka. She picked up a soiled woolen shirt. It was not large enough to belong to Jake, and it certainly was not Daniel's size. She took off her torn jacket and shirt and put it on. The material felt stiff, and it swamped her but she didn't care. Then she went through the pockets of the parka, but all she found was some plug tobacco and a penknife, nothing to identify the unknown grave-dweller. She put the parka on; it was in better condition than her own but far too large. Among the mining tools she found a piece of rope, double-wrapped the coat's excess, and knotted the rope around her waist.

She found nothing of Daniel's. There was no reason to think he had ever been here.

There was a tin deed box in the corner of the tent. It was locked. She got hold of a knife and started prising at the hinge. The screws were rusty and gave without too much trouble.

Tara opened the lid. There were five dollars, a receipted bill for thirty dollars' worth of groceries, a postcard of New Orleans with nothing written on it, a rabbit's paw, a little necklace with an Indian pendant. None of it meant anything to her. There were also several letters, stained, crumpled, dirty, addressed to names and places she had never even heard of. She threw them aside impatiently. Then she spotted handwriting she recognized. She couldn't believe it. She picked it up.

"Mrs. Tara Kane, 110 Fulton Street, San Francisco, Cal., USA," read Daniel's script.

Her mind reeling, she tore open the sealed envelope. At first she couldn't even focus on Daniel's words, she was shaking so much. Then she took several deep breaths, and spread the creased pages out on the floor so that her trembling hands wouldn't prevent her reading it.

"My own most dearest Tara," began Daniel's letter. "I do not know when you will receive this or, indeed, whether it will ever reach you. I have lost all track of time. I do not even know what the date is. I almost hope, in a perverse sort of way, that you will never read these words. Yet I must write to you, because I need you so terribly and I miss you more than words can describe.

"Things have not gone well so far and the only thing that keeps me going is the thought of you and our daughter.

"Tara, you know I have always loved you, but it was not until our separation that I realized how much you mean to me, my darling. Perhaps the circumstances in which I now find myself are the revenge of jealous gods who envy my happiness. I love you Tara. I love you as no man has ever loved a woman.

"This is a dismal hole and I am not at all sure I am on the right trail. Supplies are running low and I have developed an irksome cough. There is nothing for you to worry about. It is just an added aggravation.

"The worst thing is the dreadful isolation. I have not seen a human face for days, and at times I have a nightmare that I will forget how to talk. I never dreamed it would be like this. Perhaps I have gone wrong somewhere. I ran into some trouble and that didn't help. I've had to sell a few belongings to keep going.

"Of course I know that we will laugh at these ridiculous things one day. I so look forward to us all being together, to having our little daughter on my knee and telling her all about my travels in the Yukon.

"How is my precious Gabie? If only you could write back to me and tell me. This is hell."

Uneasiness pervaded Tara. There was something odd about the

letter. It began to ramble, almost as if it were written by a feverish man, no longer able to think coherently.

"Take no notice. We shall all be rich. One way or another. Isn't it insane how useless gold is, though? You cannot eat it. You cannot smoke it. Out here it doesn't even keep you warm. What good is it? Why, why do we worship it? Damn it. I've decided the streets of hell must be paved with it.

"One thing, though, I know now. You are the most wonderful woman in the world. I always thought you were the loveliest, but now I also know you are the most understanding, most wonderful, most desirable woman a man can find on earth.

"I will come back to you, Tara. In this world, or another. We will never be parted, you and I.

"This is such an awful place, darling, and you must excuse my writing but it is very cold and I haven't eaten much. Only one thing keeps me going, the knowledge that you are there, waiting for me.

"I love you and cherish you, my own Tara. I always have and I always will. Whatever happens, never forget me, my dearest. My love for you and our most darling daughter will never die."

Her eyes were brimming with tears as she finished reading the letter. There was no date and it was not signed, but it didn't matter. It was from him.

"Oh Dan," she sobbed, "Dan."

Through her tears she tried to reason it out: The letter looked old, months old maybe. Perhaps he wrote it ages ago when things were going badly. But how had it got here? Had he given it to the man in the grave to mail?

And what about Jake Gore? There was no mention of him or having teamed up with a partner. Or did his line "I ran into some trouble and that didn't help" say it all?

So many questions remained unanswered. How had Jake Gore got hold of Daniel's watch? Had he bought it from him or stolen it? And how did Cad Wilson fit in? Tara vaguely recalled something Jake had said before she killed him. She racked her brains to remember exactly. Then it came back to her: his words about killing her as he had told Cad he would. Could it be Cad was so insanely jealous of her that she had hired Jake Gore to lure her out here to kill her? She could hear the dogs whimpering, snarling, yapping like lost, forsaken creatures. They had not been fed for hours.

There was some dried moose meat packed among her things, but she was frightened. A terrible gale had started up, and the sound of the wind, the howling of the dogs, and the two dead bodies filled her with foreboding. She couldn't face going out of the tent, but she knew she had to feed the dogs. Without them she would never get back to civilization.

She pocketed Daniel's letter and, summoning all her courage, battled her way out to the sled and unwrapped the meat.

She knew she had to unharness the dogs before she fed them, but the noise they were making sent shivers down her spine. She could cope with her own team, they had become used to her, but Jake's malamutes were an unknown quantity. She didn't trust them; they seemed sullen, treacherous. They didn't bark but raised their heads and yowled terrifyingly.

She picked up her whip and went over to them. As she approached they growled at her and reared up, so she cracked the whip.

"Down!" she cried as one beast snapped at her ankles. She had to show them who was in command; so she hit it on the nose with the stock of her whip. It yelped, but that seemed to have a chastening effect on the others. Quickly she unwrapped the meat and then unharnessed them. She had forgotten the golden rule: each dog had to be fed individually and unharnessed one at a time to eat.

As she returned to her own sled, where the tethered dogs were getting restless, Jake's team, free from their traces, streaked across the snow like a pack of wolves.

"Come back!" Tara yelled, but they took no notice. Then she saw what had caused the stampede. The dogs were tearing, biting, ripping Jake's body, gorging themselves on the corpse. There was blood everywhere. One animal stood a little to one side, gulping down mouthfuls of what looked like a hand, eyes wary in case any of the others should spot him. Tara's own team responded by yapping and snapping with excitement, straining at their harnesses in their eagerness to join in.

For Tara it had become a hideous nightmare. Her stomach turned at the sight of this necrophageous banquet, but fear of what this maddened horde might do next overwhelmed her disgust. Where would they look for their next victim?

She knew she had little time. If the malamutes turned on her, she was finished. She ran over to Jake's sled and, with shaking hands, untied his rifle from the handlebars.

It was heavy, and she had difficulty in holding it straight. She pushed back the safety catch and, aiming as best she could, pulled the trigger. She heard the shot, but not even the sound of it stopped the pack feasting itself on the carcass of the dead man. She did not appear to have hit anything.

Tara pulled the trigger again and again and again, shooting at the horror in front of her, trying to squint through the snow the icy wind hurled against her. She kept firing until the rifle clicked, its magazine empty. She had killed two of the dogs and wounded another in its hindquarters. It was dragging itself away from Jake's body, a gob of him still in its jaws. Then, like a grisly epilogue, two of the survivors, their jaws dripping gore, launched themselves at the crippled dog and sank their teeth into his throat, his body. The third watched for a moment and then flung himself into the melee.

"Oh my God," Tara sobbed as the frenzied animals fought each other, biting and tearing. The savagery of the dog fight in the cave was nothing compared to this battle. Here was a primitive lust to kill, not spurred on by sadistic bystanders, but fed on the oldest urge of all, survival.

It did not last long. The dogs lay strewn around the snow, dead or dying. The pack had destroyed itself. And Jake was no longer recognizable. He was a shapeless mass, limbs missing, flesh eaten clean off his bones, part of his skeleton showing, his eyes, his nose, his hands gone.

She dashed to her sled and, without a backward glance at the freezing carnage she was fleeing from, cracked her whip and urged the team ahead. They pulled the sled willingly. They were hungry, very hungry, and a ravenous dog made a willing worker.

The swirling snow made visibility bad, and she could not tell which direction she was going. Although she had no map she decided she was north. She had to get back to Dawson, which she reasoned must lie to the south. She rifled through her bag and took out the compass. If she followed the opposite direction to the tip of the needle, she would be going south. Eventually, she would reach Dawson. In her confused state, it made eminent sense. How ironical that Dawson, with all its ugly memories, should be her mecca!

She pulled her woolen scarf tighter around her head, wrapping it around her nose and cut mouth to keep out the biting cold. From her bag, she took out her snow goggles and put them over her eyes. She continued traveling through the night, occasionally consulting the compass as if it could give her all the answers. Although the steady, unmovable needle was a great comfort, it was a pitiful aid to navigation.

Like a phantom team the dogs pulled through the darkness. She had become a sleepwalker, relying on the huskies to keep traveling along the right track.

In her delirious condition she thought at times that she was lying safely in bed and all this was a dream. Then she would realize where she was as she scanned the unending whiteness with bloodshot eyes. Nothing seemed to change. Once her tortured mind told her that she had been this way before. She recognized the terrain. She had been traveling around and around in a circle. She called out, and the dogs came to a halt. Maybe she was retracing her route, and she would come across the tent again and those ghastly remains.

Tara screamed with such terror that one or two of the dogs turned their heads and stared at her, their eyes puzzled.

"Somebody please help me! Save me!" she yelled dementedly to the empty landscape. "I don't want to die. Help me! Please help me!" she cried, her hand outstretched as if she were pleading with a group of people.

Then she saw it.

She watched, awestruck, as an indescribable yellow light sprang from the whiteness of the snow to the heavens above. Reality had ceased. An unearthly golden glow was spreading across the sky, streamers of brilliant, dazzling colors advancing and dancing along the horizon, bathing the sky in a wondrous, multicolored hue, a divine firework display.

The lights, vivid reds and yellows and blues, imbued the whole firmament and spread before Tara's hypnotized eyes. After the blackness, the grays, the whites, the monotones, this darting stream of color was like the promise of another land. Tara had never seen, but she had heard of, the northern lights. Standing there, a lone human figure witnessing the sky on fire, she was enraptured by its beauty and hidden meaning. It was the omen that made all the difference.

"Thank God," Tara sobbed, overwhelmed by emotion. "Oh, thank God."

Those glorious shining rays, reflecting all the brightness of all the hopes of the Yukon, more dazzling than all the gold in the Klondike, gave her faith as nothing else could have. It was a sign from heaven. There was hope.

"Yes," croaked Tara. "Of course."

She turned her back on the phenomenon and faced the direction the miracle had now confirmed was south. Although she was tired, consumed by fatigue, she gritted her teeth and thrust the sled forward, determined to make it to Dawson.

As the sled gathered momentum, prisms of light were caught and reflected by the freezing snow, making her think she was slowly traveling around the crescent of a rainbow. And in her maddened mind she thought that when she reached the apex she would be home.

CHAPTER EIGHTEEN

The woman who staggered, robotlike, into Dawson three days later had no memory of her long, delirious trek. Her limbs numb, her body frozen, she was not even aware that she had arrived at her journey's end. She stumbled down the main street unconscious of the traffic, the people, the buildings, driven by the inner compulsion that had kept her traveling through the snowy wastes. Her legs obeyed her; the dogs obeyed her; but her mind was a blank. She was ignored in her turn. Passersby didn't give her a second look, not even recognizing the frost-covered, weather-beaten, glassy-eyed soul as a woman.

She stopped. Slowly some realization began to grow. She was holding onto a hitching post, staring blankly at a wooden facade.

"The Monte Carlo," she muttered to herself.

Dizzily, her head pounding, she leaned against the post trying to recall the significance of the name. Then it dawned on her. She had reached Dawson. Before her was the most important building in the town—the place where Cad Wilson worked—Cad Wilson, the only woman who could tell Tara the truth and, perhaps, the only one who could restore her reason.

She slowly mounted the wooden steps, pushing open the swing doors of the saloon.

At eleven o'clock in the morning, the Monte Carlo looked sordid, the harsh lights illuminating the shabbiness of the decor and furniture, the filth of the floor. at the end of the room bored bartenders were cleaning the counter, washing glasses, and restocking empty shelves. The air was stale.

Tara walked with unseeing eyes toward a man in shirtsleeves behind the bar.

"Where is she?" she croaked.

The man raised his eyebrows. Tara looked like no woman he had ever seen. Her clothes were torn and stained, her hands caked with dried blood, her face weather-beaten, her lips covered with scabs.

"Cad Wilson," Tara said woozily.

He hesitated, then he saw the look in her eyes.

"Miss Wilson's upstairs, I think."

Clutching the edge of the counter for support, she made her way to the staircase and slowly climbed the stairs. Below, the man stood watching her, uncertain.

She was in a corridor, doors flanking both sides. Blindly she opened the first door. A couple were in bed, the man fast asleep, snoring. The woman sat up with a shock, trying to cover her nakedness, as Tara looked around with vacant eyes.

"What the hell," screeched the woman at Tara's departing back.

Tara made her way down the length of the corridor, looking around each room in turn, leaving angry whores in her wake and a percussive coda of slamming doors. Unaware of the havoc she was causing, only knowing that what she saw was not what she was looking for, she reached the last door. Inside was a large and ornately decorated boudoir. A crystal chandelier hung from the friezed ceiling, a large mirror dominated one wall, and tasseled curtains bordered French windows.

Tara floated across a sea of thick carpet toward a chaise longue on which Cad Wilson reclined, dressed in a multicolored kimono which had fallen apart, to reveal her long legs clad in shimmering black silk stockings. Cad stood up. From miles away Tara heard her gasp, "You!"

Then the whole ghastly nightmare came back to her.

"He didn't kill me," Tara said.

Cad Wilson was not one to lose her composure for very long.

"I don't know what you're talking about," she retorted, her lips curling into a disdainful smile. "You smell, honey. Why don't you get yourself a bath?"

She made to turn away but Tara stepped closer.

"What happened to my husband?" she asked in a low voice.

"Don't tell me you didn't find him, Mrs. Kane," Cad laughed mockingly.

Tara slapped Cad across the face. The hate-filled blow had amazing strength, and it rocked Cad. She stepped back, holding her cheek. For the first time apprehension showed on her face. This haggard, hollow-eyed, feverish apparition frightened her.

"How did you get his watch?" demanded Tara.

"I told you," shouted Cad.

Tara hit her again, and Cad fell back clumsily onto the sofa, staring up at Tara.

"You knew Daniel wasn't there. You used his watch to get me out of the way," screamed Tara. "You hired Jake Gore to kill me, didn't you? Out there, in the wild, where nobody would know? You'd do anything, wouldn't you, to be rid of me?"

"You need a doctor, Mrs. Kane," blustered Cad. "You're not a well woman."

"Only it didn't quite work out the way you planned it," Tara went on, undeterred. "Because Jake Gore is dead."

Cad looked at her, fear growing.

199

"I killed him!" Tara shrieked. "Now I only want to know one thing."

"You're crazy!" whispered Cad, standing up. "You get out of here and leave me alone."

"Just tell me where he is! Where's my husband? Where is he? Where is he?" She grabbed Cad by the shoulders and shook her like a rag doll."Where is he?" she sobbed, gradually releasing her grip. Cad sank to the floor.

"What's happened to my husband?" Tara begged, tears streaming down her face.

"I don't know," gasped Cad. "I don't think he's dead," she added hastily, seeing Tara's look.

Tara straightened up, and Cad jumped to her feet.

"You're not going to get away with this, Mrs.Kane."

Cad went to the door. "Get out before I have you thrown out."

Tara turned and looked at Cad standing beside the open door. Beyond her was a crowd of inquisitive faces, pulsating forward and backward in Tara's mind. She started toward the gaggle of whores, her head ringing, the whole room spinning one way then another.

The corridor seemed like a snow tunnel, gently descending a red-and-white slope into a large pool of oblivion. At the top of the stairs she fainted, falling down the entire flight and collapsing in a heap on the saloon floor.

She never heard the uproar. Everyone in the Monte Carlo had heard the argument. Mort had recognized Tara when she had first walked in and had hot-footed his way over to the Regina Cafe to tell Smith of her return and the state she was in. They had entered the saloon in time to see Tara crash down the stairs.

Smith dashed to where she lay and carefully turned her over, the shock at her appearance showing on his face.

"What happened?" he demanded, still kneeling beside Tara.

Cad rushed forward. "Oh, Jeff," she bleated. "I'm so glad you're here. The poor woman came to my room ranting and raving, and when I told her she was a sick woman and needed a doctor, she went quite wild, ran out of my room, and you saw the rest. I've no idea how she got here or where she's come from."

Cad Wilson was no mean actress, and the rest of the staff knew better than to contradict her story.

"Mort!" shouted Smith, getting up. "Get some blankets. I'm taking Mrs.Kane home."

Cad fussed over Tara's inert body, stroking her forehead and clucking like a concerned mother hen. Smith got some brandy and tried to get Tara to take a sip, but it was useless. She was in a coma. Gently the two men swathed the unconscious Tara. Then, very carefully, Smith picked her up.

"I'll talk to you later, Cad," was all he said, as he started toward the saloon doors.

But she ran ahead of him, holding open the door. "I hope she'll be all right," she simpered anxiously as Smith carried Tara through.

"She'd better be." Smith's voice was hard.

The sight of Jefferson Smith walking down Front Street carrying the seemingly lifeless body of a woman wreathed in blankets was unusual even in Dawson. He ignored the gaping passersby, looking down at her emaciated, scabby face, the taut skin stretched tightly over her cheekbones, the closed eyes in dark, hollow sockets. She was light in his arms, and he could feel her bones pressing against his body, despite the blankets. Her breathing was labored and beads of perspiration stood out on her forehead.

Smith mounted the steps and knocked on Mrs. Miles's front door. Her first reaction when she opened the door to him was to slam it in his face. Then she saw Tara limp in his arms.

"Good God," she gasped.

"Mrs. Kane has collapsed," Smith said quietly. "She needs your help."

"She doesn't live here any more," began Mrs. Miles half-heartedly.

"She's very ill, Mrs. Miles. She needs you desperately."

Mrs. Miles grunted and then stood aside to let him enter. Her mouth was grimly set. Even in this situation, she found it hard to let Smith cross her threshold.

"This way," she said gruffly. They mounted the stairs in silence, Mrs. Miles leading the way to Tara's room. She stood hovering while Smith gently laid Tara on the bed.

"Now, please leave my house. I don't want to see you here again."

"Of course," he agreed amiably. In the hallway he paused. "Before I go, ma'am, I want to thank you for agreeing to nurse Mrs. Kane and to assure you that anything you may require will be at your disposal. I will arrange for the doctor to stop by, and I'll be much obliged if you would keep me posted as to her day-to-day state."

"You can keep your thanks," said Mrs. Miles, puffing herself up. "Further, let me make myself quite plain, Mr. Smith. I don't want you around. If I'd been asked to look after Mrs. Kane as a favor to you, I would have refused. I know what kind of man you are; I know that Tara shares my opinion of you. It's for that reason that I'll take her back under my roof."

"Nevertheless, ma'am," Smith said charmingly, "I would be much obliged if you would keep me advised as to her progress, and I am most appreciative of everything you will be doing."

He raised his hat and bowed. "Remember, ma'am, if I can be of—" But the door slammed on him before he had time to finish the sentence.

After the doctor had examined the unconscious Tara, his face was grave. She was suffering from exposure. She had bronchitis, it could be turning into pneumonia, and she was half starved.

Day and night Mrs. Miles nursed Tara like her own daughter. She made sure her room was well heated, bathed her like a child, attended her every need. She sat hour after hour by her bedside, watching her toss and turn, delirious with fever, fits of coughing racking her thin, wasted body.

But Tara's physical condition was not the only cause of Mrs. Miles's anxiety. She could cope with bodily ailments, but something had happened to Tara over and above the physical ordeal she had endured, of that Mrs. Miles was certain. She was tormented, ranting unintelligibly, as if still trying to escape from some ghastly experience.

One night, toward dawn, Tara grew quieter and slept peacefully, her breathing increasingly regular. It seemed to Mrs. Miles that the fever was abating. Much relieved, she went to her own room and lay on the bed. She was exhausted and soon dozed off.

The scream that woke her came from Tara's room.

She rushed across and found her sitting up, wide-eyed, her hand to her mouth.

"What is it?" she asked anxiously. "What's the matter?"

Tara looked at her vacantly and sank back onto the pillow, turning her head to and fro.

"Don't!" she cried out, fending off some phantom attacker. "Don't! Leave me alone!"

"It's all right," soothed Mrs. Miles. "There's nobody here but me."

"Jake! No!" screamed Tara, grabbing, unseeing, for her.

Mrs. Miles placed a cold compress on the burning forehead. Tara was very agitated, groping around as if she were searching for something. "The gun," she whimpered. "The gun." Then she sat up, her eyes staring sightlessly, and let out a blood-curdling scream. The lodgers came rushing into the room, Doc Robbins leading.

"What's happened?" he panted, his tufts of hair standing on end.

The others crowded around, gaping.

"It's all right," Mrs. Miles whispered, ushering them all out. "The fever's broken. I think she'll be all right now."

When she returned to the room Tara was asleep. Mrs. Miles stayed with her for the rest of the night, wondering who Jake was and why Tara had wanted a gun.

The following morning Tara regained consciousness. She couldn't believe where she was, had no recollection of getting back. Mrs. Miles told her that she had collapsed in town and had been carried back to her house. She made no mention of Soapy Smith.

Tara was very weak; even holding a cup was an effort. She had hardly any appetite, apathetically picking at the food that had been so painstakingly prepared. Left alone, she shut her eyes, hoping that sleep would come, but each time she dozed weird, frenzied images haunted her dreams.

Time moved excruciatingly slowly; what seemed an eternity turned out to be merely an hour or two. She gazed into space much of the time, just thinking of Daniel. For the umpteenth time she reread Daniel's letter, trying to spot a new meaning between those desperate lines, wondering yet again where he had written it, who he had given it to, where he had gone after sealing it.

She could not stand up without Mrs. Miles's support, and when she got back in her bed, having left it only to sit on a chair while Mrs. Miles changed the linen, she was exhausted.

Tara wanted to tell Linda Miles what had happened, but she could not face the thought of reliving those terrible days, having to admit that she had murdered. Yet she knew that once she confided in the kindly woman some of her own guilt might be assuaged.

Monotonous day followed monotonous day, and still she said nothing. One day Mrs. Miles popped her head around the door.

"There's someone to see you, dear," she announced benignly, her tone indicating that she approved of the visitor. "He'll cheer you up. Come in, Reverend."

"Good day to you, Sister Tara," beamed the Reverend Bowers. Soapy Smith's henchman was perfect in word and manner, even sporting a clerical collar in place of the string tie he affected in Skagway. He was wearing his funereal black and carrying a big Bible. "I trust I find you on the road to recovery," he continued, sitting down on Tara's bed.

Mrs. Miles nodded, full of approbation.

"I'll leave you with the Reverend, my dear." She excused herself, gracing Bowers with a smile. "It's good of you to find the time to visit, Reverend." She shut the door.

"This will console you on your sickbed, Sister Tara." Bowers held out the huge Bible.

Tara looked blankly at it, then at him. She was befuddled, her head throbbed, and she had difficulty in concentrating.

"Don't rouse yourself, Sister Tara, don't rouse yourself," soothed Bowers, leaning forward confidingly. "Tell me, how do you feel?"

Her lips moved, but she turned her head away. She didn't feel like talking.

"You look fine, kid," smiled Bowers encouragingly, his role lapsing. "Couple of days you'll be your old self, eh? The boss will be mighty pleased to hear it."

Her eyes flickered. The boss?

"He wants to make sure you've got everything you want. The old dragon downstairs ain't no problem, don't you fret about that."

He picked up the coffee mug beside her bed. "Maybe a few bottles of bubbly to warm your insides?" He put the mug down again. "Best medicine in the world, fizz." Tara stared at him.

Bowers got to his feet. "Guess I'll let you have some shut-eye. Get your strength back. The boss wants you in good shape." He smiled at her benevolently, but she did not move.

At the door he turned. "Now make sure you read the good book, Sister Tara. It refreshes the spirit and cleanses the soul."

She heard him going down the stairs and saying to Mrs. Miles, "You are doing the Lord's work, ma'am, succoring that poor woman. Charity, it is written . . ." But the rest of it was lost.

Although she had not said a word, the visit had exhausted her. She sighed, then closed her eyes, trying to work out how Soapy Smith had known she was ill and why he had sent Bowers to visit her.

A couple of days later the doctor announced that Tara could go downstairs for the first time. Mrs. Miles opened the sacred parlor and lit a huge fire. Wrapped up warmly, Tara took her first few shaky steps, managing to walk without support. She sat in front of the fireplace staring at the flames' changing patterns, enjoying the sound of the logs spitting and crackling.

There Tara spent the next few days, her mind becoming clearer and her body stronger. Slowly her eyes grew brighter, the scabs cleared from her lips, and her dry skin began to glow once more.

Her gradual improvement was partially due to her decision that the nightmare events at the grave belonged to another world. As her health returned, so the terrible memories receded. Perhaps one day she would even forget what now still occasionally haunted her sleep.

She spent her time thinking out the best way to continue her quest. Where would she go from here? Although the trail might appear to have run dry she knew he was somewhere, she was certain he was not dead, and was equally certain she was getting closer to him.

Her thoughts were interrupted by a peremptory knock on the front door. Mrs. Miles was out shopping, having left firm instructions that Tara should stay in the fireside armchair. The knocking sounded again, hammering urgently, insistently. Her legs still felt shaky as she tentatively opened the front door.

"Hello, Tara," said Campbell. He was in uniform, and with him was another Mountie.

"Andrew." Tara held out her hand. It was a pleasant surprise to see him. "How have you been?"

Campbell cleared his throat. He seemed ill at ease. "May we come in?" he asked, a little awkwardly.

"Of course." She led the way into the parlor and indicated the sofa. "It's nice of you to come by," she said, sinking into the armchair and pulling the rug over her knees.

The two Mounties sat down ramrod straight. They looked stiff, uncomfortable. "This is Constable McIver," Campbell began, peering at Tara's pale face, the shadows that lingered under her eyes. He stopped. McIver sat observing her. Their authoritative manner made Tara nervous. Her heart started thumping. Perhaps they had called with bad news about Daniel.

"It's not my husband?"

"No," said Campbell. "This is official business, Tara." His grave face stared across at her. "Inspector Constantine is in Fortymile, and so I have to ask you some questions."

"What about?"

"An allegation has been made." He paused. "Constable McIver and I are following up a report that a man was murdered in Tagish territory."

Campbell waited for her to say something, then pulled out a leather-covered notebook.

"You've been out in the bush," he said, not looking at her. "Up north. In Tagish territory."

She nodded, her face ashen.

"Traveling on your own?"

"Some of the time," she replied in a low voice.

"Is there anything *you* want to tell me?" he asked.

"About what?" she mumbled, clenching her hands to stop them shaking.

"The allegation is that . . ." Campbell hesitated. "Tara, did you kill a man?"

"Kill a man," she repeated dully.

The nightmare turned into reality again. The room spun. "Oh my God," she whispered.

Campbell shifted uneasily. "I'm sorry I have to ask you these questions. I know you've been ill."

"Would you like to make a statement, Mrs. Kane?" suggested McIver.

"Yes," she croaked. "Yes. I killed a man."

"Jake Gore?" prompted Campbell.

"He—" She couldn't go on. She was trembling uncontrollably. "I didn't want to . . . He tried to . . . He made me . . ."

"He was a bad man," said Campbell, trying to be helpful. "A real bad 'un. Was it self-defense?"

"What exactly happened, Mrs. Kane?" asked McIver.

"He took me to a camp where he said I'd find Daniel, and then he . . . He got hold of me . . . but I killed him," she sobbed, burying her face in her hands.

"Tara, there's trouble," said Campbell. "You've got to help us get this cleared up."

No one heard Mrs. Miles come in. She stood in the doorway of the parlor, her coat and hat spattered with snowflakes, frowning at the distraught Tara and the two Mounties.

"What's going on?" she demanded.

"Could you leave us alone please, Linda?" asked Campbell.

"Certainly not," replied Mrs. Miles. "Not until you tell me what this is all about."

Tara looked up, her strained white face streaked with tears. "I'm sorry," she whispered. "I . . . I . . ." But her voice petered out.

Mrs. Miles glared at Campbell. "Well?" she declared.

"We're investigating a killing."

"So?"

"Linda, there's an allegation against Tara that she shot a man in the bush. There's a man in town by the name of Arne Gore who says that Tara killed his brother Jake."

"I don't believe you," exploded Mrs. Miles. "Where's Inspector Constantine?"

"He's away, that's why we've got to follow this up," said Campbell. "Gore's on the warpath. He's threatened to get the whole of Dawson on his side if we don't do our duty as law officers. You know the trouble there's been already. I got no choice."

"Was it self-defense, Mrs. Kane?" put in McIver.

"Yes," she murmured. "Yes."

"Go on," Campbell said.

Tara wavered.

"Did he try to assault you?"

She nodded.

"I've got to have this clear, Tara. Was he going to kill you?"

"Yes," she screamed, the tears pouring down her face. "Yes!"

"Oh, my dear," said Mrs. Miles, putting her arm around Tara's shoulders. "Why didn't you tell me? Oh you poor, poor thing."

"You said it was self-defense?" repeated McIver. "You were alone in the bush with Jake Gore, he tried to kill you, but you shot him dead in self-defense?"

"Yes, I shot him," she agreed, her face expressionless.

"According to Arne Gore," said Campbell, "you murdered his brother Jake, and then robbed him. . . ."

"No!" Tara cried. "That's not true. He . . ." She could not bring herself to say any more. Jake Gore's disfigured visage was imprinted on her mind. Would she ever be able to exorcize that awful memory of his eyes, the blood, the dogs?

"We got no evidence of murder," Campbell said. "Only what Arne Gore says. We'll send a patrol out there to see what we can find. As soon as we've got men available. In the meantime, you'll have to make a formal statement, Tara."

"You can't believe that man's story," Mrs. Miles protested. "You're mad to even think he could be telling the truth."

"Linda, we know what the Gore brothers are. Jake should have hanged five times over, and Arne's no better. But he's going round town telling his story to anyone who'll listen, whipping up feeling against her, saying we won't do anything because she's a woman." He paused for a moment. "I'm not going to put her in jail," he added, "but she mustn't leave Dawson."

"How can she leave, the state she's in?" cut in Mrs. Miles.

"Linda, please try to understand that I can't afford trouble. There's only us two at the moment, everyone else is out on the trail. Until Inspector Constantine can take over I've got to do it by the book. Otherwise . . ."

"The Citizens' Committee or the Miners' Court might take the law into their own hands," McIver said.

"You look after her," said Campbell, going to the door. "Bring her over to the post as soon as she's fit, and I'll take a deposition."

After they had left, Mrs. Miles led Tara upstairs and helped her into bed. She lay there silent, staring at the ceiling. Mrs. Miles sat beside her and took her hands.

207

"Why don't you tell me about it?" she said very softly. "Maybe it will make it a little easier."

Tara looked at her, and then, her voice choked with emotion, her green eyes pools of sadness, told Mrs. Miles the whole story.

Campbell had not been exaggerating when he said that Gore was stirring up bad feeling in Dawson. The next night, men carrying flaming torches gathered in front of the house, shaking their fists, yelling. Tara could not make out what it was they shouted, but it was an ugly sound.

Mrs. Miles came into the room. "Get away from that window," she ordered. "Don't let them see you." For the first time Tara could hear the words the mob were yelling:

"Tara Kane, we've come for you. Tara Kane! Tara Kane!"

"What do they want from me?" she whispered. "Why are they shouting for me?"

The mob pressed closer to the house. They were being waved on by a tall, lean man, his long hair tied back in a familiar fashion. His blazing brand illuminated sharp features, an ugly, snarling mouth. What she could see in the flickering light reminded Tara of the man she could never forget. Jake Gore.

"We're coming in to get you," the man yelled, and the crowd behind him roared.

Mrs. Miles rushed from the room, Tara following her. The lodgers had gathered in the hallway, taking it in turns to peer out at the street. They were all armed, and Mrs. Miles carried a shotgun.

"Go back to your bedroom and lock the door," she commanded. "Keep out of sight. Hurry, woman!" But Tara remained where she was on the staircase.

Fists hammered on the front door. To Tara it sounded like the knocking of an executioner.

"Open up," came a voice, "open up and hand over the Kane woman. No need for any trouble, Mrs. Miles. We only want her. Orders of the court."

"Go away, and leave us alone," Mrs. Miles shouted.

"We don't want no aggravation. We're only carrying out the committee's orders. We've come for her and we're coming in to get her if you don't open up."

A buzz ran around the lodgers.

"It's the Miners' Court," Lamore said.

Tara froze. This was the reckoning. As the Mounties had predicted,

208

the Miners' Court of Dawson had decided to settle the matter themselves.

Lamore's gaze rested on her.

"She's sick," Mrs. Miles told them through the door. "Leave this business to the Mounties."

The only reply she got was a furious pounding; then they heard a window smash upstairs. One of the Bartletts ran past Tara.

"The first man that tries to come in, we'll blow his head off," he yelled from the first-floor window.

The crowd continued shouting, their torches casting weird, eerie shadows through the windows. "Don't talk foolish," called one of the men at the door. "Just give her to us."

"What are we going to do?" asked Lamore. "They won't give up 'til they've got what they came for. They'll burn the house down."

"Linda! Open the door!" Tara said, hardly recognizing her own voice.

"No."

"Please. There's no other way," she insisted. "Put the gun away. I'd rather go out and face them."

"It's not safe. You won't stand a chance."

"What else is there to do?" Lamore asked. "They'll just drag her out if she doesn't."

Tara took her coat off the hook and wrapped it around her shoulders. She paused in front of Mrs. Miles. "I'm going out there, Linda. I'll be all right. They've a right to hear the truth, and I want to tell it to them."

Mrs. Miles, the gun still poised, her brow furrowed by worry, hesitated.

"It'll be OK, Mrs. Miles," Brock said very quietly. "I'll go along too and see justice is done. Best you open the door."

"I won't," she said fiercely. "They're after her blood, and nothing'll stop 'em proving what they want to prove."

"Linda, you know there's no alternative," Tara said, clasping her hands around the gun so that Mrs. Miles had to lower it. Reluctantly, she put the gun down and unlocked the door. As it opened, Tara saw a three-man deputation standing on the steps, and behind them a sea of torches. An awful roar went up as Tara stood revealed by the flickering light.

"There she is," yelled the tall man, holding his torch high and pointing at her. "There's the woman who killed my brother."

Tara drew back as the crowd erupted again, but one of the three men took her arm. "You'll get your say, Gore," he said. "Good and proper on the witness stand. Now shut up and let's go."

"Where are you taking me?" Tara asked, looking around for a familiar face, but the lodgers and Mrs. Miles were lost from sight, and she was alone.

"Courtroom," grunted the leader, escorting her down the steps.

The mob jostled Tara, but the three men pushed to the front, and she found herself marching with them. The whole town appeared to have turned out for this grim procession. She began to understand how Cal Mason must have felt. She prayed desperately that the Mounties would intervene as they had then.

The crowd had grown silent, and now the only sound was of hundreds of pairs of feet crunching on the frozen snow. In the glow of scores of torches she caught glimpses of hard faces, set grimly. Ahead, a sinister parade marshal, his blazing brand held aloft as he led the way, ran Jake Gore's brother. The men on either side of Tara said nothing. They marched on relentlessly, looking neither left nor right. She could almost smell the mob's eager anticipation. They knew what was coming, and they were not going to miss a moment.

Halfway down Front Street, Bowers appeared at her elbow. Under his black coat a gunbelt was visible. It was the first time Tara had seen him armed, but she was so tense it did not really sink in.

"Keep your powder dry," he whispered urgently.

"What are they going to do with me?"

"Keep cool," was all Bowers said. "The souls of the righteous are in the hands of the Lord, and there shall no tormentor touch them." He produced a bottle from his coat pocket and passed it to her. She hesitated, then grabbed it and took several gulps.

"Plead not guilty," said Bowers, taking back the bottle and drinking from it. "Whatever they say, you plead innocent, see?" He merged back into the throng marching behind them. The three vigilantes with her had taken no notice; they accepted Bowers.

Arne Gore was already standing on the steps of the Eldorado Saloon when the procession halted.

"Here she is," he yelled. "why don't we get a rope now?"

The crowd stood impatiently, Tara and the vigilantes facing Gore.

"What do you say?" yelled Gore at the crowd. "Let's save a lot of time."

The vigilante leader had his finger on the trigger of the rifle. "Stand aside, Gore," he commanded. "This is all going to be done according to miners' law."

Gore wavered for a moment, then grudgingly stood aside, and the throng rushed forward, propelling Tara and her escort through the swing doors in front of them.

Inside, the saloon had already been transformed into a crude courtroom. A table had been dragged in front of the bar; opposite it, on the empty dance floor, was another table; to its right, a lone chair. At the back the tables had been stacked and rows of chairs lined the walls. Now people stampeded wildly, pushing each other out of the way to get a good seat. On the steps outside, hundreds more were clamoring to get in.

The vigilantes marched Tara through the mob to the vacant chair.

"Sit there," ordered the leader.

Tara had the distinct impression that if an order were given for the mob to tear her apart, they would fulfill it cheerfully. Mrs. Miles had been right when she had said Tara would not stand a chance.

Cad Wilson swept in, dressed in a magnificent silk dress, her gold-nugget belt glinting, a fur cape draped casually around her shoulders. As she sat down, her eyes met Tara's.

Tara looked away, wanting not to give Cad Wilson the satisfaction of seeing how nervous she felt. She clenched her hands in her lap and willed herself to keep calm. She couldn't believe that this was actually happening to her, that she was on trial for her life in this parody of a court of law.

She looked around for a sign of hope, a friendly face, anyone who would make her feel less alone in this roomful of blood-lusting men. She spotted Bowers, his head bent down. Further along stood Lamore, Brock, and Doc Robbins deep in conversation. In the front row she saw for the first time the fat, eager face of the Grizzly Bear sitting beside Diamond-Tooth Gertie.

A white-haired man appeared at the table in front of the bar and held up his hands.

"Quiet," he yelled, "silence in court!"

The buzz of conversation ebbed. Through the swing doors a man was pushed in a wheelchair. Gold-rimmed glasses perched precariously on his nose; his skin was gray and pasty, his thin lips tinged with blue. His sharp ferret eyes darted around the assembly; the rest of his body was immobile, shrunken. A moth-eaten blanket covered his bony knees and he clutched a couple of books. The chair was being wheeled by a swarthy man in cavalry boots, two gun holsters slung from his hips.

Slowly, he maneuvered the wheelchair between the bar and table, then swung the chair around so that the withered man faced the crowd. His piercing eyes fixed unblinkingly on Tara while the white-haired man declaimed, "This court's now in session. The honorable Judge Elmer Rickless presiding."

Tara took in the judge's dirty shirt, food-stained coat, and frayed collar. His physical appearance made it clear that he was very sick as well as very old.

The man in cavalry boots opened a velvet carpetbag hanging from the handles of the invalid's chair and took out a battered opera hat. When the judge put it on his balding, greasy head it made him look even more of a grisly caricature. He searched around for something to bang the table with. The man in cavalry boots produced a hammer, and the judge rapped for order.

"Court's ready," he said in a reedy voice. "Where's the jury?"

Twelve men immediately stood up as one and trooped behind the bar. They all knew what to do. In unison they sat down on high stools, facing the saloon. They looked almost identical—tough, villainous, shifty. Tara shuddered at the thought of their being her jury.

The judge nodded at the white-haired man, who appeared to act as court usher. "Get them sworn," he snapped irritably.

The usher turned to the jury and said in one breath, "Do you swear to give a true verdict in this case without fear or favor so help you God."

"I do," they chorused.

"OK," said Judge Rickless. "Let's start. Who's prosecuting, and what's the charge?"

Arne Gore was on his feet. "I am, your honor, and the charge is murder," he said. Cad Wilson's vicious smile acted as a confirmation.

"OK," nodded the judge. He looked across the table at Tara. "She's the accused?"

So far Tara had been a detached spectator. Now she was struck by the reality of her plight. This was no charade. She was on trial for her life. "No. I didn't do it," she cried out.

Judge Rickless banged the hammer. "You can talk later," he said. He turned to the man in the cavalry boots. "Where's the refreshment that goes with this job, Billy? Or do you expect a judge to preside with a dry gizzard?"

Billy hastily put a bottle and a glass on the table. The judge poured himself a generous tot of whisky and drank it in one gulp. "OK, what's your name?" he wheezed.

"Kane. Mrs. Tara Kane."

"Married woman," muttered the judge. "No wedding ring, but we ain't interested in morals. This is a court of law." He took another drink. "Who's she killed, then?"

"My brother," spat Gore, glowering at Tara.

212

"OK." The judge took off his glasses and with a solid piece of cloth began cleaning them. "So who's the chief witness for the prosecution?"

"I am," said Gore.

"Figures," said the judge. He put his glasses on and then leaned back. His sick, white face was now slightly flushed; whether it was from the drink or the excitement of this travesty, Tara didn't know. "You got to plead. Did you do it?"

Tara stared at him blankly.

"Did you kill his brother?" asked the judge impatiently. "It's a simple question."

Tara shook her head.

"Are you pleading guilty or not guilty?" he snapped.

"Not guilty," replied Tara quietly.

He clicked his fingers, and Billy swung his chair around so that the judge faced the twelve jurors lounging behind the bar.

"You got the picture," he said. "The prosecutor says she killed his brother, but she says she didn't, so you gotta listen because one of them is lying, and then I'll ask you for your verdict. That's the law." He snapped his fingers again, and the chair was returned to its former position.

"OK," said the judge. "You got a defense counsel?" Nobody said a word.

"Maybe there's nothing to defend, Judge," interrupted Cad Wilson.

The men around her laughed. The judge frowned.

"I'll defend myself," Tara said. Although her voice was low she spoke with steadfast determination.

"You ain't qualified," rumbled the judge. "Everybody's got to be legally qualified."

"Like the prosecutor?" Tara asked.

Gore leaped to his feet. "That murdering bitch killed my brother," he screamed. "That's good enough."

"No yelling," complained the judge, hammering the table. "If you do that again I'll have you fined for contempt." He poured some whisky, leaned back in his chair, and drank it. "OK. You defend yourself. It's your neck." He burped. "So, Mr. Prosecutor. You tell us how she killed your brother."

"Sure I will, your honor," Gore said, stepping nearer Tara's chair. Instinctively, she recoiled. He was as repulsive as his brother. "She hired Jake up in Tagish country as a guide. Then out on the trail she shot him."

"For what reason?" asked the judge.

"To rob him," replied Gore. "She's a hustler who's down on her luck. Jake had sixty dollars and three ounces of gold dust. That's why she killed him," he lurched forward, toward Tara, "the murdering whore."

The judge hammered the table. "Did you witness the murder?" he asked.

"No, your honor."

"Then how do you know she did it?" queried the judge, peering hard at Gore. "You gotta prove he was murdered."

For a wild moment, Tara thought that was the end of it. His whole pack of lies would collapse. Arne Gore grinned.

"Miss Cad Wilson will testify to that."

The judge frowned and pulled over one of the books he had brought into court with him. Licking his fingers, he began thumbing the pages, moving his lips silently as he read. Then he looked up. "But there's someone who's seen the corpse, right? Law's kinda funny on that point. Without a body you don't have a murder. So who's seen the body?"

"I have," said Gore. Tara stared at him.

"Ah," said the judge. "Now we're getting places."

"I went looking for my brother," Gore said, his voice tense. "And I found what was left of him. She'd set the dogs on him." There was a rustle in the saloon, and Tara could feel a wave of hostility.

"Go on, son," said Judge Rickless. He was slumped in his wheelchair, his gold-rimmed glasses in imminent danger of sliding off his nose.

"She set the dogs on Jake," repeated Gore. "There wasn't much left of him, just enough for me to . . . to . . ."

Cad Wilson produced a lace handkerchief and sat dabbing her eyes ostentatiously. They were very dry.

"OK. That sounds good enough. Let's hear from your witness now."

Gore looked over to his table. "I call Miss Cad Wilson."

"Hold it a moment!" said the judge, turning to the usher. "Where's the goddamn witness stand? A courtroom's gotta have a witness stand."

"Judge, she's all right there," whined the white-haired man. He too had been drinking quietly in a corner, and he was swaying a little.

"You get me a witness stand, or I'll recess this hearing," yelled Judge Rickless. His bottle of whisky was two-thirds empty.

The usher dragged a wooden crate from behind the bar and put it in the middle of the floor. "How's that?" he beamed.

"Better," growled the judge. "Makes it decent and formal. OK, Miss Wilson. You take the stand."

"Thank you, Judge." As she stepped on the crate, she looked elegant, glamorous, and completely at ease.

"You swear to tell the truth, the whole truth, and nothing but the truth so help you God," intoned the usher.

"On a stack of Bibles, Judge," Cad demurely agreed, looking around the audience and smiling sweetly.

"Get on, get on," said the judge testily.

"You just tell 'em what you know," urged Gore.

"Couldn't I sit down first?" Cad asked. "It's kinda drafty up here. A lady like me ain't used to being on show like this." The spectators guffawed and clapped.

"You sit right here, Miss Wilson," said Billy, getting up and placing his chair next to the crate.

"May I, Judge?" inquired Cad coyly.

From behind his bottle Judge Rickless grunted, and Cad sat down, managing to display her silk-stockinged legs to everyone in the saloon. "Well, Judge," she began in a low voice. "It's kind of a long story, and I don't know where to begin."

"You tell the jury from the start," said the judge, his speech increasingly slurred. "You're here as a witness to the corpus delicti so take your time, my dear. Take your time."

"Yes, your honor," Cad agreed. Then she moistened her lips and took a deep breath. "She's a fortune hunter. She heard that Jake had struck it rich, and she asked me how to locate him. Later on, I heard that she and a friend of hers set off for Jake's camp. When she returned to Dawson, that maniac of a woman burst into my room and attacked me. She was completely wild, quite crazy in fact. As you can imagine, I was terrified because she threatened to kill me. She told me in front of some of my friends"—Cad nodded in the direction of the Grizzly Bear and Diamond-Tooth Gertie—"that she'd killed Jake Gore. She said she was pleased she'd murdered him and that she'd seen to it that nobody would ever find his body. Then she threatened me, saying that I'd be the next person she'd kill."

"Why did she do a thing like that?" muttered the judge.

Cad shrugged. "That sort do anything for gold."

The judge focused on her with some difficulty. "But you didn't see her do it?" he asked.

"She admitted it," snapped Cad. "Ain't that good enough?"

The judge looked at Tara. "You want to ask her something?"

Tara stared at Cad, horrified. She had played her part in the conspiracy to perfection. "She's a liar. She knows she's lying. There's no point in my asking her anything."

Cad jumped to her feet angrily. "You whore!" she screamed.

215

"Gentlemen, I appeal to you. Ain't a lady entitled to some protection from that . . . that tramp?"

The judge banged for order with his hammer. "Let's keep this dignified," he rambled. "I can't have witnesses yelling like that. This is a court of law, and it's going to be conducted in a proper manner. You are excused, Miss Wilson."

Cad returned to her seat.

"Mrs. Kane, are you ready to testify?" Tara heard the judge ask. She sat paralyzed with fear. As she looked around, not one single face seemed remotely sympathetic. There was no sign of a scarlet tunic; even the lodgers and Bowers had forsaken her, blending in with the pleasure-seeking mob. It was up to her to win over this kangaroo court, and her only defense was that she was the one person who knew the whole truth.

"Mrs. Kane, take the stand," ordered the judge. Tara stood, slowly walked over to the chair recently vacated by Cad Wilson, and sat down. In a low voice she repeated the promise to tell the truth.

"So what happened?" asked Judge Rickless.

"I killed Jake Gore, but I didn't want to. I had to kill him because otherwise he would have killed me." She stopped. Scores of hostile eyes were dancing in front of her.

Judge Rickless held up a thin hand.

"Are you saying it was self-defense?"

Tara nodded. Cad Wilson emitted a high, sneering laugh.

"OK, OK," said the judge. Billy turned him to face the jurors behind the bar.

"If a woman says she killed a man in self-defense," he told them, "that makes it justifiable homicide, and she ain't guilty of murder. That's my ruling, but she's got to prove it was self-defense."

Billy swung his chair around again and he said to Tara, "Did you have any choice?"

"No," whispered Tara.

"You'll have to explain to the court, Mrs. Kane."

Tara swallowed. "I've been searching all over for my husband. That woman came to see me and brought me my husband's watch."

Cad shook her head angrily.

"Go on," prompted the judge. His whisky bottle was now empty.

"She told me that if I went up north, to Hell's Kitchen, and asked for Jake Gore he'd take me to where my husband was prospecting. Naturally, I was impatient to get there and set off almost immediately with a friend. I found Jake Gore, and the first thing he did was cold-bloodedly kill a man in front of my eyes. I knew he was dangerous, but

216

I didn't care because he said he was my husband's partner and that he would take me to where they were camped, which was all that mattered. But when we reached the camp site there was no sign of Daniel."

"Who's Daniel?" burped the judge.

"My husband."

"Get on with it, Mrs. Kane," the judge grumbled.

"The camp was deserted, and we were utterly alone. Jake Gore took me around the back and showed me a grave and told me that it was my husband's. I couldn't believe that Daniel was buried there in that anonymous hole, but Jake boasted that he'd killed him. Then he grabbed me and we struggled. During the fight I killed him."

"Billy! Another bottle. Doesn't sound like self-defense to me," growled the judge, peering at Tara. He looked over his shoulder at the jury. "That's not good enough. She'll have to do better than that to prove self-defense."

Cad Wilson and Arne Gore were smiling complacently. Gore's cruel, evil face brought back to her Jake's look when he had attacked her and the words he uttered just before she shot him.

"He didn't just grab me," she said, not taking her eyes off Gore. "He attacked me. He was going to rape me. Kill me. He forced me to the ground, and started tearing my clothes off. I tried to fight him, I screamed, but he laughed at me." She was white-faced, her voice shaking. "He said he was going to, to take me, do what he wanted, then kill me. Just as they had planned." And her glance swung around to Cad Wilson, whose smile had frozen. Momentarily there was a hint of fear in her eyes.

Tara tried to control herself. She paused, and then she noticed Jefferson Smith. He stood to the side of the crowded room, and he was watching her closely. This time there was nothing mocking in his expression. His look seemed sympathetic; no hint of arrogance, no cynical smile. She wondered how long he had been standing there.

"What happened then?" she heard the judge ask.

"I couldn't get away from him," Tara went on, her voice very low. "I struggled, but he kept hitting me and laughing. He was enjoying himself. I screamed and screamed but it only got Jake more excited. I was alone. There was no one around for miles, no one to hear me, to help me." Tara was sobbing. "So, so I pulled out the gun and I shot him. There was no other way, unless he killed me."

The saloon was silent. Smith raised a cheroot to his lips, and his face was obliterated in a cloud of smoke. One or two of the spectators shifted uneasily as Tara wept.

217

"Don't believe her," yelled Gore, stepping forward. "That's a pack of damn lies. She robbed him, that's why she did it."

The judge leaned forward. "Did you take his gold, Mrs. Kane?" he hiccupped.

"What gold?" mumbled Tara, the tears streaming down her cheeks.

"Look at her," cried Gore venomously. "Putting on her big act. She set the dogs on his body, I tell you. I saw it. I saw what was left."

"That's not true," shouted Tara, standing up, and confronting Gore. "You know that's not true."

"Calm yourself, lady," said Judge Rickless, reaching for his bottle.

"After I had shot your brother, I passed out, and when I came to a terrible blizzard had started," she continued. "I didn't know what to do, but I had to find out who was in that grave, and so I—" She stopped, the horror of the moment coming back to her. "Under that frozen ground was the body of another man who'd been murdered. He had a hole straight through his heart, and your brother probably put it there."

"Oh sure," sneered Gore. He was finding it difficult to contain his hate for Tara.

"I was going to feed Jake's dogs, but when I unharnessed them, they went crazy. They rushed for Jake's body and tore it to pieces. They were wild, insane, so famished they even started eating one another." She buried her face in her hands, sobbing uncontrollably.

Cad Wilson raised her hand to her mouth, in a studied gesture, to stifle a nonexistent yawn. But few people saw it; their eyes were on Tara.

She looked up, her face tear-streaked. Even the judge had stopped drinking. Smith's eyes stayed on Tara.

"It was a hideous sight," she said in a trembling voice. "What was left of Jake Gore was . . ." Despite herself, she shuddered. Then she raised her head. "Do you think I'll ever forgive myself for what I did? Do you think I killed that man for pleasure? Do you think I'll ever be able to wipe from my memory what I've been through, what that man did to me? I've been haunted day and night by what happened. I'll never forgive myself for taking a human life, never. But Jake Gore had taken many and he would happily have taken mine. And if he had he wouldn't be standing here now, would he?"

Then Tara pointed at Cad Wilson. "That woman," she accused, "that woman planned it. She hired Jake Gore to kill me. His only mistake was he wanted to get some fun out of it first."

"She's lying," screamed Cad, getting up and starting toward Tara. "She's lying, I swear it."

"Order, order," hammered the judge. "Return to your seat, Miss Wilson."

His bleary eyes blinked at Gore. "Prosecution wants to cross-examine the accused?" he inquired.

Arne Gore smiled coldly, and shook his head. "Hell no, Judge," he said. "No point. Guess she's condemned herself in anybody's language. She don't even deny she killed Jake." He looked at Tara. "As for the rest, don't believe a word the woman says. Can't you see what she is? Just look at her. She's acting helpless, but that's not how she was when she blew Jake's face apart. When she fed the dogs on his body. That's how she's decided to play it now, relying on her looks, on being the poor, defenseless woman. She only calls it rape when she don't get paid for it."

He walked past the judge and addressed the jury, his sharp features feverish. His black hair tied at the back was like an evil plume. "I say she's a murdering whore and I want justice. I want justice for my brother's death, and I'm going to see that I get it. I went to the Mounties, and you can see what they did about it." He spat on the sawdust-cover floor.

"You know why? They couldn't care less if a Yank gets killed. They don't want us here. They ain't got the right flag here. If you're not a Canuck, you don't get justice, but it's your duty as true Americans to see that I get it. It's up to you to see that this woman gets what she deserves. She's a murderess. I say we should hang Tara Kane!"

"OK, Gore. You've made your point," the judge intervened. "Sure, you're sore as hell. Couldn't be anything else, boy. A man who ain't sore about his brother's death ain't worth calling a man."

He paused as footsteps echoed around the silent saloon. Jefferson Smith had come forward and stood near the front row of tables, his arms folded. Cad looked up at him, her face strained, but he ignored her.

Judge Rickless cleared his throat. "However, there's two sides to every story. Now the accused here, she says Jake did terrible things to her and she shot him. Does her credit. What kind of woman is it who lets a man do such things and then kisses him goodbye, eh?"

The jurors grinned and shifted in their seats. They had been sitting a long time.

"Arne Gore says it was robbery and murder, and she says it was self-defense. Now it's up to you to say who's telling the truth. You men go away now and consider your verdict. Guilty or not guilty. Come back when you made up your minds, but don't take too long 'cos these folks want to use the saloon. Court's recessed."

219

The men behind the bar did not bother to move. One of them, a lanky, bearded individual in a tartan shirt, stood up. Tara got the impression that they had not even consulted each other.

"OK, Judge," he said. "We're decided."

"So what's the verdict?" asked Judge Rickless.

"Not guilty."

There was pandemonium in the saloon. Many people applauded; others booed. Tara sat slumped, only half aware of what was going on, thanking God it was all over and that she had survived. They had believed her, and perhaps there was such a thing as divine justice. Against all the odds she had somehow managed to convince these twelve roughnecks that she was not a murderess.

An aromatic perfume pervaded the air. Glancing up, Tara saw Cad Wilson standing in front of her. "You'd better get out of town," warned Cad, "fast. You're not going to be very popular."

"You're late for work, Cad," interrupted a cool voice. Smith had appeared by her side.

She whirled around. "Jeff," she began.

"Time's money," cut in Smith. "You're wasting it. Get going."

She glared at Tara, her mouth curling with contempt, then sauntered off, wrapping herself up in the fur jacket. The Grizzly Bear and Diamond-Tooth Gertie followed like two faithful hounds.

"Sister Tara," said Bowers, coming up to her and taking her elbow. "I think you need a little sustenance to celebrate the victory of justice. The righteous shall conquer, and you have conquered."

He steered Tara over to a table in an alcove.

She sat down in the shadows, her head pounding, her mouth dry, confused by the noise, the people, the rushing around. Suddenly the Eldorado was its old self again, the piano tinkling away, the faro wheels clicking, people laughing and shouting. It made the whole experience all the more unreal.

"Drinks on the house," shouted Smith, from the middle of the floor. He walked over to the bar, where the jurors were standing in a group. "Gentlemen," he declared, "you've served the town well. Order whatever your pleasure is and it needn't just be rotgut."

They laughed and gathered around him as Smith poured champagne and raised his glass with them. But his eyes looked beyond them at the corner table, where Tara sat, still dazed, with Bowers. And his eyes never left her. By the bar also sat the judge, in his wheelchair, a glass in his hand, calling for more drink, his top hat on his lap, his hair now wildly awry. Billy went behind the bar to help speed up the service.

"Good man, the judge," remarked Bowers. "Mighty good lawyer, until he had his accident."

"What accident?" asked Tara vaguely.

"A client caught up with him," said Bowers. "Pity when you think of it, because he might have made a real lawyer one day." He saw her puzzled look. "Sister Tara, he ain't even an attorney. But he makes a damn fine judge. Best in Dawson I reckon. You should hear him hang a man."

He poured two glasses of champagne and passed one to her. Tara stared at the glass. Everything was becoming too much.

"Please, I want to leave," she said quietly.

Bowers took a drink, then got up. "Sure. I'll take you home."

Tara stood, her legs almost buckling as she held onto the table. She was exhausted and yearned for the peace of her own room. Bowers took her arm, and they were edging their way through the celebrating crowd when, unexpectedly, they came face to face with Arne Gore. His bunched-up hair had come loose and was hanging down his shoulders like a woman's. He stood in front of Tara, ignoring Bowers. A hush descended over the festivities, and only the occasional click of the roulette wheel broke the oppressive silence.

Tara shrank back from the venom in his eyes.

"You!" spat Gore. "You're dead." She stared at him, mesmerized.

"That's enough, friend," intervened Smith.

Gore took no notice. He continued to confront Tara. "You won't even have time to make a will, bitch," he snarled, "because I'm going to get you. You think you've got everybody in your damned pocket, you fucking whore. Well, you're going to find out."

Almost casually, Smith reached out and grabbed Gore by the collar, pulling his face close to his. In various corners of the saloon, armed men, men who were Smith's shadows wherever he went, began to move forward.

"You get out of here and keep walking. Don't you come back," said Smith, quite pleasantly. "You leave now, right now." He hurled Gore away, throwing him against a nearby table. Gore tottered, his eyes shifting uneasily. Then he turned and slunk toward the doors of the saloon.

"Mr. Gore," Smith called out. Gore froze, his back rigid. Slowly he turned, his eyes transfixed on Smith's face. Several armed men appeared behind him, but Gore was unaware of them.

"You forgot something," said Smith, his voice bantering. It was misleading; his eyes had become chips of ice. "You forgot to apologize to the lady."

221

A nerve twitched in Gore's face.

"We're waiting," smiled Smith.

"I—" Gore swallowed. Smith eyed him lethally.

"I'm sorry," Gore said through gritted teeth. There was an audible sigh of amazement.

"I imagine the lady will accept your apology," said Smith suavely. "Now get out, before she changes her mind."

Without another word, Gore turned and walked swiftly out, everybody stepping aside to let him through. The swing doors of the Eldorado banged as he disappeared into the night.

"I haven't had a chance to congratulate you, Tara," drawled Smith. "After you said your piece, the jury couldn't give any other verdict. You had every man in the room on your side. When they hang me, I'll get you as my counsel."

"I only told the truth," she said quietly.

"I know. And it won you the day, as it should have. You can be proud of yourself. Now I'll escort you home."

"That won't be necessary. Mr. Bowers has already offered."

Smith turned to Bowers. "That's very kind of you, Reverend, but I know how anxious you are to continue your work converting the sinners of Dawson, and I wouldn't dream of letting you miss this God-given opportunity."

"Thanks, Boss," grinned Bowers. "See you around, Sister Tara."

"My apologies for that little incident," Smith continued after Bowers had left them. "We have some highly undesirable characters in town."

"I know," said Tara.

"Some are more undesirable than others," he said as he walked Tara through the crowded saloon. Outside, on Front Street, he offered her his arm.

"I can manage," she said.

"Don't be so damn female." Smith took her arm. "You're shaking." They walked in silence.

"Didn't I tell you to be careful about Cad?" Smith asked. "She isn't somebody who forgets, let alone forgives. I warned you, and now I find out this has all been her doing."

"Didn't she tell you? I thought she'd confide in a friend."

"She's an employee, Tara," said Smith, "and after what I heard this evening, even that's in question."

"I'm really not the slightest bit interested," said Tara.

He smiled crookedly. "No?"

They had reached Mrs. Miles's house, and on the steps he withdrew his arm and faced her. "Tara," he began.

"Goodnight," she said, turning to go, but he caught her hand.

"Come on. Can't we at least be friendly?" he asked.

"I don't think we've enough in common even for that," she replied.

He looked amused. "Guess I'll have to find something, then." His tone changed. "Do you still have that gun?"

She nodded curtly.

"Keep it handy," he advised. "And keep out of Arne Gore's way."

She closed the door, but Smith did not move for a long time. He stood staring after her. Then, slowly, he made his way into the dark town. There was a smile on his face.

CHAPTER NINETEEN

Tara entered Constantine's bare little office. He was sitting, immaculate as ever, writing a report. The only sign that he had been on the trail, whipped by blizzards, was a more weather-beaten face and lines of tiredness around his eyes. He seemed harassed, and if Tara had expected sympathy for her ordeal, he quickly disillusioned her.

"I was hoping you'd have quit," he said. "You might not be so lucky next time. It might be for real."

"So you would have let me hang, would you?" Tara asked.

"Who are you trying to kid, Mrs. Kane?" he said frostily. "You weren't in any danger. It was a carnival, and you took the starring role."

"What on earth are you talking about?"

"Why are you getting so worked up? Nothing was going to happen to you. It was all carefully staged."

"Staged? By whom?" asked Tara incredulously.

"The man who rigged the jury. Your protector, Soapy Smith."

"I don't believe you," gasped Tara.

"Please yourself," Constantine shrugged. "They got well paid, so I understand."

"No," breathed Tara. "That isn't so. That wasn't why."

"Oh no?" He smiled coldly. "You tell me why they let you off so easily then. They were on the rampage. They wanted blood. So why the change of heart? Because they liked the look of you? You're lucky you got that sort of friend."

Tara winced. "No," she said again. She didn't want to believe it. "They let me go because, because I convinced them."

"Have it your own way," remarked Constantine dryly.

"Why should he do it?"

"Maybe you'd better ask him," Constantine said, his unwavering eyes boring into Tara. She could feel his contempt for her.

"I, I never knew," she said quietly.

"Does it matter?"

"Yes," Tara said fiercely. "It does. To me."

Constantine pulled out a file from his desk drawer, studied a handwritten sheet inside, then stared at Tara.

"I have here a report about the death of Jake Gore," he said slowly. "The answers you gave my officers weren't very satisfactory."

She looked at him blankly.

"A patrol found the place." He glanced at the sheet again. "Who is the man in the grave?"

"I don't know," she said in a low voice.

"It's not your husband, then?" he asked.

"No," said Tara. "Thank God."

He nodded. "I'll send the facts to headquarters. Maybe we'll find out all about it one day."

"You don't want a statement any more?" she said. "You're not going to . . ."

Constantine shut the file.

"Mrs. Kane," he said. "I want you out of Dawson. Out of the Yukon. That's all. I have no authority to expel you, I can't make you go. All I can say is that since you've been here you've been nothing else but trouble, big trouble, and I don't need it or want it. And remember, your benefactor may not always be around."

"Damn him!" Tara said fervently and stormed out.

Locating Jefferson Smith, during his periods in Dawson, was usually no problem. If he wished to be found, one only had to ask. Those who looked for him to make trouble found him more elusive. Hard-eyed men would study them, unsmiling, and shake their heads. So, when Tara marched into the Monte Carlo after seeing Constantine, Mort greeted her as one of the accepted.

"Where is he?" she asked haughtily.

"In his office."

"Where's that?"

"Over at the Regina."

Tara resented the familiar way he eyed her. "Thank you," she said coldly, and marched out, her head held high.

She strode through the town and into the four-story building. The two men behind the desk were hardly hotel managers. Both wore guns. One had an unlit cigar stuck in his mouth. They were bodyguards; she could smell it.

"I'm looking for Mr. Smith," Tara said.

"Sure, Mrs. Kane," said the one with the cigar. "I'll take you up."

They knew who she was. They probably thought they knew *what* she was, and in the mood she was in that annoyed Tara even more. She followed the man up the staircase and along the corridor she remembered. He knocked on a door, stuck his head in, and said, "Mrs. Kane, Boss."

Tara marched into the room, then came to a dead stop. Smith was not alone. He rose from behind his desk, flashing her a welcoming smile. Sitting on a chair opposite him was Joe Lamore. Tara's resolution wavered momentarily. What she had come to say was for Smith's ears alone.

"Tara, my dear," Smith said, seeming genuinely delighted to see her. "Please come in."

Smith pushed an ornate chair forward for her. The office was certainly not the sort Tara expected a racketeer to have. On one wall was a framed map of Alaska and a portrait of President McKinley. In a corner, on a flagstaff, was the Stars and Stripes. The overall effect was, to say the least, opulent.

Lamore sat, his mouth open, looking a little heated.

"You know Mrs. Kane," Smith said, "don't you?"

"Of course." Lamore gave Tara a sickly smile. "How are you, Tara?"

"I'll come back," Tara said.

"Our business is finished." Smith's hooded eyes turned to Lamore. "Isn't it, Mr. Lamore?"

"Well, I don't know." Lamore took out a huge white handkerchief and mopped his brow.

"I think it is," Smith said firmly. "Except, maybe, for the formalities." His teeth gleamed. "Please make yourself at home, Tara. I insist." Tara wondered what on earth Mrs. Miles's respectable lodger, solid businessman, owner of a sawmill, was doing with Soapy Smith.

"I'll pay you interest," Lamore offered, sounding desperate. "Won't that do it?"

Smith chuckled. It was a pleasant laugh. He picked up some pieces of paper from his side of the desk and, one by one, dropped them in front of Lamore's dazed eyes. "Five thousand, two thousand, six thousand, three thousand, four thousand, two thousand. That makes it twenty-two thousand dollars, Mr. Lamore. I want it. Now."

"I haven't got that kind of dough in cash. I can let you have ten thousand, but the rest . . ."

"Can you let me have the balance," said Smith, consulting his watch with its dangling charms, "in, say, half an hour?"

"Half an hour!" exclaimed Lamore. "My money's in Seattle. You know that. It'd take two or three months."

"You've had your pleasure, now you must pay for it," Smith said. "And I mean *now*." He opened a drawer, took out a large foolscap sheet of paper, and placed it before Lamore. "I have it ready. Just sign."

"Hell, that's not fair," Lamore protested. He was sweating. Tara tried to imagine what Mrs. Miles would say if she could see shifty-eyed Joe Lamore now.

"Fair?" smiled Smith, "If you'd won, you would have grabbed my money and laughed. Supposing I'd said I hadn't got it, eh? I can just see you running to your friends howling how Soapy Smith had welshed on you."

"Jeff."

"You're a four-flushing cheat, Lamore," Smith said pleasantly. "I don't like four-flushers. Sign."

"But . . . but the sawmill . . . it's worth five, ten times . . ." Lamore stuttered.

"You put it up as collateral," Smith reminded him. "Sign."

Lamore started to croak something, but the sight of Smith's expression strangled his words. He picked up the pen Smith thrust at him and scrawled his name. Then he looked up, hate in his eyes. "I won't forget this, Smith."

"Good," Smith said. "It's first-class education, my friend, and that doesn't come cheap." He looked at Lamore's signature and then pushed the paper toward Tara, holding out the pen.

"Please," he said. "You're the witness."

"No," Tara said. "It's got nothing to do with me."

"I'm only asking you to witness what you've seen."

"With you, I don't believe what I've seen," she said coldly.

Smith shrugged, got up, went to the door, and called, "Jeb."

The man with the unsmoked cigar came in.

"Jeb," Smith said. "You have just seen Mr. Lamore here sign this document in your presence."

"Sure, Boss."

"Now please be so kind as to witness that fact."

"Right." Jeb took the pen and bent over the paper. Then he looked up.

"Which name should I use, Boss?"

"The one your mother gave you," Smith sighed, indicating the spot on the document. Jeb signed.

"Thank you," Smith said. "Now, will you show Mr. Lamore out."

Lamore was on his feet, red-faced.

"That mill, it took me two years to—"

"Good day to you, Mr. Lamore."

Lamore turned to go, then stopped in front of Tara. "You, you're not going to mention . . ." he said.

"No, Mr. Lamore," she said quietly. "I won't tell Mrs. Miles or the others that I saw you paying your gambling debts."

Smith grinned, and Lamore departed, followed by the bodyguard. Tara sat stiffly, but before she could say anything, Smith waved a hand.

"How do you like my office?"

"To hell with your office. I think you're contemptible. You're a cheap, rotten crook. You think you can bribe and corrupt, buy anything and anyone with money. Even your kangaroo courts."

Smith sat behind his desk and started playing with his dice. The clicking infuriated her. "Maybe you're right. I needn't have fixed the jury, you did so damn well. I reckon those sons of bitches would have let you off, no matter what."

He reached into a bottom drawer and brought out a bottle of brandy and two cut-crystal glasses. He poured two and pushed one across to Tara. "Let's drink to it," he said. "To the course of true justice."

"True justice!" She took a breath. "You, you damn . . ."

"Rogue?" suggested Smith, mockingly. "Trickster? Operator? Oh, come my dear." He raised his glass.

"You hypocrite," spat out Tara angrily. He inclined his head, amused. It was one word he hadn't thought of. "You make everything cheap. Even the truth. Everybody believed me, you said, everybody was on my side, and all the time you'd bought them, you bastard, bribed the jury, bought the court, rigged the verdict."

"Well, you got off, didn't you?"

"So you didn't believe me either! You thought I was lying! That I robbed and murdered a man!" She stuttered with rage. "Is that why you bribed them? You've made me as cheap as yourself."

227

"Tara," he said gently, "hold your horses. You spoke the truth. Every word. I know what you went through. I know what happened."

"Well, then." Her face was flushed.

"I didn't fix that trial. Your lady friend did. Cad Wilson. She bribed the jury. To find you guilty. They've never lynched a woman in Dawson, but she wanted to make it a first time. Sure it was all fixed."

Tara stood, astounded.

"So, I figured I ought to assist the course of justice. I bribed those twelve men good and true not to let themselves be bribed. Not guilty costs a little more than guilty, but I figured it was worth it. That pretty neck of yours deserves a better fate."

Smith took a drink of brandy and set the glass down.

"Truth is," he said, "that once they got going there would have been a goddamn riot if somebody had tried to stop them having their fun. But you handled it beautifully. I'm proud of you. You didn't need anybody's help. Here's to you."

She glared at him, hating him and yet believing him, wanting to tell him what she thought of him, yet feeling he had spoken the truth.

"Goodbye." Tara went to the door and opened it.

"Tara," he called.

She looked around. He was standing by his desk in his debonair, arrogant fashion, but his eyes looked straight at her. Something about them seemed to be sad.

"Goodbye," she said once more and went out, closing the door behind her.

YOUNG WIDOW ACQUITTED!

Not Guilty of Murder

by Our Own Correspondent

A miners' court, convened in Dawson City, declared Mrs. Tara Kane, a young, comely widow, innocent of the slaying of one Jake Gore. Mrs. Kane, who moved the court with her account of how she fought for her honor on an isolated trail in Tagish country, was unanimously held to be not guilty by a jury of twelve citizens. After the trial, Mr. Jefferson R. Smith, speaking as head of the citizens' committee, said it proved yet once again that justice prevailed in the Yukon. He declared that this innocent widow, all alone in the world, was a shining example of how right will be done by anyone, be they poor or humble, friendless or abandoned.

Mrs. Kane said afterwards that she was grateful to the citizens who had brought a just verdict and for the fairness of the trial. Mr. Smith declined to discuss the matter further, but we understand that the poor widow lady did not have a cent and Mr. Smith personally paid all her costs. A gentleman, he told our reporter, does not talk about such things, but obviously it was a matter of honor that the lady have the best defense money could buy. Mrs. Kane is very appreciative, he added.

Tara glowered at the paper. She considered going down to its office and telling the creature who called himself the editor what she thought of him and his rag. Or maybe she should write a letter to him, setting out the facts. But what was the point; they would never print it, and her frustration would only serve to amuse Soapy Smith.

"Young widow, indeed! Grateful and appreciative! Damn you, Mr. Smith," she muttered, tossing the newspaper to one side.

As it fell to the ground, her eye was caught by a photograph of Front Street. The caption read:

The above pictorial study of our main drag was taken only last week by the well-known German photographer, Ernst Hart, who has returned to Dawson after a round trip of the territory and has set up a studio next to the barber shop. He will be open for business on Wednesday.

Since she had been back, Tara had been so preoccupied that she had hardly thought of Hart once. Now she could not wait to see him. So much had happened, there was so much he didn't know. He must have been under the illusion that she had been reunited with Daniel.

Hart had gone up in the world, she realized, as she gazed at the painted wooden sign. "Photographs!" it proclaimed. "Alaska Views, Portraits. E. Hart, Exclusive Work Undertaken," all in a handsome yellow script on a black background and much more impressive than the barber's shop next door. Admittedly, Hart's frontage was smaller, but there was a glass showcase displaying portraits of his various sitters, dominated by a large print of an innocently smiling Cad Wilson.

Tara tightened her lips and went inside.

A bell tinkled announcing her entry, but no one appeared. From behind a curtain, which partitioned off half of the store and the studio and darkroom area, she could hear a woman's voice saying, "That picture you took is swell, but I need some more. For professional reasons, if you get my meaning." It was Cad Wilson.

229

She laughed, and Tara heard Hart say, "Absolutely. Perfectly."

"After all, I'm a working girl, and a couple of good sassy pictures help to bring in the customers. When do you want to take 'em?"

"Any time to suit you, Miss Wilson."

"Call me Cad," she purred. Tara decided that this was not the right time to call on Hart.

That afternoon he arrived at the lodging house. When she opened the door he held her close. She eased herself away gently and invited him into the kitchen. As he sat down stiffly at the table he said, "My dearest Tara, I am so sorry. It is such terrible news. I had thought you were together, and now I read this awful story. Poor Daniel. What happened?"

For a moment she was frightened that he had heard something she had not.

"I just read of your bereavement in the paper," he went on. "It was such a shock."

Her face cleared. "*That*," she said, "that is Smith's handiwork. I'm no more a widow than you."

"I don't understand," frowned Hart. "I did not dream you were even in Dawson until I picked up the paper. I thought you had found Daniel. Why were you on trial for murder? What murder?"

He poured out an endless stream of questions, each one following the last so quickly that he gave Tara no opportunity of replying. She waited until he had run out of breath; then she told him what had happened, most of it. He listened, polishing his spectacles, never taking his blue eyes off her face.

"My God!" he said finally. "What terrible things you have been through. I blame myself, I should never have let you go off alone with that man." There were tears of shame in his eyes.

"Dear Ernst," she said softly, "it's over. None of it matters now. The important thing is that Daniel is still alive."

"Of that you're sure?" he asked, his voice quiet.

"Of course, Ernst. I don't quite know where to go from here, but I'm carrying on looking. I'll find him, never fear. I promise you I will."

"You've said that a lot," he reminded her. "You keep saying it."

"You believe me, don't you?" she asked him fiercely. "I will find him."

He said nothing as he replaced his glasses. Then he smiled at her. "I have thought of you so often and so hoped that we would meet again."

"First thing this morning I stopped by your studio to see you, but you were otherwise engaged."

"Please?"

"You had a customer."

"Well, why didn't you wait or leave a message or something?"

"Because I thought you'd be fully occupied for some while with Miss Wilson."

Hart went quite pink. "Oh, Cad," he began, trying to cover his embarrassment. "But there was no need for you to leave. She and I, it is pure business—I am taking her portraits, I mean."

"If you'd been around the night they tried to lynch me, I guess you would have just stood happily and photographed me hanging from a tree!"

Hart looked hurt. "Please, Tara, do not say such things. I was out on the trail. Anyway, Cad tells me she is leaving Dawson. That is why she needs more photographs."

"Oh, really?" said Tara.

"Yes," went on Hart enthusiastically. "She may go to Skagway, maybe even Seattle or Frisco. She is parting company with . . ."

"Mr. Smith," prompted Tara, acidly.

"I don't know what it's all about, but she tells me she is going to entertain in clubs and . . ."

"I am relieved to hear she won't be around any more."

Hart gave her a quizzical look.

"She tried to kill me. She arranged the whole expedition to Hell's Kitchen. She paid the jury to hang me. She wants me dead."

Hart was horrified. "I had no idea," he muttered.

"Well, I won't have to worry about her crazy jealousy any more. Tell me about your work."

"I have taken the most fantastic collection of photographs," he told her, his eyes shining. "Such material. I am just printing them. They are really what I wanted. At last I have got the collection I wanted. You must see them."

"Soon," promised Tara.

"What are your plans? Where will you go from here?"

"I'm not too sure," she sighed. Then she brightened. "But you know my motto, Ernst. One day at a time."

Hart took her hands. "And Tara, remember I will never stop looking either," he said, kissing her lightly on the forehead. His question resounded in her head as she watched him walk down the street. Where now?

The first commandment of Dawson street life, as Tara had learned, was "Thou shalt not interfere." People looked, stood and watched, but they never became involved. The first time Tara stepped over a drunk lying face down in the mud, she felt a pang of guilt. Now she kept herself to herself. It was wiser—and safer.

So she had no intention of stopping when she saw the crowd outside the harness shop. Then she heard the agonized yelp of a dog. It was more than a yelp. It was a scream of agony.

Again the dog howled, a mixture of terror and pain. Unable to help herself, she ran over and pushed her way through the crowd. A sled had stalled in front of the store, piled high with supplies. One of the dog team lay exhausted, too weak to help pull the huge load. Horrified, Tara saw the sled driver kick the wretched animal again with his hobnailed boots.

"Get going, you bastard," the man snarled. He was huge, a thickset fellow with a fleshy face and close-set eyes.

The crowd stood watching impassively. They were not enjoying it, but the sight of the mountainous giant was enough to make them think twice about saying anything.

The dog yelped piteously once more. Its ribs must have been broken by the kicks, thought Tara. The giant bent down, unfastened the dog's collar from its harness, and kicked it again. "I'll teach you," he growled.

"Lay off," said a voice, and the throng parted to let Jefferson Smith through. Smith was white-faced. There was fury in his eyes. The huge prospector stared at him dumbly. Smith stood with his fists clenched. "You touch that dog just once more."

The giant spat contemptuously, picked up the dog by the tail, swung it over his head, and crashed the animal down on the ground. The dog was heavy, but the giant did it effortlessly. There was a ghastly thud as the dog smashed hard on the frozen mud. It lay silent.

Smith stepped forward and swung a fist. It was not so much the weight of the blow but its suddenness that caught the prospector off balance. He slipped and crashed down.

"OK, mister, you're next," the giant roared, scrambling to his feet. It was incongruous, the sight of Smith, dressed in his city clothes, facing up to the prospector, who weighed maybe forty or fifty pounds more. But the prospector's blow missed. Smith ducked, and his right shot into the bully's mouth. The man just shook his head, like a bear.

"You're going to get what I gave that mutt," snorted the giant. He hit out again, and though Smith ducked he did not escape entirely, and Tara saw blood coming from his lip.

The crowd, excited, started to murmur. Smith, bobbing and weaving, kept raining blows at the man-mountain, and the man's bulk made him so clumsy he avoided few of them.

Smith launched himself at the bully like a man possessed. To Tara's surprise, the giant backed away, cursing. His right hand reached behind his back, and when it appeared again he was holding a huge knife. Smith stood panting, blood on his face, and then, unexpectedly, his foot lashed out and caught the prospector in the groin. The man grunted and dropped the knife. Again Smith lashed out, and this time the giant held himself, howling in agony, sounding just like the dog in its pain. As the bully swayed, Smith smashed his fist into his face, flattening his nose into a bloody pulp. The prospector folded to his knees and collapsed, knocked out cold. He lay just a couple of feet from the body of the emaciated husky he had kicked to death.

Smith was breathing hard, swaying slightly. Blood was dripping onto his shirt. Tara pushed forward. "Here," she said, "use this." She gave him a handkerchief.

"Thank you." He was still unsteady. He glanced at the prone figure, then turned his back on him. "I think I need a drink." For the first time he seemed to take her in. "And I guess you do too."

She had had no intention of coming to his assistance; it had been an automatic reaction when she had seen him bleeding and dazed. "All right," she said quietly.

"Over there." He indicated a small bar across the way.

They sat down at a wooden table, and she studied him curiously. The last thing she would have expected Smith to do was risk getting knocked to kingdom come for the sake of a dog. He was still dabbing at his mouth with her bloodstained handkerchief. "Guess I owe you a new one," he apologized.

A bartender appeared looking quizzically at Smith; not many had seen him in this state.

"Two Scotches, Jerry." Smith felt his jaw. "Jesus, he packed a punch."

He saw her look. "What's so funny?"

"You can be very surprising," Tara said.

"Don't like to see people hurting dogs."

Jerry came over with two glasses and started pouring from a bottle.

"Leave it here," ordered Smith.

"Yes, Boss." So this is one more of his establishments, thought Tara. He had a bigger hold in Dawson than she knew.

"Just taste it," said Smith. "It costs me seventy-five bucks a quart to import." He raised his glass to her and took a swig, wincing as the whisky burned his cut lips and mouth.

"I'm glad goodbye wasn't goodbye. I hoped we'd get a chance to talk." He shifted on his chair. His body was bruised. "Not like this of course." She sat looking at him.

"Tara, I think I owe you an apology for a couple of things."

"You don't owe me anything," she said coldly.

"Whoa. Just hear me out. I've been sort of thinking about you. You got guts. No screams, no hysterics. No tears, leastways not where people see them. A mighty proud lady, aren't you? Only one trouble."

She raised an eyebrow, dangerously.

"You don't know how to look after yourself."

"You've no need to worry about me. Mr. Smith."

"But I do," he said gently. So gently she looked up, surprised. "Damn, he darn well walloped me." He dabbed his cut lip again. "I don't worry about much, I can tell you. That's not my style. But I keep thinking, if I'm not around you ..." He tossed back the remainder of his Scotch. ". . . you get into trouble. And hell, you do."

"I can handle it," she said.

"Like up in Tagish country, eh? With Gore? Like when Cad tried to half kill you?"

He leaned forward. "Listen, Tara, it makes bad odds. Figure it out. Figure out if you can afford it."

"Afford what?"

"To be without me," he said simply. He was speaking quite soberly, and for once he was not play-acting.

"You mean the widow needs a protector," Tara suggested.

He didn't rise to that. "I have plans, Tara. Big plans. I'm going to do things, great things." He poured himself another drink and lit a cigar.

"It's not going to stop here, I promise you. There's a hell of a big future ahead. I aim to grab a large slice of it."

"More saloons, bigger and better dives? More rackets?"

Smith grinned. "I'm not interested in penny-anteing, Tara. I'm talking about big things. Politics. The railroad. The future of Alaska."

This was yet another Jefferson Smith who had never revealed himself before.

"Sure, it sounds crazy, but a man can do anything he sets his mind to, provided one thing." His cheroot had gone out, but he took no notice. "Provided," he said softly, "he's got the right woman beside him."

"I hope you find her one day," Tara said.

He seemed about to say something but changed his mind. Instead he poured her another whisky.

"It's all out there waiting for us. Hell, do you realize what's waiting to be grabbed with both hands? Why, we could even make Alaska the center of the map. Yes, sir." He lowered his voice. "Tara, it could

234

be done. A railroad directly connecting this place with Paris, New York . . ."

"Why, that's impossible," Tara said. "Paris? How about the ocean? A railroad on the ocean?"

"All it needs is a tunnel. Twenty-seven miles under the Bering Strait. Right across Russia, across Europe, into France. You step onto the train in Skagway, or Dawson, and a few days later you're in gay Paree. Last stop in Alaska, Stewart City. And you can build a track that links up all the way on land across the United States. One week you're scratching yourself in Lousetown, next month you're having breakfast on Fifth Avenue. Never touch the ocean."

He saw he had made an impression, and went on, "The linkup with the Trans-Siberian Railroad is no problem. The Czar will give his consent."

"Will he?" Tara asked, bemused.

"Sure. I'll go to St. Petersburg and sign a treaty with the Russians myself."

She glanced around the shabby saloon, the roughly dressed men drinking at the bar. It was so remote from these grandiose schemes.

He seemed to read her mind. He topped up his whisky. "I'm returning to Skagway," he said putting down the bottle. "First, I'm going to put that little place on the map. In a big way. It needs me, and I need a first lady. Every senator needs a first lady. Every governor. Every president." He relit his cheroot and blew out the smoke. "Governor of Alaska," he said, his eyes lost in his own vision. "Why not? Alaska, the Yukon, tell me, why not?"

"Alaska a state?" she asked, amused.

"I'm going to add that star to the flag," promised Smith. He raised his glass. "Here's to great days," he proposed.

She hesitated.

"Hell, Tara, you're not drinking." There was a plea in his eyes. She picked up her glass.

"To great days," she toasted.

"So," went on Smith, as if it had all been decided. "I want you to come to Skagway with me. My pappy always said when you've got something really important to say, make sure you pick the right time and the right place." He looked around the drab, seedy bar and gave her a twisted smile. "I guess this ain't either, but I can't wait, Tara. Time's too short. How about it?"

She looked him straight in the eyes. And she made her decision. "All right. I'll come to Skagway if you'll help me to find Daniel."

He threw back his head and laughed. "I talk about opening up the

235

world, and you just talk about him. Now you listen. I'll do anything for you, Tara." He was still smiling, but there was a hardness behind it. "You only have to say. But that's one goddamn job you got to do all on your own. I'll help you anywhere, any time. You're a woman I'd do anything for. Anything but that."

He downed his drink, his eyes never leaving her face. "Well," he said. "Are you coming to Skagway with me? Are you going places with me?"

"No," replied Tara. He nodded. "I play long odds," he said.

"There are no odds, Mr. Smith."

He grinned, a little painfully. His lip was swelling. "I'm a born gambler, Tara. And I never lose."

CHAPTER TWENTY

The arrival of Spring and the thawing of the Yukon River would also herald the opening of the '98 lucky strikers' season. Those already prospecting staked extra claims to make sure the new arrivals, when they turned up, would not get the chance to find a fortune they themselves had missed. Claim markings shot up all over the sprawling creek land from its mouth to far beyond its sources, along its right fork, its left fork, along every tiny stream and rivulet that emptied into the basin of the Klondike, Indian, and McQuesten rivers.

There was no further news of Daniel. No one had replied to the various requests for information Tara had posted in the general store, the stables, the harness shop, or the gunsmith's. Although she knew there was little chance of finding him there, she decided to visit the creeks and ask for herself. Then, perhaps, she'd stop feeling so impotent. So she borrowed a horse, got together some supplies, and rode out to Bonanza.

The sheer effort of scouring eight hundred square miles of gold claims was daunting. In whatever direction Tara looked, tents dotted the landscape, fires burned everywhere to thaw out the ground, and men toiled and sweated melting the ice, gouging away at the frozen earth and streams so that they could pan the gravel.

Tara discovered that these hard-headed men, who eyed her suspiciously when she asked about Daniel and who never turned their backs, were, in fact, superstitious at heart. And she herself found there was something eerie in these miles of creek land, the will-o'-the-wisp fires burning day and night, and men silently looking, searching, panning, the remoteness of it all.

Some of the friendlier sourdoughs talked of the gold lore: how gold water had its own flavor, how you had to stay on the right side of the Yukon, no good going too far upriver or looking for gold where the moose roamed. Trees had to lean the right way; trees at a wrong angle meant no gold.

"There's going to be trouble in the spring," one old man told her. "Gold's running out." Tara stared at him bewildered. "Come the thaw," he rumbled on, "what with newcomers, there ain't going to be enough to go around."

"But that's crazy," Tara said. "There's talk of millions to be found. A man in Dawson sold his claim for seven hundred and fifty thousand dollars and said he'd already had a million out of it."

The old man shrugged. "You want to see some real gold?" he asked. From a pouch he took a bundle wrapped in cloth, which he carefully and lovingly undid. "There," he said triumphantly, holding out to Tara a bundle of tallow candles. "What do you think of those? You know what they cost? Three bucks each. There's thirty dollars' worth here." He wrapped them up again. "*That's* gold for you. Next week they're going to fetch double, and the week after even more. When they're all sitting around shivering, no food, no gold, no heat, I'll have a shack full of candles, then I'll clean up." He tottered off, laughing to himself.

For days Tara rode through the claims. She studied the miners' faces, read the names of the owners scratched on wooden boards nailed to the stake poles, asked if anyone had seen or heard of Daniel Kane. But each man she spoke to either ignored her question or shook his head.

It's hopeless, she thought, as she paused at the foot of Cheechakoo Hill by a tree on which had been hammered a weather-beaten, primitively carved notice:

> To whom it may concern!
> I do, this day, locate and claim, by
> right of discovery, five hundred feet,
> running upstream from this notice.
> Located this 17th day of August 1896.
> G. W. Carmack

Below her she could see men toiling away at their claims, the smoke from their fires curling in the frozen air.

So this is where it all began, she thought, gazing at the little board. On this spot, Carmack, Skookum Jim, and Tagish Charley had found

237

the nugget that started it—less than two years ago. Here had been discovered the wild dream that had brought thousands to this wilderness, that had lured Daniel away, that had led her to this.

Tara turned her horse around, and began her long, despondent ride back to Dawson.

She took one last look at the legions of men who, soaked and freezing, had spent months in back-breaking labor, hauling up tons of muck, hacking fiendishly at the frozen soil, depriving themselves of the most basic comforts, week after week, month after month, shoveling gravel in creek after creek, always their eyes straining for any sign, any speck of that telltale yellow metal.

They did not give up, and neither would she. No matter what, she would find her man. By the time she rode into Dawson she no longer felt defeated, just travel-weary and extremely stiff.

She returned the horse to the livery stables and began trudging back to Mrs. Miles's house. After the long hours she had spent in the saddle, it was a relief to stretch her legs, and the exercise warmed her. She began to feel more human again.

Passing Hart's studio, Tara was surprised and pleased to see the number of people waiting. "My goodness," she exclaimed when she saw him, "at this rate you'll be needing an assistant soon."

"It's amazing," he chuckled, delightedly, "I never dreamed I would be this busy. I'm making lots of money." Then his expression grew serious. "Any luck?" he asked quietly.

Tara shook her head.

"What's going to be your next step?"

"A bath, then a meal, followed by a decent night's sleep," she replied, with a brave attempt at a smile. "But I will find him, Ernst. I know I will."

"Of course you will," he agreed, patting her hand. "By the way, I've finished processing my photographs. Please, can you come over tomorrow? You will be the first person I'll have shown them to."

His genuine concern for her opinion was obvious.

"Of course. I'll come after supper tomorrow night."

"Hey, do you want our business or don't you?" interrupted a surly sourdough.

"Until tomorrow, then," Tara said, hastily pecking Hart on the cheek.

There was a package waiting for her at Mrs. Miles's. It was a very small parcel, not much larger than a matchbox, wrapped in brown paper. Her name and address were penned in neat but unfamiliar writing. She tore off the paper to reveal a small, plain box. Inside there were two beautifully carved red dice. Nothing else. No note. But she knew who had sent them.

For a moment, she turned the dice over in the palm of her hand, then she threw them across the surface of her dresser. They rolled, and stopped.

Seven. Lucky seven.

Was her luck about to change?

As Hart spread each print in front of her, it was as if Tara were looking at the whole of the Gold Rush unfolding in one long panorama. Some of the photographs showed vast, sweeping views, like the White Pass seen from Cutoff Canyon, with rolling snow as far as the eye could see and, just in one corner, a tiny figure of a man with his sled. She relived her journey through Dead Horse Gulch, Hart's lens having magnificently caught the awful macabre graveyard of pack animals. A bare skeleton in the foreground, a half-rotted cadaver in the distance. Hart's sensitive eye had effectively recorded the small and personal as well as the vast and endless. There were photographs of a weary gold prospector who had fallen asleep as he panned, a saloonkeeper standing behind his counter, a good-time girl grinning brazenly at the camera as she lifted her skirt to show her legs. Hart, Tara realized, was an artist, using his photographic plates like a canvas, light and shade like paints.

"Well?" he asked eagerly.

"I've never seen pictures like these," she replied. "They're superb, truly marvelous."

He was enormously pleased. It seemed especially important to him what she thought of them.

She looked at pictures he had taken among the claims, of gold-laced rubble being raised by a windlass and dumped in piles to be washed later. "Where is this?" she asked.

"French Hill. Just above Tom Lipp's claim, on Eldorado."

She remembered it. She recalled the rawboned, weary men whose faces now looked out at her.

Hart worked methodically, indexing the location and technical details of each photograph in a little black book. "That's Trail Gulch," he explained, handing her another print, "and this one was taken at Hunter Creek. Do you recognize where this is? Just outside Lousetown. I took this a mile from Five Finger Rapids. Him? Oh, he's a Scottish trapper I found at Lake LaBarge."

His fascination for characters emerged in his studies of the men and

239

women of the Yukon. He would see two sourdoughs in front of a tent and photograph them, simply to capture their expressions. A man having his hair cut, two miners playing cards, a bearded prospector making batter, a few drunks slumped over a table. He had also exposed the stark hardships of the life, men gnawing at slabs of frozen bread, or trying to warm themselves around stovepipes and inadequate fires. His action photographs showed the sourdoughs working, trekking, climbing, fighting. He had scenes from dance halls, gambling dens, saloons, brothels, general stores, anywhere he could set up his camera. Diamond-Tooth Gertie, the Grizzly Bear, and the other ladies of Dawson's night life had preened themselves for his lens. He showed them having a tea party and then in their familiar surroundings, drinking and gambling in the Monte Carlo, the Dominion, the Golden Nugget.

"The night you and Cad had your argument, I wish I'd had my camera with me," Hart sighed. "I haven't yet got a good picture of two women fighting."

He was particularly proud of his photograph of Jake Gore standing beside Hank's body after he had knifed him. "Came out well, didn't it?" he said. Jake's face had become an indistinct blur in Tara's mind, but the photograph brought it back in all its ugliness. She cast the print aside with distaste.

"What are you going to do with all these?" she asked.

"Take them back to the States, show them in exhibition. That's what I've intended all along. Then, maybe one day, perhaps someone will publish my entire collection. A pictorial history of the Gold Rush."

He said it wistfully. He had a craving for immortality, and Tara knew that these pictures were his hope of it.

Hart had stacks more photographs. He had picked out the ones he thought his best, but he was so pleased with them all that he wanted Tara to look at the rest. She saw his views of Miles Canyon, of Windy Arm on Lake Tagish, of Mount Halcon, of prospectors building boats on Lake Bennett while waiting for the thaw, of Mounties high up on mountain patrol, of Indian guides squatting mournfully in front of their tepees, of snow-covered shacks, of lonely graves, of . . .

Tara stopped. She stared at a photograph in her hand.

"Where did you take this?" she asked very quietly.

He glanced at the photograph she was holding. "Oh, that one, at Sheep Camp, I think. Why?"

"That man," she said, her hand shaking.

"What about him?" He looked at the picture again. The man was

240

in front of a tent. He was perched on a crate, his right leg stiffly extended. He was holding a crude crutch. A dog team was beside him, the huskies sitting on their haunches.

"That's Daniel," she exclaimed. "I'm sure that's Daniel."

"Are you certain?" asked Hart.

"When did you take this?" Tara almost shouted. He turned the pages of his little book, while Tara waited, her heart pounding.

"A few weeks ago," he told her. "On my round trip. Sometime in January, I think."

"Sheep Camp. Where is that?" Her excitement was growing. This was Daniel, no doubt about it—his eyes, his mouth. Despite the straggly beard, she could tell it was he.

"It's on the Chilkoot Pass," Hart said. He looked at the photograph again. "Is that really him?"

"Yes, yes!"

Hart was barraged with questions. How did he come to take the picture? Did he talk to Daniel? What was he doing there? Did he say anything?

"Tara," said Hart, raising his hands, *"nicht so schnell.* Slowly, my dear."

"Think back," pressed Tara. "Tell me."

He consulted his book again, and shook his head. "I did not take his name. I simply photographed him because I thought he looked like, like a man marooned. He'd broken his ankle. He couldn't continue up the Chilkoot until it had mended. I felt a little sorry for him. The Gold Rush was passing him by."

She wanted to kiss the photograph, to hold it to her heart, to make it talk.

"He was all right, otherwise," Hart reassured her hastily. "He had plenty of supplies."

"But if he couldn't walk . . ."

"He could hobble around on his crutch, but until the bone set he couldn't tackle the rest of the pass. So he just had to sweat it out."

"Ernst, he must be there now." Her eyes were shining with excitement.

"Tara, I have no idea. It was weeks ago." He could see the frantic plea in her eyes. "Of course it takes a long time for a broken ankle to heal. I suppose he could be."

She kept staring at the photograph. It was her first sight of Daniel for so long. After all this, there he sat, looking straight at her. It was wonderful.

"Can I have this?" she asked.

"Of course."

"I have to get there. I have to get to Sheep Camp as quickly as possible."

"That's foolish, Tara," Hart said quietly. "He'll probably have left by the time you arrive."

"I don't care. You said he couldn't move." She looked at him for confirmation. "Well, he may still be there now. He may not yet be able to travel far. I can probably catch up with him. Or someone may know where he's gone to." She saw his face. "It's no good trying to dissuade me, Ernst. My mind's made up."

Hart shrugged resignedly, and Tara took his hand. "Ernst," she said softly, "you've brought me luck."

"Tara, my dear. I haven't done anything."

She held up the photograph so that they could both look at it. "You've found him," she said, her eyes filling with tears of happiness. "You've found him, alive."

"You won't be coming back, then," Mrs. Miles said sadly when Tara announced her plans the following morning.

"No," Tara said. "It's goodbye to Dawson. There's nothing more for me here. Daniel's at Sheep Camp, and I'll pick up his trail from there. You can't imagine how excited I am."

"Can't I?" Mrs. Miles was looking at the photograph. "He's a handsome man, I'll say that, and a mighty lucky one too. I hope he doesn't forget it. I can't think of many women who would go through what you have." She sighed. "Sometimes I wonder if men really appreciate a devoted woman, or just take her for granted, like mine did, bless him."

"Daniel's not like that," said Tara with conviction, and Mrs. Miles had to smile. "The thought of being with him again is all that's kept me going all these months. And your kindness, of course, Linda," she added, hastily. "Without you, I don't know what would have happened to me."

"No, you would have managed," broke in Mrs. Miles. "You would have survived. Mind you, I didn't think that when I first saw you, I didn't really believe you had it in you. But now, I don't worry."

"I wish I felt half as confident," said Tara.

"You know, over the past few months I've seen you gradually turn into one of us," Mrs. Miles reflected. "You belong now. I've watched you become capable of dealing with the hardships of this place, and yet you've remained very much a woman. That's what I mean when I say you belong."

"Thank you," Tara said as Mrs. Miles fussed over the coffeepot, embarrassed by what she had said.

"Supposing," Mrs. Miles suddenly began, handing Tara a mug of coffee, "—what I mean is I know all you want to do is to return to the States with Daniel, but have you ever thought that maybe, you could, well, you could help me run this place on a permanent basis. I've got to know you, Tara. Didn't much like you at first, figured out you were a cheap little hustler, but I've learned better. And now, well, if I had a daughter to leave all this to . . . ."

Tara stared at her, completely dumbstruck.

"I've made a good little business here," Mrs. Miles went on. "I give good value, the lodgers pay on the nail. I've got a little nest egg stashed away. It's not a gold mine, but it's enough to keep me in my old age. Well, if we became partners, maybe opened up a second lodging house, or a little hotel. A decent, well-run place, not a dive or a cheap saloon but a respectable place for honest folk. Don't you think together we'd do very well?" She stopped, looking at Tara almost pleadingly.

"Linda," Tara said gently, "that's the nicest proposition anyone has ever put to me. It's just that . . . ."

"But think of what might happen," Mrs. Miles continued, then hesitated.

"What do you mean?"

"Only that if things don't work out for you . . ." Seeing Tara's expression, Mrs. Miles let her words die on her lips.

"What exactly are you trying to say?"

"Only that you've always got a home here, whatever happens. If you find Daniel . . ." She paused. "Well, face it, you haven't found him yet. Sure, you've spotted him in a photograph, but you don't know where he might be now. You came across his watch and his letter, but what happened?"

Tara was very tense. "Are you trying to tell me that he won't be at Sheep Camp?" The tone of her voice was more like a challenge than a question.

"Of course not," Mrs. Miles replied hurriedly. "I know you'll find him. All I'm saying is that if ever, if anything goes wrong, come back here."

"There'll be no turning back, Linda," Tara said very quietly. "I'm very grateful to you, but now I have to move on. I *know* I've found

243

him. I *know* where he is." She picked up the photograph and gazed at it. "I know he's waiting for me."

"Sure he is," agreed Mrs. Miles, but not sounding so convinced as Tara felt.

Later that day she went into Tara's bedroom and found her poring over a map Hart had given her. Next to it was the little compass.

"How do you plan on getting there?" Mrs. Miles asked.

"I'll take a dog team."

"By yourself?"

"Of course."

"You make it sound like a day's hike. It's not even Spring yet. It's no journey for a woman by herself."

"Shame on you, Linda," Tara laughed, "when you've just told me I'd made the grade. If they had a post office, I'd send you a card to say I've arrived. I'll be in Sheep Camp by the end of March. That's only a few weeks off." She looked at the map. "See, it's a straight trail. I'll make my way down to the lakes and through the Chilkoot Pass. Sheep Camp is a few miles beyond the state line and that's where he is."

"But you should wait. You should wait till the thaw," cautioned Mrs. Miles. "You can take the boat then, and you'll be able to join up with other people. There'll be dozens of prospectors leaving Dawson when the river thaws."

"*Wait!*" exclaimed Tara. "Until then? Linda, you don't know what you're saying. He might have left. I simply can't wait. *You* wouldn't, would you?"

"No, I suppose not. But I still think . . ." She shrugged; she knew it was no good. Once Tara had made up her mind, it was pointless trying to argue.

"All right. I'll buy your supplies," she said.

"Certainly not," Tara protested. "You've done more than enough. I'll hire a dog team, and I'll get everything I need."

"Don't be ridiculous," Mrs. Miles scoffed. "Those storekeepers would charge you the earth. You know what prices are now. I'll talk to Mr. Brock and get them at cost, you wait and see."

Mrs. Miles could be just as determined as Tara and, as she had proved so many times, she always kept her word.

Just at the point when the *Klondike Nugget* predicted that the spring rush would make Dawson the largest city north of San Francisco and west of Toronto, just as an outfit called the Yukon Telegraph Company strung its first wire between Dawson and

Lousetown, at the very time Dawson could boast two banks, two newspapers, and five churches as well as the biggest red-light district outside the Barbary Coast, Jefferson Randolph Smith decided to sell out.

With the anticipated influx of thousands of lucky strikers, saloons, bars, and gambling dens sounded attractive and profitable propositions, so the news of Smith's unexpected departure swept around the town like wildfire.

Tara heard people say that Smith could not have chosen a better time to pull out and that the prospect of a civilized Dawson made him realize that his rich pickings were over. The railroad was becoming a reality. Slowly, mile by mile, it was going to forge northward soon, and its arrival would mean a different Dawson, a place where Smith would find his buccaneering more restricted, fast communication curtailing his scope. And there was a rumor that the Dawson detachment would be increased to eighty Mounties.

Tara knew how Smith would describe it. "Limits free enterprise," he would say. "Cuts down a fellow's chance of showing some initiative."

And Tara also remembered Smith's talk in the bar about governors, senators, and presidents. The flag in his office, McKinley's picture; his vision of a rail link all the way to Europe; his political aspirations; his boast that he was returning to Skagway to "put that little pile on the map." She was certain that when he talked about his ambitions, he for once meant what he said.

The likelihood of Senator Smith, Governor Smith of Alaska, President Smith of the United States seemed absurd in that raw wilderness, and yet Tara had to admit that Smith had the nerve.

The political friction between the United States and Canada was increasingly discussed in Dawson, and even Tara, engrossed with planning her forthcoming journey, became interested in the debate. Mrs. Miles's boarders said the government was going crazy. Canadian officials, with the exception of Constantine and his handful of men, were called grafters and worse. And to the Canadians, the American gold seekers were a growing horde of greedy parasites and unruly roughnecks.

Although Dawson was a Canadian city, four-fifths of its population owed no allegiance to Queen Victoria. When the gold royalty was suddenly upped by Ottawa to twenty percent of any mine's output exceeding five hundred dollars a week, the Yanks had rebelled. Any move to make the Yukon American would have to start at Skagway, where the Stars and Stripes already flew. There the United States

245

faced a blurred, unclear frontier line between Alaska and British Columbia. If anyone wanted to wipe out that line, he had to begin where Soapy Smith was now heading.

Not that Jefferson Smith was idealistic enough to put patriotism before profit, and it was true that his opportunities for exploiting the needs of Dawson's community were getting, one way and another, more cramped. He had always been proud of his Dawson postal service, his phony telegraph line in Skagway and his Fortymile post office which sold only United States stamps, all part of his campaign to Americanize the Yukon. But now Constantine had cracked down, and the North West Mounted Police took over handling Dawson's mail.

Already, too, there was talk of crude tramways being built in the creeks, shifting buckets on cables anything up to three hundred feet high. Gold mining was becoming mechanized, reducing the openings for the likes of Smith, boosting the flow of supplies.

Luckily for Smith, just as he started selling his major Dawson assets, the various establishments on Front Street and the Regina Cafe fortuitously increased sharply in value because some of the competition disappeared, literally, in smoke. Arkansas Jim Hall saw his Greentree Hotel, long a rival of Smith's places, go up in flames. Charlie Worden and Big Alex McDonald stood helpless as their hotels burned down before their eyes. The temperature was forty-five below, the water frozen hard; ice had to be melted for the hoses, but it solidified again long before it reached the nozzles. Despite frantic attempts, each wooden building collapsed in showers of sparking splinters.

So, naturally, when Smith went to Arkansas Jim and Charlie Worden and Big Alex McDonald and asked if they were interested in acquiring the Monte Carlo, the Golden Nugget, the Eldorado, and the Regina Cafe, together with his other little ventures, they made very good offers. It was that or being out of business. Smith's decision to quit Dawson had turned into one of his sure things.

Before she departed, Tara went to say goodbye to Charles Constantine. "Well, Inspector," she said, after he had asked her gruffly to sit down, "you'll be pleased to learn that you won't be seeing me in Dawson much longer."

"I know," he said. "You're leaving. Good luck."

"Who told you?" she asked, puzzled.

"Your friend, Soapy Smith."

"He can't have," said Tara. "He doesn't even know."

"Oh, he knows all right, Mrs. Kane. I suppose I should be thankful that Dawson loses two headaches at once, you and Mr. Smith. He's wise to get out of British Columbia, believe me."

"Where did Mr. Smith say I was going, since he knows so much?" asked Tara.

"Oh, he just mentioned it as an aside," Constantine replied. "He said that he would see you in Skagway eventually. I gained the impression that was the arrangement."

"There is no arrangement," Tara snapped.

Constantine inclined his head, like someone saying, have it your own way. "I take it you're not asking for a police escort this time," he remarked, getting to his feet.

"No, thank you." Tara blushed at the memory. "I'm going under my own steam."

"Well," he said, "pity my wife never had an opportunity to meet her sister." The chilly eyes almost twinkled for a moment. Then he held out his hand. "Good luck, Mrs. Kane. Travel safe." He actually means it, she thought, as they shook hands.

Outside, by the wooden hitching post, stood Campbell.

"I hear you're leaving us," he said.

"Everybody seems to know," she smiled. "Yes, I am. I've found my husband."

"That's great. Where is he?"

"Near Sheep Camp."

"Just listen to you," chuckled Campbell. "Quite the Yukon traveler."

Tara noticed for the first time that he had been given his three stripes back. "I'm glad you've got those again," she said.

"Oh," he shrugged, "the Inspector's so short of men they'd make a jackass a sergeant."

"I don't think that's true, Andrew," she replied.

He walked along with her. "Are you going to miss us?" he asked, as they crossed the street.

"Dawson, no," she said. "Some of the people, yes." He slowed his pace so that it was easier for her to keep up with him. "You remember the last time you marched me through the town?"

"How could I forget? The Inspector was real mad at you."

"The looks people gave me," she recalled. "I often wonder what they thought I'd done."

"Take care, Tara," was all he said when they stopped at the corner of Third Street. He looked her in the eyes, nodded, and walked off.

Tara hurried on to the lodging house. She still had lots to do. When she arrived back, she was surprised to find it quiet. At five-thirty Mrs. Miles was usually in the kitchen, bustling over the preparation of the evening meal. But today the kitchen was empty, although large pots simmered on the range, emitting inviting aromas.

"Linda, I'm back," she called, but there was silence.

Perplexed, Tara went to her room, washed her hands, straightened her hair, and put on her apron. She was half way down the stairs before she realized she had not come across a single lodger. Usually "Doc" Robbins and Mr. Brock were back by this time, closely followed by the Bartletts and Lamore.

There was still no sign of Mrs. Miles when Tara returned to the kitchen, so she decided to get on with laying the dining-room table. She went to the cupboard where the condiments were kept, but tonight they weren't there.

"That's odd," she muttered to herself.

The cutlery drawer was also empty, and the glasses had gone from the shelf.

"Tara, you're late!" came Mrs. Miles's voice from the dining room.

When Tara opened the door she was greeted by a blinding magnesium flash and cheering voices. For a moment she stood, totally bewildered, colored lights dancing in front of her eyes. Then she saw Hart emerge from under his black camera hood.

"Ernst, what . . ." she began, then stopped short.

The boarders and Mrs. Miles were seated in their usual positions at the table, but there were three extra places. Mrs. Miles was sitting opposite a most unexpected guest. The Reverend Bowers smiled benignly at Tara while Hart grinned at her.

"It's a surprise farewell party," smiled Mrs. Miles, getting up, obviously delighted that her plan had worked out so well.

"Oh, Linda." Tara was so overcome with emotion she felt like crying. Instead she threw her arms around Mrs. Miles's ample shoulders and kissed her on both cheeks. "I just don't know what to say. Thank you, thank you so much."

"And we've got a special treat for dinner too." Mrs. Miles patted Tara's hand and led her to a vacant chair.

"First, I must take another photograph," Hart insisted, again disappearing under his black hood. "All please smile."

Everyone sat stock still, grinning somewhat self-consciously while Hart focused the lens. Tara couldn't help glancing out of the corner of her eye at Bowers. Now she understood how it was that Smith knew she was leaving town. It amused her that Mrs. Miles and the others, who prided themselves at knowing everything about Dawson's community, were not aware of his role in Smith's setup.

248

There was another bang and a great deal of smoke as Hart immortalized Tara's farewell dinner, after which everybody started talking at once. From under the table Mr. Brock produced a bottle of whisky and cast a rather sheepish look at Mrs. Miles.

"Well, just this once," she agreed good-naturedly. Then she got up and went into the kitchen while Mr. Brock passed around the bottle and everyone filled their glasses.

"Sister Tara," said Bowers, raising the bottle, "are you partaking?"

"I won't, thank you," replied Tara.

"Perhaps you and Mrs. Miles would prefer something more refined." So saying he placed on the table a bottle of champagne. "Compliments of one of my flock who particularly asked to be remembered to you." Tara arched her eyebrows, but he was too busy opening the bottle to notice.

"Dinner is served!" Mrs. Miles carried in an enormous plate on which sat two roast capons. Compliments flowed as she placed the delicacy in the middle of the table.

"Linda, how on earth did you manage to get those?" exclaimed Tara.

"That's our little secret, isn't it, Mr. Brock?" chuckled Mrs. Miles.

Before Mrs. Miles served up, she turned to Bowers and said, "Reverend, if you please."

A hush descended over the festivities as Bowers, his face straight, lowered his head, and intoned, "We thank you dear Lord for the food you have provided, and may we always show our thankfulness now and forever."

"Amen," they all chorused and Tara wondered, since she had never heard that particular form of grace before, whether he had made it up on the spur of the moment.

Everyone was in high spirits as they tucked into the meal, which Mrs. Miles had obviously planned with special care.

"Dear Tara," Hart said, hardly audible above the hubbub, "I'm going to miss you a great deal."

"As we all are," piped up Bowers, who rose and addressed Mrs. Miles. "Madam, please don't think I'm in the habit of drinking or leading Christian women astray, but may I request that just this once I pour you a glass of champagne, so that on this very special occasion we may toast the future happiness and success of Sister Tara."

Mrs. Miles inclined her head. "Only a little, though, Reverend," she said, and Tara felt her mouth drop open.

"Gentlemen," Bowers said, "may I ask you to be upstanding to toast two gracious ladies." He paused as the men got up. "To Mrs.

Miles, our deepest thanks for her generous and kind hospitality and for inviting us to be her guests. And to Sister Tara, may God speed your journey, and I pray you find the happiness and contentment you so richly deserve and have so laboriously pursued."

"Mrs. Miles and Tara," echoed the ensemble.

Tara had to admit that Bowers carried off his role with aplomb.

"You'll stop by before you leave tomorrow, won't you?" she heard Hart saying.

"Of course, Ernst."

"I'll have your sled loaded up and ready at the store," Brock said, his mouth full of chicken. "Come around ten-thirty."

The remainder of the course was spent discussing the news from the outside: the outrage of the battleship *Maine*, the inevitability of war with Spain. The conversation grew louder and more patriotic as more bottles were produced and passed around.

Tara helped Mrs. Miles clear the table, and once they were in the comparative quiet of the kitchen she said. "Linda, there aren't enough words to say how grateful I am to you. I'm really touched by your thoughtfulness. I'm only sorry to be leaving you," but she could no longer control her tears.

"There, there," soothed Mrs. Miles, taking her in her arms. "I'm going to miss you so much, my dear, but as you said it's time for you to move on. I just didn't want you to leave without the memory of something nice happening to you in Dawson."

Tara fished in her pocket for a handkerchief. Suddenly Mrs. Miles was also crying. As they both dried their eyes they realized how funny they must have looked and started laughing. In spite of the months they had spent in one another's company, this was the first time they had shared a joke together.

For dessert, Mrs. Miles had opened some of her precious cans of fruit, and Hart insisted that he take yet another photograph and that they have something to go with the coffee. He burrowed in his camera case and from its depths brought out a bottle of clear liquid.

"Schnapps!" he cried, and everyone giggled a little drunkenly. "Finest Ansbacher."

Coffee was served in the sacred parlor, which, for once in its life, had a warm and informal ambiance. The men started telling each other risqué stories, and Mrs. Miles was in too good a humor to object. She and Tara returned to the kitchen and began cleaning up. They had drunk enough to make the work easy.

Hart and Bowers left together, both of them thanking Mrs. Miles effusively, Hart reminding Tara to stop by the studio in the morning.

Bowers's farewell was more religious. "May God bless and guide you," he said, placing his hand on her head solemnly. "I've a strong feeling I'll be seeing you again." With a conspiratorial wink he left.

When Tara climbed into her bed that night, she felt tired but happy. She looked around the room with all its familiar furniture and sighed. It had become a haven for her. "Oh, little room," she whispered, "I'm going to miss you." She buried her head in her pillow and cried.

How sentimental, she scolded herself. Very soon she would be with Daniel.

Lamore and "Doc" Robbins said their farewells immediately after breakfast Tara had got up very early to finish off her bit of packing. "Don't forget to recommend me if you meet anyone heading for Dawson with a toothache," Robbins said. "And thanks for everything," he added, pressing something into the palm of her hand. Tara had never been tipped in her life, but she was not too proud to accept a five-dollar piece.

Lamore's leave-taking was more oily. Tara came face to face with him on the landing, and there was no escaping his wet kiss.

"Thanks for not mentioning what you saw," he said, when at last she managed to free herself.

"That's all right, Mr. Lamore," she said. "Hope you get the sawmill back soon."

Mrs. Miles walked with her to Brock's store, where the Bartletts had taken the sled and team. It stood outside, piled high with equipment and provisions. Tara tucked her sleeping bag, filled with her belongings, under the tarpaulin, then turned to Mrs. Miles.

"Linda, you've got me enough stuff to last a lifetime. How can I begin to thank you?"

"Don't begin," she said, tears in her eyes. "Come on, let's go inside."

Brock and the Bartlett brothers stood like a reception committee, each with a gift for her. The Bartletts presented her with another pair of goggles. Brock gave her a little jar of honey, a very valuable commodity and worth a good deal of money.

Still accompanied by Mrs. Miles, Tara took the sled over to Hart's studio. He was waiting for them outside, his camera already set up.

"This is one photograph I'll always have in my own album," he told her.

Tara and Mrs. Miles posed with their arms around one another before Hart's lens, and then he took pictures of them separately.

"Dear Tara," he said after he had exposed several more plates, "I

251

refuse to say goodbye to you because I know we will meet again. I will be leaving for San Francisco in the Spring, but no matter what, I will always ask if anyone knows your whereabouts in the hope . . ."

"Ernst," Tara began, but Hart put two fingers lightly on her lips.

"Tell Daniel when you find him that he's a lucky man and I envy him greatly. You are an amazingly remarkable woman, I love you dearly, and I only hope that he feels for you as I do." Then he took Tara in his arms and kissed her, his lips pressing against hers firmly, lingeringly, filled with love but not passion. She had not been kissed like that in a long while and, for a moment, her heart beat faster.

"*Auf Wiedersehen,*" he choked, and without a backward glance rushed into his studio, leaving his precious equipment in the street. Tara looked after him.

"*Au revoir,* Ernst," she said, very quietly.

"Everything ready?" inquired Mrs. Miles after Tara had regained her composure.

"Yes," she replied with a watery smile. "Oh, Linda," she suddenly sobbed.

"Come, come, woman, pull yourself together," Mrs. Miles said firmly. "You're behaving like a child. Now you're sure you've got everything?"

Tara nodded. "Then you're ready to leave, my dear." They embraced. "God speed, travel safely. Keep in touch, even if the letters do take months to get here." She pressed Tara's hand reassuringly.

Tara walked to her sled and picked up the whip. She turned and waved to Mrs. Miles, at the same time shouting, "Mush!"

The dogs moved off, and Mrs. Miles slowly receded behind her. As Tara drove through Dawson, she realized how it had grown since she had first laid eyes on it. There were new thoroughfares, Well Street, Broadway Avenue; the population had doubled with the prospect of thousands more arriving. There were now stores selling things like patent-leather shoes, cribbage boards, opera glasses. The town was changing, and at night it was louder and there were more lights winking from new buildings. But it was still a lawless community pretending to be a town, and she was not sorry to leave it. Soon, she told herself, soon she and Daniel would leave this cold, bleak, savage land. Soon they would be on their way home.

CHAPTER TWENTY-ONE

Sheep Camp was so named because, it was said, a group of hunters had once camped there, seeking mountain sheep. It lay in a deep basin scooped out of the surrounding mountains, the last staging point beyond Dyea, and four miles from the evil, treacherous Chilkoot.

The White Pass was terrible, but the Chilkoot had a cold, fearful majesty all its own. It turned men into pigmies, insignificant dots on its huge surface. An endless line of men climbed the slippery slope of the Chilkoot, each one following the footsteps of the man ahead, draping the steep incline to the summit of the mountain like a human garland.

They were going north, to the destiny they were all dreaming of, the gold fields of Dawson, Eldorado, Bonanza, and beyond. Always northward.

Tara's route was in the opposite direction, down Long Hill, along the Scales to the outpost they called Stone House. Near there was the spot Hart had identified. He had drawn a crude map of the place where he had photographed Daniel.

The snow steadily got heavier as Tara began descending a gradient of thirty-five degrees. It became almost impossible to guide the dog team, and she had to leave the animals to make their own way. At times she fell on her hands and knees but still seemed upright. Dizzily, she grabbed hold of the sled again and clung to it, wondering frantically when all would crash down into the abyss. A thick blanket of heavy flurries blinded her as she slipped and slithered down the steep terrain.

Exhausted, battered, soaked to the skin, and freezing cold, Tara reached the settlement at the foot of the hill. Although she was only a few miles from Sheep Camp, her body and the gray, threatening sky told her that she could not go on. She would have to wait until she felt stronger and the weather had cleared.

Around her, angry prospectors were arguing with Indian guides who refused to take them up the Chilkoot because of the worsening conditions. She knew she had no alternative but to hole up too.

She found a protected spot and, as if battening down a ship before a storm, she tucked away the sled, covered it, tied down the tarpaulin, made sure the dogs were safely fastened, rigged up the tent, and crawled inside. Curled up in her sleeping bag, waiting, she was

253

reminded of those fearful moments on the *North Fork* when the crew strung up the lifelines and shut the hatches, and the passengers sat helpless, anticipating the worst.

When the blizzard came, it charged with the ferocity of a tornado. The wind howled; gusts tore at the guy ropes and pummeled the canvas. Tara thought the tent would be torn free, and it was little comfort knowing that she would have to stay there for as long as the storm raged. Daniel was so near, but she couldn't get to him. He would be sheltering too against this onslaught. If only he knew how close she was, how she needed him, what the calm would bring.

Outside the tent it was neither dark nor light. It could have been early morning or late evening; it was a blur of snow whipped along by a shrieking, whistling wind. Then, after what seemed like hours, the howling eased. In the sudden quiet, she thought she heard one or two distant rumblings that sounded like faraway artillery fire, some ghostly bombardment in the Chilkoot.

She closed her eyes and prayed that when she woke up the weather would have cleared enough for her to continue the last few miles to Daniel. Tomorrow she would make up for lost time, she promised herself, and then she fell asleep.

The date was Saturday, April 2, 1898.

She woke early on the Sunday morning. When she emerged from the tent it was curiously calm. The sky was clear, and there was even a hint of sunshine. Hastily she bolted down her breakfast. She was anxious to get moving, but she knew better than to set off on an empty stomach. Then she fed the dogs, dug out the sled, and loaded up her tent and supplies.

The going was slow, the snow so deep that the dogs and the sled sank into it. After an hour, in which she had been able to cover no more than a few hundred yards, she heard the same dull rumbling as the night before. This time it seemed louder, threateningly sinister. Was it her imagination or was the ground shaking slightly? She urged on her dogs. Daniel was ahead; nothing else mattered.

Gradually, spreading a few miles in front of her, was the sprawling sea of tents, shacks, hovels that was Sheep Camp. All over the basin, against a backdrop of mountains, swarmed black flecks—people.

From where she stood, Sheep Camp looked quiet, peaceful, and orderly. Hart had told her the place was a madhouse of nearly fifteen hundred people, some halting on their way north, some passing through to Dyea, others just resting, broke. It had its permanents and its transients; it wasn't a town, yet it wasn't a camp either.

Over on the far side, on the slopes leading down to it, were other dwellings. That was where Hart had photographed Daniel, the actual spot he had drawn in the map for Tara. She was too far away to make out anything other than a few dots on the mountainside, which she assumed were the cabins and shacks.

Once more, the ominous rumbling echoed and vibrated in the strangely muffled stillness.

Three hours later, she entered Sheep Camp, driving her dogs along the slushy, slippery camp road that would lead to the slope where, judging by Hart's map, she would find Daniel. She guessed it could not be much more than a mile away. Although she was exhausted, and the last few hours had been more grueling and frightening than the whole of the journey, she did not care. Within a matter of an hour she would be with Daniel at last. She kept staring at those huts and tents on the slope. She was close enough to see people moving around, and the smoke rising from chimney-stacks and open fires.

"Oh, thank God, thank God," she muttered to herself, her eyes riveted on the mountainside.

Then it happened.

She could feel the tremors under her as the rumbling thunder reverberated like the kettledrums of hell, crescendoing in a tremendous roar, a fearful crashing sound.

Before Tara's disbelieving eyes, the top of the mountain she was heading toward slid twenty-five hundred feet down and enveloped everything in its path—huts, tents, cabins—consuming the specks of life on that slope.

Tara screamed as she saw people tossed aside, sucked under the expanding white tide, flung high, and disappear. The avalanche roared on and on, blanketing all below it. As if to make sure no one escaped, more snow crashed down from the top, burying what had been the slope encampment under thirty feet of snow and ice. It was all bare, white, crushing and suffocating those who were entombed under its weight.

In the eerie silence that followed, Tara stood numb with horror. She could not believe what she had witnessed.

All over Sheep Camp people had come rushing out of shacks, makeshift saloons, shabby tents. They stood shielding their eyes, staring, gaping at the awful spectacle of the avalanche's terrible destruction. Slowly, a cloud of snow rose, a cold funeral pyre. Then they rushed forward, stumbling, groping, sliding, panting in a frenzied attempt to get to the slope.

255

Daniel, Daniel, Daniel was the only thought that pounded through Tara's head. He's there, I've got to get to him, I must get him out before it's too late. Daniel, oh my God, Daniel.

The unnatural stillness was shattered by shouting and the clanging of makeshift alarms. Tara was staggering along with the crowd; more appeared every second, all stampeding forward wildly, carrying spades and pickaxes, sinking deep into the snow but dragging themselves on.

Tara stumbled on blindly, silently moaning, sobbing, praying that she would find Daniel.

People were digging frantically, not knowing if they were reaching anyone, by the time she got to the slope. It was a terrible sensation, to be standing on tons of snow, sinking into it, knowing that under it who knew how many people were buried, some dead, some slowly suffocating.

She rushed from group to group asking whether anyone had been found, but they were all too busy digging to answer. Then the first body was brought out. He was dead, his limbs stiff, his body icy, his face set like a man blissfully asleep. They laid the corpse on the snow. Tara ran over, but the man was not Daniel. She sobbed with relief, but it was short-lived.

All the time more rescuers were arriving from Sheep Camp, some bringing supplies of spades, pickaxes, and gold pans, anything to dig with.

"Here!" yelled a man, waving a pickaxe. "I can hear somebody." He started hacking away furiously and soon others joined him, trying to gouge airholes into the snow so that whoever was down there could at least breathe.

Tara grabbed a gold pan and, almost possessed, began digging, shoveling, forcing apart the frozen layers. They could heard a voice coming from the depths, a man's voice. They all stopped and listened. No one could make out what he was shouting; but they all began attacking the snow with renewed vigor. They dug and hacked and then stopped again to listen, but this time no sound came from underneath. Finally they lifted him out. He had been alive, but they were too late.

A few women from Sheep Camp were now running up, sobbing, screaming, crying, tearing away with their bare hands at mounds of frozen snow, staggering about calling out their men's names.

"Mike!" yelled one of them, passing everyone unseeing, "Mike, where are you?"

Corpses were gradually dug out and laid in lines like dead soldiers on parade.

Tara counted the bodies—six, ten, fifteen, twenty—studying each face, young and old, clean-shaven and bearded, calm and terrified. She was appalled by the happiness she felt that none of them was Daniel.

One man, who seemed to have made himself the leader, was shouting orders for more tools, hurricane lamps, blankets, brandy, tents, for fires to be built. He was collecting around him a whole army of rescuers, for every able-bodied person in Sheep Camp was coming forward to help dig out the victims.

"Mister!" called out Tara. "Where do I find Daniel Kane?"

He stared at her angrily. "How the hell should I know?" he yelled.

Death had not been dignified for many of the victims. Some bodies were dug out frozen into a running position, as they had fled from the oncoming avalanche. One man had been buried head down, another in a praying attitude, but most of the bodies were stiff and crushed, the snow having entombed them so tightly that they had had no room to breathe or move, only to die.

Despite her desolation, Tara tried to help out. One man carried the frozen body of his crushed partner and dumped it in front of her.

"He's OK," said the man, "he's OK. He only needs a drink. You got some brandy?"

"He's dead," Tara said.

The miner stared at her and then at his buddy. "No," he said, gathering up the body in his arms and staggering off with it.

A few minutes later they dug out the first survivor. Gently, Tara wrapped him in blankets, gave him brandy, and rubbed his wrists. She could feel a faint pulse and she kept saying, "You'll be fine, you're doing great."

He turned his face toward her, dazed, his eyes blank. He was shivering and his teeth were chattering.

"Been buried for three hours," explained one of his rescuers. "Thought he was a goner. He's a lucky son of a bitch."

"What's your name?" Tara asked, and the man rasped, "Kelly."

"Was anybody with you?"

"Five, six, maybe more."

"Was one of them a man called Daniel Kane?" Kelly stared at her dully and the rescuer shot her a withering glance. Plainly he disapproved of the selfishness of her question.

For how many hours Tara worked on the bodies and the survivors, she had no idea. She lost count of the number of eyelids she closed for the last time, the missing heartbeats she tried to find, the expressionless, frozen faces she covered with blankets. Her physical and mental strength to endure such a gruesome ordeal was only possible because of her dogged determination not to leave before she knew whether Daniel was among the victims.

In the bitter cold, groups of men were still digging for survivors, but mostly they found dead men. For every living person there were ten or twelve corpses. The avalanche had swept away many more people than anyone had first realized. Unbelievably they hauled an ox out alive. Somehow the animal had managed to trample itself a little tunnel in the deep snow. Once rescued, it seemed quite contented.

The avalanche had also taken its toll of the few survivors. Some had severe frostbite; others had been driven mad by the experience of being buried alive. One man cursed his rescuers in the name of Jehovah and warned them that this was only the beginning of the wrath of the Lord. When they tried to guide him to a sled so that he could be transported back to Sheep Camp, he fought off their helping hands and, cursing and singing at the top of his voice, started running back up the slope. One or two rescuers ran after him, but he raced off at such a speed that it was hopeless.

Tara was unutterably weary. The horror, the misery of the catastrophe, her anxiety about Daniel, increasingly enveloped her. As corpse after corpse was laid out, she felt more and more desperate. Here she was helping others, but nobody was helping her. She was too tired to stand, too distraught to cry, too hoarse and cold to talk, but she could wait no longer for news, she had to find out for herself.

She tried group after group of rescuers, who were now digging by the light of hurricane lamps.

"Have you found my husband? she demanded, her voice unnaturally high-pitched as she tugged frantically at men's sleeves. They shook her off and didn't bother to answer. "Has anyone come across Daniel Kane?" she shouted. Again, there was no reply. "Daniel! Daniel! Daniel!" she screamed hysterically, running around in circles.

No one took any notice. There were too many like her. They had become immune to the desperation of the victims' relatives, friends, and partners.

Tara sank to her knees. "Oh God," she cried, the tears freezing on her face, "please, please help me. Somebody please help me find my husband!"

Then a hand shook her roughly. "You!" barked a gruff voice. "Get up. We need you." A black-bearded man glared down at her.

"Leave me alone," Tara said. "I've done enough."

"Get up." The man yanked Tara to her feet.

"I said leave me alone. I'm not going to help any more. I've had enough of helping other people. Why won't somebody help *me?*" she shouted at him hysterically.

He slapped her hard around the face. "Take a grip of yourself," he ordered. He waited for her sobbing to subside. "There's a woman over there about to give birth any second. Go help her."

"Get someone else!" she sobbed. "I'm not helping any more until someone helps me—helps me find my husband."

The black-bearded man grabbed her by the shoulders and shook her violently. "Pull yourself together for Christ's sake!" he said, not letting go of her. "Everyone's doing their level best to dig out those poor bastards, and you're not helping any by screaming and ranting like a maniac. That woman over there needs you. Get her to Sheep Camp before it's too late."

"I'm not leaving," Tara said, "not until I know what's happened to Daniel. Somebody else can do it. Get somebody else. Why doesn't her husband look after her. He's responsible, isn't he?" she shouted.

"He's down there," the man said, pointing at the snow, "just the same as yours is. Now, are you going to help her?"

She felt totally ashamed.

Unexpectedly the black-bearded man put his arms around her. "I know what you're going through, lass," he said. "Come on, follow me."

The woman had been covered with a fur pelt, but Tara could clearly see the outline of her swollen belly. She bent over. The woman was pale, with blue-tinged skin stretched over prominent cheekbones, mauve shadows under her eyes. She gave a cry of pain and clutched Tara's hand, tight.

"My baby," she whimpered, "my baby."

Compassion flooded through Tara as she placed her hand on the woman's stomach and felt the baby move within. Amid so much death, this woman was going to give life.

"You, you, and you," Tara said wearily to the bystanders, "get her onto a sled. Carry her very gently, and don't drop her, for God's sake. Hurry up!"

She turned to the black-bearded man. "Daniel Kane. Remember the name, please. Any news, anything, I want to know, no matter whether it be good or bad.

"You'll be told," he said, turning away.

"So don't you forget, I want some help too," she called after him.

The three men had strapped the woman onto a sled and were ready to move off when Tara caught up with them. She held the woman's hand as they gingerly negotiated the slippery descent to Sheep Camp.

259

Tara glanced back at the rescue parties, illuminated by the flickering lights of a hundred hurricane lamps. From a distance it looked like a pretty snow scene, with the grim truth well camouflaged.

They took the woman to a tent. Inside was a pallet, over which one of the men draped the fur pelt. They lifted her onto it, and Tara covered her with a blanket. The three men stood looking on, uncertain of what to do next.

She turned to them. "You can make yourselves useful," she said. "I need hot water, plenty of it. Get me a stove, pans, extra blankets, a knife, anything sharp. And I'll want a crate or a drawer, something to put the baby in."

"If it lives," mumbled one of the men.

Tara glared at him. "Get going." She had taken charge with such authority that they did not even hesitate.

"See if there's a doctor here," she called after them, but she knew that was unlikely. Then she knelt down by the woman and loosened her coat. "Everything will be all right," she said, trying to sound reassuring.

The woman moaned again, but when she opened her eyes and looked at Tara, there was gratitude in them.

"My husband," she whispered. "How is my husband?"

"They're looking for him, don't worry," Tara said. The woman clutched her hand and bit her lips as the labor pains grew stronger.

"What's your name?" Tara asked.

"Suzanna, Suzanna Lacey." She had another contraction. "It isn't due for another six weeks." She was sweating, and the pains were growing in intensity. "We thought we could make it before. Then the avalanche."

Tara tried desperately to recall everything she knew about the birth of a baby. "What do you want, a boy or a girl?"

"I don't mind," Suzanna smiled wanly. "Are you a nurse? Do you know about babies?"

Tara nodded. "I should," she said, well aware of how important it was for the woman to have confidence in her, even if she had none in herself. "I've been a mother too, and my father was a doctor. So this isn't a new experience."

Suzanna groaned and turned her head from side to side.

"Hold my hand and squeeze it every time you have a pain," Tara told her.

Suzanna gripped her hand, her eyes opening wide. "I'm going to die."

260

"That's nonsense, you're going to have a beautiful baby, and I'm going to help you."

Suzanna smiled at Tara, her eyes full of trust. "Promise me," she said, and she held Tara's hand very tight.

"Promise you what?" Tara asked, wiping the sweat from Suzanna's forehead.

"Promise me that you'll look after my baby."

Tara squeezed Suzanna's hand. "I'll promise you that you won't die."

"But if I do," she whispered, "until they find John, promise me you'll take care of the child." She looked beseechingly at Tara. "I believe I'll die, but I don't mind so long as I know that my baby will be safe. With you."

"You've got to believe that you'll live," Tara said. "It's very important for both of us and the baby."

"But you promise," entreated Suzanna, "if I don't . . ."

"I promise."

"Thank you," sighed Suzanna. "I'm not worried any more." She closed her eyes and fell into a light doze, a little smile hovering around her lips.

For the first time Tara noticed how young Suzanna was, no more than seventeen or eighteen. She stroked the burning forehead, brushing back long strands of light brown hair, which clung to rivulets of sweat trickling down her face and neck.

Then the men returned with a portable stove, a variety of cooking pots, and blankets. "Here, take this," one of them said, "it's the best I can do." He handed her his pocketknife.

"OK," she said. "Now light the stove and fill the pots. Has one of you got a watch?"

They eyed her suspiciously. She realized that her request would probably deprive one of them of his most treasured possession. None of the men spoke; they just busied themselves with banking up the stove and filling the pots with snow.

"I just want to borrow it," Tara added after a long pause. "I'll have finished with it by the morning."

"Ain't got a watch, got a clock though," the burliest of the men said grudgingly. "And I want it back!"

Reluctantly, he undid his coat and removed from a piece of string tied around his waist a large brass clock with two enormous bells and a glassless face. Unwillingly he handed it to her.

"Does.it go?" she enquired.

261

" 'Course," he snapped.

The men were getting restless, longing to get away from the quietly moaning Suzanna and this woman who had become not only authoritative but demanding. All of them were plainly uncomfortable at having anything to do with such an intimately feminine affair as this.

"Is there no doctor around who could help?"

They looked at each other and shook their heads. Then they all walked, nearly ran, out of the tent, leaving Tara to cope single-handed.

"Stay with me, mother," whispered Suzanna.

"I'm Tara," she said gently, "I won't leave you."

Tara began preparing things, melting the snow on the stove, ripping one of the blankets into thin strips, all the while going over her little practical knowledge of childbirth.

As she wound the clock she remembered her father's watch and all her other treasured belongings left abandoned on the other side of Sheep Camp. Would she ever find them again? When the disaster had happened she had rushed off, not even grabbing her sleeping bag, between the layers of which she had carefully stowed Daniel's letter and photograph, and her father's watch. It did not work, but it would have comforted her, having a part of her father, a part of Daniel, close at hand.

Tears welled up in her eyes; her throat ached as she thought of Daniel, of Gabie, of her father, all the people in her life whom she had loved so much. "God, give me strength," she prayed, closing her eyes, willing herself to keep going.

The labor pains had started again, and for a while Tara had no chance to think of herself. Perhaps someone had heard, was guiding her, was helping her.

She covered Suzanna with extra blankets and carefully removed her underclothes, all the while soothing her, talking to her, comforting her.

According to the clock, the contractions were coming every seventeen minutes. At each one Suzanna tossed and turned, fighting against their natural progression. Sitting beside the girl, holding her hand, waiting for a new life to make its appearance, Tara felt unutterably sad. Why, in the midst of joy and life, did sadness have to be so close?

She would never forget that first glorious moment when they had put Gabie in her arms and she had looked down at that tiny face, only minutes old. She had wanted to smother her with kisses; she had wanted to hold her so tight, to never let her go. Everything had

262

seemed so glorious. Daniel's expression as he had held Gabie, and the way he had smiled at Tara, were the happiest moments in her life.

"Hello there. It's Hal. How is she?" asked a voice.

Tara glanced up. It was the black-bearded rescuer, looking down at them with some awe.

"I need a doctor," Tara said quietly. "I don't think I can do this alone."

"We got forty dead out there and a dozen dying ones and the nearest sawbones is at Dyea," he said. "Sorry. Guess it's up to you."

"Have you any news for me?"

He shook his head. "We're doing our best," he said, then changed the subject quickly. "You'll be OK, I'm sure."

"What about her husband? If you could find him."

He cut her short. "We're digging. That's all we can do."

"Is there a woman who could help me, when the baby comes?"

"I'll try and find you someone."

"And if someone could bring my sled—it has supplies that would be useful now."

"OK," he said, relieved at having an excuse to leave, "I'll look for it when I can."

A little while later the flap of the tent was pushed aside and a wide-eyed blonde came in and stared at Tara. Her face was heavily rouged, and around her scrawny neck was a string of pearls. She wore moccasins on her feet and, incongruously, black silk stockings.

"Is that her?" she asked, walking warily over to Suzanna, who was lying with eyes closed, breathing heavily. "Hal said you wanted someone to help you."

"Yes," said Tara, "I think the baby's coming soon."

Suzanna let out another agonized cry.

"Jesus!" said the woman, looking at Tara appalled. "Oh my God, is she dying?"

"Have you ever helped at a birth?" Tara asked her.

"No siree," the woman said proudly. "I dug out a few slugs in my time, and a knife blade when Chuck Hamilton got it in the kidneys, but kids? No. Never."

"When it happens, we'll have to move quickly. There'll be a lot to do," said Tara. "Don't worry about the blood."

The woman paled under her rouged cheeks. "Sounds messy," she grimaced.

"It's the most natural thing in the world. Babies get born every second and it's no messier than cutting bullets out of men. What's your name?"

"Laverne," replied the woman, looking at Suzanna resentfully.

"Well, Laverne, we'll need lots of hot water. Pour it into that jug and those two basins on the floor. Keep it coming. Don't worry about a thing. I'll deliver the baby, you just do what I tell you."

Suzanna shrieked with pain, tossing her head from side to side.

"I think it's coming," whispered Laverne, horrified.

Tara swept into action, scrubbing her hands as best she could with the tiny piece of soap she had been given. She washed them a second time to make sure they were clean.

"I don't want to see it," announced Laverne. "It's going to be awful. All the mess, blood, and screaming. I don't want any part of it."

"Laverne," Tara said quietly. "I need someone to help me. The baby will be here very shortly."

"I'll be sick," complained Laverne. "I know I'll be sick. You do it. You know all about it. I want to get back. I got work to do ... the saloon."

"Laverne, look," Tara began.

"I can't stand screaming females," she said, and fled from the tent.

There was nothing Tara could do, for now the pains were coming faster and faster, and Suzanna was exhausting herself just tossing and turning.

"Relax," Tara told her. "Save your strength until the baby needs it."

"Stay with me," sobbed Suzanna, clutching Tara's hand so tight she nearly crushed it.

"I'm here," Tara said quietly. "I'm with you all the time. Don't worry, I'm not going to leave you."

Gently she released Suzanna's grip and lifted the blankets that covered her. She saw the tip of the baby's head beginning to thrust its way out of Suzanna's bloated form. She tried desperately to remember how it was done.

Suzanna was panting, her mouth wide open; her eyes stared upward at the canvas of the tent. Tara did not even notice the sweat that was pouring down herself.

"Try to help it by pushing, Suzanna," Tara said. "Push. Keep pushing, now, again, again. It's coming, it's coming, push harder, harder."

The head emerged, gently aided by Tara's rough, calloused hands firmly gripping the crown. Very quickly the rest of the baby followed. Tara tied two strips of the torn blanket around the cord that had been feeding it for so many months. With the knife, already disinfected in

264

the flames of the portable stove, she cut between the knots, thus separating mother and child.

Tara's major concern was to make sure this minute body would live. It was a boy, and as she held it high by its heels it began to cry.

"It's a boy," Tara announced, and the baby howled in protest. Tara hastily wrapped him in a shirt and bundled him up in a blanket.

"Look," she said when she had finished, placing the infant in his mother's arms, "hold your son. Isn't he perfect?"

Suzanna smiled weakly as she cradled the child, but she was too exhausted to speak.

"Hold him tight," Tara told her, wiping Suzanna's ashen face with a damp cloth. "He needs you to keep him warm, to make him secure, to love him." She tucked the infant beside his mother so that the warmth from her body gave him an effective form of insulation. Then she began to prepare for the delivery of the afterbirth. Suzanna was visibly declining, and she was worried that this part would truly finish her.

Suddenly, blood spurted everywhere. In seconds, she and Suzanna were saturated by a hot sea of gore. Suzanna's eyes opened wide with fear and horror. She knew that the hemorrhage was the beginning of the end. The look she gave Tara confirmed that fact.

Tara tried to stem the flow, but it was hopeless; within a matter of minutes Suzanna would be unconscious, and there was nothing she could do. She tried to make the woman as comfortable as possible, willing herself to believe that the inevitable would not happen.

"Tara," came a whisper from Suzanna. Her voice was so low Tara could hardly hear it. "Love John for me."

Tara nodded, too full of emotion to speak.

Suzanna's eyes stayed on the baby lying beside her. For a moment there was a glint of anxiety.

"He is all right, isn't he? There's nothing wrong with him?"

"He's beautiful," Tara replied, putting him closer to Suzanna so that she could feel him. "Your son is quite perfect." Suzanna sighed and closed her eyes, at peace with herself as life slowly oozed out of her. Tara felt desperate as, minute by minute, Suzanna moved closer to death while she stood by helplessly.

"Thank you," whispered Suzanna. She made a feeble gesture, as if she was trying to pick up the baby, but she hadn't the strength and her arm flopped limply. Her lips moved soundlessly, and Tara bent closer to hear what she was trying to say. It sounded like "John." Then her eyes flickered open again. "Always," she whispered. "Always keep him, no one else."

"Please don't die," begged Tara, clutching Suzanna's hand as if that link would transfuse life into the dying woman. "Please live. *Please.*"

Suzanna's head fell to one side. As Tara stared down at her she stopped breathing. Frantically Tara felt for the pulse, but it had ceased. She sank to her knees, exhausted. Death seemed to be everywhere around her, and now she felt lifeless herself. A terrible fatigue swept through her, making it impossible even to keep her eyes open. She wanted to die too. She wanted to be out of this terrible world, freed from the imprisonment of the Yukon. She was too tired to cry, too spent to hear the baby whimpering as he lay next to his dead mother, too drained to move from where she had collapsed on the floor. She just wanted to sink into oblivion, to sleep and never wake up.

She was brought back to consciousness by someone roughly shaking her shoulder. Dimly, she could hear a voice commanding, "Lady, lady, wake up!" but her eyelids felt too heavy with sleep. When she did eventually manage to force them apart she could remember neither where she was nor what she was doing there. She tried to focus on two indistinct figures that peered down at her. The black-bearded man shook her shoulder again, and Tara sat blinking, trying to comprehend what it was he wanted or was trying to tell her. She looked down at a tin plate he was holding under her nose.

"I've brought you both food," he said. "What happened?"

Gradually, the nightmarish memories returned. "She's dead," Tara whimpered. "I did everything I could, but she's dead."

"What about the baby?" he asked.

"A boy. I don't know if he'll survive. I don't really care any more. I'm so tired. I can't go on. I don't want to go on."

The two men walked over to Suzanna's body and awkwardly removed their fur hats.

"That's tough," said Hal. He went back to Tara. "What happened to Laverne?"

"Who?"

"Guess she don't know much about babies," he said, almost to himself.

"Laverne!" the other man grinned. "You can say that again."

"Mister," Tara said to Hal. "Have you found the father?"

"Yeah," he said uncomfortably.

"Listen, lady," said the other man, glancing at Hal. "That's what we came to tell you."

"We found him," said Hal. "He was close to where we dug her out."

"And?"

They both shook their heads. "He's dead. Crushed by two tons of snow."

"Guess we'll bury them together," Hal added. "Rough on the kid."

"What will happen?" asked Tara.

"Search me," replied Hal. "Don't know nothing about them. They spent a night down at the camp, then moved up there. Making for Dawson, I guess. Crazy with her in that condition. Don't even know their name."

"Lacey," Tara said. "John Lacey was his name. Hers was Suzanna. What about their belongings?"

"What belongings?" asked Hal. "Hell, everything got swept away. Maybe they had a team, I don't know. We ain't found a thing."

"Real tough," agreed his companion, and put on his fur hat again. Hal rubbed his nose.

"What the hell's going to happen to the kid now?" he mused. "Somebody's got to look after it."

"I will," Tara said quietly. "I promised I would, though God knows how."

Hal put his hand on her shoulder. "You're strong enough, Mrs. Kane," he told her. "You'll feel stronger too when you've got some grub inside you. When you've eaten and slept, life won't seem so bad."

Tara glanced up. Under the thick, black brows his eyes were sincere. She believed him because it was easier and she was too despondent to argue.

"We'll be back," he went on sympathetically, "to get the mother. Eat, then try and sleep for a while before we return."

She toyed with the plateful of beans listlessly. Then, as if she had suddenly remembered something, she looked up at him again, her unspoken question evident.

"No," he said, "there's no news. Perhaps we'll have some soon, but I can't promise."

After they had gone, Tara sat alone and mechanically chewed mouthful after mouthful of the tasteless beans. From where she sat, she could see the dead woman and the bundle in her lifeless arms, his tiny hands and feet moving under the heavy blanket. She got up and went over to the pallet. Suzanna looked like someone peacefully asleep, her skin a fluorescent white. There was no sign in her serene expression of the pain she had suffered, and the blankets concealed her bloody death.

Gently Tara touched the baby's wrinkled face.

"Don't worry, John," she said. "You'll be safe. I swear it. I promised your mother."

Perhaps this was what fate had intended all along. She had been robbed of her own child; she had failed to find Daniel; maybe, unknowingly, she had even seen him die. Everything seemed to have been taken from her.

Until now. She picked up the baby and rocked it to and fro.

"We've got one another," she told him, "we need one another." And that was the truth of the matter.

The rescue operation continued. Silently people from Sheep Camp watched and waited. There were those who would not admit defeat. When the body of someone they knew, a partner, a friend, a man they'd played poker with, someone who had shared a cabin, was brought down stiff and lifeless, they manipulated their arms and legs, tried breathing warm air into their lungs, even slapped the rigid, frozen faces in a vain attempt to find a flicker of life.

Although every hour that passed lessened the chances of anyone coming out alive, there were miraculous exceptions. One man emerged from his snow tomb after twenty-three hours still alive, still conscious. Here and there the rescuers thought they could hear faint sounds and renewed their efforts. But mostly those who were brought out into the cold air were dead: suffocated or crushed.

In the tent Tara cradled the baby, determined about one thing: Little John was going to be a survivor. Not just because of a promise she had given a dying woman, not just because there was no one else, but because she had been given a second chance, someone to love, to cherish, and for her the baby had become a symbol. More than anything, Tara needed him; she needed to be needed.

She tried to recall every detail of the first few days after Gabie's birth. God, how easy it had been compared to this. How little she had appreciated the security of a midwife, a comfortable bed, a loving husband, a doctor, fresh linen, all the things she had taken for granted. She looked down at the serious, frowning face of little John Lacey. He was asleep, but soon he would need food and she had nothing to give him.

She asked Hal if, by some amazing chance, there might be a nursing mother in Sheep Camp.

"You serious? A wet nurse out here?" was his reply. Then he told her that her sled had apparently been stolen.

For the first three days she could just about get by. She boiled snow, added sugar, let it cool, then soaked a piece of linen in the liquid. She knew melted snow was not as pure as boiled water, but John sucked hungrily at the syrupy cloth.

Tara kept the baby close to her at all times. Cuddling him at night, she would stare into space, experiencing an apprehension she had never before known. It was not fear, but a gnawing anxiety. She had been entrusted with a life. How was she going to provide for it? Yet she knew she could not afford to lose John. If that happened, there would be no point in her continuing; it would set the final seal of failure on her life.

She was so involved with the child that she lost touch with what was going on outside. Her only contact was Hal, who would call in occasionally to see if she needed anything and to tell her there was still no news of Daniel. One day he told her that the death toll might go as high as two hundred and that many of the bodies would remain unfound until the thaw.

She knew also that some cabins had been turned into morgues and that they had taken Suzanna's body to one of them. Within a few days there would be a mass funeral.

Tara had lost all sense of time; she could not remember how long it was since the avalanche. Not that it really mattered; milk for the child was what was important. All Hal had been able to find for her was one can of condensed milk. She had to look herself.

With the baby bundled up in blankets inside her parka, Tara ventured out. For a moment she stood blinking, unsure, trying to acclimatize herself to the freezing wind and the snow flurries that had once again sprung up. On the distant slope she could see people still working, still shoveling aside thousands of tons of snow, even if it was becoming increasingly pointless. A wagon creaked past her; in it, covered by a tarpaulin, lay two bodies.

The catastrophe overshadowed the entire camp. People stood in groups, talking in subdued tones. Some of them were gathered around a log cabin, staring at a newly painted sign nailed to the door. Tara went over and read the sign, which said, CORONER.

She had not realized that officials were already in Sheep Camp. The news of the disaster must have spread all over the Territory.

Tara knocked on the door of the cabin, but there was no answer. She tried the door; it was unlocked, so she went in. Inside was a trestle table, on which lay a thick ledger, an inkwell, and a stack of papers. Behind the table sat Soapy Smith.

It was the first time Tara had known Jefferson Smith to be speechless.

"Tara!" he gasped at last. "Tara," he said again, his eyes suddenly full of delight. Then he glanced down and saw John Lacey's head protruding from her coat. "My! I had no idea it had been that long since we'd seen one another," he grinned. "What in tarnation are you doing here?"

"I want to see the coroner," she said flatly.

"Oh, surely not," he said. "Not the coroner. I'd have thought you'd more likely want to see the Registrar of Births." He studied the baby. "Who the hell is that?"

"That's no concern of yours," she replied. "I'll come back when the coroner is here."

There was a flash of white teeth. "But he is, Tara. The coroner is right here." He stood and bowed, the charms on his watch-chain tinkling mischievously. "I'm sort of acting coroner for the Chilkoot division of the Territory."

"Self-appointed, I suppose?"

"Of course." He had a lopsided smile. "Well, somebody had to take on the onerous task, and since everybody else had been running around in circles I guess I was the right man for the job. As a public-spirited citizen, I saw it as my duty. Sort of honorary, you see. There's a lot of work here." He dismissed the subject with a wave of his hand. "Much too grim for us to discuss. I want to hear about you, Tara. What happened? What are you doing here? And who is that?" He peered down at the top of the baby's head. "Is it a he or a she?"

"His name is John Lacey," she said coldly.

"Do I know his father?" he drawled, taking out a cheroot. He bit off the end, then stopped. "I guess he wouldn't like all the smoke," and he put the cigar to one side. "Why don't you sit down, Tara, and tell me all about it?" His tone was concerned.

Tara sank into the chair.

"His father was killed in the avalanche. His mother was dug out, and I delivered him, but she died." She stopped, then glanced up, staring Smith straight in the eye. "He needs milk," she said fiercely, "and he needs it quickly. If he doesn't get some soon . . ."

Smith contemplated her. "I've heard of a joker in the deck, but this— What are you going to do with him?"

"Look after him. Make sure he survives," she replied. "But he won't if he doesn't get some milk."

"All right," Smith said, standing up. He went over to where Tara sat, crouched down, and studied the baby's face. "He looks worried, doesn't he?" Then he laughed out loud.

"What's so amusing?" he asked.

"You. Your latest role. Fairy godmother. I'm not sure if it's the right casting. I'd have thought the merry widow was more your line."

Tara glowered at him. "You bastard," she said, getting up. "Don't you respect anything? Do you think I came to this godforsaken hole to amuse myself? Do you think I'm still here because it's such good fun? You know how many people died in that avalanche, and my husband might be one of them. He was here, and now I don't know if he's among the dead still buried on that slope or gone before it happened." Tears came to her eyes. "I hate you, Mr. Smith. In the past I've disliked you, but now I hate you." She turned to go, brushing away the tears.

Smith got up and caught her arm. "I'm sorry," he said. "Tara, please believe me. If it helps at all, I don't think they've found him, but then there's a lot of people still out there twenty foot down. I promise you one thing, if I do hear anything, anything at all, you'll be the first to know. Please forgive me for having hurt you, I should never had said what I did."

He walked around, put his fingers under her chin, and tilted her head back so that their eyes met.

"Forgiven?" he asked. Tara nodded. He squeezed her hand lightly, then returned to the table, sat down, and, from the pile of papers in front of him, extracted a form.

"Fortunately, in my official capacity, I'm not only the coroner but also registrar of births and deaths."

"As of this moment, of course."

"Naturally," Smith agreed, as he opened a thick ledger. "Father's name John Lacey," he recited, glancing at her for confirmation, "that's right?"

"Do you have to do that now?"

"It won't take a minute," he said smoothly. "Mother's name was . . ." He looked at her questioningly.

"Suzanna."

Smith went on writing, first in the ledger and then on the form.

"There, I think that makes him legal," he said, handing over the form. "Now he officially exists."

She stared at the printed birth certificate, wondering how he had got hold of it. The date of birth had been filled in as April 3, 1898, place, Sheep Camp, Yukon Territory, District of British Columbia, father John Lacey, profession prospector, mother Suzanna Lacey, married woman.

And the name of the child was listed as John Jefferson Randolph Lacey.

"What are these?" asked Tara, baffled.

"What are what, my dear?" he inquired innocently.

"These names, Jefferson Randolph?"

"Well, after all, I am his godfather," Smith said. "Only fitting that a boy should have his godfather's names too."

She stared at him, but he was serious.

"It's quite customary for a child to have a godfather, you know," he chuckled.

"A godfather," Tara pointed out, "looks after his godchild's spiritual and moral welfare. I wouldn't have thought you were much up to that kind of responsibility."

Smith grinned. "Maybe that'll be your department. But I've got a few talents he'll find useful, believe me. Anyway, he needs a father figure, and I've appointed myself. For the time being," he added hastily.

"Coroner, postmaster, pawnbroker, law officer, civic leader, and now godfather. All by self-appointment."

"Sure," he concurred. "Who else is going to do it in this wilderness?"

"God help the poor little mite," she murmured, putting the form in her pocket.

"I'm sure He will, but there's no harm in giving Him a helping hand along the way."

"Well, somebody better had quickly," said Tara, "because John is starving."

"Exactly. Now that my status has been established, I'm in a better position to provide for him."

Tara wished that she could tell him that neither she nor the baby needed his help. But it would not be true, and in a way she felt tremendously relieved that some of the responsibility for John's survival was being shared with someone else, even if it was Soapy Smith.

Back in the tent, she wondered if she was deluding herself. Despite enormous misgivings, she was placing a certain amount of faith in Smith's ability to help her.

The baby's hungry crying didn't help her to think more clearly. She picked him up, cradling the small doll-like body, and stroked the tiny hands waving aimlessly in the air, the minute feet kicking out at nothing. Her soothing voice and comforting arms, all she could provide, could no longer placate him.

The flap of the tent was pulled aside, and Smith stood there, silhouetted against the outside whiteness. "Mother and child," he

272

laughed above the din. "Delightful. Pity your friend Hart isn't here to record for posterity such devoted maternity."

"Did you just stop by to entertain yourself?" Tara asked.

"Not at all, my dear. I've got a present for my godson."

For the first time Tara noticed that Smith was holding a piece of rope. Her heart jumped as he tugged hard on it, and then stood aside. On the other end of the line was a goat.

"I'm not going to bring Eleanor in, because she'll stink up the place to high heaven," Smith explained, tying the animal to a tent peg, "but there it is. There's your milk."

"A goat!" exclaimed Tara.

"Madam will forgive me if I haven't been able to lay hands on a herd of Jerseys," Smith said. "The Territory isn't exactly dotted with dairy farms. But Eleanor here has a lot of milk, and no doubt our godson will get used to it. Mighty nourishing, goat's milk."

John seemed to sense that food was on its way, for his yelling subsided, and he was less fretful in Tara's arms.

"Where did you find her?" Tara asked.

"Now, now, my dear," he grinned, "you must never ask a fellow to give away trade secrets. But I'll tell you, it took some doing. I never figured a darn goat was so difficult to acquire. Now if young John there could feed on some bubbly or smoked salmon or roast duck, there'd be no problem. But Eleanor is something again, aren't you old thing?" he said, patting her on the head.

The goat stood motionless, regarding Tara thoughtfully through the tent door.

"How do I get the milk?" she asked timidly, eyeing the animal with trepidation.

"You milk it," Smith replied. "How else?"

The goat looked friendly, and Tara refused to appear totally helpless. "Here," she said, getting up. "Hold him firm." She handed John to Smith.

Smith took the baby somewhat gingerly. He then sat down, keeping a very straight face, while Tara gathered up a crate and saucepan and went outside. She placed the saucepan under Eleanor and began, as best she could, to emulate the pastoral paintings she had seen of plump, rosy-faced young milkmaids. She put her hands on the udders and pulled. Eleanor turned her head, stared at her balefully, and walked off. Only the rope by which Smith had secured her prevented her escape.

"Come here, you son of a bitch," she muttered.

273

"You got it all wrong, Tara," Smith said. "That's one thing that critter ain't."

"Why don't you come and do it?" she challenged.

"Oh no, certainly not. You're John's godmother, and milking Eleanor is your job. Now me, I'm needed to look after John's finer talents. Ain't I, John?"

John gurgled, his saliva trickling down Smith's sleeve. Smith started to say something, but changed his mind. "He's going to be a fine boy, Tara," he said blandly.

But Tara was engrossed with Eleanor and when, half an hour later, she had managed to fill the saucepan with milk, she felt triumphant.

Smith sat opposite, lighting a cheroot, watching Tara feed the baby. "I calculate he'd better get used to this," he said. "No godson of mine can get used to Havana smoke too early." He picked up his hat. "I'll be back, my dear," he said, sniffing the air. "Sorry about the smell."

"On the contrary," she said. "Thank you. Thank you for the goat."

He stopped at the tent doorway. It was the first time she had ever thanked him for anything. He stood and looked down at her strangely as she fed the baby.

"Thank you," he echoed, very quietly. For an instant their eyes met. Then a jaunty smile flashed across his face. "Look after our godson. He's all we've got." He waved and walked off.

Tara was kept fully occupied with John. From time to time Smith came in to see them, but she was lonely. Her months of separation from Daniel had served only to prove how much she missed him, how much she loved him. Her heart ached for him. During these dark hours she found herself wondering, over and over again, about a possibility, the shadow of which she had always shut away. Supposing he were dead?

Never before had the thought been allowed. Now the seed of doubt had been sown, a doubt that she could not shrug off. Supposing, that ugly inner voice kept nagging, supposing he really were dead? Had she been sentenced to a monotonously gray future without her husband's love, without the only man who mattered to her? Tara sat staring into space, trying to imagine what she would do, how she could come to terms with life as a widow. A cold sensation crept through her, like the one she had experienced when she had entered the coroner's office to find out the truth and yet had been afraid of hearing it.

Over the past few months, her life had been mechanical, her only aim to survive until that moment when she was in Daniel's arms again, feeling his love. She had never contemplated that their eventual reunion would not be. What if it had all been for nothing?

"God, please don't make that true, let him come back to me, please, please," she sobbed, burying her head in her hands. "Daniel! Daniel!" she cried, holding herself tight as if embracing a phantom, remembering how it felt to be held by him. "My darling, I need you. I need you so desperately."

"Tara, Tara, I'm here," said a voice, very softly.

Startled, she looked up. Jefferson Smith was standing in front of her. She had no idea how long he had been there. She had not heard him come into the tent.

"Go away!" she pleaded, distraught, but there was no conviction in her tone.

Smith had never seen Tara like this before. She—who had always proudly stood up to him—despondent, broken.

"Tara," he said again, his voice full of compassion.

She looked at him through tear-filled eyes. "I have to be alone," she begged, fresh tears caught in her thick eyelashes. "Please, Jeff."

It was the first time she had used his name. But if he felt a triumph, he showed no sign. Instead, he said, very gently, "Tara, it has to stop."

He knelt down, trying to see her face. She said nothing, just sat with her head bowed, lost in her own sadness.

"Somebody has to look after you," he said, covering her scarred hands with his. If she had looked up she would have seen his eyes saying, I only want to help you, I only want to do anything I can for you.

She shook her head. "I'll be all right," she sniffed. "I'll sort things out."

"No, Tara. It's not just you," he said, nodding at the crate in which the baby slept. "It's him too you must think about."

She knew she was being selfish, thinking of herself and not the baby. Had she not thanked God for the chance of having someone in her life who needed her? But at this point she could only consider what it would mean to her having to face the future without Daniel.

"You've got to get to some kind of civilized place," Smith continued. "You can't bring up an infant in this shantytown. You can't get by on goat's milk and baked beans with a baby."

"Why not?"

Smith smiled. It was a warm, friendly smile. "Because you and I have a responsibility toward that little man," he said. "There's nobody else to look after him but us." He paused. "I want to get you both to Skagway. To make sure you've got a decent roof over your heads, to make sure you get what you need. I can't do it without you. You can't do it without me. Together."

He knelt closer. "I beg you," he said.

"Beg me? Why, Jeff? You don't need us. You've got it all. Money, power. Why do you want to do this?"

"I think you know, Tara." The rest remained unsaid.

"Are you going on with it?" he asked after a little while, "with searching for him?"

He avoided mentioning Daniel's name; she could sense it.

"I don't think there's any point. Not now." He said it flatly.

She closed her eyes. Hearing someone else voicing her thoughts sounded like a death knell. "Jeff," she said, her voice very low. "You must know he'll never be dead. Not for me. Not, not in here." She pressed her hand to her bosom.

He reached over and put his arms around her. Tara did not resist the comforting warmth of his body. He held her tight, and she felt him stroke her hair, his lips brush against her still-damp cheeks. Her eyes closed as he hugged her. He was more comforting, more kind, more reassuring than she would have thought possible.

Gently he released her, and sat back regarding her with passion and warmth. It was the moment when he could have destroyed her newborn trust. But he did not. What he said was, "I stopped by to tell you that we're burying John's folks tomorrow."

"Yes," said Tara. "We'll be there."

"And afterward?"

"I'll take everything one day at a time." But Tara knew that there was no alternative. She and John would have to go to Skagway with Jefferson Smith. Fate had decided for her.

The next morning dawned gray and cold, and the cemetery of Sheep Camp was as colorless as the handful of mourners. Tara stood next to Smith, young John in her arms, staring down at the single grave the Laceys now inhabited. The victims of the avalanche were buried in neat rows. Sixty bodies had been recovered, but how many more were buried under the huge frozen mass of the collapsed mountaintop nobody knew.

There was little ceremony about the funeral. Smith's men, who had taken over Sheep Camp, stage-managed the burials with the help of a priest who read a short prayer as each victim's coffin found its last resting place.

For a while after the short service, Tara remained, gazing at the cross hastily inscribed with the Lacey names and reflecting on another grave, another funeral, across the ocean. She held John tighter as she recalled the moment she had said goodbye to Gabrielle. The grief of that moment was still alive within her as if it were only yesterday. She sighed, turned, and started making her way down the hillside, back toward the town.

"Tara!" Smith called out. She waited until he caught up with her. "Now that's over," he said, pressing her arm, "we'll leave for Skagway tomorrow."

"Tomorrow?"

"Sure. The sooner we leave here the quicker we get there."

"Jeff," said Tara, "before I go there's something I must do."

He stopped in his tracks and looked at her.

"What?"

"It won't take long but I want to check their belongings. I've got to make sure that Daniel wasn't among the unidentified bodies."

"I've already told you, Tara, he wasn't. If he'd been among them I would have known, and I would have told you, you know that. You can take my word for it. I saw each body."

"You don't know what Daniel looks like."

"Tara," Smith held Tara's eyes with his own unwaveringly, "I do know what he looks like, and I tell you he wasn't among them."

"How could you? You've never met him."

"I've seen a picture. Ernst Hart showed me one."

"Ernst! But why?"

"Because I asked him to."

Tara was stunned.

"He was drunk," Smith explained almost contemptuously, "and I made a deal with him. I saw that photograph too. And I can positively tell you that he wasn't among the unidentified, if that man in the photograph was your husband."

Smith started to walk on, as if the matter were closed.

"I'm not satisfied," Tara said, catching up with him. "It's too neat. What about the victims' belongings. There might be something among those."

"You can check with my men," he said. "They're safeguarding them."

He saw her look. "My dear Tara, somebody had to look after them until we locate the next of kin. The poor folk would expect it of us. Anyway, most of the stuff could have belonged to anyone, so there's really no point in your wasting time. It's all been taken care of."

Now she realized why Smith had appointed himself coroner. There were rich pickings to be had. "And of course you're taking particular

277

care of any valuables the victims might have had," Tara said dryly.

"Do I detect a note of cynicism?" he inquired. "That's hardly worthy of you, my dear."

"I know your liking for personal effects," she said fiercely. "Don't think I've forgotten you still have my wedding ring."

"I'm looking after it for you Tara, that's all. Looking after it better than Daniel Kane looked after his wife."

"You hate him, don't you?"

"On the contrary," Smith said. "I admire him for having had the good taste to marry you."

She ignored his sarcasm. "Then tell me why you're trying to stop me finding him."

"I'm not, my dear. I'm just trying to stop you hurting yourself further. Why subject yourself to going through a pile of meaningless belongings when I can assure you there's no point? Now what you've got to do is get yourself and our godson ready to go south—back to Skagway so that we can get away from this place and enjoy ourselves again. See some life."

"I don't think I could ever enjoy life without Daniel," Tara said, staring into the distance.

"Tara, that's something you're going to have to learn," he said, turning her face so that she could see his warm, friendly smile. "And remember, I'll be there to help you."

CHAPTER TWENTY-TWO

When Tara had arrived in Skagway in 1897, Smith had been the unchallenged town boss. But during the first three months of 1898, industry and commerce began to make their mark, encouraged by the town's designation as the starting point for the forthcoming rail link with Whitehorse. With the completion of the first stage of the track, future prospectors would be able to reach the summit of the White Pass by train, and those who could afford it were being promised the opportunity of traveling to Lake Bennett along a narrow-gauge railway in July 1899.

As a result of the disaster at Sheep Camp, the White Pass was now considered safer than the Chilkoot. So thousands of sourdoughs who had been holed up in Dyea waiting for the new thaw thronged the trail to Skagway, to prepare for their journey to Dawson via the easier route. The prospect of work constructing the railway further swelled the population of the already bulging town.

Since Tara had been away, the amenities of Skagway had improved to keep up with its growth. The town's residents were now provided with better entertainment, better hotels, and even better opportunities to lose their money. Skagway was as lawless as ever, but as the respectable element prospered, so they became more sensitive to the complaints of theft, double-dealing, and sharp practice, and increasingly critical of the likes of Soapy Smith and his men.

It had taken Smith and Tara three days to reach Skagway from Sheep Camp. Tara had sat in the sled, driven by Smith, young John warmly wrapped up in her arms, lost in her unhappiness, trying to sound enthusiastic when Smith told her of his ambitious ideas. Eleanor trotted along behind.

Throughout the trip, Smith behaved like the gentleman he had always pretended to be. He made no demand on her, had not attempted to take advantage of her presence. She had not forgotten his kiss, she could still feel the warmth of his embrace, but he left it at that, and she was grateful. And she had to admit a curious contradiction. She, who had grown so fiercely independent, who had so enjoyed the sensation of whipping her dog team through the vastness of the Yukon, found it a great relief not to have to worry about anything, not to have to negotiate the route, not to have to look for shelter when they arrived.

Smith, she knew, would take care of everything. "You leave it all to me," he had said, and very willingly she had.

As they neared the end of their journey, Smith was in high spirits. But if he had expected a welcoming committee, he was in for a shock.

During his absence at Sheep Camp the storekeepers and some of the townsfolk had decided it was time to clean the place up. And to this end they had printed a notice which read:

> Warning.
> A word to the wise should be sufficient. All
> con men, bunco and sure-thing men, and all other
> objectionable characters are notified to leave
> Skagway and the White Pass road immediately and
> remain away. Failure to comply with this warning
> will be followed by prompt action.

Smith stood in front of the first poster he came across, visibly seething. Then he smiled, but not genially. He ripped down the notice, crumpled it up, and threw it in the mud.

"Guess even being away for a couple of weeks is too long," he said, as he walked back to the sled. "That's the trouble with newcomers," he went on, "always getting too big for their breeches. Maybe the businessmen of the town will have to do something about that."

She knew the kind of businessmen he meant. They were more familiar with guns than with ledgers.

Everywhere there were new buildings. Near the harbor a company called the North American Trading and Transport Company had constructed impressive offices. As they drove down the main street, they passed a host of new saloons, making an even greater mockery of the territory's prohibition laws. The Blaze of Glory, The Hungry Pup, The Mangy Dog, The Red Onion, The House of Hooch were particularly obvious because of their freshly painted signs and facades. More to her taste, Tara saw hotels offering their guests hot water and clean sheets.

The sidewalks teemed with prospectors, trappers, and traders. For the first time in the Yukon, Tara noticed a new class—the business-man. City clothes peeped from under their parkas and fur coats, and polished high-button boots gingerly side-stepped the slushy puddles of Skagway's main drag. Nervous eyes blinked behind steel-rimmed glasses or out of clean-shaven faces. The city slickers looked uncomfortable, out of place amid the unwashed masses of Skagway. But the spending power of the lucky strikers was not to be ignored. They needed things, from dog teams to whores; they gambled, they drank, and they put healthy profits into the businessmen's pockets.

Tara could sense Smith assessing all this fresh competition. She wondered how his existing establishments were faring against so many new enterprises, how he had come to terms with the situation.

Smith supplied no answer; he merely drove on slowly, his eyes noting each new attraction, each gimmick, each added saloon.

"My, it's changed," Tara mused, trying to elicit a reaction from him.

"Hasn't it," was all he replied.

There was the sound of hoofs from behind them, and Tara turned to see a man galloping toward them.

"Hi, Boss," he called out. "Good to see you again." He eyed Tara and the baby but said nothing. "The boys will be gald to know you're back in town."

"Where's Colson?" Smith asked without ceremony. "Haven't seen him about."

The name struck a chord in Tara's mind. Of course—the Marshal, that boorish creature who upheld what was jokingly referred to as Skagway's law—Smith's stooge.

The man on the horse leaned forward. "He's dead," he said in a low voice. "He got shot at Fay's place."

"The hell he did." Smith turned to Tara. "Excuse me," he said, and the man dismounted so that he could talk more confidentially to Smith. "So what happened?" Tara heard Smith ask.

"Well, Boss, a guy called McGrath walked into the saloon. One of the men working on the new toll road. Put down a bill for a drink, and Fay wouldn't give him change."

"So?" shrugged Smith, "what's wrong with that? Local custom ain't it?"

"Yeah, I know. But McGrath started a ruckus, and Colson rushed in. Fay kind of lost his head and there was shooting. That's when Colson got his."

"And McGrath?"

"Oh, that's OK, Boss," said the man. "He's dead too."

"Ah, well," Smith sighed, "guess we'd better get ourselves a new marshal. And get rid of those damn posters. I want them down. Understand?"

"Sure, Boss." The man galloped off.

"You see what happens the minute I turn my back?" remarked Smith, returning to the sled.

"The baby and I need a place to stay," Tara said coldly. Soapy Smith's racketeering had suddenly been forcibly brought home to her.

"Sure," he agreed. "Got to get the important things done first."

And although he seemed preoccupied, he meant it.

Half an hour later he had installed Tara in a log cabin. It was surprisingly neatly furnished: bright Indian rugs covered the rough floorboards, curtains at the windows, a roomy wooden bed, a rocking chair, and a range. To Tara, used so long to roughing it, it was a small palace.

"Whose is this?" she asked, looking around. She was delighted. Here she could be warm and comfortable and make a home for herself and the baby.

"Yours," Smith said.

She wondered just how he came to have it, but after the long journey she was tired and John was fretful. The questions would wait until later.

"My men will bring you wood, food, and supplies, and I'll get a cot for John. Eleanor can stay around the back." Smith paused. "This is OK for you, Tara, isn't it?"

"It's the nicest place I've been," she smiled. "Thank you."

"I've got things to do," he said, pulling on his gloves. Then he stopped and gazed into her eyes. "You'll be safe here, Tara. I promise."

"I know," she said.

At the door of the cabin he paused. "Tara," he said. She looked at him questioningly.

"It's good to have you here," he said simply. Then he was gone.

Maybe it was as well that Tara had a great deal to do; it allowed her little time to think.

A couple of hours later, Smith's men arrived with food, cooking utensils, kerosene lamps, bed linen, every household item she could possibly have wanted. As she was putting it all away she heard someone hammering outside the cabin. There was no one around, but a poster had been nailed to the cabin wall.

> Public Warning:
> The body of men who have been usurping civic authority
> are hereby notified that any overt act committed by
> them will promptly be met by the law-abiding citizens
> of Skagway, and each man and his property will be held
> responsible for any unlawful act on their part, and
> the Law and Order Society, consisting of 317 citizens,
> will see that justice is dealt out to its fullest extent
> as no blackmailers or vigilantes will be tolerated.
>   JEFFERSON R. SMITH
>   *The Law and Order Society*

Soapy Smith had declared war. It had not taken him long to warn Skagway that he commanded an army, an army of 317 followers, and that he ruled the town once again.

Tara ripped down the handbill, tore it into a thousand pieces, and threw them to the wind.

Even the luxury of lying on a feather-filled mattress and pillows, between crisp sheets, covered by thick blankets, did not help Tara sleep that night. She knew she had to tell Smith that her acceptance of his hospitality and kindness did not indicate approval of his lawless way of life. He had asked her if she would be his first lady in Skagway and, although she had never agreed and he had never asked her again, she had the distinct feeling he had taken for granted that her presence here confirmed she was with him, that she condoned and had joined his entourage. Something Linda Miles had said months before kept echoing in her mind: Soapy Smith never helped anyone unless, in so doing, he helped himself.

The next day Smith turned up at the cabin with a Moses basket. "Here," he said, maneuvering it through the narrow doorway. "This should be just right for Johnny boy."

Tara pushed in a pillow to serve as a mattress, and he gently placed the baby in it.

"Isn't that neat," said Smith, standing back admiringly. "How about that? Safe and snug. What do you think?"

"It's exactly right," she said.

"Got another surprise for you," cut in Smith, disappearing outside again and almost immediately returning with an Indian woman. She was young, no more than sixteen, her thick black hair braided in two long plaits. She stood smiling broadly at Tara, her dark, round eyes shining.

"Here's your milk supply," Smith said. "She's got it all laid on. Her papoose died. Meet Lydia."

"Lydia?" echoed Tara, looking at the Indian woman in surprise.

The girl nodded, her smile broadening to reveal uneven rows of stained teeth.

"She'll take care of John, give him his milk, and look after him when you're not around. She's honest and godfearing and you can trust her. And don't worry about Johnny getting Indian milk—hell, I had a wet nurse blacker than the ace of spades."

"Do you speak English?" asked a startled Tara.

"Not a word," intervened Smith, "but she's perfect with the baby talk. Now, you introduce her to John."

Lydia cooed with delight as she and Tara bent over the cot, then she picked the baby up, and he gurgled happily as she rocked him in her arms.

"There you see, they get on perfect," Smith said, leading Tara a little to one side. "Just don't leave any whisky around. Lydia's folks have a weakness for firewater, and we don't want it to get mixed up with Johnny's milk, right?"

"You mean she drinks?" Tara looked at Lydia thoughtfully.

"Hell, she's an Indian, isn't she?" snorted Smith. "Sure she drinks. But if there's no bottle around, she's as sober as a judge. You can trust her fine."

"I hope so," Tara said.

"I wouldn't take any chances with our boy, would I? Anyway you need her around the place."

"Why? I'm perfectly capable of managing on my own."

"Sure you are, but how the hell can I take you out if little Johnny here is yelling for his milk?"

"I don't remember saying I was going out," Tara said stiffly.

"You're dying for it," said Smith flatly.

"Seeing that you think you know what I need and what I'm dying for," Tara said, aggravated by his self-assurance, "no doubt you'll also be aware that I think it's time you and I had a serious talk."

"It'll be my pleasure, my dear," Smith beamed, "but not just at the moment. There's business I've got to attend to first. We'll get together very soon, I promise you, and then we can talk to our hearts' content. I'm taking Eleanor with me. I'll be seeing you soon," he said briskly. Tara was left staring at the closed cabin door.

She stood for a moment, muttering angrily to herself, then turned to the Indian woman, who was bouncing John on her knee.

"Lydia," she said.

The flat-nosed girl flashed her teeth.

"Would you like some coffee?" Tara asked.

The smile broadened.

"I guess you would," Tara said.

It was then that she saw a plain white envelope lying on the table. She picked it up and ripped it open. Inside were fifty one-dollar bills and a note with just one word written on it: "Housekeeping."

Tara held the money, at first undecided what to do. There were things she needed to buy for the baby. Material to make John a dress, proper diapers instead of the torn towels he'd worn since his birth, oils and ointments for his chapped skin. .

"All right." Tara folded the money and put it in her pocket. "I'll take it. I'll take it because John needs things, but, my goodness, Jeff Smith, don't think fifty dollars can buy me."

That afternoon Tara went out shopping, accompanied by Lydia, with John on the Indian girl's back wrapped up like a papoose. The mild temperature and the excitement she felt at gazing in shop windows lifted Tara's spirits. Not until now had she realized how tired she was of being constantly cold, always surrounded by the monotonous monochromes of winter, never anything colorful on which to feast the eye. There was so much to look at, so many varieties of stores had opened since she had been away. There were milliners, dress shops, and even a Viennese pastry shop. Skagway was becoming a place where one could buy fripperies.

At the drygoods store where she bought the materials and thread she needed, she was treated with a deference that impressed her as much as the array of satins, taffetas, linens, and velvets they displayed. Standing at the highly polished counter in her shabby trousers, her thick hair hidden beneath the old hat she had bought in Dyea when she first arrived, engulfed in her stained and torn parka, she toyed with the idea of buying herself a few yards of the brightly dyed fine wool the shop had to offer. The salesman noticed her eyeing the huge bolts, so he pulled one down and festooned the counter with yards of crimson, inviting her to feel the material. It was soft to the touch; Tara could hardly recall the last time she had fingered anything so fine.

If she gave Smith an inch by indulging herself, she knew he would take a mile. No, it was all right to use his fifty dollars for John, but never, never would she use the money on herself, at least not until Smith knew the score.

"I'll just take five yards of white toweling and three yards of the white flannel," she told the slightly crestfallen assistant, who had hoped he was going to make a much larger sale.

Next they went to the pharmacist, where Tara purchased olive oil and ointments for John's skin. By the end of the expedition she had five dollars left. As they passed the pastry shop, she could not help stopping to look at the chocolate éclairs and cream puffs. Lydia waited beside her, also ogling the amazing cream-filled pastries.

"They're fattening," Tara announced righteously, but Lydia continued smiling expectantly. "Oh, dear," Tara sighed, "you really don't understand a word I'm saying, do you?" She walked on, followed by the faithful, and now despondent, girl.

Soapy Smith's posters were much in evidence. The people gathered around them appeared hostile as they discussed them among themselves. She shuddered as she heard one man complain to another, "Damn blackguard. Must think he owns the place."

"He'll learn he doesn't. He'll get his comeuppance soon," prophesied the other.

Within a few minutes of their return to the cabin, there was a knock on the door. Lydia was preparing to feed John but was not in the slightest abashed by the three men who staggered in, two of them manhandling a sitz bath filled with boxes, the third carrying a folded screen and a copper kettle.

"Compliments of Mr. Smith," puffed one of them, handing an aghast Tara a small envelope. Without further ado, they all left.

Tara opened the envelope and read the card inside. "This isn't meant as an insult. Just pamper yourself," Jefferson Smith had written in his neat script.

She unfolded the screen, which was stained rosewood, upholstered in padded damask; it looked elegantly incongruous in the log cabin. Next she undid the boxes and gasped as, item by item, she took out an extravaganza of feminine luxury. There were jars of bath salts, bars of soap, oils, talcum powder, and several bottles of perfume. Lydia, still feeding the baby, watched, her eyes full of wonder, as Tara unpacked the costly collection.

"Aren't these fantastic? Just take a sniff of this," enthused Tara, getting up and waving a little bottle under the Indian's nose.

"Good," muttered Lydia, nodding hard to make her point.

"Very good," Tara agreed, smiling at Lydia's attempt to speak English.

Lydia beamed, then she mimed drinking from a bottle. "Very good," she echoed.

Tara was horrified. "No, no," she protested, waving her hands frantically. "Not firewater. Not drink. To bathe in, to smell nice."

But Lydia didn't understand. She just kept nodding and smiling.

"Ah well," shrugged Tara. "You're sure to be ill if you think this is whisky."

Inside the second box was an enormous white turkish towel, some smaller ones, a washcloth, and a sponge.

"I don't know if you're hinting, Jeff Smith," Tara smiled, pressing the soft material to her face, "but this bath will sure be a treat."

And it was. Tara scrubbed and massaged her sore and tired body, feeling the grime and muck of the past weeks float off her. She hadn't enjoyed a bath so much since she had last been in Skagway. Then too, Smith had supplied the means to indulge in such luxury. The price that time had been her wedding ring, and she wondered what it was going to be now.

She stepped into the comforting warmth of the huge, thick towel and briskly rubbed herself dry. Then she washed her hair until it squeaked.

Afterward, sitting in front of the range wrapped in the enormous towel, combing her long, deep-auburn tresses, Tara felt good. She tingled from head to foot with pleasure as she dropped into the soft bed and stretched out. Her last thought before falling into a deep sleep was that tomorrow, when she put on her freshly laundered clothes, boiled by Lydia, she would look like a different woman, one ready to confront Jefferson Smith.

The following morning Smith called for her. "I'm taking you out," he announced.

"Where?" she asked with ill-concealed suspicion.

"Somewhere private, to a place where we can have that serious conversation you wanted."

With evident pride he walked her through the center of Skagway, stopping a few feet off Broadway at a restaurant with a white, immaculate facade which, it turned out, was as false as its air of respectability.

This was Jefferson Smith's Oyster Parlor, his seat of power in the town, which stood in a small thoroughfare, the number 317 over the portal. She remembered his Law and Order Society with its 317 members.

He saw her glance. "Yes," he nodded, "that's right. Three hundred and seventeen. Nobody can beat that." He said it like a gambler who has put all his faith into one combination.

He held open the door, and Tara entered a barroom, complete with flags of American states, a big mirror over the polished mahogany counter and, to Tara's astonishment, electric light. Bare electric bulbs hung from the ceiling.

"Figure they might as well know we got electricity," explained Smith. "The generator cost me enough, and I don't aim to disguise the only electric light in Skagway under fancy shades and frills."

Next door to the bar was the restaurant, with fretwork screens, artificial palm trees, and framed photographs of bosomy actresses providing the decor. All over the establishment, clothesbrushes hung from hooks.

"Got to give the fellows a chance to brush down and turn themselves into gentlemen," he said.

Unbelievably, there were waiters in boiled shirts and white bow ties, their immaculate appearance somewhat spoiled by one or two of them having blackjacks stuck in their belts.

"Only to discourage drunks," was how Smith put it.

"Where's the gambling?" inquired Tara, looking around for the green baize tables, the roulette wheels, and the other paraphernalia.

"Gambling!" Smith looked shocked. "My dear, this is a high-class restaurant. An oyster parlor."

But there was more to the place than food, Tara found out. Like the back room, "cozy as a lady's parlor," draped in satin and velvet, heavy with gilt, reserved for "special parties only." And there was the secret exit, which Tara did not learn of until later. It led straight from the parlor into a back yard enclosed by a high fence with a concealed door through which people could disappear, leaving pursuers baffled.

They were greeted by a sinister, soft-spoken man in a blue suit, with diamond cufflinks. He had disconcertingly staring eyes, which never seemed to blink.

"Yeah Mow," Smith said, "this is Mrs. Kane. Anything the lady wants, any time, she has. Understand?"

"Sure, Mr. Smith," said Yeah Mow diffidently.

"She speaks for me when I'm not here," Smith went on.

There was the faintest flicker of surprise in the man's eyes. "Certainly, Mr. Smith," he said. He bowed to Tara. "Ma'am."

"What did you say his name was?" asked Tara, following Smith to the back of the parlor.

"Yeah Mow. It's Chinese," Smith told her, leading the way upstairs. "Means Wildcat. He bodyguarded some Chinese Tong lords in Frisco—the only American who used an axe better than the Chinks. Guess Frisco got too hot for him or perhaps he ran out of axes." He laughed. "You ever get bothered by anyone, just say the word to Yeah Mow. You won't be bothered again."

Tara hoped she would never need him. There was something about him that recalled Jake Gore.

Smith opened the door of his office, then stood back to watch her reaction as she stepped in. It was palatial, dignified, impressive, even more so than Smith's other statesmanlike office in Dawson. On the wall was another picture of President McKinley, and next to it a framed photograph of a fierce-looking individual.

"Who's that?"

"Ah," Smith said, ushering her into a huge leather armchair in front of his magnificent desk. "Meet José de la Cruz Porfirio Díaz."

"Who?"

Smith shook his head sorrowfully. "For a lady who is going to move in high society, you'll have to brush up on these things," he said, not allowing her a chance to object before he added, "Señor Díaz. President of Mexico."

He went over to a silver cigar box and selected a cheroot.

"In case you're interested, I happen to be a colonel in the Mexican Army."

"But you're an American citizen."

"Honorary, strictly honorary, Tara. I organized their foreign legion."

"And how much did that cost them?" she asked crisply. Smith looked startled. Then he smiled. "Splendid, Tara," he chuckled delightedly. "You get the point of things. I asked eight thousand pesos, he paid me four thousand. That's why I'm here and he's in trouble. I kept the rank. He didn't mind. Doesn't cost him anything."

She looked around and took in the picture of George Washington, the map of the North American continent, the framed copy of the Declaration of Independence, the florid decoration, complete with jewels and a silk ribbon, in a glass case (another memento from Señor Díaz, she guessed), the bust of Julius Caesar on a shelf.

"Well, my dear, what is it that you wanted to talk about?"

Now that she had a chance to state her case, Tara was uncertain how to begin. "Jeff," she said falteringly, looking down at her hands, "I think it's time you and I got things straight between us." She glanced at him, expecting him to interrupt, but he just raised an eyebrow quizzically.

"First," she went on, "I want you to know I'm very grateful for the cabin, for the help you've given me with John, for your thoughtful gifts, and for your friendship, but I want to make it absolutely plain it's just that. I don't want you to think that because I might appear helpless at the moment or without funds, even reliant on you, that indicates I approve of the sort of man you are or the things you do."

"And tell me, my dear, what sort of man is it that you think I am?" he asked softly.

"The sort that doesn't respect the kind of woman I am. You think that because I came here with you, because I've allowed you to be my, my, benefactor, that means you own me."

"Own you?" grinned Smith. "Come, Tara, how do you work that out?" He leaned back in his chair. "Why act the righteous little woman with me? Who are you trying to kid?"

"Jeff Smith, you know, I think you're a crook. You take advantage of innocent people."

"And what are all the others doing?" he demanded, his eyes steely. "Everyone here has come to use someone, something, somehow. The sourdoughs are here to tear the Territory apart so that they can make themselves rich on its gold. The city slickers are here to cash in on the sourdoughs. The railroad's coming to profit from the sourdoughs going to the gold fields. And I'm here to entertain those poor suckers. But they needn't be entertained by me or by any other rogue, as you so charmingly put it, unless they want to."

"And you think that makes you decent? You believe you're doing them a service, cheating them before anyone else has a chance?"

"Tell me, Tara," said Smith very softly, regarding her from under his heavy lids, "haven't you ever used anyone? I seem to recall a certain incident when the use you made of some poor, unsuspecting Mountie cost him his stripes. But that didn't occur to you at the time, did it? You know why. Because you wanted to get to Dawson. You wanted to get there so badly you didn't mind whose neck you trod on."

"That's not true," she retaliated, blushing at the memory. "I never wanted Sergeant Campbell to lose his stripes. I didn't hurt him on purpose."

"But you did," pointed out Smith. "He was a means to an end, so that sort of puts you in my league right away."

"Your league! How on earth do you think that my one mistake puts me in with the likes of you? I'm not a cheat. I've never swindled or stolen from anyone!"

Smith made no reply for a while. Instead, he picked up a paperknife from his desk and toyed with it. "Whatever I've done I've thought, in that situation, at that moment, was the right thing to do."

"So that makes it OK, does it? You make me laugh, Jeff Smith, you really do. You're always right, aren't you? Always above suspicion, always within the law!"

"Of course, Tara," agreed Smith, "especially when the law doesn't exist."

"And what about Sheep Camp? Why did you take it upon yourself to act as custodian for the few pathetic belongings your men 'took care of'?"

He puffed at his cheroot.

"If anyone comes forward to claim them they can have them. As soon as they prove they've a right to them, of course. Got to protect the deceased, you know that. And if I hadn't arrived at Sheep Camp when I did who else would have organized the burials? You saw how well I made the arrangements. There were no complaints that I can recall. I don't remember you being too upset to see me. You sure as hell needed someone to help."

"I had no alternative."

"No alternative?" echoed Smith, laughing derisively. "Me being there suited you, Tara Kane, and don't you deny it. You know what the trouble is with you, you want it all ways, and however I play it, I can't win. If I help you it's because I want to own you. But if I'd left you to fend for yourself, and pretty useless you would have been at that point too, I'd have been a scoundrel. You're so conceited and arrogant, all the things you accuse me of being, that if I provide you with food, a roof over your head, which I can easily afford, it's so I can woo you into a lawless way of life. If I was after you, I trust I'd be able to show you in a more spectacular fashion than by lending you a cabin and a wet nurse, giving you fifty dollars and a few bottles of perfume. I'd like to think I'm bigger than that."

She looked at him challengingly.

"Well, why did you help me, then?"

"Because I wanted to," he said quietly.

"I don't believe you, Jeff, because I don't believe you've ever done anything without an ulterior motive."

"What a pity that such a kind-hearted woman has so little faith," he mused, smiling sadly. "I bow to your superior knowledge, Mrs. Kane. I can see you know it all. But before you go I'm going to put you straight about me. You think educating suckers to watch their dough is my ambition in life? Owning faro games? Running shell games? Well, dear lady, you're wrong. As wrong as if you think you came to these parts to find that missing husband of yours."

"So what am I here for?"

"You ran away to find yourself, to learn something you would never have found out back in San Francisco. That you can tackle anything. That you can stand on your own feet and own the world."

Tara was taken aback. She had never questioned her reason for coming to the Yukon. Surely that was not it. Surely not.

"I have—I have no interest in owning the world. I couldn't care less about power. That's your desire, not mine."

"We'll see," said Smith. From a drawer he brought out a heavy object. It was a piece of rock into which was set a brass plate. He put it on the desk, in front of Tara. Some words were engraved on the plaque.

"Read it," he ordered.

She leaned forward.

"Jefferson Randolph Smith," it read, "Governor of Alaska."

"Another sure thing?" she asked acidly.

"Exactly," he said. "Alaska, the Yukon, the Klondike. All under one flag. The richest slice of real estate in the world."

"All built on your profits from the Gold Rush?" she suggested.

"No! You don't think gold's all there is, do you? People look at the ice, the snow, the frozen rivers, and they think there's nothing else there. I tell you, one day they'll know the real truth. Once this place opens up and the railroad's established, you wait and see. And I aim that the whole territory will belong to the United States."

"And to you?"

Smith's eyes twinkled. "Sure. A few acres will. Commission, so to speak."

"And just how do you intend to go about this mighty mission?"

"I've already begun," he said softly. "I know the most important thing already."

He carefully knocked the ash off his cheroot. "I know that, as much as you hate to admit it, you believe in me, Tara, and that's fine for starters. And I'm going to offer you a job," he went on heedlessly. "A chance to earn money, clean money. Not by drudgery like in Dawson, not by being a dance-hall hostess or a play-for-pay girl. Be my right-hand woman. Help me achieve what's proper and decent for this godforsaken territory—a future. How about helping me set the record straight?"

His eyes were bright as he spoke. Tara was lost for words.

"If you're the woman I think you are, Tara, you'll take up my challenge. That way I can't own you. That way perhaps you'll stop being ashamed of having a friend in Jefferson Smith. I know you value your self-respect and I'm giving you the opportunity of proving it. This way we can help one another because you've got the one thing I lack. The one thing I haven't got you can give me."

"What's that?"

"Class," he replied.

"Jeff."

"I don't mean you clean your teeth, wash behind your ears, and don't eat with a knife. I mean class. Real class."

He laughed a little wryly. "I got no illusions about myself, Tara," he continued. "I know what I am. No matter if I wear city duds, flash my gold, smoke my Havanas, there's a hell of a lot of people who don't find me proper and won't accept what I aim to be." He looked at her earnestly. "You can make me something else. You can make me respectable."

"By sitting here and licking envelopes?"

He threw his hands in the air.

"Goddamn it, Tara, don't play dumb with me. You know darn well what I'm talking about." He glared at her angrily. "You don't have to do it, you know. Jefferson Smith isn't going to be beholden to anybody, believe me. I just thought . . ." He paused.

"Yes," said Tara, "you thought what?"

"I thought maybe you'd like to see me get places," he said, staring into her eyes. "Guess I was wrong. You're so damn superior about the way I operate. I've seen it again and again, that look. Now I'm telling you I think you're right. Sure, I've played them all for suckers. I'm an operator. I've had to do a little bit of conniving here and there." He saw her expression. "OK, some lying and cheating and hustling, but I'm not ashamed. The difference is that I'm trying to become something other than a tinhorn gambler. I can do things for people. I can go places. I thought maybe you'd like to see me do that. So I was wrong. Don't worry, sister, I'll get by."

292

Then he got up, went to the door, and opened it. "Think over what I've said. Don't give me your answer straight away. Consider my proposition carefully, but let me know soon."

In a daze, she moved toward the opened door. She had never intended this to be the outcome of their conversation. As she passed him, unexpectedly, he took her hand and kissed it.

"I've got faith in you, just as I know you've got faith in me," he whispered. He walked back to his desk, leaving Tara to find her own way out.

On the corner of Broadway, Tara felt far from satisfied. She knew she had played straight into Smith's hands. He had won. After all, he had done most of the talking and she had hardly got out half the things she had meant to say.

Yet, strangely, she felt stimulated by Smith's words. Was it because he had offered her an opportunity of proving herself? But if that was the case, to whom? And what was it that she wanted to prove? That she could stand on her own two feet? That she could be financially independent? Were those things really important to her, or was it that they were important to Jefferson Smith?

"Oh goodness," she sighed, her mind filled with a thousand different questions, none of which she'd ever asked herself before.

She dug her hands deep into her pockets and started making her way back to the cabin, brooding over what Smith had said about her coming to the Yukon to find her own identity. He seemed to have taken it for granted that she had given up her search for Daniel, but that wasn't true, and he wasn't going to be given the satisfaction of winning on all fronts. Gradually, a plan of campaign began to form in Tara's mind.

If Daniel had survived Sheep Camp and all the ghastliness that was part of a sourdough's lot, if he had managed to find gold or even if he had been unsuccessful and had just given up, if he was still alive, then he must be in the Territory somewhere.

There was only one way for him to get back to San Francisco and that was by sea. He would have to pick up a boat in Juneau, Dyea, or Skagway, the only ports serving the Gold Rush, or he could sail direct from Dawson, but that would only be possible when the Yukon River thawed. Therefore it stood to reason that he could come to her. Boats would be leaving those points very soon, but that still gave her time to implement her plan.

The key to it was the *Skagway Intelligencer* and Smith's five dollars.

She located "The Klondike's Biggest Little Paper" easily. Like the town it served, it had grown. Clearly, the paper had acquired not only one but several office boys as well as reporters and editors, because the minute she stepped inside the shop, Tara was caught up in a hive of activity. Behind the counter people were coming and going, men were pounding away furiously at typewriters, the presses were clattering, and everyone was shouting above the noise.

Tara stood at the counter, ignored by all. She rang a large brass bell, but in the din nobody heard. She rang it again and shouted, "I want to place an advertisement."

Eventually one of the men glanced up. "OK, hold on a minute."

Grudgingly he got up from his typewriter, ground his dead cigar into the floorboards, pulled out a thick wad of paper from under piles of photographs and proofs, took a pencil from behind his ear, and came over.

"Make it quick. We're hellish busy today," he said, shoving to one side the odd pieces of paper, pots of glue, and scissors that littered the countertop.

"What are the rates?" Tara shouted to make herself heard.

"Display or classified?"

"Display."

"Two twenty-five a week."

"All right," said Tara. "Two weeks."

"What do you want to say?"

" 'Daniel Kane' in bold type across the top, and underneath, 'a reward will be paid to anyone knowing the whereabouts, having any information, or able to inform him of this notice. Contact his wife Mrs. Tara Kane urgently care of box number,' etcetera. Does the paper sell in Dyea too?"

"Sells all over," the man replied, checking the advertisement. "Even in Juneau. I've seen them read *The Skagway Intelligencer* as far afield as Dawson, so don't expect an instant reaction. It could take months."

"That's all right." Tara handed him four dollars and fifty cents. "I'll still be here."

"First insertion next week and the second the week after," he confirmed, putting the money in a little tin box. "See you next week, Mrs. Kane."

When Lydia took John out later that afternoon, Tara began slowly drafting a letter to Jefferson Smith.

Dear Mr. Smith,

With reference to your offer of employment, I am writing to advise you that I would be happy to accept the post of assistant to yourself, provided the following terms are agreeable:

I understand in being offered this vacancy, and you appreciate in my accepting it, that my exclusive employer will be yourself, Jefferson Smith, and that I will not have to deal with any business appertaining to Soapy Smith.

I would require a remuneration of one hundred dollars per calendar month with free board and lodging for myself and John.

If I am to work for you, and if my stipulations are acceptable, then I would still need the services of Lydia, for which I will not be able to pay.

I can commence working for you when it suits you and put in whatever hours you wish, within reason. I am not an experienced assistant and can only promise to do my best.

I look forward to hearing from you if the above arrangements are acceptable to you.

Yours faithfully,
Tara Kane, Mrs.

Tara read and reread the draft, trying to work out what Smith's reaction would be. She was filled with doubts. Supposing he turned her down? Supposing he said she was asking for too much? Supposing he said that he had changed his mind and that he thought she had a hell of a nerve? What would he say if he found out that she was just using his offer as means of getting herself and John back to San Francisco?

"Well, he'd be a fine one to talk on that score," she muttered to herself, nibbling the end of the pencil. "If he turns you down you'll have to think up another plan, and as for using him, you're only doing something he taught you."

So she pulled out a clean sheet of paper and carefully copied her draft. Then she sealed it in the plain brown envelope and addressed it. She made her way back to the Oyster Parlor hoping and praying that she wouldn't bump into him.

She was in luck. The place was almost deserted; even the frightening Yeah Mow was nowhere to be seen. She thrust the letter at the barman saying, "Please give this to Mr. Smith as soon as he comes in."

She went back to the cabin and nervously awaited the bombshell.

"Tara, you're incorrigible!" were Smith's first words when he walked into the cabin.

She looked up, startled by his arrival and his bonhomie. Since delivering the letter, she had been engrossed in working out a detailed budget for each step of her plan. Quickly she gathered up the sheets of

295

paper, completely covered with her laboriously calculated sums, and pushed them out of Smith's sight.

"Have I interrupted something?" he inquired.

"No," smiled Tara. "I was just brushing up on my arithmetic, trying to get my brain going again."

Smith didn't seem that interested.

"Can I get you some coffee?" she asked, nodding at Lydia, who, under Tara's eagle-eyed supervision, sat by the crib stitching dresses for John from the material they had bought.

"No, don't bother. I'm here to talk business." He reached in his pocket and pulled out the brown envelope. He sat down, slowly unfolding her note and reading it to himself. "Well, now," he said after a while. "I think we have a basis for discussion. There's only one problem."

Tara stood silently, anxiously waiting for him to go on, but Smith was well versed in milking this kind of situation.

"What's the problem?" he made her ask.

"Money. I intend to pay my assistant a minimum of two hundred dollars a month."

Tara's eyes opened wide. "Two hundred dollars," she repeated with some awe.

"You'll have to be my hostess when necessary and to be available to work whenever I say. Naturally, I'm willing to pay for any inconvenience that may cause. And I want your company whenever I please."

"You're asking for more than an assistant," she remarked frostily.

"Of course. That's why I'm willing to pay for the additional socializing required."

"So all you *do* want is another play-for-pay girl. Me this time."

"Tara. I didn't say I wanted to sleep with you."

She suddenly felt foolish.

"This is strictly business," he went on quickly, like a gambler rapidly playing his trumps. "You need a job. I need somebody I can trust, to be around me, to keep my books, to do my letters, to travel."

"Travel?" she broke in. "Travel where?"

"Business trips, what else?"

She tried to avoid his eyes.

"Well," said Tara slowly. "I can do your accounts. I'm a reasonable bookkeeper, I suppose."

"Sure, and you'll make a fine hostess at a business function," he interjected.

She shook her head.

"I'm not worth two hundred a month. And I don't want special favors either. I'll take half that. If I can do the job."

"If you insist," said Smith. "But you'll get a dress allowance too." He raised his hand to silence her when she began to say something. "Can't have my assistant looking like a ragbag."

He rose and smiled. "Well, Mrs. Kane, you're on the payroll now." For a moment, Tara felt a twinge of guilt. "Here." He pulled out a bundle of notes, and peeled off four of them. "Get yourself a dress and a decent coat," he said, pressing the money into Tara's hand. "You start at nine o'clock sharp tomorrow morning. At the Oyster Parlor."

Without a backward glance, he went.

When Tara opened her hand, she saw he had given her two hundred dollars. A handout from Soapy Smith, she began to say to herself savagely, and then stopped. She did need clothes. She couldn't look like this as his, his what? Secretary? Assistant? Hostess? Companion?

All that would have to sort itself out. Right now she was going to spend the money.

Tara had exactly a dollar and seventy-five cents of Smith's money left when she arrived at the Oyster Parlor the next morning. The chocolate-brown velvet dress, the thick woolen cape, the silk underclothing all had been imported from New York, and their price had rocketed the moment they arrived in Skagway.

But she knew she looked well, that the lustrous velvet set off her green eyes and her deep auburn hair, which was now pinned up in a chignon.

Smith eyed her appreciatively and led her to a small writing table which had been placed opposite his desk. It was covered with writing materials. "How do you like it?" He pulled out a tapestry chair from behind the table. "Go on," he said. "Sit down and try it."

"What's all this for?" she asked a little nervously.

"So that you can help me with my correspondence. If there's anything else you want, just say the word. I'll get you a typing machine, if you prefer."

"I wouldn't know how to use it."

"That doesn't matter," he assured her. "If you want to, you can teach yourself. The main thing is that your just being here helps me. You know, Tara, I've already got a lot of important things going. There are letters to write to Washington, to congressmen and editors, and that's what you're going to do. Put them into the right language."

Tara frowned. "Jeff, I don't know anything about writing to politicians. I've never met a congressman and I've never been to Washington in my life."

"Don't worry. You'll soon learn."

"Well, if you think so, I'm willing to try."

"Good. You've got spirit, Tara, and you're keen. That's how I manage too." He sat behind his desk and picked up a sheet of paper.

"OK. I want to write to this guy," he said. "He runs *McClure's*, some magazine. He wants to do a story about me."

Tara selected a pen from the inkstand. "Go ahead," she said.

"He's called Cy Warman. I guess I want to say something like this." He stuck his thumbs in the arms of his vest. " 'Dear Mr. Warman. Mighty kind of you to want to do a piece about me, but I shun publicity.' "

Tara glanced up but said nothing.

" 'I figure that a man in my civic position finds it kind of unseemly to appear as if I'm interested in the limelight. This may be important for a man with political ambitions and a first step on the road to Washington, but I have no such desires. If you happen to be in Skagway, I'll gladly buy you a drink, but I reckon I don't really want to be publicized.' How's that?"

"What you mean is you're dying for him to do a story about you, how you're wasted out here, and how the country needs you."

"Jackpot," he chuckled. "I told you you understood."

"It's all right, Jeff," Tara said dryly, "I'll convey your sentiments."

Smith blew her a kiss, reached into his desk drawer, and took out two curious brass objects. He fitted one of them around the knuckles of his right hand, punching the air with his fist. Brass knuckles.

"How about that, eh?"

Tara sat stony-faced.

"An outfit in St. Louis makes them. Big business," Smith said. He pulled a catalogue over. Harrison and Frisby, St. Louis, Missouri. You got the address here, Tara. You write and order me four dozen. OK? Cash on delivery."

Tara put down her pen. "No," she said.

"What's wrong?"

"Those are murderous things."

He laughed. "Gentle persuaders, honey, for my men. They got a rough job."

"And I'm having no part of it. Nor your rackets either. I thought there was going to be a new Jefferson Smith. The man who cares. The

298

man who wants to go into politics. I refuse to have anything to do with Soapy Smith, Jeff. I'll work for you, but not for him."

"You're crazy, Tara."

She shrugged. "You may think so, but that's the way it's got to be. And if you don't like it, too bad. Now we've settled that point, I'll quite understand if you want me to quit."

Smith sat watching Tara tidy up her desk as if preparing to leave.

"OK," he said eventually. "Forget it. But, Tara, you're not going to start preaching to me, are you? I don't want no damn sermons."

"Anything else?" she asked.

He said nothing. He got up and walked out of the room, banging the door hard as he left.

Tara finished the letter and put it, together with the addressed envelope, on Smith's desk. There seemed nothing else for her to do, and she sat at her writing table wondering if Smith had not returned because he was sulking about the brass knuckles.

There was a light tap on the door and a waiter came in carrying a silver tray, on which were a silver coffeepot, cream jug, and sugar bowl, together with a delicately painted bone-china cup and saucer.

"Is Mr. Smith downstairs?" Tara inquired as the waiter put the tray down in front of her.

"No, ma'am," he replied. "He went out. Said he wasn't sure what time he'd be back but that you were to be served with coffee and lunch up here."

After the waiter had gone, Tara sat sipping her coffee, unsure of what she should do until Smith came back. She got up and wandered about the room. On Smith's desk lay a big leather album, bound in red morocco, with his initials embossed in gold on it. Idly, she began reading it.

Before her unfolded the making of Jefferson Smith. Or, at least clues to his life. There were photographs, newspaper clippings, even leaflets. Page after page of mementos, articles, stories, even small paragraphs, clipped out of dozens of papers and periodicals. Only a man with an enormous ego could have so painstakingly kept such a collection. She could visualize him, cigar clamped between his teeth, cutting out each item, and carefully pasting it into the album, beaming.

There were faded photographs of an elderly couple. His parents, Tara guessed: the father, white-haired with a goatee, proud, very much the gentleman; and the woman, dignified, handsome. Hard to believe that the offspring of this genteel, even aristocratic-looking couple was the notorious Soapy Smith.

299

There was another photograph of the old man, even more yellowed, in the uniform of an officer of the Confederate Army.

On a page by itself was a very old postcard-sized picture of a magnificent colonial mansion. It was not hard to imagine the carriages pulling up in front of it, the guests mingling on the lawn. Was this where Smith grew up?

There were photos of Smith himself: one as a little boy, in lace, looking so angelic that Tara had to giggle; another of him, a grown man, in a flamboyant uniform, presumably playing his role as an officer in the Mexican Army. A crumpled and half-torn photograph showed young Jefferson Smith, sporting a deputy's badge no less. He was smiling broadly.

Many of the clippings appeared to date from 1892. One of the earlier ones was a curious article suggesting that Smith had avenged the killing of Jesse James by setting up Bob Ford, the man who had shot James in the back ten years previously.

In Denver, Smith had apparently lectured to a learned body of academics about the evils of gambling. According to the newspaper report of the gathering, "Mr. Jefferson Smith, a well-known social worker, described an establishment he ran as 'an educational institution affording its patients release from the curse of gambling.' No one, Mr. Smith explained, had a chance of winning, and this taught them the folly of indulging in gambling." Tara arched her eyebrows. It sounded familiar to her. The amazing thing was that, according to the clippings, a body as respectable as the Keeley Institute had actually consulted Smith about his "scientific findings."

There were clippings from the silver-mining town of Creede on other pages. Smith had become a leading member of the community, apparently dabbling in politics. But he left the town without being given the benefit of a big write-up. Or at least, that clipping was missing.

The album left Tara with a mixed impression of Jefferson Smith. A man, apparently from a well-to-do family, who had roamed all over the place, involving himself in all kinds of activities, sailing near the wind more than a few times. A man who loved play-acting, dressing up in uniforms, having his picture taken.

A man who now had made the Yukon his kingdom.

Behind that smooth, debonair exterior was a fine brain. Smith, despite the rackets he operated, the gang he ran, had ability, vision, nerve. If only he could apply his wit, his intelligence, to a good purpose.

If only he could be persuaded to change.

300

CHAPTER TWENTY-THREE

Smith enjoyed entertaining on a grand scale, and the dinner party he was planning was clearly intended to be an elaborate and an impressive affair.

He barely noticed Tara's arrival at the Oyster Parlor that morning. Like a theatrical producer arranging a gala performance, he was busily instructing Yeah Mow on the wine that was to be served, who was to wait on table, and when they were to retire.

For a while, Tara stood by, watching the waiters come and go as they prepared the private dining room at the rear of the restaurant, not certain whether she was supposed to join in the general activity or to leave them to it. She mounted the stairs to the first floor, where at least all was quiet.

On her writing table was a box, and on top of that lay a newspaper with an item circled in blue crayon. Her advertisement in the *Skagway Intelligencer* had caught Smith's eye, and for some inexplicable reason Tara felt embarrassed that he had seen it.

"You'll never give up, will you?" Smith remarked, going over to his desk. Tara glanced up. She hadn't heard him come in.

"No. Not while I believe there's a chance."

"If you want my opinion, you're wasting your time and your money."

"Thank you for your words of wisdom, Mr. Smith. I don't recall requesting your advice."

Smith, searching for something on his desk, made no answer.

"What's in the box?" she inquired.

"A dress. I want you to wear it tonight."

"I don't need another dress, thank you," she said, "and if I did, I'm quite capable of buying one myself."

He found what he was looking for and went over to her.

"Don't let's argue. Wear it," he instructed. "You'll have just the right effect. I aim to cash in on it."

Tara glared at him.

"Here's the menu," he went on, handing her a sheet of paper as if the matter of the dress had been settled. "I want you to do four copies of it, then do the place cards. After you've finished those, check the seating arrangements with Yeah Mow. I'll be out for the rest of the day. You sort out any problems here and then go home and change,

301

but be back by six-thirty. We'll be eating at seven sharp, and I don't want any hitches tonight."

"Off to wheel and deal again?" suggested Tara, arching her eyebrows.

"I'm negotiating, Tara," Smith said loftily, "and for your information it's all going very smoothly. This dinner may well clinch the whole thing, so I trust I can count on your co-operation."

He put on his coat. "In that dress you'll look stunning., See you tonight. Six-thirty, don't be late." He picked up his hat and was gone.

"We'll see about that," Tara muttered at the closed door. He had just fired a string of instructions at her. He had not bothered to tell her what it was all about.

While she copied out the lavish menu, the wine list, and the place cards, Tara wondered why "Sir Thomas Tancrede" and "Mr. Michael J. Henney" warranted such extravagant consideration, what exactly they were going to clinch, as Smith had put it, and if they were aware of the sort of man they would be dining with.

It struck Tara that he had given her a splendid opportunity to educate him in the same way he taught other people. What fun it would be, she thought, to show up that arrogant scoundrel in front of two people he was falling over himself to impress. He would learn that Tara Kane was not a woman to provide light relief, to dazzle the suckers while he conducted his shady deals. She could open Sir Thomas Tancrede's and Michael J. Henney's eyes to the type of crook Smith really was, and she would enjoy doing it.

Once home, Tara undid the dress box and took out a most sensational black taffeta evening gown, with a plunging neckline.

"Quite out of the question. Why, it's positively unwholesome," she laughed to herself, returning the exotic creation to its box. To think Smith intended her to preside over an all-male dinner party in it. No wonder he was so optimistic about the successful outcome of tonight's business. It was her duty to the community not to distract Smith's guests with such a décolletage.

She took painstaking care with her hair, sweeping it up but leaving wisps to frame her face, and dabbed perfume behind her ears. Then she put on the old trousers and shirt she had worn on the trail.

Her only concession to Smith was to wear the brown cape. Kissing John lightly on the forehead, well aware that she was going to be at least fifteen minutes late, she left the cabin.

Like any leading lady about to make her entrance, Tara felt nervous. For the first time, she was going to defy Smith, not just in words but in deed, and she faced the prospect with butterflies in her stomach.

When she finally entered the Oyster Parlor, twenty minutes late, Yeah Mow rushed forward, for once nervously.

"The guests are already here, Mrs. Kane," he said, looking at her anxiously. "Mr. Smith has been asking after you."

"Has he?" Her tone was haughty.

"The boss wants dinner to be served at seven sharp," he added reproachfully.

Tara swept past him, dropping her cape on the floor.

Outside the private dining room, she swallowed. There was no retreat. She would have fled if she could, but her pride would not let her.

Without knocking, she opened the door and stepped into the candlelit room. Smith, who was wearing evening dress, looked around, but not a flicker on his face betrayed his surprise at her appearance.

"Ah, Tara," he said smoothly, his diamond cufflinks twinkling in the subdued lighting, "you're just in time."

He turned to the two well-dressed gentlemen standing in front of the fireplace.

"Gentlemen, may I present Mrs. Tara Kane."

She smiled brilliantly, partly to cover her embarrassment. In truth, she felt slightly ridiculous, but she would not give Smith the satisfaction of knowing that.

"This is Sir Thomas Tancrede," he went on, indicating a beanpole of a man with thin lips, who seemed to have a permanently sardonic smile.

"Enchanted, my dear," said Sir Thomas in a clipped English accent, proffering his hand, which she shook limply. "What a surprise."

"And this is Mr. Michael J. Henney." Smith glanced at him. "Known as 'Big Mike' to his friends."

The granite-faced man did not smile but nodded curtly.

"These gentlemen are on the board of the railroad," explained Smith.

Now she knew why he had gone to so much trouble over the dinner. This was the get-together at which he intended to make his bid for a share of the White Pass and Yukon Railway. She was not in the slightest sorry for having messed up his well-laid plans.

"My goodness, Jeff, you should have told me," Tara said. "If I'd realized this was going to be such an important occasion, I would have dressed more formally."

Smith did not blink an eyelid. "Mrs. Kane is a real pioneer lady," he said, turning to his guests. "She is the kind of woman, gentlemen, you will never meet in the parlors of London or Boston. She is more at home with a rifle and a dog team than with the frills and fol-de-rols of the salon. As you forge your railroad into the interior, you'll meet more of them in the settlements. Don't let their sex fool you. They're as tough as nails."

"I wouldn't say tough, Jeff," laughed Tara. "It's just we're more used to dealing with the practicalities of life than to being treated as pretty ornaments to be indulged by the opposite sex."

Smith's eyes raked her, then he reached for the bellpull.

"Shall we eat?" He smiled coldly at Tara. "We're a little late, but you probably had to feed the dogs first."

"Jeff, how you exaggerate!" She turned to Sir Thomas. "Why, at this rate, you'll have your guests believing everything you say."

Smith did not reply. This side of Tara was completely new to him, and tonight he was taking no chances.

They sat down at the large oval dining table, resplendent with crystal glasses and silver cutlery. It was a beautifully cooked meal. Smith had seen to it that the menu, the wine, and the service would not have disgraced a luxury hotel. These men had money, but it was a sure thing, thought Tara, that they hadn't had a dinner like this since they had stepped ashore in Alaska.

Throughout the four courses, Tara acted the perfect dinner companion, keeping up a spirited conversation, playfully bantering with Smith, and all the time stopping him from getting down to the business at hand. But he went along with her, attentive, amusing, a gentleman very much at ease, all the while watching her like a hawk.

Big Mike had little to say for himself, but the Englishman was thoroughly enjoying the dinner, and Tara's company particularly.

"Are you really such a tough lady, Mrs. Kane?" he inquired,

"Oh no," she replied. "You mustn't let Mr.Smith or my appearance deceive you, Sir Thomas. It's simply that I've had to learn to look after myself. You've no idea how hard life can be for a woman alone, particularly in this neck of the woods."

When they reached the brandy stage and the cigars came out, Tara started to leave.

"No, Tara," Smith said firmly. "You know this territory. You know the people. I'd like you to stay."

"Absolutely," insisted Sir Thomas. "Won't be deprived of the pleasure."

There was political talk. Of the war with Spain and how long it would last. In the United States, there were patriotic rallies, "Remember the *Maine*" had become a national slogan, and Teddy Roosevelt was raising a band of volunteers to fight in Cuba.

"Is it going to be a big war?" asked Tara.

"By American standards," said Sir Thomas lazily.

Smith was about to say something, then restrained himself; it wouldn't help matters to quarrel with the Englishman.

"I heard somewhere you'd been a military man, Smith," remarked Henney. His tone was challenging.

Smith smiled deprecatingly. "I saw some service," he said modestly, "in Mexico."

"Fascinating," murmured Sir Thomas. He poured himself another brandy. "Remarkable man, Mr. Smith, isn't he?" he said to Tara.

"You think so?" she said, and Smith flashed her another look. "Mr. Smith says so many things."

Sir Thomas blinked and then cleared his throat. "Why don't we get down to business? People say you're interested in our railroad." He rolled the brandy around the glass. "Is that right?"

"Damn right," said Smith. "I know a good investment when I see one."

Henney cut the niceties short. He waited until the waiters had left; then he said curtly, "What exactly is your proposition, Smith?"

For a moment, Smith looked pained. That kind of direct talk seemed more suited to the sawdust-and-spit world of the cheap bars than to this elegant supper table. Carefully he knocked the ash off his cheroot.

"We all have a dream, gentlemen, you and I," he said after a while. Anybody less like dreamers than this trio would be hard to find, thought Tara, but she waited, amused. She wanted to hear his pitch.

"The dream is to make this territory a great land, a land which can make more money for all of us than anyone has imagined," he went on. "The key to that land is the railroad. Open up the territory, and you shrink it to a manageable size. Cut the distances, and you've conquered it."

"I say, Mr. Smith, you wax quite poetical." Sir Thomas winked at Tara. "He can dress up things, can't he?"

"Well?" cut in Big Mike, unimpressed.

"The point is, Mr. Henney, I'd like us all to be partners."

Smith leaned back, beaming at them. His watchchain and diamond cufflinks danced in the candlelight.

"Sorry," said Henney gruffly. "No deal."

Smith remained unruffled. "But you haven't heard me out."

305

Sir Thomas sighed. "Mr. Smith, we're an Anglo-Canadian consortium. I raised my half of the money in the City of London and Mr. Henney got the rest in Ottawa. I don't think we really want American involvement. No offense, of course."

Smith nodded."Aren't you forgetting that the starting point of your railroad is on American soil?" he asked mildly.

"And aren't you forgetting, sir, that under the '71 Convention, Canada has the transit rights she needs?" retorted Henney. "This is a Canadian project, to serve Canadians on Canadian soil."

"A little more brandy, gentlemen?" suggested Tara.

"I propose we leave that all to the politicians," Smith said, clearly aggravated at her interruption. "We're businessmen, all of us. I know you have the capital, but since when hasn't some extra money been useful? You got big costs coming."

"Maybe," grunted Henney. "But we don't want you in, Smith. We don't want any part of you."

Smith sat stone-faced. Sir Thomas looked a little worried.

"What Mike means . . ." he began.

"I know what he means," snapped Smith.

"Then you know why we don't want your kind of money," went on Henney.

"So you don't think my dough's good enough," said Smith very quietly, his lips drawn into a thin line. "You don't want to soil your hands. You only like nice clean capital. Virgin dollars." He laughed mirthlessly. "Tell me, Sir Thomas, how did your folks make their dough? Never shipped any slaves? Never conquered any colonies? Or you, Mr. Henney? Earned it all by the sweat of your brow?"

"I don't need lectures from a brothel owner," spat Henney.

Smith's eyes blazed. Tara knew that at any other time there would have been violence. But with an effort he remained seated.

"Mike didn't mean that exactly," conciliated Sir Thomas. He looked embarrassed.

"Sir Thomas, one thing we've got to get clear if we're going to be partners," said Smith. "You have to stop telling me what Mr. Henney does or does not mean. I can figure it out for myself."

Sir Thomas pulled out a beautiful silver hunter.

"It's been such a marvelous dinner, I hate to break it up, but perhaps we ought to retire now."

He smiled at Tara, seeking an ally.

"Gentlemen, maybe you forgot a couple of things," Smith said, ignoring Sir Thomas. "You need a lot of supplies, a lot of men, a lot of horses to build that one hundred and eleven miles of railroad. You haven't got any of it."

"Right now, Smith," Henney said triumphantly, "ships are on their way to Skagway with every damn thing we need, laborers, supplies, timber, horses. We got it all organized."

Smith nodded. "Of course. They're due in a couple of weeks, and within twenty-four hours of their arrival you'll start laying the track. Eight weeks later you hope to have the first four miles of the line open."

Henney's eyes narrowed. "What are you getting at?"

Smith grinned smugly.

"Your point, sir," said Sir Thomas crisply.

"I have a certain, let's say, influence on the waterfront. The men listen to me. I dare say, gentlemen, that if I didn't get a look into your railroad, they might not unload any of your ships."

Henney pushed back his chair unceremoniously and stood up. "Now you listen, Smith," he snarled. "I thought you'd start blackmailing us. Well, sir, our railroad has the blessing of the authorities. They want it built. You try and hold us up, you try to stop us unloading, you start your bully-boy tricks, and we'll have a battalion of United States infantry in Skagway so quick you won't know what hit you. And I'll tell you something else, your hired guns aren't going to be much use against Army bayonets."

He glanced at Sir Thomas. "I think it *is* time we went."

The Englishman stood up and bowed to Tara. "I do apologize, dear lady," he said. "Business can get so tedious."

"Business, Sir Thomas," she replied, smiling politely, "is never tedious. It interests me enormously."

Sir Thomas looked slightly nonplussed. "We'll see ourselves out," he said, nodding at Smith. "Thank you for a highly entertaining evening. Good night."

Smith did not stand up as they left the room.

For a while Tara and Smith sat in silence. It was perhaps the first time she had known Jefferson Smith not to have the last word. Yet she did not exult. She actually felt rather sorry for him.

"Well?" she asked at last.

"I'll get there. I'll get my way. You'll see. It'll happen. It might just take a little longer than I'd thought." He sipped his brandy. "What do you think, Tara?"

She looked at him in surprise. Smith was talking to her as an equal.

"Do you care?" she asked.

307

Smith was pacing up and down, contemplating his brandy as he rolled it around inside the large balloon glass. He stopped and looked at her.

"Yes," he said. "Yes I do. Very much."

It was up to her, she realized. He wanted someone to advise him, someone he could depend on, someone he could trust. She knew it was time for her to be his friend.

She had the power to guide Smith. He was a leader, not a follower, so if she were to succeed then she must encourage him to make the right decision by allowing him to regard it as his own.

She glanced up. The dying candles highlighted his chiseled features and the steely grayness of his eyes.

"How can I help you?"

Smith frowned. "You sure you want to?"

"Yes. If you'll let me."

"Well," he said accusingly, "what about this evening? Why the hell didn't you help me then?"

"You musn't take me for granted," murmured Tara.

"You put on a great act. That Limey really appreciated you." He imitated the stiff English accent. " 'How quaint, my dear.' But you know you did your best to make a fool out of me, damn you." He scowled at her. "And another thing, look at yourself. Some hostess. What stopped you wearing the dress?"

"Jeff, I will not be an ornament. I didn't wear it because you only wanted me to be a pretty doll, making the right noises. That's not me."

"Mighty independent, aren't you—at my expense?" he growled. "You really did a hatchet job. More or less called me a liar. Sure I want your help, but not this way."

"It didn't make any difference, so don't fool yourself," she said quietly. "They'd made up their minds before they got here. You know that."

For a moment he stared at her.

"I just wanted to prove to you that snapping your fingers doesn't work with me. I'm not Cad Wilson. I'm not a plaything."

Smith thought for a moment. Then he lit another cheroot, exhaled the smoke, and paused.

"All right," he said at last. "If that's the way it's got to be." He gave his twisted grin. "Kind of expensive lesson. That dress cost me two hundred and fifty bucks. Imported from France, and I thought I was doing you a great turn. The latest Parisian fashion in Skagway." He became serious. "OK, you and me got a lot in common. So let's share it. You want me to tell you things, I'll tell you things. But you got to help me too."

He told her of his various schemes to secure control of the railroad.

Tara became increasingly uneasy. For she began to realize that if Smith did not achieve his means peacefully, he would do it by force. If he couldn't use a dock strike to win a say in the railroad, he would bring in his hired guns. Skagway would be ripped apart by bloodshed. The railroad would have its own little army, and the town would become a battlefield.

Whatever it took, he had to be steered away from violence.

"They're not going to beat me, Tara, by God they're not. Sooner or later they'll crack."

"You can't blackmail the railroad," Tara said. "It won't work. Suppose they break the strike?"

"I'm a gambling man, Tara. The cards are stacked right. You wait, after a ten-day strike, I'll more than likely be offered a partnership on a silver plate. They'll do anything to get the waterfront moving. And if they play rough, they'll meet with a reception they hadn't bargained for. I'll fight them if they make me, but by jingo I hope they don't."

"Force never solved anything," Tara said very softly.

"It's the only way. What alternative have I got?"

"To give in."

Smith threw back his head and laughed derisively. "You crazy?"

"Jeff, if you're serious about achieving your political ambitions, that's your only course. You must prove to them and the townsfolk that you're after the best for Skagway, not just the best for Soapy Smith. If you allow the railroad to go ahead without a fight, show everybody what kind of man you really are, you'll gain their confidence. They'll look on you as somebody worth voting for, a man worthy of their respect, perhaps even a governor. Bring in gunmen, tear the town apart, destroy its prosperity by fighting it out on the streets, and you'll be hated and despised. And when you get killed, as most certainly you will, they'll all cheer. So what can you get out of that, people calling you a racketeer, a power-grabbing gang boss, a man who spilled blood for his own profit?"

Tara went over to Smith and knelt down beside his chair.

"Jeff, you wouldn't want that, would you?"

He looked down at her, his face expressionless.

"You told me about your vision for Alaska and how you wanted the best for it," Tara continued. "If that was the truth, if you really are against harming anyone, then don't murder and plunder to reach your goal when diplomacy can reward you so much more."

Smith sighed wearily. "It's late. Let's call it a day."

Tara's last thought before she drifted off that night was that she had less than two weeks in which to prevent Smith destroying Skagway, and himself.

"Mrs. Kane. I say, there."

Tara stopped and looked around. Sprinting across the muddy thoroughfare with an agility that did credit to the playing fields of Eton was Sir Thomas Tancrede.

"Dear lady," he panted, lifting his shiny silk hat and kissing her hand at the same time. "What a marvelous coincidence. This *is* a pleasure."

Tara had the distinct impression that it was no coincidence.

"I did so enjoy our little dinner party," he smiled. "How nice to see you again."

"Yes indeed," said Tara. She gathered her cape around her. "It was very pleasant." She gave him a polite nod and walked on, but he kept up with her.

"Mrs. Kane," he said, his tone more urgent.

She stopped. "Yes?"

"I'd like to have a few words with you," he said. "It won't take long."

"I'm late already," began Tara, but he cut in: "My hotel is only two blocks away. We can talk over a cup of coffee."

She shook her head. His look was hard and his brown eyes unwavering.

"If you'll forgive me," she began, but he interrupted, "I don't think I ever would."

He was smiling, but not with those eyes.

She hesitated. Curiouser and curiouser, she thought. He wants something. Badly.

"All right."

On the way to the hotel, he gave her a little sideways look and smiled. "I see you're wearing your town costume today." She realized that it was the first time he had seen her looking more like her usual self.

The Princess Hotel was full of railroad men. They were the vanguard of the little army that would soon begin to lay the iron track

310

northwards. The air was humming with the buzz of their conversation.

Tara perched on the edge of an enormous armchair in Tancrede's grand suite and unbuttoned her cape.

There was a tap on the door and a man entered dressed in a black morning suit.

"Ah, Rogers," said Sir Thomas, handing him his coat, cane, and hat, "Mrs. Kane and I would like some coffee. After you've served it, I don't want to be disturbed until I instruct you."

"Certainly, Sir Thomas," said Rogers plummily, bowing as he left the room.

An English manservant, thought Tara. Now that's something that would impress Smith. "Did Mr. Rogers come with you from England?" she asked.

"Rogers," corrected Sir Thomas, "has been with me for years. Simply couldn't travel anywhere without him. A perfect gentleman's gentleman, don't you know."

"My goodness," smiled Tara, "this town must seem mighty strange to you both. So different from the drawing rooms of London."

"You have a strange picture of an Englishman's life," chuckled Sir Thomas. "I might be a baronet, but I'm also a businessman. Rogers and I have journeyed, building railways in India and Australia, studying them in the United States, and now financing them here. One day this age will probably be regarded as the most inventive and exciting in history, and I've always enjoyed thinking of myself as one of its pioneers."

Rogers returned bearing a tray, served them with coffee, bowed again, and retired. Tara was amused by the man's circumspect solemnity.

"Now, Mrs. Kane, tell me about your husband."

She was completely taken aback. "My husband? Why?" she asked.

Sir Thomas took a sip of coffee. "Because you're a very charming lady, and I would like to help you find him. I saw your advertisement in the Skagway newspaper."

"But how can you help me? Surely you haven't heard anything about him?"

"Not at present. However, as the railroad progresses I could keep an eye open, mention his name to my foreman, get a bush telegraph going, if you'd like me to."

"Sir Thomas, I can't begin to thank you. I'd give anything to know exactly what's happened to him, even if it's bad news. It's this terrible uncertainty that I find so unbearable."

"It'll be my pleasure, Mrs. Kane. What better cause is there than a lady in distress?" He cleared his throat. "Is Mr. Smith a friend of your husband's?"

"Oh no," said Tara. "They've never met."

"I see. So Mr. Smith is your . . ." Sir Thomas sought for the correct word, "patron?"

Tara felt herself blush a deep crimson. "I wouldn't call him that, Sir Thomas," she replied a little haughtily. "He's simply a man for whom I work. I'm his assistant."

"His assistant," he repeated, a cynical smile curling his lips. "And pray what precisely do you assist him with?"

"I don't see that as any of your business, Sir Thomas," she said frostily, putting her empty cup on the table that stood between them. "I think it's time I was going."

"Ma'am, I trust I haven't offended you," cut in Sir Thomas, pouring her more coffee. "Please don't leave without giving me a chance to redeem myself."

Tara felt uncomfortable. She was not sure she liked Sir Thomas Tancrede. He did not seem quite the gentleman she thought he was.

"You see, my dear," he went on, returning to his seat, "you strike me as a woman after my own heart. A pioneer, a person with spirit, someone who doesn't mind defying the rules of convention."

Tara couldn't think what he was getting at.

"How long have you been working for Mr. Smith?"

"Not very long."

"But you've known him for some time."

"Yes."

"I suppose I must seem very nosy to you, Mrs. Kane. My interest in Smith is purely a professional one, I assure you. I find him rather a queer fellow, and I'm only asking you about him in view of his desire to involve himself in our railroad project. Mr. Henney isn't too keen to have him in, you know."

"So I gathered."

"I'm just anxious to clear up a few points about his pedigree, you understand. I find him a bit of a rough diamond, don't you?"

"Mr. Smith or Mr. Henney?" inquired Tara.

Sir Thomas chuckled.

"It's Mr. Smith we were talking about. He has a great deal of authority in this town, doesn't he?"

"What is it you want to know, Sir Thomas?" asked Tara bluntly.

"Mr. Smith's plans."

"If you're so interested, why don't you ask him?"

"Because I don't think Mr. Smith would be completely truthful. You're his assistant, so who better to put my little proposition to than you?"

"Proposition?"

"Yes. What I would like to suggest is that you and I help one another."

"Indeed. How would you like me to do that?"

"I've already outlined how useful the railroad can be in tracking down your husband. Obviously I cannot guarantee results, but what I would also like to do is offer you a small, shall we say, retainer in return for your help."

"My help?"

"A little service, shall we say?"

"I see," said Tara.

"I'm sure you do," said Sir Thomas smoothly. "It is my opinion that Mr. Smith will do everything within his power to disrupt the construction work."

"Which would cost you a lot of money."

"Exactly."

Tara was quite cool. "So you'd like me to keep you informed of his plans. He's bound to confide in me, and then I can pass anything useful on to you."

"Dear Mrs. Kane, you've taken the words out of my mouth," he said gratefully. "It's quite a simple thing, really, isn't it?"

"Oh, quite simple."

"Of course, we would, ahem, reward you. As I say, a little retainer. Say, three hundred dollars a month? How does that sound to you?"

"It sounds like a lot of money," said Tara, practically.

"And of course, the resources of the company will be available to you to search out Mr. Kane."

He waited a moment; then he leaned forward. "I mean, you know the kind of man Mr. Smith is. Forewarned is forearmed, eh?"

Tara nodded.

"To a lady of character like yourself, some of his underhand dealings must be a little distasteful."

"Oh, yes."

"Well, then. I'm so glad we've agreed on our little arrangement."

"But we haven't," Tara said.

"My dear Mrs. Kane!" His eyes narrowed. "Perhaps the money— shall we say, another fifty dollars?"

Tara stood up. "For your information, sir, I know nothing of Mr. Smith's intentions, and if I did I wouldn't tell you." Her voice was cold and disdainful.

"Come, come, Mrs. Kane."

"You know something else, Sir Thomas, I think I prefer the roughnecks in the saloons. When they want to buy a woman, they don't dress it up in all this." She waved a dismissive arm round the room. "I am not for sale," she added. "My loyalty isn't, either. I don't spy on people. And I think your suggestion is a hell of an insult."

"You're getting very vulgar, Mrs. Kane."

"If you are a typical English gentleman, then I can only thank God that you're the only one I'm ever likely to come across."

"Don't you think you're being a little naïve, Mrs. Kane? You're already working for a crook. You're part and parcel of his villainy."

"That's a lie."

"Then why don't you take up our offer? Your intelligence could possibly stop this town being plunged into a bloodbath. Because, let me make it quite clear, Mrs. Kane, if Smith lifts a finger to stop those boats landing or to impede the railroad's progress, we'll bring in the infantry, the Mounties, and anyone else who'll come, and we'll have Smith shot down before he knows they're even in town. You could stop that, perhaps even save his life."

She faced him defiantly. "Let me tell you something, Sir Thomas. I have faith in Mr. Smith and his dream for this territory and a damn sight more respect for him than I have for you. Mr. Smith has many faults, I believe I know most of them, but unlike you he doesn't mind dirtying his own hands. If you're looking for a Judas, don't come to me."

She walked toward the door and opened it. "Good day, Sir Thomas," she said, slamming the door behind her. Her heart was still pounding as she walked along the corridor.

In the lobby Tara saw a man whose face and build were familiar. For a moment she could not think who he was; he had frizzy ginger hair under his black bowler, and his muscular body seemed to be fighting to escape from the confines of his brand-new, loudly checked suit. He looked affluent in his coarse fashion, as he swaggered toward the reception desk, puffing at a large cigar. As Tara reached the foot of the stairs, she heard him ask the clerk for Sir Thomas.

"He's expecting me," the man said, flicking ash onto the hotel carpet.

His voice left Tara in no doubt. Now she knew who he was—Clancy, the very man Smith was relying on to keep the waterfront strikebound

314

should it turn out to be necessary. Someone was being double-crossed.

Tara picked her moment carefully to tell Smith that he was being outflanked. She broke the news to him almost casually.

"I've been made an offer," she said.

"Oh?" He looked up from his Seattle newspaper. "What kind of offer?"

"Sir Thomas Tancrede has put a proposition to me."

He took his cheroot out of his mouth. "Has he now?" Smith blew out a cloud of smoke. "Well, fancy that. So that limey does have some red blood in him." He wasn't outraged, just slightly amused.

"It's not that kind of offer," said Tara.

"What else?" he asked. "Go on."

"He wants to pay me three hundred dollars a month."

Smith was impressed. "That's some offer. What do you have to do for it?"

"Spy on you," Tara said.

For a moment he sat quite still. Then he burst out laughing.

"Three hundred bucks! That's a lot of dough. I hope you took it."

"Took it?" echoed Tara, horrified. "To spy on you? Of course I didn't."

"Why on earth not? You disappoint me, my dear." He was rueful. "I thought I'd been educating you."

"You mean I should have sold you out?"

He laughed again. "Sweetheart, you haven't even learned lesson one, have you? Just because you accept the guy's dough doesn't mean you have to earn it. It's a hell of a good offer."

"You can't be serious," Tara said incredulously. "You simply can't be."

"Know what your problem is?" Smith shook his head sadly. "You're too honest. I thought with a little help from me you could get cured. But I guess you're still stuck with it."

"Money wasn't all he offered," Tara said.

"Ah!"

"He promised he'd help me find Daniel. Using all the resources of the railroad."

Smith whistled softly. "For a limey dude, Tancrede ain't a bad boodler. He knows how to play his hand, I'll give him that."

He did not ask her whether that nearly swung the deal. He was watching her keenly. Then he said, "There's something else, isn't there?"

She nodded.

"Maybe it isn't important, but . . ."

315

He made an impatient gesture for her to go on.

"You know the hotel's full of railmen? Well, I saw Clancy there."

Suddenly Smith was very alert.

"He seems to have gone up in the world," she went on. "He's got new clothes. He was smoking a fat cigar. And he had a meeting with Tancrede, after I left. He seemed pretty much at home."

"Well!" He examined the tip of his cheroot. He was almost talking to himself. "That explains a lot. It sort of looks as if our friend Clancy has been bought. I wondered why he's been avoiding me. Now it figures."

He stood up and went to the window, staring out in silence.

"Jeff," Tara said quietly.

He said nothing.

"You can't fight the railroad. You can't blackmail them either. They're too big."

He swung around. "Nobody's too big for Jeff Smith in Skagway. I mean to have myself a piece of that railroad, any way I can."

"They won't have you, Jeff. They won't let you get a look-in."

"You'd be surprised what can go wrong when you build a railroad. Accidents. Landslides. Explosions." He smiled. "Believe me, Tara, a few armed men and a load of dynamite, they might find it cheaper my way."

Tara recalled the cold, calculating eyes of Tancrede. "Jeff, if you try to stop them—they'll kill you. They'll hire somebody, and—"

"Maybe I will too," he retorted grimly. "Maybe I got a little more experience at that kind of game."

"No," Tara said. "Not while I'm around. Where would it end? No, Jeff. That's not the way."

"I got a lot at stake." He looked into her eyes for a moment, but it seemed much longer.

"OK, I'll do it your way. We'll keep the waterfront moving. They can build their railroad. But, I'll get what I want . . . eventually."

She was surprised at how readily he agreed. Soapy Smith was not a man to change his methods so casually. "How?" she asked.

That crooked, disarming grin appeared. "Not sure I should tell you," he said. "Might be you'll hotfoot it over to his lordship and spill the beans."

"Damn you!" Tara was furious.

He was pleased at her reaction. "Where's your sense of humor, woman? Can't you see I'm joking?" He stubbed his cheroot out and came over to her. He put his hands on her shoulders and gazed into her eyes again. "Tara, you know I trust you. With everything I have.

316

Maybe your way's the right way. And if that's your price—" He stopped.

"I don't have a price," Tara whispered. "I don't ask anything. Only I don't want to see you with a bullet in your back."

He kissed her, a sudden, warm embrace, holding her tight for a fleeting moment. Then he stepped back and smiled. "I've got to be careful, Tara." He stroked his mustache. "Mighty careful. If I don't watch it, you'll be teaching me. And hell, it's me who's supposed to be educating you."

It was that afternoon, as Tara was about to open the door of the cabin, that the voice hissed, "Forget that."

She froze. Even after all these weeks, even after all that had happened since, his hateful voice was still familiar. She turned around slowly.

Arne Gore had a pistol in his hand. The expression in his eyes reminded her frighteningly of his brother's.

"Get going," he ordered, waving his pistol.

She hesitated, looking into his mean, hate-distorted face.

"If you scream you'll never find out if anybody heard you," he added.

That was the last thing she would have done: the Indian girl and the baby were in the cabin; she could hear John crying. Even greater than her fear was the desperate need to keep him away from them.

"Move," he snarled, giving her a push. "Keep walking ahead of me."

"You won't get away with this. People will see you," Tara said.

Gore shook his head. "So what? It's our little reunion. You're all by your own little lonesome self."

He was keeping the promise he had made in Dawson. All this time, he must have been stalking her.

He seemed to have read her thoughts. "Thanks for coming home," he sneered. "Saved me a whole load of trouble."

He was walking just a step behind her, and she could feel the muzzle of his gun pressing into her spine. "Just keep walking," he commanded. "I got horses waiting for us."

"Where are you taking me?" she croaked fearfully.

"Some place Mr. Soapy Smith can't save you. Don't slow up," Gore warned. She felt the pressure of the gun again.

"This is madness," she told him. "Don't you see?"

"Shut up," he growled. They crossed into State Street. "The only reason I don't kill you now is that I aim to live to tell the tale. I don't need no upright citizens on my back."

317

A man was crossing the street, and Tara's heart beat faster as she recognized Mort.

"Say, Mrs. Kane," he called out.

Tara stopped, Gore standing behind her saying nothing. She sensed his finger twitching on the trigger of the gun.

"Mighty glad to see you, ma'am," Mort greeted her. "I just got into town and heard the news." His voice trailed off as he realized who she was with.

Gore looked at Mort coldly. "Me and she are getting together," he said. "We got no hard feelings, see? That's right, ain't it?" The gun poked into her sharply.

Tara gave a wan smile. "No, of course not," she replied, her face strained with fear. "No hard feelings, we're great friends."

Mort looked from one to the other, uncertain. "Well, that's fine," he said dubiously.

"Mr. Gore and I are going away," added Tara. "Together."

"Going where?" asked Mort.

"Places," Gore snarled. "Let's go." The pistol jabbed into her again. again. They started moving off.

"Goodbye," Tara called, turning to wave at Mort, who was staring after them.

"Shut up," spat Gore.

Tara's heart sank. She had hoped that Mort would tackle Gore. But he had just stood and done nothing.

"Take a good look," said Gore. "You won't ever see Skagway again." He laughed.

She tried to nerve herself to run. She knew he would kill her, but that would be better than being dragged off by him to some lonely spot. She guessed what he had in mind first.

Then, a few yards ahead, she saw Jefferson Smith emerge from a doorway and casually saunter toward them, puffing nonchalantly at the eternal cheroot.

She heard Gore's gun click as he cocked it. "One word, and you're dead," he hissed into her ear.

Smith had seen them, but his face betrayed nothing. As always, he was not wearing a gun belt. He appeared totally unconcerned.

Please God, prayed Tara silently, he must realize. He must know what is going on. But he raised his hat, politely, his hooded eyes not even flickering.

"Good afternoon, Mrs. Kane," he said formally, nodding briefly at Gore. Tara could not believe it.

318

"Enjoying your little walk?"

"We're in a hurry," Gore said gruffly, pressing the gun against Tara. She knew she was a hair's breadth from death.

"Well," Smith said, "in that case I mustn't keep you. My pleasure, Mrs. Kane. Hope to meet you again soon, sir." He nodded to Gore and walked on.

Incredulous, Tara looked after him.

"You ever seen anyone so dumb as Soapy Smith," laughed Gore, the muzzle of his gun propelling Tara forward.

They were about to turn the corner by the harness shop when Gore suddenly stopped and stiffened. Tara turned and looked at him. A surprised expression crossed his face. He staggered and his pistol thudded on the wooden sidewalk as he fell, face downward, across the boards. One of his legs twitched, and then he lay still. In the middle of his back was a single hole, a red stain gradually spreading around it.

Tara stood rigid, a hand pressed to her mouth stifling a scream. She had not even heard the shot. She leaned against the hitching post, feeling faint, trembling.

Smith ran up to her. "Are you all right?" he asked, anxiously, his eyes full of concern. "Are you sure you're all right?"

"Yes," Tara whispered, staring at the little gun still in his hand, then at the body of Arne Gore. "Oh God."

"I know, in the back," he muttered. "Not the way a gentleman shoots somebody, but then he wasn't a gentleman either." He bent down and picked up Gore's pistol. It was a black Colt, ugly, deadly.

"No class at all, but useful," Smith said, stuffing it into the pocket of his fur coat.

"He was going to kill me," Tara said.

"Yes, I know. Mort saw you. Mort isn't dumb. He came running."

Two or three men began gathering around.

"He drew on me," Smith explained to them. "Had to shoot him in self-defense. You men saw it."

They all eyed the bullethole in Gore's back, but nobody argued.

"Get him a coffin. I'll pay," he added, taking hold of Tara's arm and gently guiding her away.

She was still shaking when he poured her a brandy in a saloon across the way. Her face was pale. "I was so frightened," she whispered. "How did he find me?"

"A bastard like that doesn't give up easy. My fault. I should have had him picked off in Dawson."

She was too shocked to react to the cold-bloodedness of his remark.

"Thank God he didn't get to the baby."

Smith smiled. "Like I told you way back, you need a protector."

And she knew, whatever she said, she had one.

CHAPTER TWENTY-FOUR

Once a week Tara stopped by the *Skagway Intelligencer* to see if there had been any replies to her advertisement. This was her fourth visit and, like the previous times, she nodded resignedly when the clerk told her there was nothing for box thirteen.

"See you next week then," she said, turning to go.

"Mrs. Kane?" asked a man, stepping in front of her.

Tara regarded him quizzically. He was well spoken, educated. "Allow me to introduce myself," he went on, fumbling in his pocket. He pulled out a card. "I'm Edward Cahill. Edward F. Cahill." He handed her the card, but his name meant nothing to her. He waited expectantly.

"Special Correspondent," he explained. "From Seattle."

"What is it you want?" she asked.

"To talk to you, Mrs. Kane." She noticed how he was studying her. He was appraising her, taking in everything about her, her manner, her looks, her attitude.

"And why do you want to talk to me?" Tara asked.

"If you would allow me to walk with you."

There was something persistent, even determined about him.

"Al right." She shrugged.

He said nothing at first as they walked together down Holly Street toward Broadway.

"Well, Mr. Cahill." Tara glanced at his youthful, freckled face. "What is this all about?"

"I've come here to do some investigating, and I'd like to ask you a few questions," he said, carefully side-stepping a broken duckboard.

"Investigating what?"

"Mr. Smith" he said.

She looked at him closely.

"We've been hearing all kinds of—well, stories about Mr. Smith. My editor has sent me up here to find out what's going on. To name names, to . . ."

"What kind of stories?" Tara asked warily. She wondered if Smith knew this man was in town. He hadn't mentioned anything.

Cahill smiled. "What kind do you think, Mrs. Kane?"

"So why have you come to me?"

He pursed his lips and selected his words carefully. "I'm sure you know. . . . I mean no one knows Mr. Smith better than you, do they?" he said delicately.

"Says who?"

"You're his closest friend, aren't you?" Cahill smiled knowingly, and Tara could see that this man was looking for trouble.

Cahill noted her hesitation. "What do you say, Mrs. Kane?" he prompted.

"Did Sir Thomas Tancrede suggest you talk to me?" Tara asked.

Cahill looked puzzled.

"Are you working for the railroad, Mr. Cahill?"

"Good gracious no," he exclaimed.

"I think, Mr. Cahill," Tara said, "that if you want to know anything about Mr. Smith there's only one person who can help you."

He smiled at her eagerly. "And that is . . ."

"Mr. Smith," Tara said crisply.

He smiled again. "Well, you see, Mrs. Kane, some of the stories . . . well, he might not want to talk about them. They say there's been a lot of lawlessness. They say that he—"

"You'd better find out from him, hadn't you," Tara cut in firmly.

Cahill stopped in his tracks.

"Hasn't there been any mention of a Mountie detachment passing through Skagway?" he asked.

Tara regarded him. "I've no idea what you're talking about," she replied.

Cahill politely raised his hat. "I appreciate our little chat, Mrs. Kane."

"I regret I haven't been of much assistance."

"Oh, I wouldn't say that," he said carelessly, and he strolled off in the opposite direction, leaving Tara wondering why a Mountie detachment coming through Skagway was so important.

Smith's career as a civic philanthropist began the spring day when, on a startled town, he launched "Adopt A Dog" week. He set about it in style. Posters appeared on walls, notices went up in stores, urging every decent-minded citizen to adopt a stray.

"Adopt a *what?*" Tara laughed when he told her.

"The streets are overrun with stray mutts," he declared. "Poor critters, starving, homeless, friendless. It's a real shame, and a disgrace to Skagway."

There was a fine actor lost in Jefferson Smith. Tara looked at him closely, but his face was serious.

"What's brought this about?" she asked.

"We have an obligation to our dumb friends. There must be a couple of hundred dogs running loose, and if two hundred citizens each adopted one, there'd be no more suffering," he declaimed, as though he were addressing a public gathering.

"What's the idea, Jeff?" Tara asked suspiciously. "What do you get out of it?"

"You do me an injustice, Tara. This is just a humane campaign to alleviate suffering."

For a moment his straight face almost took her in. Then his lips twitched, and he roared with laughter. "Also one of my smartest ideas, you got to admit. But I don't get a red cent out of it, Tara," he added hastily.

"Soapy Smith, public benefactor, animal lover, dog welfare campaigner?"

"Jefferson Smith," he corrected. "Soapy's retired."

"I wonder."

She heard that Clancy was dead two days after he had been found in a side alley. Nobody mourned him, least of all in the saloons. Clancy had been playing with the wrong cards, people agreed. He had sold out once too often.

But she was troubled. "How did he die, Jeff?" she asked.

Smith shrugged. "Heard he had a weak heart."

"How convenient."

"God almighty, Tara," he said, "he's no loss. You could buy that bum with a two-dollar bill. Can I help it if he boozed himself to death?" And that was Clancy's epitaph.

Overshadowing the talk in the bars, the barbershops, the stores, was the war with Spain. It was far removed from Alaska, did not touch the life of the gold miners, but as the news filtered through, patriotic fervor grew.

For Jefferson Smith, it was a sure thing. In the Oyster Parlor, additional miniature Stars and Stripes sprouted everywhere, even in the artificial-palm pots. Uncle Sam posters appeared. A picture of Teddy Roosevelt hung prominently over the bar. Free drinks flowed on occasion, with Smith standing on the bar counter, leading raucous patriotic songs, and toasting the avenging of the *Maine*.

"I got to get into this war," he told Tara.

"Are you volunteering?"

"Maybe," he said thoughtfully. "Maybe."

Jefferson Smith fighting his way through the Cuban jungles? Or in the mountains of the Philippines?

"Perhaps it'll all be over soon," Tara suggested.

But he hadn't heard her. "There's more than one way of volunteering," he said, almost to himself.

She was increasingly convinced that Soapy Smith was far from retired, whatever Jefferson Smith assured her.

That was the last she saw of him for forty-eight hours. When she arrived at his office on the morning of the third day she stopped dead in her tracks. The door had been forced. Inside, it was chaos. Drawers had been pulled out of his desk, a metal deed box had been jimmied open, letters were strewn all over the floor, ledgers lay about. The chair behind his desk was overturned, and her own desk was in confusion, papers scattered everywhere.

Tara started to tidy up the mess, trying to sort out what had been taken. But nothing seemed to be missing. In fact, the cash-box in her desk had been opened, but the six dollars had not been touched. She was stacking the ledgers back on their shelf when Smith appeared in the doorway.

"What the hell," he began, looking around. "Are you all right?"

"Somebody broke in," Tara said. "I don't think anything's been stolen. They've even left the change."

"They would," Smith said tersely, taking off his coat.

She looked at him, puzzled.

He went over to his desk, pulled open one or two drawers, and smiled coldly. "They must be dumb."

"Who's they?" Tara asked.

"Oh, the guys who did this," he said lightly—too lightly. His eyes were darting all over the room.

"Jeff," said Tara. "Do you know what they were after?"

"Maybe," he said, without looking at her.

"What?"

He shrugged. "Could be anything, couldn't it?"

"They weren't after money," she pressed. "So what were they looking for?"

He glanced at her with an expression of studied innocence. "How do I know, honey?" He paused imperceptibly. "Have they taken any papers?"

"I don't think so. They want through everything. I think they even read the ledgers, but they left them."

"They wouldn't find anything there," he said, and he looked pleased.

"Find what?"

She kept his ledgers. She knew about his accounts. She knew he listed his illicit liquor shipments as timber, but who would care about that? The liquor laws were a joke in Skagway. She could think of nothing which could interest anyone.

But he was playing it so casually that she began to get an uneasy feeling that maybe she did not see everything. Maybe there were documents he kept hidden away. Maybe that was what the intruders had been after.

He did not answer her question. Instead he said, "Listen, me and the boys are going to have a little council of war. No need for you to be here."

That meant Bowers, Yeah Mow, Mort—the inner circle.

"Jeff, is there anything wrong?" Tara asked.

"Now what could be wrong?" he countered. "You come back after we've had our little powwow."

But from then on, an armed man hovered outside the office, day and night. He would always nod to her politely, sometimes, if her hands were full, courteously open the door for her. At other times he just leaned against the wall, his arms crossed, watching impassively. New locks had been fitted to the office door and to the drawers in the desk. For the first time there was a safe in the office, and Smith kept the key to it on his watch chain.

"Merely precautions," he explained. "You'd be surprised how many rogues are in town."

"Would I?" Tara asked dryly.

He didn't rise to it. "You keep your eyes open too," he instructed her. "If you don't like the look of somebody, you tell the boys."

"Jeff, what are you afraid of?"

"Nothing, nothing. I just don't like people poking their nose into our affairs. Can't have that."

"*Your* affairs," she reminded him firmly.

She saw the large Mountie detachment riding into Skagway with a string of pack horses. The lean, sharp-eyed officer at their head was Inspector Zac Wood. When she had met him on her way to Dawson with Campbell's patrol, he had seen through her from the start.

"Do you know why so many Mounties are here?" she asked Smith.

He laughed. "Do I know? Honey, it's me you're talking to. Sure I know."

"What do they want?"

"Say, what's bothering you?"

"Oh, nothing."

"Relax. They're not after you, believe me. Tell me, did you notice their kitbags?"

"No. Why should I?"

"Ah," Smith said knowingly, "they're mighty heavy, those kitbags. Heavy as hell. Practically heavier than the men."

She still didn't understand what he was getting at.

"You want to know what's inside?" he went on teasingly. "Gold. Pure gold."

She looked at him open-mouthed.

"Yes, my dear. That detachment has brought in a hundred and fifty thousand dollars worth of gold. All the way from Dawson."

"Whose gold?" Tara asked.

"The Government's. Customs duties and fees collected from the miners."

Things were beginning to fall into place.

"Why bring it here?"

"Because they're shipping it to Vancouver Island. And once it's locked up there, nobody will get their hands on it. The *Tartar* is lying at the wharf now. The detachment's booked on her."

"And you're going to make sure it never gets on board," she cut in.

"Oh come, Tara," he protested.

"Aren't you?"

"Well," he said slowly, "I got to admit it's a mighty attractive proposition. A hundred and fifty thousand bucks don't grow on trees."

"You know what will happen if you try." Her voice was taut. "There'll be shooting. If any Mounties get killed . . ."

He took out his dice and threw them across the table. "There, you see. The luck of the game. It all depends how the dice fall, doesn't it."

"No, Jeff. I know what you like to call it. A sure thing. Well, I'm going to tell you a sure thing. You hijack that gold, and they'll hang you."

"Don't worry your little head," Smith began.

"And don't damn well patronize me," Tara shouted. "I'm telling you for your own good, forget the idea."

He stroked his moustache.

"You got to have a better argument than that before you start giving me orders," he said.

"I have," she snapped, and before he could say anything she had walked out, slamming the door.

Tara entering the Oyster Parlor two hours later with a tall Mountie officer brought sudden silence. Ignoring the looks, she walked over to Smith, who was standing at the bar.

"Jeff," Tara said as he stared at her transfixed. "This is an old acquaintance of mine. Inspector Zac Wood. Inspector, I don't think you've met Mr. Smith, have you?"

"Not face to face," murmured Wood. "But I've heard of you, sir. As you can guess."

Smith had poise, she had to hand him that. He had been shaken, but he recovered at once.

"Welcome to my establishment, sir," he drawled. "May I offer you some hospitality?"

All around the bar, they were staring at Smith and the policeman. Mort hovered at the back.

"Some other time, Mr. Smith," Wood said politely. "As a matter of fact, I've only come by because our mutual friend here,"—he smiled at Tara—"suggested we might have a few words. Purely informally you understand."

"Let's go upstairs," Smith said, Tara, her heart beating, watched him closely. She had taken a big gamble. If it went wrong . . .

"No need for that, sir," Wood said. "I'm merely here to put you in the picture. My detachment sails in the morning."

"On the *Tartar*, I believe," Smith remarked.

"Correct, sir. Well, I wonder if I can enlist your help. Mrs. Kane tells me you are always anxious to uphold law and order."

Tara admired the poker-faced way Wood said it.

Smith gave a slight bow.

"You hear everything that goes on in town. So tell me, Mr. Smith, have you picked up this rumor that somebody might try to bushwhack us? Before we ship out?"

Smith's hooded lids covered his eyes. "Surely not," he said.

"Then you think it's just idle saloon talk?"

"Of course," Smith replied. "Who'd tangle with a dozen Mounties? They'd be crazy."

Taylor smiled. "I'm obliged, Mr. Smith. I thought it was just a rumor. Which is just as well, of course."

"Really?" Smith's voice was very soft.

"They'd get a hell of a warm reception, if you'll forgive the expression, Mrs. Kane. Until we sail, we have riflemen on the wharf, the pier is covered, and we have sharpshooters along the route to the waterfront. So you see, Mr. Smith, they wouldn't have a chance."

Smith's cheroot had gone out. Now he relit it. "That's a load off my mind, Inspector Wood," he said, puffing. "It reassures us businessmen that the law is so wide awake. But there's one thing that puzzles me. Why on earth should anyone want to ambush your outfit?"

"I thought you knew," the Inspector said smoothly. "We're carrying a little gold."

Smith gave another bravura performance. His eyes widened with surprise. "Well I never." He looked at Tara. "Did you ever guess that?"

"Government gold," interrupted Wood.

"Well, Inspector, one thing's for sure," Smith said magnanimously. "Nobody's going to try and hijack it. Hell, they'd be real foolish to try, with you all prepared for it."

"Exactly." Wood smiled. "It's been a pleasure, sir." Then he turned to Tara. "And we're mighty obliged to you, ma'am. You're a smart woman, Mrs. Kane."

As he turned to leave, Smith called after him: "Why not hang around for a day or two? I'm sure I could set up some entertainment."

"That'll have to wait for another time, Mr. Smith," Wood said and walked out. Dozens of pairs of eyes followed him.

Tara waited for the explosion.

"You still seem to have some good friends in the Mounties," was all Smith said.

"Jeff, I wanted you to know what you're up against," Tara said. "You made a promise, remember? No killing."

"Good God, woman, you didn't suspect that I was planning anything?"

She stared right back at him. "How could I?"

"You had me worried there," he said innocently, and it would have fooled most people. "I got bigger fish in mind, and they're strictly legit."

The *Tartar* sailed the next day. Armed sailors lined the railings, and the Mounties were at battle stations. But not a shot was fired, and the ship steamed over the horizon with one hundred fifty thousand dollars worth of gold safe in her hold.

Little could surprise Tara about Smith, or so she thought. Then during another of Smith's mysterious absences, a hand-painted sign appeared on his door. "Office of the Commanding Officer," it read.

At least, she said to herself as she unlocked the door, life was never dull around him.

He made his next entrance in the uniform of a U.S. Army officer.

He saw her astonished reaction and burst out laughing.

"You never seen a soldier-boy before, Tara?"

He turned around slowly, showing off his uniform. "Well, how does it look?"

He had a good military bearing and the uniform fitted well. He snapped to attention. "Captain Jefferson Smith, ma'am, commanding officer, Company A."

"Company what?" Tara asked. "Jeff, what are you playing at?"

"Company A, First Regiment, National Guard of Alaska, that's what."

"I don't believe it!"

"We're at war, woman," he replied, loftily. "I'm raising my own outfit, Skagway's own national guard company." He walked over to the mirror and studied his appearance from every angle.

"Does the Army know? The War Department? Washington?"

"I'm enrolling a citizens' militia in the country's hour of need, and you want me to wait for the paper shufflers? Hell, Tara, it might all be over by then."

"You mean you're raising your own private army," she said.

He stroked his mustache. "A National Guard outfit. There's nothing private about it." He sat down and put his smartly booted legs on the desk. "It's a volunteer unit. Patriots answering the call. Hell, guys are busting down the door wanting to enroll."

"And who made you a captain? Where did you get your rank, Mr. Smith?"

"It's, it's . . ." He sought for the right word. "It's an acting rank. Acting Captain. I figure that an ex-colonel in the Mexican Army qualifies for an acting captain in the National Guard. Satisfied?"

She knew he had some motive other than strutting around in a uniform. Playing soldiers wasn't his object in life.

"We may even have a lady's auxiliary," Smith went on breezily. "Yes sir. You'd look mighty fetching in soldier blue. Maybe I'll make you an acting lieutenant."

"No thank you, Captain Smith. I'm not the military type."

He became totally committed to Company A. Recruiting posters went up in town overnight, replacing the fading ones left over from "Adopt a Dog" week. He dictated to Tara a flamboyant order of the day, urging all "red-blooded Americans to follow the summons to arms in our country's hour of need." Near the Oyster Parlor, a recruiting marquee was raised. He had calling cards printed with his rank on them.

"Why so modest?" asked Tara. "Why only Captain? Why not Colonel?"

"Tara," he said warningly.

"Or why not General?"

"Goddamn it, Tara, stop being so aggravating," he snapped.

Along with many others, Tara went to the recruiting rally at Jackson's music hall. Smith was on the platform, dressed in his uniform. He pointed dramatically at a crowd of unshaven, tight-lipped characters, lounging in the front rows, and told them: "You are fine and brave men, each and every one of you, and I'm sure you will unhesitatingly follow me anywhere and at any time."

Everybody cheered. Tara guessed that that was true enough, since she recognized a number of members of Smith's gang among them.

Then Mort and some other men went around the audience with collection boxes. When he came to Tara, Mort said hastily, "That's OK, Mrs. Kane." He started to move on, rattling the box, but Tara stopped him.

"What are you collecting for?" she asked.

"It's the welfare fund. For the company's orphans and widows."

"Yours must be the only unit in the world collects for its widows and orphans before it's even got recruits," Tara said to Smith afterward.

"Absolutely," he agreed. "But you got to make provision. No good collecting when it's too late. I got to think ahead."

He handed her a little wad of paper. "Here," he said. "Like you to sell some of those. Dollar a ticket. It's a lucky draw."

"A benefit for the widows?" she inquired.

Smith nodded. "If we sell fifteen hundred, it'll be a good day's work."

"What's the prize?"

"Seventy-five bucks," he said. "Not bad, for a dollar, eh?"

"Who keeps the other one thousand four hundred and twenty-five dollars?"

"Who do you think? The company paymaster," Smith said.

"I wonder who he is?"

"I can see you ain't going to sell any, so I'll keep 'em myself."

Smith transformed Skagway. Huge banners declaring "Freedom for Cuba" and "Down with Tyranny" spanned the streets. All over town, people were wearing gold, white, and blue buttons reading "Remember the *Maine*, Compliments of Skagway Military Company, Jeff R. Smith, Captain."

If there were some who questioned how it came about that the notorious Soapy Smith, of all people, was raising a National Guard outfit, they kept their qualms to themselves. Smith, in fact, gave no one much chance to collect his wits; every day there was a new rally, benefit, or appeal. He even hired the Skagway Silver Temperance Band to give open-air concerts.

The community's new paper, the *Skagway News*, was virtually controlled by him. Stroller White, the editor, was a close crony of Smith's; he never had to pay for his drinks or his meals in the Oyster

Parlor. Now Stroller and his sheet began to repay some of their obligation. He front-paged the creation of the Skagway Company, and printed laudatory editorials about its commander.

Not that the town saw much outward evidence of Smith's Army. He discouraged too many questions.

"Why be so mysterious?" Tara asked.

He smiled at her. "Skagway's going to see plenty of its militia when the time comes. You'll have something to cheer about, I promise you."

All that was swept from her mind when, next day, Mort came into the office at the Oyster Parlor. Tara was on her own, working on the ledgers. She looked up from the rows of figures she had been trying to balance.

"Yes?"

"That German fellow is here. The guy from Dawson. He's asking for you."

"The photographer? Herr Hart?"

Mort nodded, unenthusiastic. "I'll tell him to go away, OK?"

But Tara was already rushing down the stairs, and there he was, his blue eyes lighting up behind their glasses when he saw her. She ran toward him.

He opened his arms to her, embraced her, held her tightly. Gently she released herself.

"Oh, you don't know how good it is to see you, Ernst," she said. She started going toward a table. "Come, sit down."

"Tara," he said, slowly, looking at her solemnly.

"Yes?"

"We must talk." He glanced around the bar. "Not here. Somewhere quiet."

He seemed nervous, almost ill at ease. He had never been like that with her before.

"Let's go upstairs," she said.

He did not even glance around the office. He perched opposite her, on the edge of the armchair, and she sensed his uneasiness.

"What's the matter, Ernst?" she asked, frowning. "Tell me, how did you track me down?"

"I heard you were with Smith." He shrugged. "It wasn't difficult."

She had a lot to explain, she knew that. "Ernst, I didn't find Daniel," she began, but he cut her short.

"I know." He said it very softly, almost sadly.

"You know?" Tara was puzzled.

"Yes, Tara," he said quietly, then stopped.

"Who told you?"

"Nobody." He licked his lips. they were dry.

"What do you mean?" she asked.

"Tara, Daniel is dead."

It seemed an infinity before the words assumed meaning and her brain managed to grasp what he had said.

"No. He can't be." Tara's voice faltered. Her hands were icy cold.

He sat, slumped, and then he said in a low voice, "Do you think I would tell you such a thing if, if it wasn't true?"

"How do you know?" she whispered.

He reached for her hand. "You must be brave. You did all you could to find him. I know better than anyone."

"Where?" she cried. "Where did it happen?"

"He was murdered in Circle City. Somebody knifed him. He was found in a back alley."

"Oh my God."

"Inspector Constantine identified him himself. From this." Hart pulled out a handkerchief and neatly unfolded it. In it was a gold ring—a wedding ring.

"Here," he said.

She took it, her fingers curiously steady. She could see the inscription inside the band. "Tara to Daniel." It was his ring, the twin of the one she had worn.

"No," Tara moaned, her voice full of despair. She looked at the ring mesmerized, and then buried her face in her hands. She was racked by sobs, while Hart sat helpless, took off his glasses, rubbed his eyes nervously, bit his lip, shifted in his chair.

"I'm sorry," he whispered, but she never heard him. When she looked up, her face was ashen.

"How . . ."

"Constantine recognized the names on the wedding ring. Then he realized who the man was."

He fell silent. Tara held the ring in a frantic, tight grip.

"The Mounties are doing all they can to trace the killer," Hart said gently. "I told the Inspector I'd try to find you. So he gave me the ring."

But all Tara asked was, "Where is he buried?"

"In Circle City. We put his name on the cross." He looked awkward. He did not know how to put it. "It's a nice grave, Tara. They have a little timber chapel and . . ."

"Who did it?"

"Nobody is sure. Some people said there was a trapper, but the Mounties are also looking for an Indian guide. They—they haven't even got a proper description." Hart paused. "I think it must have happened very quickly, Tara. He had no pain, I'm sure. It was done, yes, very quickly. . . ."

"Did you see him . . . afterward?"

Hart moved toward her. "Please, Tara. There is no point . . ."

"Ernst, did you see Daniel?"

He nodded. "I was traveling with Constantine's patrol. Yes, I did see the body. He looked very peaceful."

"Go on."

He shrugged. "What can I say? He had been stabbed in the side. Just below the birthmark."

Tara spun around.

"Please, Tara. . . . This is morbid," mumbled Hart. "Don't torture yourself."

"You said birthmark. . . ."

"Yes," he said reluctantly. "The knife wound had just missed his birthmark. The funny-shaped one, under his left arm. . . ."

"That's not Daniel," whispered Tara. "He had no birthmark."

He stared at her dumfounded.

"Did you see his eyes? What color were they?"

"Blue."

"Daniel has hazel eyes," Tara cried triumphantly.

"Then . . ."

Tara was sitting half laughing, half crying.

"That man was not Daniel." She leaned back and closed her eyes. "Thank God."

"But the Mounties are sure he must be Daniel."

"I tell you they're wrong," she snapped, almost savagely. "Daniel has no birthmark, no blue eyes. That man was not my husband!"

"Please, Tara, this is not good. You must not delude yourself. You must face up to it." He was nervous, taken aback by her fierce reaction.

"I *know* it's not Daniel," she insisted.

"The ring is proof. . . ."

"The hell it is," Tara cried. The energy that the shock had drained out of her was coming back. "What does a wedding ring prove? You tell me that? I haven't got mine have I? Maybe he sold it. Maybe it was stolen from him. Maybe."

She became rational. She asked him what other identification the man had. Nothing, Hart said. Just the usual things a man carried with him. A knife. Tobacco. Nobody in Circle City knew him. He had come in off the trail.

They sat in silence, and then Hart stood up and said, "I am sorry to

332

have given you such a shock. And if you're sure it is the wrong man . . ." He frowned. "I just wish we knew how he came to have the ring."

"We'll find out," Tara said confidently. "We'll find out when I am reunited with him. Won't Daniel have some stories to tell?"

"So will you," Hart said.

That evening, Tara sat in her cabin, gazing into the dancing flames of the fireplace, and seeing a dozen strange patterns form and disappear in as many seconds. It was like her quest. Each time she picked up his trail, fate seemed to upset the jigsaw again. Was she chasing a phantom? Was she bewitched by an obsession? Was she fooling herself, she wondered over and over again. Tara stared into the flames a long time, as if the answer would emerge from the hot embers. But when she curled up to sleep she was no nearer to the truth.

When she saw Hart again, he told her he had written to Inspector Constantine, informing him that the man had been wrongly identified, and that the body they had buried at Circle City was not that of Daniel Kane.

Like a bad dream they wanted to forget, they didn't talk about it any more. Instead, he gave her all the news from Dawson.

With Hart, she started to feel relaxed. She even found herself laughing at his rather ponderous jokes. Perhaps it was the pleasure of being reunited with an old friend who had shared in so many of her adventures.

"Well, I must say you're looking very chic, Mrs. Kane," he said, eyeing her admiringly. "You might not have found Daniel, but it would appear you've struck gold."

"Don't let's talk about me, Ernst," Tara said, hastily changing the subject. "How is your picture-taking coming along? How long are you staying in Skagway?"

Hart held up his hands. "You have not changed, my dear," he chuckled. "Always questions, too many to be answered all at once. We are going out to celebrate our wonderful reunion, and then we will talk because I have much to ask you too."

They walked down the street arm in arm, chattering animatedly, interrupting one another with questions, laughing together until they reached the Blaze of Glory. It was still early and, apart from blackjack, faro, and roulette games in progress at the rear of the saloon, the place was quiet enough for them to talk. Hart insisted on ordering champagne.

"On such an important occasion, only champagne is good enough," he told her.

The waiter filled their glasses, then Tara raised hers and toasted, *"Prosit!"*

"And well met," added Hart, looking into her eyes. "Now I want to hear everything. From the very beginning."

She told him what had happened at Sheep Camp, but she did not mention the baby or Jefferson Smith. Somehow she was reluctant to admit to Hart the role Smith had been playing in her life or how he had helped her with the child. She realized he would have to know eventually, but this seemed the wrong moment.

A second champagne bottle was empty, and Hart's conversation became oversentimental. Tara felt it was time to leave. She did up her coat and smiled at his slightly glazed expression.

"Ernst, I must go now."

"Why?" he asked. "We haven't seen each other for so long. I'm so lonely, Tara, please don't leave me."

"We'll meet again very soon," she promised.

He blinked at her across the table. Then he came out with it, a little woozily, the one question Tara didn't want him to ask.

"One thing you haven't told me, *Liebchen*. What are you doing with Smith? What is it between you and him?"

If he hadn't been such a good friend, she would have been very curt. As it was, she said lightly, "Oh, I do a little clerical work for him. He needed a bookkeeper, somebody to do his paper work. . . .'"

It did not sound right, and she knew it.

"He pays you?"

"I have to earn my keep," said Tara. "I'm a working woman, Ernst, and never you forget it."

He shook his head, and burped.

These were all the things she had not wanted to say at this moment, and there was only one way out of it.

"Ernst, I have a little cabin now. Come over, on Sunday. Have some home cooking."

He blew her a kiss across the table. "That's more like it," he said. He raised his glass to her. "Just us. I'll count the hours."

Tara smiled and rose. He stood up too. He still had his glass in his hand, and he toasted her again. "You are sensational, Mrs. Kane," he hiccuped, and the patrons of the Blaze of Glory gawked at them.

"See you Sunday at noon," Tara said and fled.

The next day Smith was in a foul mood. When he turned up at the Oyster Parlor, he snarled at the bartender, thumped upstairs, crashed into his office, slamming the door, and flung himself into his chair. He had not been around for the best part of three days, and he glowered at Tara.

"What's that booze-hoister hanging around for?" he rasped.

She raised her eyebrows. "Who?"

"Goddamn it, Tara, you know who I mean. Sir Galahad with the tripod. Herr Hart." He spat out "Herr Hart" with surprising venom.

"Ernst is passing through Skagway, so he looked me up."

"Yea, I heard. Drinking in the Blaze of Glory. That's a low-class dump, Tara." She couldn't resist a smile at that. "Nobody takes a lady there. And you brought him up here, into my place. I don't want him in here, you got that?"

"Anything else?" she asked coldly.

Their eyes locked, and he got up and left the room without a word. Tara decided that she would finish her work as quickly as possible and go for the day. The Oyster Parlor was too small for both of them.

But he came back after an hour and stood looking at her. She ignored him, her pen scratching in the ledger she was balancing.

"Tara," he said at last.

"Yes?" She did not glance up.

"Sorry I bit your head off.

"That's all right."

He threw a chamois leather bag in front of her. It was small, but it fell with a thud.

"What's that?" she asked, surprised. For the first time she raised her head.

"Gold dust. Six ounces."

"Whatever for?"

"Salary," he grunted, and turned away.

"Thank you," said Tara, and went back to work.

He walked around the office like a man making up his mind about something. Then he faced her. "I haven't seen anything of you." He produced one of his cheroots and lit it.

She put her pen down. "You've been away," she pointed out.

"And I missed you a hell of a lot. So let's all take a day off and go somewhere. You and me and the kid. Get out of this joint, get out of Skagway. We'll have a picnic, out in the country. All day Sunday."

Inwardly, she groaned. "Sunday?" she said, awkwardly.

"On the seventh day ye shall rest, as Bowers says. Anyway, I want to make it up to you. I owe you some fun."

"Jeff, not Sunday," Tara said.

He took his cheroot out of his mouth and stared at her. "What's wrong with Sunday?"

"Well" said Tara, "we can make it any day you like, can't we? It doesn't have to be Sunday, does it?"

He looked down on her with his hooded eyes. "What are you trying to say?"

"Ernst is coming to have a meal. He won't be in Skagway for long and—"

"Oh, I see. Herr Hart himself. A little tryst with Sir Galahad."

She stood up, papers scattering about her, flushed, trying to control herself. "Damn it, what's it to you anyway?" she cried. "I don't have to ask your permission, do I?"

"You're wasting your time with a gump like that," Smith said. "You can do better than him, honey."

"He's a *friend*," she yelled at him, "a friend! You don't even know what that means. And don't call me honey."

He frowned a moment. But, like a passing shadow, it was gone, and then he inclined his head, as if in agreement.

"OK," he said mildly. "Why not? Have a good time. The guy needs feeding up, I guess. We'll have our picnic some other time. You enjoy yourself Sunday. If you need any booze, you know where to get it. For free. I'll get the boys to deliver some."

"No," said Tara. She put the bag of gold dust in her purse. "I'll manage very well."

She opened the door and without another word walked down the stairs. The gunman on the landing nodded, but Tara had already swept past him.

CHAPTER TWENTY-FIVE

She had rehearsed in her mind how she would introduce the baby to Hart. Yet, as the time approached for his arrival at the cabin, she became increasingly uneasy. Something told her that things were about to go wrong.

Hart showed up clutching two bottles of wine. He had eyes only for her, and he apologized for being late. If he sensed her nervousness, he gave no sign. He handed her the wine, and then, for the first time, he noticed the Indian girl, holding little John in her arms.

"I didn't know you were sharing this place," he remarked, puzzled. "Who is she?"

Tara took a deep breath. "I'm not. Lydia works for me, and the baby is mine."

He stared at the baby, then at Tara. "Yours?" he gasped.

"By adoption, so to speak."

She took the baby from Lydia. "Here, Johnny," Tara said, "come and say hello to Uncle Ernst."

John gazed seriously up at Hart.

"You've adopted him?" repeated Hart at last, incredulously.

She nodded and gave John back to Lydia, who went and sat in a corner.

"Why didn't you tell me?" Hart's tone was reproachful. He removed his glasses and polished them, gazing at her owlishly.

"Ernst, there is a great deal I haven't told you."

He put his glasses on again. "Well," he said, "you'd better start."

He listened intently, his eyes never leaving her face. When she told him about the avalanche, and how she brought the baby into the world amid all that death and horror, he glanced across the cabin, to where Lydia was rocking John in her arms. When she finished, he sat silently for what seemed to Tara an interminable period.

"I'm sorry I didn't tell you before," she said quietly. "So much has happened. So much has changed."

"Has it?"

"He has changed it," she said, nodding at John. "I have to think of him now." She looked at him questioningly. "You are not angry with me?"

"Why should I be? No, I admire you. Taking in that child, keeping him alive, looking after him. Now I understand."

"Understand what?"

He looked away as he replied. "Why you are with Smith. Why you take his money."

"Ernst. I am not with Smith. I do not take his money. I am working for him. I needed a job, and he gave me one. I earn my wages."

"Of course," he said. "That is what I meant."

"Good," Tara said firmly. For a moment, there was an awkward silence. "The food's ready," she said. "I hope you're hungry."

But he didn't answer her. Instead he leaned forward. "Tara," he said gravely. "You must get away from him. He is a bad man."

"You don't have to worry, I know all about Mr. Smith," she replied dismissively, getting up.

"I don't think you do." The way he said it made her stop. "There are rumors. He is planning something. Something dangerous. I hear stories."

"I'm not interested in gossip," she retorted.

"No, you must listen," Hart said urgently. "He is raising an army. Shipping in weapons. Ammunition. Training men."

"That's his little hobby. He likes playing soldiers. He'll come to you any day now for a photograph of him in his pretty uniform. You're taking it all too seriously, Ernst."

"Don't you understand?" Hart was getting excited. "He plans a *Putsch*, a revolt. When he has enough men and enough guns, he will take over the town, the railroad, maybe Dyea, seize the Chilkoot, the White Pass."

"That's crazy!" she cried.

"With his army, who can stop him? A couple of deputy marshals? By the time they send troops, he'll control everything."

"Ernst, you're being ridiculous."

"I beg you, Tara, you must leave here. Before it's too late."

"Ernst, I don't believe any of—" she began, but he cut her short.

"I will protect you from him," he burst out. "He won't be able to do anything. You can rely on me. I will look after you and the baby. You need not have anything to do with the man ever again."

Tara said nothing. He was speaking rapidly, emotionally, his spectacles steamed up. He grabbed her hand. "You will tell him you are leaving him. You will tell him you have found a man who makes you happy." Tara's jaw dropped. "I will arrange everything. Your worries are over, and one day, God willing, we will marry, and we will be so happy, my dearest, together always."

Tara looked at him, unbelieving. Hart, encouraged by her silence, raised her hand to his lips and kissed it. "And the little baby, of course, he will be my son too. Thank God, *Liebchen*, it has happened this way, and I can save you from Smith."

"No." Tara pulled her hand away.

Hart looked startled.

"You've got it all wrong. I don't want to live with you. I don't want you to look after me. I'm married, and if I wasn't I wouldn't marry you. Not ever."

His wounded expression reminded her, ludicrously, of one of Mrs. Miles's ghastly prints. She softened. "Oh, I don't mean to sound unkind, Ernst. Believe me, you're the last man I want to hurt. But this, this is absurd."

He sniffed. "Tara, you're upset," he said, rising. "Of course, what a *Dummkopf*. I should have realized. After what you've been through. Well, don't worry. I will take care of everything."

"I don't want you to," Tara said.

"So," he said, and there was bitterness in his voice, "you prefer that hoodlum to me. You like Smith better."

She stared at him amazed. "Jeff has been a friend to me, don't you understand that? He's given me a chance to prove myself, to find a new life with the child. I know what he is. I know what people say. To me he has been generous, kind. I'm grateful to him."

Hart was white-faced. "No. Never. How often you told me how you hate him, his arrogance, the way he treated you."

"Ernst, I like him." Tara stopped. It was the first time she had ever admitted it, even to herself. "For all his cheating and double dealing, he's been straight with me. He's asked nothing from me. I think deep in him is a man nobody has yet seen. I get mad at him, I could throw things, but I like him. I'm sorry."

"He is a *Schuft*, a scoundrel, he . . ." Hart was trying to control himself.

"You're jealous," Tara said gently.

"He's always tried to come between us." There were tears in his eyes. "He knows I love you."

To Tara's horror, he fell on his knees in front of her and clung to her dress. The Indian girl stared, fascinated. Truly these people had weird customs, the man kneeling at the woman's feet.

"I love you," Hart whimpered. "You're the only woman I have ever met who's meant anything to me. Please, please say yes. I'll do anything, anything you ask, oh, I love you so."

"Ernst," she said, "for heaven's sake, pull yourself together. You're being ridiculous. I don't love you. I never have, I never will. I like you, Ernst, but I don't love you. Please get up, please, compose yourself, I beg of you."

At that moment the cabin door opened. Tara turned to see Jefferson Smith standing on the threshold, a bunch of flowers and a bottle of champagne in his arms. He stood and contemplated them. "My, my, what a touching scene. All we need is the orchestra."

He kicked the door shut with his foot and put down the flowers and the bottle.

"Amateur theatricals, is it? I must be there on opening night."

"What do you want?" Tara demanded.

Smith's voice brought Hart to his senses. He got up, assiduously brushing specks of dust from his trousers in an effort to cover his embarrassment. Lydia stared, her black button eyes wide with astonishment.

339

"Have I arrived at an inopportune moment, my dear?" Smith asked, solicitously. He sniffed the aroma from the stove. "Smells good. Yes, I think I'd like some lunch. How kind of you."

Tara saw Hart's face and wished the floor would swallow her. "Jeff, I don't recall inviting you," she began, but he handed the flowers and champagne to her.

"I'm sure you meant to," he said blandly.

"I'll get the food," she sighed, pleased to find an excuse for doing something.

"Shall I open the bubbly?" Smith called out. He turned to Hart. "A drink to our hostess, Mr. Hart?"

"Tara." Hart cut Smith dead. "I'm not staying for lunch. I don't think I can. I'll see you some time."

"Oh, for Pete's sake, there's plenty of food for everybody. You're staying, Ernst. Please. And you're going to behave decently, aren't you, Jeff?" She hastily laid an extra place at the table.

"How's my godson?" Smith asked. Out of the corner of her eye Tara saw the two men glaring at each other. Like two enraged bulls, she thought. Men could be so absurd.

"Godson? I thought Tara had adopted him," Hart said coldly.

"We both did," Smith smiled. "Sort of a joint stake."

The two men did not speak to one another while Tara served the soup. Smith sampled it and pronounced it delicious. He turned to Hart. "Taste it. Isn't she a great cook? I tell you, she reveals new talents to me every day."

Hart's face was taut. Tara wondered how on earth she was going to get through the meal without an explosion. Smith walked around the table, pouring the champagne.

"I hope I wasn't interrupting anything by bursting in on you folks," he said casually.

Hart looked at him viciously. "I have asked her to marry me," he said.

Smith did not even stop pouring. "Have you?" he murmured mildly. "My pappy always said there's no harm in a pig looking at the moon as long as it doesn't think it can fly there."

Hart clenched his fists. "Jeff," Tara said warningly.

There was a further silence while they ate.

"Never reckoned moose could be so tender and tasty. My compliments to the chef," Smith said.

Hart pushed his plate away.

"Why, you're not eating, friend," Smith said silkily.

"I'm not hungry," Hart muttered.

Smith took a drink of champagne. "I reckon that's a real insult to our hostess," he said, putting the glass down.

For Hart it was the final straw. "Goddamn it, I have had enough of your patronizing insolence," he thundered, and his fist smashed down on the table.

Tara closed her eyes. This was what she had dreaded.

Hart stood up. "You're scum, Smith." His eyes were blinking rapidly behind his glasses. Tara had never seen him so outraged. "I have had enough of you, you crook. You . . ." He was searching for a word. Smith remained seated, a smug, benign smile on his face.

Hart turned to Tara. "How can you have anything to do with this scoundrel? Where's your pride?"

Tara opened her mouth to speak, but Smith cut in. "Your manners are appalling, sir. Or is it just you were never taught any?"

"Now stop it, both of you," intervened Tara hastily. God, it was going to become a saloon brawl. "You're both behaving like a couple of overgrown stupid schoolboys. Ernst, sit down. And you, Jeff, you'd better leave."

"I'll go when I'm good and ready, as the guy said to the hangman. Relax, honey. Don't tell me you take this fellow seriously?"

"Tara!" burst out Hart. "How can you sit there and take his insults? Why do you let him talk like that?"

"Please," Tara begged.

Slowly Hart sat down. Smith contemplated him. "You're very lucky that I'm a gentleman and in company of a lady and that you're just a jackass. Otherwise, I'd ask you to step outside and continue this discussion privately."

Hart flushed. "I tell you what you are," he said tightly. "You are a swindler. A cheat. A hoodlum." He was mentally translating the words from German.

Smith nodded. "Good enough. You care to repeat that some place?"

"You name it. Place. Time, Weapons."

"For God's sake," Tara interjected, but they ignored her.

"Guns," said Smith. ".45s."

"What time?"

"Tomorrow. Five o'clock."

"Where?"

Smith shrugged. "I don't mind killing you any place."

"Where?" repeated Hart, fists clenched.

"Back of my saloon?"

"So your gang can shoot me in the back? No. Neutral territory. I insist."

"You name the place," said Smith.

"There'll be nowhere," Tara shouted. "You two aren't going to fight a duel any place. What on earth for? You're both in the wrong."

"Stay out of this. It's nothing to do with you," Smith snapped.

"It has very much to do with me." Tara's eyes sparked angrily. "You do this, and I'm through with both of you. If you idiots live."

"It is a matter of honor," Hart insisted stiffly.

"Get out, both of you," Tara yelled. "Go away, take your precious honor, fight your damn duel, kill one another. Leave me alone. I think I hate you both."

She got up and ran behind the screen, threw herself on the bed, and gave way to the tears that had almost choked her.

There was silence for a long while; then Smith cleared his throat.

"I think we both owe our hostess an apology," she heard him say.

"For speaking the truth?" Hart asked.

"Mr. Hart, no matter what you think of me personally, I consider myself a gentleman, and the last thing I want to do is distress Tara. The duel's off. Tara was right, it would be insane to fight over nothing."

"I wouldn't fight a duel over nothing, Mr. Soapy Smith," hissed Hart. "Could it be you're afraid of dying, that you're a coward at heart? Frankly, it's my opinion that you should crawl away and do it yourself, you parasite. I'd be doing the Territory a service if I killed you."

Suddenly John woke up and began howling. Tara was amazed that the child had slept through all the previous noise.

"Take him out," she heard Smith order. "Lydia, take him for a walk."

Smith and Hart waited for the Indian girl to leave. As soon as the door closed Smith said, "Mr. Hart, if you weren't Mrs. Kane's friend I'd take you apart limb by limb for what you've just said. However, I've made it a rule to turn the other cheek to the cheap insults of clowns. And that's what you are. A clown."

He was speaking without heat, quite casually.

"You want to marry her, protect her? Jesus, you couldn't look after a lame cat. She goes on the trail with you, and gets back alone, half out of her mind, two thirds dead, and on a murder charge. I'll never forgive you for that."

342

"I, I couldn't stop her," Hart said in a low voice. "she went off on her own. What could I do?"

"I could tell you, friend. If I'd been in your boots nothing in the world could have stopped me staying with her. No, you were too busy taking your pretty pictures. You're not worth a woman like that."

Hart was silent, and Tara heard Smith continue, "She staggered into my saloon, and when I saw her, out cold, nearly dying, when I picked her up and carried her home, I wanted to kill you, Hart. Jesus, I never felt so much contempt for a man before."

Tara was startled. Not until this moment had she known that Smith had taken her to Mrs. Miles. Every time she was in trouble, he had stepped in and got her out of it. She felt ashamed for the way she had always denied his kindness to her, felt sorry for herself and never grateful to him.

"She's told me a few things about you. Like the way you made a fool of her at Fortymile," Hart said.

"I don't intend sitting here trading scoring points with you, mister."

She heard the sound of a chair being pushed back and footsteps approaching. Smith appeared round the screen. "Tara, I'm sorry about all this. I had no idea he was going to ask you to . . ."

She sat up and smoothed out her dress.

"You're not going to take him up on it?" he asked and suddenly stopped. He was staring at the wedding ring on the middle finger of her left hand.

She followed his look and nodded. "Yes, Jeff. It's Daniel's. Ernst brought it to me from Circle City. They found it on a dead man, but it wasn't Daniel."

He took her hand, and studied the ring. "What happened to him, then?" he asked.

"I don't know. " He released her hand, and she touched the ring.

"One thing's for sure, Jeff," she said gently. "I'm not marrying anybody. I'm married already."

"Well." He looked into her eyes and gave a wry little smile.

"I hope I'll see you tomorrow," he added, his voice sad. He smiled wistfully at her, and then disappeared around the screen. He left the cabin without saying a word to Hart.

She heard Hart moving around, so she straightened her hair and prepared herself to brave the inevitable. Hart was by the door, putting on his coat.

"I'm going now," he said when he saw her.

"Yes," said Tara quietly. "I think that's best."

343

"You won't come with me . . ." he said, his eyes appealing to her.

Tara shook her head.

"Then I don't think we should see one another again," he went on, his voice faltering. He opened the door, then paused. "Take care, dear Tara. I will always love you, and I only hope and pray you have made the right choice.

"There is no choice, Ernst," she said, looking him in the eyes. "There's only one man I love, one man I'll ever love."

Hart nodded. "Yes, Mr. Smith."

Immediately Tara was on the defensive. "Of course not!" she exclaimed.

Hart shrugged. "You know, my dear, I think you are hoodwinking yourself. In your heart, I believe you have fallen in love with that man."

"You're wrong," she snapped, but although her voice was firm she could not meet his gaze. "It's simply that Jeff knows and accepts how I feel about Daniel but you don't. I don't think you ever could. I'm sorry. . . ."

Hart inclined his head. "Goodbye and good luck."

"Goodbye Ernst, and thank you. Thank you for everything," she whispered as she watched him walk away.

She was sad for him, but there was no other way.

Smith was already pacing up and down his office when she walked in next day. The air was thick with his cigar smoke.

"I've been waiting for you," he said. He helped her off with her cloak, then put his hands on her shoulders. "I was counting every minute."

Tara tried to avoid his eyes, but they compelled her to look at him. "Oh, get along with you, Jeff." She tried to say it lightly.

"You're mighty important to me, and that joker made me realize it . . . more important than I'd ever figured. Tara, I need you."

Before she knew how it happened, he was kissing her on the lips, first gently, then more passionately, and suddenly Tara did not resist. She closed her eyes and, for an instant, luxuriated in the sensuousness of his embrace, in the excitement of his closeness, her body yielding to him, her arms folding around him.

Then, slowly, he released her.

"Don't you forget that," he said in a hoarse voice.

They stood looking at one another, the atmosphere between them charged. He was imbued with a magnetism, a power, an animalism she had never felt in him. It left her breathless, dizzy, flushed.

His hand cupped her chin, and he slowly raised her head so that their eyes met. "You're a man's woman," he said slowly. "And there ain't no greater kind." And he kissed her again.

There was a knock on the door. Smith ignored it, but Tara disengaged herself. Again the knock came.

"Yes?" Smith called out irritably. His eyes were on Tara. She was trying to take advantage of the interruption to collect herself.

Yeah Mow came in and stopped when he saw the two of them.

"Well?" Smith demanded. His voice was sharp.

"I didn't know you were busy, Boss," grunted Yeah Mow, "only they're going to start unloading." He stopped. "The cargo will be coming ashore soon. Thought you'd better know."

"OK," Smith said curtly, "I'll be there."

She could tell something was being kept from her. Yeah Mow closed the door, and Tara asked, "What cargo's that, Jeff?"

Doubts were crossing her mind, and echo of what Hart had said, "When he has enough men and enough guns."

"Christ, honey, we got more important things to talk about than that," he said. Suddenly, he seemed guarded.

"No. I want to know."

She sat down and looked at him challengingly. Her softness had gone. She was tough, businesslike.

"You don't make sense," he replied. Under his hooded lids, his eyes were wary.

"You keep disappearing for days on end. Nobody sees you. Then all these cargoes that arrive. You keep going to the waterfront. What's so important about them? You keep that gunman outside your door. Your office gets burgled. What's happening? Your right hand wants to know what's happening.

He hesitated, then he shrugged. "I'm training my men. Hell, I'm the CO of the outfit. I'm whipping them into shape. I got to spend time with them. And those cargoes, why they're just supplies. Military supplies. Uniforms. Boots."

"Arms?" Her voice was quiet.

He didn't blink. "Sure. Rifles, sidearms. I'm having them shipped in, and I don't aim to see them go astray. So I keep an eye on things. You don't want my soldier boys to have wooden swords, do you?"

He laughed as if that was a good joke. He opened a drawer and took out some sheets of paper.

"Now while I'm gone, I'd appreciate you copying these out. Just for me and a couple of the boys."

He passed them over to her.

She glanced at them, uneasiness growing. "What are these lists?"

"It's the payroll. If the men get called out, if a state of emergency is declared."

"You mean martial law? In Skagway? Who'd declare that?"

"I like to be safe."

"Safe from what, Jeff?" she pressed.

"Safe from other people's interference."

She stood up, putting down the lists. "But all this is illegal. Recruiting private mercenaries in the name of the United States, shipping in arms, wearing uniforms, giving out ranks. National Guard, indeed!"

Smith looked amused. "He's put you up to this, hasn't he? That lousy photographer made your beautiful hair stand on end? Right?"

"I can use my own eyes," Tara said. She didn't want to bring Hart into this.

He grinned. "Now you listen. Congress has rushed through a bill authorizing the immediate enlisting of volunteer troops for the war. Here." He went to a chair, picked up some Seattle and San Francisco newspapers. The headlines were there. They were recruiting men for the Spanish War.

"What's good enough for Teddy Roosevelt is good enough for me," went on Smith.

Tara shook her head. "You'll have to try harder than that. You're raising a private army, and I want to know why."

He strode across the room to the newly installed safe. "Goddamn it, Tara, you can be the most aggravating female," he shouted. He took out a sheet of paper and thrust it at her.

"Private army, indeed," he growled.

The paper had an officially printed letterhead embossed with the legend: Office of the Secretary of War, Washington, D.C.

Dear Captain Smith, [it read] The President has passed over to the Department of the Army your letter and asked me to reply on his behalf.

He joins me in commending your patriotic spirit in forming your militia unit You and your volunteer forces and the enthusiasm with which you have rallied to the colors in this hour of your country's need are a tribute to the people of Alaska.

Your offer to put your unit at the disposal of the United States Army and to lead your men in an invasion of Spanish Cuba is greatly appreciated, but I can assure you that the forces we have available are adequate and there is no need for the War Department to require your services overseas.

I am, sir, your obedient servant,

And it was signed Russel A. Alger, Secretary of War.

"Well?" He stood beaming at her. "You still think I'm planning to start some cockeyed private war?"

She had to admit that it was not what she had expected. She hadn't known that he had been in touch with Washington. She thought he was doing it all on his own here, thousands of miles away. Maybe he was right, she thought. Maybe Hart had wanted to paint Smith in the blackest colors. She gave him back the letter.

"How many men have you got now?" she asked.

"Two, three hundred," he said, going out of the door.

Washington knew what Smith was up to, and they had raised no objections. What was really going on? Was it just that Hart was jealous of Smith's attentiveness to her? Or was she, as Hart had said, hoodwinking herself? Was she seeing only what she wanted to see because she was falling in love with Jeff Smith?

"No," she muttered to herself. "I can't be. It's Daniel I love. Only Daniel."

But she colored when she thought of the way Smith had kissed her and of her own reaction. "Oh, God, I don't know what I think any more," she said aloud. "I've got to give myself a chance to work it all out. I've got to prove to myself that Daniel is still alive and that I love him more than anyone."

That afternoon she told Smith she was going away for a few days.

"Is that so?" he drawled. He tried to appear indifferent, but for once he was a bad actor.

They were downstairs, in the saloon, and one of the bouncers came over and handed him a scrap of paper. Smith looked at it, then glanced over to a group of cardplayers by the wall.

"OK," he said, and scrawled his initial on the I.O.U. "He's good for one hundred, and not a cent more."

The bouncer nodded and disappeared at the back. Smith turned back to Tara. "You still haven't told me where you're planning to go." He attempted to make it sound casual.

"Juneau," Tara replied.

"You'll get seasick," he grinned, but she didn't smile. "What's it all about, Tara?"

"You know damn well," she said.

347

"Ah." He shook his head. "Still wild-goose-chasing, eh? You won't learn, will you?"

"If you know anybody there who may have come across Daniel, I'd appreciate you telling me," she said. "I can look them up."

"No, I told you before. You can have anything you want, but not that. It's time you faced facts." His eyes were hard. "How long are you going to waste your time?"

"I don't see it as a waste of time. That's my only reason for being here." She pulled on her gloves. "I'll see you when I get back," she said and started to go.

"What about the kid? You going to drag him along?" he asked disapprovingly.

"You leave that to me," she retorted and left him frowning after her.

Tara left little John in the care of the Indian girl. Lydia had picked up enough English to understand, and Tara had learned to trust the girl. Even so, she had misgivings as she stood on the deck of the little steamer that was to take her from Skagway to Juneau. The baby was so much of her life now that even a short separation left her anxious, her thoughts constantly with him.

When she came ashore at Juneau, Tara was agreeably surprised. It was unlike Dawson, unlike Skagway, unlike any of the rough-and-ready sin cities with which she had become so familiar. There were prospectors and sourdoughs here too, but the community was overshadowed by its commerce. She passed two big cigar factories. Two breweries were going full steam. There were several millinery shops, confectionary stores, steam laundries, pharmacies, nine hardware stores, a hospital, even an opera house.

Of course there was another Juneau too. If there were four churches, there were also nine saloons. That at least it had in common with Skagway.

Tara breathed in deeply. The air was cleaner; the people in the streets seemed tidier; she liked Juneau. She realized why: it was not part of the Soapy Smith empire; he did not rule the dives and the saloons and the back alleys.

And there were children. Tara looked at them with delight. On her travels, she had come across little Indian youngsters, but children in the Klondike were rarer than garden roses. Now for the first time she saw groups of boys and girls running along the main street, laughing, skylarking.

Juneau boasted no less than three schools, and as Tara stood and watched the youngsters troop in when the school bells tolled, she found herself smiling. Suddenly Alaska was a much warmer place.

Tara checked into a hotel (there were three, all neat and respectable, and she was even shown to her room by a maid in a lace cap). Then she set out to make her inquiries about Daniel.

There were more than five hundred claims staked around Juneau, not only gold, but quartz and other precious metals. Tara patiently followed up the trail. She went to the claims registrar; she visited the town's newspaper, the *Juneau City Mining Record*; she went to the U.S. Marshal.

It was certainly different from her experience in Skagway. The Marshal was a businesslike law officer, who listened to her, checked records, opened files, talked to two other law men. Eventually, he shook his head.

"I'm sorry, Mrs. Kane," he said. "We've never heard of him. No reason why we should, come to think of it."

Next morning she was at Juneau's biggest fish cannery because she had been told they took on a lot of casual labor. The Frenchman who ran the place looked up his pay ledgers, but finally he too came up with a blank.

Still she refused to give up. She visited the shipping offices and the breweries, posted notices in the general stores, asked at the livery stables and the gunsmiths, but no one had heard of Daniel Kane.

She had had no grounds for thinking he had been here. Smith's words echoed in her mind. Was she wasting time? Was she really ducking the truth that stared her in the face?

Tara made one important discovery in Juneau. It was about herself. Until now nothing had been more important than seeking out her man. Now, something seemed to hold greater urgency for her. It was the baby. Unexpectedly, she felt a mother's need to see her child, to hold him in her arms. She had been away long enough.

Tara sailed back to Skagway. As she looked out at the splendor of the shoreline, the snow-capped mountains, the aloof beauty of Alaska, she realized that she had found something of what she had been seeking. She had found, again, a meaning in her life.

The smile the baby gave her when she entered the cabin and held him in her arms was the homecoming welcome she needed. She kissed him, and her delight at being reunited with him pushed aside the guilt she felt about her possessiveness for another woman's child. Sure, fate had brought John to her, she was only fulfilling a deathbed promise, but the truth was that Tara now looked on him as her son. If Suzanna

349

Lacey had suddenly appeared in the cabin, Tara would have resented her like a mother protecting her child against a stranger.

Tara tucked the boy into his basket.

"Has everything been all right?" she asked Lydia. The Indian girl nodded vigorously.

"Very fine, very OK. Mr. Smith he come to look at boy. Very pleased. He come lots."

"Oh, did he," murmured Tara but said no more.

"Man bring this letter; Lydia added, handing Tara an envelope.

It was from Hart.

My very dear Tara, [he wrote] By the time you get this, I will be sailing back to San Francisco. I have over 1,000 pictures of the Gold Rush, and my work is finished. Also, any reason I have had for staying is over. It is all finished.

Tara sighed. He was very melodramatic.

I am so desolated. I had looked forward to taking you back to Germany and introducing you to my parents as my magnificent American bride [at this Tara's eyebrows shot up]and of course the little baby would have been like my son, and you would have given me a very fine heir too.

This is not to be. But I want you to know that my love for you lives on. After San Francisco, I will go on to Chicago and then New York, and I will always tell the German consul where I am, so you know I am waiting. You know *auf Wiedersehen* means to see you again next time. So I do not say goodbye. I say *auf Wiedersehen*.

Always I will have affection for you. Come to me if you change your mind.

In my dream, my beautiful Tara, I embrace you eternally and always. Ernst.

Slowly Tara folded the letter. It was such a pity. He was a nice man, and he adored her. But what he had offered would have driven her crazy.

The coming of summer flooded Skagway with the new invasion of hopefuls. The Klondike veterans eyed these johnny-come-latelies with a degree of disdain; they had missed the first onslaught; they had not had the guts, so it seemed, to plunge into the unknown when the Gold Rush had begun the year before. Now they had made up their minds at last, but the pickings were going to be fewer and serve them right.

Tara, who would never have considered herself a Yukon pioneer, found herself looking at the newcomers through curiously similar eyes. She recognized so much about them: the new clothes, the shining pots and pans, their eagerness to get north, their vain attempts to delude the locals that they were not as green as they seemed when they came off the boats.

On the surface, they appeared to know more about what to do and where to go. Back home, the books and guides and pamphlets were pouring out. The Yukon had become an industry; some stores even advertised the services of retired prospectors, those, needless to say, who had not struck it rich, to advise the greenhorns on equipment and clothes.

Smith, she knew, was well aware of it all. His men mingled with the new arrivals on the waterfront, in the bars and hotels. They watched, listened, and reported everything.

Bowers specialized in counseling greenhorns on the evils that lay in store for them in this Babylon, and then promptly guided them to the real dens of iniquity for further education.

Tara, although she knew many of the gang by sight, was constantly surprised at the people who turned out to be part of Smith's network. She met one curly-haired youth whose frank blue eyes and open countenance were the picture of innocence. But "Slim Jim" Foster, every mother's favorite son, was the operator who lurked, on behalf of Smith, at the foot of the gangway when a new ship docked. He would pick on a likely-looking prospect, offer to carry his luggage uptown, and install him in a Soapy Smith establishment.

And she was quite taken in by the gentle, white-haired, stooped little man with whom Smith had an occasional quiet drink. "Old Man" Webb, playing the role of the veteran gold miner down on his luck, won the confidence of eager newcomers with his offers of advice and local lore. By the time they realized he had taken them, and their money, for a ride, he had disappeared.

Mort and Yeah Mow were kept in the background. Their role was more sinister. They were the chief enforcers.

One thing they all had in common. They treated Tara, when they met her, with great respect. These men, who would slap a saloon girl across the face, kick a man insensible, lie, cheat, booze, smash up a bar, were always impeccably correct to her. She was the boss's lady, and they knew better than to forget it.

Smith displayed his letter from Washington proudly. It hung in a prominent position in the Oyster Parlor, reverently framed. Only Tara knew that he had cut out part of the letter and neatly joined the two other pieces. There was no mention of Washington brushing him off; only the grateful thanks of his President and the War Department. He had also put up some new notices around the bar. "Watch out for card sharps and tinhorn cheats," cautioned one. "Be on guard against affable strangers trying to take you for a ride," warned another.

In between drilling his militia company and disappearing on his mysterious trips, Smith had a new preoccupation. On the calendar in his office he ringed the Fourth of July with red.

"It's going to be the biggest, fanciest, dandiest Independence Day Alaska has ever seen," he announced. The streets would be decorated. There would be a huge carnival, flags on every building, red-white-and blue streamers across the streets, military bands, and a parade.

"*That's* when we unveil the militia," he declared. He was going to invite every important citizen—the railroad people, the bankers, the businessmen, even Governor Brady.

"They'll all be our guests, Tara," he exulted. "I want you to send invitations to everybody. I got the names here." He waved several sheets of paper. "The politicians don't care a damn about Skagway or Alaska, so I'm going to fly the flag so high they'll see it in Washington."

"Jeff," Tara said quietly, "you may be putting yourself out of business."

"Eh?" He stood rock still. "What do you mean?"

"You make too much noise and you could be finished."

"I don't see that."

"Don't you realize you can only get away with what you're doing because this is the back of beyond? It's the last frontier. Once there's law and order . . ."

She left the rest unsaid.

He nodded. "OK. I like that. I've never turned down a challenge yet." She hadn't seen the dice for a long time, but now he brought them out and played with them as he talked. "Listen, you know what I really enjoy?"

She shook her head. Her green eyes regarded him gravely.

"I'll tell you. Facing a roomful of bastards who'd like to shoot me in the back and haven't got the guts. I like to play high stakes with a son of a bitch who's so greedy he'd take the shirt off my back if I let him. So I'm going to put on a show the like of which they've never dreamed of."

He grinned crookedly. "I'm a very ambitious man."

"I never would have guessed."

352

"It's the same with you. You can't take no for an answer either. We're both stubborn cusses."

Then he stopped.

"Go on," prompted Tara.

"Not now. Sometime, but not now." He nodded at the lists on her lap. "Now start earning your keep and write those invitations."

It was both Tara's strength and weakness that she found it difficult to compromise. Sometimes she had to, and she would justify it on the grounds of necessity. Afterward her guilty feelings nagged her relentlessly.

Smith was a racketeer. She had to face up to that. But she also had to admit that he was honest about his dishonesty. She read the newspapers that came in from the States avidly, and there was no denying that a lot of politicians were giving this virgin land a shabby deal. If Smith was a crook, some of them were no better.

She read of proposals to impose taxes on Skagway's lodging houses, banks, pool halls, saloons, bowling alleys, every foot of railroad, every ounce of gold. Taxation for what? No telegraph service. No post office. No jail. Corrupt law officers. Illicit liquor trafficking. No sanitation.

She tried to tell herself that she was attempting to rationalize her involvement with Smith. She could surely not equate his fleecing of the Gold Rush with the politicians' greed for revenue from a territory for which they had done nothing.

No, forget it. Trying to justify the way Smith did things was impossible. You're looking for the man you love, she lectured herself. Don't think about Smith. Keep looking for Daniel. Make sure there's nothing you've missed.

Her mood was buoyant as she rode along the trail to Dyea. She had traveled this route with Bishop Beauchamp and his obnoxious wife, unwittingly smuggling Soapy Smith's liquor. Then it had been cold and windy, and the countryside had been white and freezing. Now it was warm and the wasteland was ablaze with flowers. Goldenrod, daisies, buttercups, poppies, and bluebells jostled with a myriad of various ferns. The sun would not set until after ten o'clock; even then, there would only be twilight. How incredible that, in three or four months, this lovely world would disappear, to be replaced once again by a freezing white blanket and perpetual night.

Dyea had changed too. Unlike Dawson and Skagway, it did not seem much more prosperous, but there was more of it. The sprawl of makeshift habitations was even uglier. There was also something else that was different. The U.S. Army had moved in. The soldiers in their dark-blue uniforms were everywhere. Tara wondered why they were there.

She left her horse in the stables next to the blacksmith and started to walk along the street. She intended to check at the local lodging houses, ask around the stores, try to find someone, anyone who might know something.

She made many inquiries, but they got her no further. If Daniel Kane had been here since her arrival in Alaska, no one knew about it.

She had a meal in an eating house, and here at least Dyea had improved. There was a checked tablecloth, the cutlery was clean, and the food was nicely served.

Just as she was paying her bill, the door opened, and an army officer came in. He was a tall man, with the silver bar of a lieutenant and the insignia of the infantry. He stood looking around, and as soon as he saw Tara he went toward her and saluted.

"Mrs. Kane?" he said, very politely.

"Yes?" Tara was startled.

"Colonel Bradshaw's compliments, ma'am. The colonel wonders if you could spare him a few minutes." His manner was formal, correct, somewhat distant.

"I don't think I know the colonel," Tara said. "What is it about?"

"I'm sure the colonel will tell you himself, ma'am. If you'll follow me."

She had the uneasy feeling that it was not so much an invitation as an order.

At army headquarters Tara was ushered into the colonel's office. She noticed, as she walked through, that two officers and a sergeant at a desk in the outer room looked at her curiously as she passed.

"Mrs. Kane, sir," announced the lieutenant, and Tara found herself facing two men. The colonel, a gray-haired man with sharp eyes, rose from behind his desk.

"Thank you, Mr. Evans," he said to the lieutenant, who saluted and left. "Sit down, Mrs. Kane."

The other man, who had also risen, sat down again on a chair near the colonel's desk. He was a civilian, in a city suit, with gold-rimmed glasses. His eyes never left Tara's face, and she found him disconcerting.

"I appreciate your coming here, Mrs. Kane," said the colonel without warmth. "I'm Colonel Bradshaw, and this gentleman is Mr. Wilkins."

Tara nodded. What did they want with her? She said nothing and waited.

"Mr. Wilkins is from Washington," added the colonel, as if that explained everything. "From the War Department."

He sat down again and looked at her. He cleared his throat.

"What actually is your, ahem, purpose in visiting Dyea, Mrs. Kane?"

She stared at him, perplexed. "Purpose, colonel? I don't follow what that has to do with the United States Army."

"You must have a reason for coming here, ma'am," Wilkins said. His voice was soft. "You've been wandering all over town, here, there, and everywhere. To what end?"

"And what business is that of yours?" she demanded indignantly. She was suddenly aware that they must have kept her under surveillance since she had arrived. "Why are you so interested in me?"

The two men exchanged looks. "Mrs. Kane," began the colonel. He stopped. He was picking his works. "There is a reason for our presence here. The government has moved in the army because—well, in case of certain eventualities."

"Let's put it this way, ma'am," interrupted Wilkins. "You are an, an associate of Mr. Smith. In Skagway."

"I know Mr. Smith," she said curtly. "What's that got to do with it?"

"Are you here on Mr. Smith's business, ma'am?" asked the colonel crisply.

"Of course not—" she began.

"If so," he disregarded her reply, "we'd like to know what it is."

"Gentlemen," she said, and her tone was hard. "I have no idea what this is about, but I take exception. If you must know, I'm here on a private matter, but that's got nothing to do with you either. Is that all?"

She was about to get up, but Wilkins intervened.

"I beg your pardon, Mrs. Kane, but what exactly is the nature of the private matter?" he insisted.

"Sir, you're being presumptuous." Then she shrugged. "Since you're so anxious to know, I'm trying to locate my husband."

To her surprise, the colonel said. "Yes, his name is Daniel, isn't it? A prospector, I believe?"

"You know about him?" Tara leaned forward eagerly. "You've got some news about him?"

"We merely know that you've been looking for him."

"How?" Tara tried to keep the disappointment out of her voice. "How do you know?"

"We're interested in Mr. Smith, in his activities, and the people

355

around him," Wilkins said flatly. He allowed himself a thin smile. "And we're interested in what they're interested in, if you follow me."

"Why?"

The colonel sighed. "You know why, Mrs. Kane."

"Mr. Smith's activities are of very little concern to me," declared Tara. She stopped. Certain things were coming back to her, things Hart had said about the militia and the shipments. Apprehension began to grow.

"Go on."

"No," she said quietly. "I don't know anything."

"Well, Mrs. Kane, whatever you're doing here, you can give Mr. Smith a message." The colonel's voice was icy. "You can tell him the government has moved a battalion of infantry into Dyea. Their orders are to keep the peace and to uphold law and order. You can tell him that we're on twenty-four-hour alert."

"That's right," Wilkins said. "You tell him just that. Then you won't have had a wasted trip."

The colonel opened the door for Tara. "Good day, ma'am," he said.

She let herself into her hotel room to find a man sitting on the edge of the bed, facing the door. It was Cahill, the Seattle newspaper reporter. He stood up, unabashed.

"Forgive the intrusion, Mrs. Kane," he began, but Tara cut him short.

"Exactly what do you think you are doing here?"

"Waiting for you," he replied blandly.

"Please go," Tara said. She turned to open the door, but he made no attempt to move.

"I think you'd better listen, Mrs. Kane," he said. His tone made her close the door again.

"Listen to what?"

"Do you mind if we sit on the bed? This establishment seems to be lacking chairs."

"What do you want?" she asked.

"Well, I guess I could tell you I'm just an inquisitive reporter on the scent of a big story."

"Sir, I'd be obliged if you left. I don't want to embarrass you by having to call."

"My dear lady, you don't embarrass me in the slightest," he broke in. "I think it's in your interest as much as mine that we talk here in private. Away from people. No risk of getting interrupted."

Cahill's manner was purposeful, authoritative. Tara hesitated, then sat on the other side of the bed.

"Well?"

"How did you get on with the military gentlemen?" he asked with a smile.

So he knew about that. The man must have been following her all over the place.

"It's none of your business. That's what I told them, and that's what I'm telling you, Mr. Cahill."

"You know, I think I do believe you," he said, after a pause.

"And what does that mean?" she demanded, bristling.

"Maybe you don't really know what's going on. You've got yourself in bad company, Mrs. Kane. We've sort of checked on things and . . ."

"We?"

"Some of us wondered what your real role is. Go-between? Courier? This story of yours didn't convince some of us."

"What story?" She stared at him, her eyes smoldering.

"About your looking for your husband. They figured it might just be a neat excuse, to justify you turning up wherever you wanted. Juneau. Here. Anywhere.

"Justify what? What are you trying to say?"

"So we started looking for Mr. Kane too," he went on.

"We?" she repeated. "Your newspaper?" He shook his head.

"No, Mrs. Kane," he said quietly. "The government. The U.S. Government."

She sat stunned.

"You see, I work for the government, Mrs. Kane. That's why I'm so interested in Jefferson Smith."

"But what's that got to do with me? With Daniel?" she almost shouted. "What do you want from me?"

"Well, ma'am, if you'll pardon me, your association with Smith." He stopped. "You're very close to him. It seemed to us you might be working for him. What I mean is, a good-looking woman like yourself, well, it's easy for her to travel around, ask questions, gain people's confidence, find out things."

"What things, Mr. Cahill?" Her voice was tense.

He shrugged. "Information. Gold shipments. The plans of the railroad. The strength of the troops here. Anything he needs to know."

"Spying for Mr. Smith, you mean?" Her face was pale.

"Well, let's say we weren't sure."

But he had said something that was much more important to her, more important than the anger his words aroused.

"What do you know about Daniel?" she asked, trying to keep her voice steady. "What have you found out about him?"

357

"That you were telling the truth. There was a Daniel Kane. He was your husband. He landed at Skagway last August on the S.S. Humboldt. He trekked to Dawson. He started prospecting." Cahill stopped.

"And?"

He saw her anxious, pleading eyes. "Then the trail sort of petered out," he said lamely.

"Do you know where he is?" she cried. "Now?"

"Mrs. Kane." He fell silent. "He's dead," he said at last. "He was murdered in Circle City. I would have thought the Mounted Police . . ."

She laughed, a wild unexpected laughter. He thought it was the shock of the news, but it was the laughter of relief.

"Mrs. Kane . . ."

"That wasn't my husband," she almost shouted at him. "They made a mistake. That wasn't Daniel."

"Mrs. Kane, the Canadian authorities are quite certain. The wedding ring."

She held up her hand triumphantly. "This is it," she cried. "Yes, it's his ring. But that man wasn't Daniel. Thank God," she added, almost to herself.

He looked doubtful. "Well, I am very glad," he murmured. Then he rose and went over to the window.

"You must help us, Mrs. Kane," he said. "We suspect Smith is planning to take over Skagway by force of arms. We think he wants to seize the railroad once it is operating, the passes, maybe Juneau, Dyea. Control the routes to the gold fields. Take over Alaska, maybe invade British Columbia, seize the Yukon. Pretend he's claiming it for the United States."

Tara sat motionless.

"It's a disputed border anyway, and you can guess what that would do. Maybe war between us and the Canadians. Anything could happen."

"That's rubbish. All he wants to see is Alaska as part of the Union," intervened Tara.

"He wants to control the gold that's coming out of the Klondike," said Cahill brutally. "He wants to squeeze the prospectors by controlling the whole place, the ports, the supplies, the transportation. He'll levy tolls and demand payoffs and take his cut out of every ounce of gold that's found."

"How could he?" Tara asked.

"What do you think he's raising his phony National Guard for? It's nothing but a private gang, four hundred tough, hard mercenaries, dressed up in army uniforms to fool everybody. Bogus, the whole bunch of them." He stood in front of her. "He's shipping in arms, Mrs. Kane. Not just small arms. We suspect bigger things. Maybe Maxim guns. Maybe even light field guns."

"No," Tara said. But she wished she really felt it was untrue.

"We suspect he's got an arsenal somewhere in Skagway. A warehouse maybe. We're trying to find out."

"We?" she asked. "Who else?"

"We've got an agent in Skagway."

Several things made sense to her now. "This agent of yours, did he break into Smith's office at the Oyster Parlor?" she asked.

He said nothing.

She knew he was now going to ask her to betray Smith, and she also knew what her answer had to be.

"Mr. Cahill," Tara said slowly. "You must understand one thing. I don't have any part in all this. Sure, I've heard rumors, but he doesn't involve me in any of it." She licked her dry lips. "And I don't want to know. I'm terrified of what you say he's doing, it's crazy. But you must also know this. He's been a good friend to me. A kind friend."

Cahill seemed surprised.

"I have a little baby to look after. He's done everything possible for him. I know he's a rogue. I know his reputation. I know some of the things he's done." She swallowed. "But he's been generous and good to me, and I can't repay it by, by . . ."

The strain was showing in her eyes. "I'm sorry," she ended.

Cahill said nothing for a moment. He looked at her gravely. "All right," he said at last, very quietly. "It's a fair answer. I believe you. Only," he looked into her eyes, "remember one thing. We're not talking about marked decks of cards or rigged faro wheels. This is insurrection. Armed rebellion. Don't put your neck in a noose, Mrs. Kane."

He went to the door. "Be careful, Mrs. Kane. Skagway is going to be a mighty dangerous place."

Then he was gone.

CHAPTER TWENTY-SIX

Tara could almost smell the tension when she returned to Skagway. Men were standing around in clusters, grim-faced. Yet the usually crowded streets were strangely quiet. The town really looked no different, but the atmosphere of unease was unmistakable.

It was even more evident outside the Oyster Parlor. Here there was a cordon of Smith's men, cradling shotguns and scrutinizing strangers with unfriendly eyes.

They let Tara through. Mort, standing by the long mahogany bar, gave her a nod. He had his sixgun buckled on. "Welcome back, Mrs. Kane," he grunted without warmth.

She looked at the empty tables, and the bouncers sitting near the door, one of them with a Winchester across his knees.

"What's happened?" she asked.

"Oh, nothing much."

"I want to know, Mort."

"Well." He contemplated Tara. "There's been a shooting. Some guy got his."

It was not all that unusual. Guns were part of the scene all over, Dawson, Fortymile, Skagway. Even a periodic shootout was not unknown. But this was different. Whatever happened, people were angry and resentful. Something was simmering.

"Who was it?" Tara inquired.

He shrugged. "Some greenhorn. The whole thing was a mistake, I guess."

She looked around the saloon, at the bouncers.

"But why all this? Why the men outside?"

"Better ask the boss," he said. He appeared anxious to end the conversation.

Smith was no more forthcoming at first, but slowly she got it out of him.

"Jeff, tell me what happened?"

"Yeah Mow got trigger-happy," he said.

"Who was the man?"

"A pain. A real pain. The stupid son of a bitch got in the way." Then he saw her reaction. "No, you're right. That's why I'm so riled. There was no need to plug him. Yeah Mow forgot where he was."

The shooting had taken place in broad daylight. In front of dozens of passersby, Yeah Mow had shot down an unarmed man.

"What a damn stupid thing to do," Smith said again.

"Who was he?" repeated Tara once more.

"Fellow called Ashbury. Glen Ashbury. The stupid jerk. Been hanging around the place." He shrugged. "It'll pass over. Folks are pretty worked up at the moment, but they'll soon forget. It was one shooting too many, but don't worry about it."

"Do, do you know anything about Ashbury?" she asked nervously.

"Why should I care?" Smith retorted. But she could see he was worried.

He snapped his fingers suddenly. "I got an idea," he declared. "Maybe I'll fix a trial. Maybe we'll get Yeah Mow acquitted by a jury, and then it's all official, and everybody will calm down."

He waited for her reaction, but all she said was, "I've seen enough of your trials, Jeff."

Ashbury's killing was a big mistake. For the first time, Tara saw a slogan whitewashed on a wall: "Hang Soapy." People kept away from the Oyster Parlor.

Smith announced, on the front page of his *Skagway News*, that he was personally paying for the funeral of the dead man, and that the townspeople could rest assured that a full investigation was taking place.

"And if there has been the slightest violation of the law, the culprit will be punished as decreed by law," Smith was quoted as saying.

Three days later he told Tara that there had been an inquest. "Verdict's self-defense," he announced, straight-faced. "Yeah Mow got cleared. Six witnesses testified they saw Ashbury draw a gun first."

"But he wasn't armed, you said so yourself."

"I wasn't there, honey. These guys saw it."

There was a celebration that night in the Oyster Parlor, with Yeah Mow the guest of honor. Those who were curious enough to follow the verdict up—if there had been anyone—would have seen the six witnesses drinking with him. They were all men whose faces were not unknown in the establishment.

The town did not forget the Ashbury shooting. Smith knew it. Nobody said anything to his face, but they glowered at him when he walked past and they talked about him behind his back.

He showed himself defiantly in all kinds of places, like a man challenging them to stand up to him. It did not help.

There was no more mention of the shooting of Glen Ashbury in the town paper, Smith saw to that. The funeral took place at an early hour with no one around. But the memory of it would not go away.

At a time when the town promised to be the most important landing stage for the gold fields, thanks to the rail link with Lake Bennett, Smith's regime was threatening everything. Prospectors would not want to use the port if it got out that they were unlikely to leave with their caches intact. The traders, the railroad, the backbone of the community knew that the news of Soapy Smith's hold over Skagway would reach Seattle and San Francisco. That could put an end to the town's prosperity.

So, no one was ever going to forget what had happened; that was, as Smith himself would put it, "a sure thing."

All the more reason for making the forthcoming Independence Day the biggest, noisiest, most dazzling event in the history of the Klondike.

The replies to the invitations were coming in, including the refusals. Tancrede and the rest of the railroad bosses were not coming. Some of Skagway's more respectable citizens turned up their noses, too. But, to Tara's surprise, Governor Brady, the ex-Methodist missionary turned politician, accepted.

She was sorting out the pile of letters on the desk when she came across some papers she had not noticed before—bills of lading, consignment notices, cargo manifests. She picked one up. It was for "kitchen equipment," shipped in from Seattle, to the amount of five thousand dollars. That, she said to herself, is an awful lot of kitchen equipment.

Smith must have forgotten to put the documents in his drawer. She found that he was importing "gardening gear," $4,000 worth; "bakery ovens," for $2,000; "sports equipment" to the tune of $7,000. What use did he have for gardening gear and sports equipment? She knew what she was looking at. Consignments of arms.

Tara had been keeping her ears open, too. Several times she had heard mention of "the warehouse." She had never been there. When she asked Smith, he had said something about storing his liquor there. There was only one way to find out if Cahill had been right about it being the arsenal.

The warehouse stood by itself at the side of a disused lumber mill. She dismounted from her horse and concealed herself behind a tree. The place looked deserted. Suddenly she froze. A man with a rifle came around the corner of the warehouse, looking about him, like a sentry on patrol. He leaned against the wall, his rifle by him. Then he got bored, picked it up, and disappeared around the other side.

How long she watched, Tara didn't know, but she was getting cold. She had found out nothing. Sure, it was a warehouse. But what did that prove? It was guarded by an armed man. If illicit spirits were hoarded there, it made sense that it was guarded. She had to get inside.

In the distance, she saw a mule train approach. Slowly the animals came along the path to the site, two armed horsemen accompanying them. Each mule was weighed down by two heavy crates. Tara watched as they came to a halt in front of the depot. The sentry appeared and unlocked the door. The others began to unstrap the heavy crates and carry them inside. When the mules had been unloaded, the men disappeared into the big shed. Tara stepped out from behind the tree and crept over to the warehouse. The door was ajar, and she could hear voices. She peered through the gap. The three men were busy stacking the crates. She caught her breath as she saw rifles, and boxes of ammunition, row after row of them. And something else she had never seen before: Maxim guns, ugly weapons, on tripods, their muzzles pointing dumbly, their magazines covered. Six machine guns which, in a few moments, could kill scores, hundreds. There was even a piece of artillery that looked powerful enough to sink a ship, with the shells stacked nearby in neat rows. Tara tried to open the door a little wider and it creaked.

The three men glanced up and saw the woman watching them. Tara tried frantically to think of a reason for being there.

"You shouldn't be here, Mrs. Kane," Yeah Mow said. She spun around. She hadn't heard him come up behind her. "Nobody's allowed here. Boss's orders." He had a pistol in his hand, and it was pointing at her.

"Put that away," Tara ordered, and her voice, luckily, didn't betray her panic.

Yeah Mow slowly returned the gun to its holster. His diamond cufflinks glinted. "What are you doing?" he asked softly.

"Mr. Smith," she began.

"Does he know you're here?" His unblinking eyes held her trapped.

"Of course," she lied.

"You sure the boss said it's okay?" His tone didn't hide his disbelief.

"Why don't you ask him?" Tara replied. The other three men were watching them both. Their faces were unsmiling.

Yeah Mow nodded. "You got a horse here?"

"Yes."

"OK," he said. "You and me are going to take a little ride. So you can say hello to the boss."

He nodded to the others. "You fellows stay here, and keep on your toes. Just in case she's got friends. Lead the way, Mrs. Kane."

They rode back to Skagway in silence. Yeah Mow spoke only once. "You're a pretty lucky lady, Usually, when people go snooping round that place, we shoot first and ask questions afterward."

"Like the way you killed Glen Ashbury?" Tara asked.

"He asked for it. Guys don't break into the boss's office and get away with it."

Then she knew they had killed a U.S. Government agent.

He shoved Tara into a back room of the Oyster Parlor. It was the storeroom for the bar, stacked with crates of whisky and gin, and the only light came from a hurricane lamp hanging from a hook in the ceiling. Electricity was strictly reserved for the front of the house.

"Get Mr. Smith right away," blustered Tara. "He's going to be mighty sore at you."

"Don't worry," Yeah Mow smiled coldly. "You'll see him all right."

He shut the door, and she heard the key turning in the padlock. She was left in semidarkness, staring at the crates of smuggled liquor. As time passed, she started to feel more apprehensive. The magic of being Smith's consort appeared to have waned.

Finally she heard a key in the padlock, and Smith came in. Yeah Mow was behind him, carrying an oil lamp. He put it down on a crate.

Smith looked at her. Then he turned to Yeah Mow.

"Leave us."

"But I told you, she was snooping."

"You heard me," snapped Smith.

"You gave orders." Yeah Mow's eyes were glittering venomously in the light of the lamp.

"I'll deal with it."

They were left alone. Smith stood, just staring at her. "What's the game, Tara?"

She stared back at him defiantly. "Don't you think that's for me to ask? Get me out of this hole." Fear had been replaced by smouldering anger. "And then you'd better do some explaining."

Smith walked slowly over to one of the other crates, and sat down on it. "What were you doing there?" His tone was quiet, unmoved.

"Finding out the truth for myself."

"You could have asked me."

"Oh, really? And be told another bunch of lies? Get fobbed off again with parades and drills and training your weekend soldiers?"

For the first time he smiled.

"Who's lying, my dear? Maybe you haven't told me everything." The smile stayed on his face, but his eyes bored into her.

Tara took a deep breath. "What's that supposed to mean?"

He waved a hand. "Oh, you know. Your little visit to the army. You haven't been very talkative about your Dyea trip, have you now?" He saw reaction. "Why did you have to sneak off to the arsenal? Why didn't you tell me you wanted a look? And what did you see? Exactly what I've been telling you. I've been shipping in arms for my little outfit. That's what you found."

"Some little outfit. Those aren't a few arms. There's enough there to equip a small army. To kill thousands."

He grinned. "You should know that when I do things, I do them in style."

If he hoped to shrug it off lightly, he failed. He knew that when he saw how grave she had become. "Jeff, I'm frightened," Tara said in a low voice. "The whole thing frightens me."

He sat studying her. "Let's go upstairs," he said. They walked through the saloon, Yeah Mow and Mort watching, intrigued. Her face was pale, tense. In silence, they went up the stairs to his office. "So," Smith said at last. "What's so frightening?"

"You."

"Really?"

"You didn't start this whole business to fight in the Spanish War. You did it for a different reason."

"I think," he drawled, "you're really getting yourself excited over nothing."

Tara tensed herself to say it. "I know what you've got in mind and so does the army," she finally whispered. "I'm scared. For you. For all of us. For . . ."

"Well, then maybe you'd better tell me what I'm plotting."

She drew a deep breath. "You're planning to seize Skagway. The railroad. Dyea. The passes. Maybe the Yukon. You're planning rebellion."

She waited for his reaction, but none came.

"I want you to deny it," Tara said, and her eyes were pleading with him. "I want you to say it isn't going to happen. I want you to say no, I'm wrong."

Smith stared at her. He said nothing. He sat rigid, unmoving.

"I'm waiting," she said. "Deny it. Please. For God's sake deny it."

She could see he was making a big decision. It came quickly. "Why should I?" asked Smith. "It's the truth."

She got up and slowly went over to his desk. "No. You can't be that cold-blooded." Her voice was controlled, quiet, her hands clenched. "Don't tell me you don't give a damn for what will happen. The people you'll kill. The bloodshed. Don't tell me you don't care if they hang you." She leaned forward. "Jeff, the government knows what you're up to. They've got troops ready to move in. I've seen them. Ashbury was no greenhorn. He was investigating you. He was a government agent."

He kept his composure.

"Come on now, that's mighty emotive talk. I ain't going to get hanged for a lousy government spy. Yeah Mow might but not me, and nobody's moving in troops. All they need is a little persuasion—like a good front-row view of Skagway's finest—and they'll get that all right on the Fourth." He laughed. "It'll all be finished before they know it. There ain't going to be no shooting, unless somebody else starts it."

"They will, Jeff." She sat down. "That's why those troops are in Dyea. You know what they'll do the moment you take over. Thank God I won't be there."

"What's that?"

"I'm pulling out, Jeff," she said very quietly. "I'll be in San Francisco when they hang you. I don't want to see any of it. I've had enough. I'm going back."

For the first time he looked worried. "You can't," he said. "I won't let you. Never." He stood and faced here. "You don't really mean it, do you?"

She nodded.

"I see," murmured Smith. "When?"

"As soon as I can."

Smith frowned and paced around the room. "Well, there's still time for you to change your mind," he muttered. "I'll persuade you. I know I can."

"You've no chance, Jeff. Not even if you try to use force."

"Do you think I'd force you to do anything against your will?"

"I never thought you would, but now I'm not so sure."

Smith went over to her and took her hand. "Look at me," he said. She kept her eyes cast downward. "Tara, look at me," he repeated, tilting her head back so that their eyes met. "As God is my witness, I'm never going to harm you. You must believe that because it's true."

She was drawn toward him as if by a magnet. He took her in his arms and stroked her hair, and she didn't resist, she didn't want to. She closed her eyes, accepting the comfort of his arms around her. She did not stop him as he kissed her neck. He turned her face and put his lips on hers.

"You're too important to me, Tara," he said softly, holding her close.

"If that's true, Jeff," she said, gazing into his unwavering eyes, "give up your crazy scheme. Prove to me you are the man I think you are, kind-hearted and generous. Promise me you'll never use your men against this town, the Territory, anyone."

"Why do you care so much?"

"I," she began, but he interrupted. "OK, there'll have to be a deal. Between you and me. I'll think about things, I promise you. Maybe ..." He looked into the distance. Then turned back to her. "All right, stay until the Fourth. More than anything I want you there. You'll be the hostess, the first lady. Please. If you do that ... well, maybe I can do it all your way."

"You mean that?"

366

"Sweetheart, I'll start a whole new deck of cards if that's the only way I can keep you here. I'll pay the price, any price."

"I've told you before. There can't be any price, Jeff. I want nothing."

He shrugged. "Jesus, I never met a woman like you." Then, much more softly, he added: "Oh, Tara." He took her hand and kissed it.

"Well?" he said. "Is it a deal?"

She nodded.

"Yes," she said slowly. "I think it is."

The Gold Rush itself had caught its second breath. What had started out, less than a year before, as a stampede by lone wolves, had turned into a veritable industry. The claims up and down the Territory now numbered thousands.

Tara had often tried to visualize Daniel returning from a bonanza strike, loaded down with gold, rich beyond their dreams, a wealthy man for whom money was no longer an object. It would be wonderful to see him realize his dream. It would make their separation, the hardships, the pain and loneliness, all worthwhile.

Yet she wondered what effect it might have on them. Gold could destroy people. The thought preyed on her after the Polack came to Skagway.

She never found out his name. To look at, he was the image of the ordinary, shabby, hungry sourdough, chasing a forlorn hope, too broke to stop looking for his elusive lucky strike, too broke to give up and turn back.

Now, the whole town knew the Pole had returned. Tara, drawn by the swelling noise, the people running, saw him standing on a barrel, flinging gold nuggets to the mob.

He was drunk, an inane smile on his face. He swayed on his precarious perch, and he kept throwing his gold to the forest of outstretched, grasping hands.

Before her eyes, he was tossing away hundreds, thousands of dollars. Gold that had cost him agony, privation, frostbite, hunger to find. Gold for which he had labored like a galley slave.

You fool, thought Tara, when you're finished, they won't even say thank you. He had run out of gold apparently but only for a moment. He bent down and picked up another sack and dug into it.

Tara heard later when they were all talking about him in the saloons and hotels, that he had certainly struck it rich. He had returned from his El Dorado with ninety thousand dollars worth of gold. And within forty-eight hours he wasn't worth a sou.

367

His last gesture was the traditional one of lighting his cigar with a dollar bill. For two days he stood hordes of strangers drinks and kept open house in the Bucket of Blood. They drank his hooch by the gallon, and when he threw his gold on the sawdust-covered floor, they scrambled for it. The Polack, eyes glazed, watched and roared with laughter. He danced with a saloon girl, and each time they waltzed around the room, he stuffed a hundred dollar bill down her cleavage.

After an hour, she was a rich hustler.

Smith stood beside Tara, watching him stagger down State Street. Nobody took any notice of him. The bystanders who had cheered and applauded him as they scrabbled for his handouts ignored him. Once again, he was destitute.

"Now there goes a guy who marked his own cards," commented Smith acidly.

Tara felt sorry for the man, but Smith turned on her. "Don't you be sorry for him. He's had the best two days and nights of his life."

She made no reply. She was thinking of Daniel. She wondered if the gold madness could ever destroy him.

In a different way, she had already struck it rich in the Yukon. She had John. He was showing signs of growing into a handsome child. Dark curly hair surrounded his small oval face, and his deep brown eyes were fringed with thick black lashes. Tara thanked God that the baby had survived and was healthy. Every night she kissed him on the forehead, then gently rocked him to sleep, all the while quietly lullabying him with songs she used to sing to Gabie. These were the moments of contentment, and Smith for a long time did not understand why the gift of the Chilkoot avalanche was so important to Tara.

"You see, you can't understand, of course, but I've been given a second chance," Tara said one night.

Smith stared at her. "Second chance?" he repeated. "What second chance? What the hell are you talking about?"

"He's my second child," she said, "given to me after losing mine."

She told him about Gabrielle, how the baby had given Tara's life a purpose, especially after Daniel's departure, how she had fled to the Klondike from the emptiness and desolation caused by Gabie's death. Tara spoke quietly but with fierce intensity. When she spoke of Gabie, of the last time she saw her little baby, of that awful gray moment when her coffin disappeared into the earth, her eyes brimmed with tears. She felt drained by reliving those traumatic days, but it was a relief to talk about it again.

They sat in silence for a while. Then Smith said, very gently, "You should have told me before, Tara."

"Why?" she asked. "It wouldn't have made any difference."

"Well, it would have explained a few things."

She brushed an errant hair away. "Such as?"

"Such as something I could never figure out. What the hell you've been really chasing . . ." He nodded to himself.

"Yes sir," he said, "it really would have explained a few things."

"You know why I'm here. To find my husband. Nothing else."

"Daniel?" He laughed. It was almost contemptuous. "The wonderful, magnificent, irresistible Daniel Kane? You came looking for him?" He laughed again.

"Jeff," Tara was trying to keep her voice steady. "He may not be wonderful or magnificent or irresistible, but he's the man I love."

Smith tightened his lips angrily. "Now I'm going to tell you the truth, Tara. You didn't come to find anyone. Not goddamn Daniel. Nothing. You came here to escape. You've been running so fast you haven't given yourself a chance. You haven't been trying to find the past, you've been trying to get away from it.

"Suddenly the whole damn shoot figures." He saw Tara's pale face and went on: "I knew a guy once, back in Colorado. Nice guy. Damn good poker player. Well, one day he got into an argument with a real crooked cardsharp. This guy didn't pack a gun, see, and the cardsharp was going to blow a hole in his head. Well, some bystander wasn't going to see this happen, and he sort of stepped between them, and he got a hole in the head instead. Turned out he had a wife and three kids. The guy I knew, he just drifted after that. He never settled down again. You know why? He kept feeling guilty. He kept thinking it was his fault the other fellow was dead. He kept running from himself, the goddamn fool."

"I can understand that," said Tara, more to herself.

"Can you? Jesus, if he was that overcome with his sensitive conscience, he should have stopped running and married the goddamn widow and fed the kids," snorted Smith. "Now you, you haven't got problems like that. You just feel bad about losing your little girl. That was tough. You got dealt a lousy hand. Now forget it. Stop running away."

"That's not what it's about at all," Tara whispered.

"No, I know, you're looking for the man you love," he said bitingly. "I got all that. Well, I say you've been running away faster than a rustler from a posse, and what's more, you're about to start again. Running away. That talk about going back to Frisco. Still running."

She tossed her head. "Don't be ridiculous." She paused. "What am I supposed to be running away from now?"

He did not reply. Instead he stood up. "Let's sleep on it," he said.

369

"We'll talk about it again soon. Then you can tell me if you're still in the same frame of mind."

Tara handed him his hat. "I will be," she said. "I told you. I've made my decision. There's just one thing, Jeff." She hesitated, then took the plunge. "If I ask you to help me, will you? Please. As a friend?"

He feigned surprise, but his eyes were watching her.

"You know, that's the first time you've ever called me that. Your friend."

"Well, aren't you, Jeff?"

He smiled, like somebody who has just drawn a good card. "That's something else I'll have to sleep on too," he replied.

Tara, for one, did not sleep well that night. Her dreams were filled with weird fantasies. She relived Gabie's funeral, only this time, as the coffin was lowered into the ground, she followed it and found herself running down a long, featureless tunnel, following a man dressed completely in black. She knew it was Daniel and she kept calling his name, but he did not stop or even look around and she could not catch up with him. Then a shadowy figure appeared at her side. She turned to it but its face kept changing. At first it was Hart, then Smith, finally it was Gore, Jake Gore, and he smiled at her villainously.

"Don't worry, Mrs. Kane," the apparition said, "I'll get you to your husband. I'll lead you to him eventually."

CHAPTER TWENTY-SEVEN

Long before the big parade was due to begin, Skagway was carousing. Red-white-and-blue bunting waved from rooftops, windows, and flagpoles, and the streets were filled with people in their Sunday best. The saloons were overflowing onto the sidewalks, the drinkers singing and shouting and sharing their bottles with passersby. Prospectors shot off pistols and rifles. Skagway's only set of church bells pealed; a man with a wooden leg was playing the accordion outside Casey's saloon; steamships in the harbor sounded their whistles.

Tara could hear the sounds of revelry as she put the last pin in her hair and dabbed perfume behind her ears. She stood back to check her appearance as best she could in the small mirror. She was wearing a new printed cotton dress she had bought a few days earlier. For Smith's important day, she wanted to wear something different, something that would surprise and please him. It had startled her when she realized that she wanted Smith to admire her, to be proud of being her escort. It was an admission that had brought her up with a jolt.

The only men Tara had ever wanted to admire or compliment her in the past had been her father and Daniel. Until a few days ago, the only man she had ever truly kissed had been her husband. Now things had changed.

When Smith had taken her in his arms and kissed her, she had enjoyed it. She liked it when he touched her, when he was close to her. He possessed a magnetism which excited her and made her want to react.

At first she had felt like an adulteress. Then she told herself she should not be guilty or ashamed, but happy at having found someone for whom she felt affection. But her conscience could see only her unfaithfulness, her betrayal of her husband's love, even her defilement of his memory. Her other voice had whispered: "But supposing you are a widow? Are you always going to cut yourself off from the admiration of other men? If Daniel's dead, is it natural to stay faithful to just a memory from now to forever?"

"I belong to Daniel," she cried out aloud in reply. "I'll always be faithful to him. There'll never be anyone else, never." But she knew that that was what Smith had meant when he had accused her of running away.

There were moments when she had gone as far as blaming Smith for his corruptive influence in awakening these dormant emotions in her. But then she had recognized he was not to blame. She alone was responsible for her actions; she alone had to sort out her feelings.

Tara knew Smith loved her, and that was why she did not want to hurt him. It was a love that Tara felt, given time, she could reciprocate but one which, because of her circumstances, she had to stifle.

Yet here she was now, dressed in a new frock, looking pretty, her deep auburn hair swept up, her green eyes bright with excitement and happiness.

John's crying roused her from her reverie. She went over to the cot and picked him up. Lydia had already left to see the festivities, and now it was time for Tara to prepare the baby so that they would be ready when Smith arrived to pick them up.

She dressed him in a little suit Lydia had made for him and wrapped him in a big embroidered shawl.

"My John," smiled Tara, balancing him on her knee, proudly, "you look nice enough to take the salute yourself." She kissed him and he smiled up at her.

"We're all that matters to one another, my precious," she said with feeling as she hugged him.

"I need you as much as you need me. Together we can face the world and cope with anything. As soon as I can, I'm taking you home, my darling, and there you'll have a proper life. I want to be a good mother." She paused, swallowing the lump of unhappiness that always formed in her throat when she thought of her dead little girl. "I am your mother, and you are my son," she told the small infant, whose wide eyes stared up at her solemnly. "No one can come between a mother and her son."

When Smith came for them he was wearing his army uniform, complete with sword. He gave a military salute that was more of a theatrical flourish. He looked handsome. Tara thought people could be forgiven for believing he really was what he pretended to be, an officer and a gentleman.

For a moment he stood and admired Tara openly. "You look beautiful," he said reverently.

"Why, thank you, sir," Tara smiled, her mood buoyant. "You look pretty smart yourself."

"Ah, but I'm a very lucky man." Smith was in high spirits. "I've not only got the honor of escorting a lovely woman, I've also got the company of an extremely stylish young man." He stroked the baby's cheek. "If you're both ready the carriage awaits," he announced formally, opening the cabin door.

Smith was not joking. Outside stood an open four-wheeled carriage drawn by two magnificent horses and complete with a driver. Such elegance was new to Skagway, but then she was going to see a lot that day that had never been seen before in Alaska.

Smith helped her into the carriage, and they set off through the streets of Skagway, Tara holding the baby and Smith bolt upright beside her, performing to perfection his role of military commander, civic leader, and would-be statesman.

As the carriage passed, onlookers, many of them holding small Stars and Stripes provided by the Smith organization, stared in amazement. Such handsome, elegant, fashionable people simply did not exist in the Klondike. Smith nodded benignly in their direction and waved his hand like a passing potentate. "Smile, Tara," he instructed through a fixed grin. "Hold little John up high so that everyone has a chance to see him."

"He's fine where he is," Tara replied out of the corner of her mouth.

"What's the matter, my dear?" asked Smith as the carriage progressed down the street.

"I didn't realize you were planning to make an exhibition of us," she whispered. "I knew it was a parade, but I didn't know John and I were going to be part of it."

"So I'm showing you off," Smith retorted, waving at the crowd outside the general store. "What's wrong with a man showing off a woman he's proud of? I'm showing off you and the boy because I want all these people to see what a lucky son of a bitch I am." He turned to her with a dazzling smile. "And I am, too," he added.

Outside the Music Hall, Babe Davenport and some scantily clad girls screeched and waved as the carriage passed. "Jeff, darling," shouted Babe, resplendent in a glittering tight-fitting dress. Smith waved at her, and she blew him an enthusiastic kiss. One of the other girls held up a placard announcing "Everything's Free Today," and Tara guessed that that didn't just mean liquor.

"Cad would have enjoyed all this," she remarked. "She'd have probably been more at home with all this attention than I am."

"Who's Cad?" Smith asked casually, saluting some more enthusiastic supporters.

The carriage was approaching a dais draped in red, white, and blue, dominated by a giant Stars and Stripes. Behind the platform the crowd was thick, and along the whole length of Skagway's main street were lined thousands of people. As the carriage stopped in front of the dais, a loud roar rang out, and Smith stood acknowledging the town's welcome. Then a brass band began playing *Dixie*.

"My signature tune," Smith grinned crookedly, as he helped Tara out of the carriage.

He led her to one of the three chairs that had been placed on the platform, another one of which was occupied by a bearded man in a frock coat. He rose as they approached.

"Governor," Smith said, "may I present Mrs. Kane."

The governor bowed, and Tara held out her hand to the man Smith wanted to kick out of the Territory.

"My pleasure entirely," said the Governor in an expansive voice, giving Tara a rather limp handshake. He laughed nervously. Tara could see that he was afraid of Smith.

"Governor Brady," purred Smith, "used to be a missionary." There was a wealth of contempt in his voice. "As you know, my dear," he went on, "the Governor is doing us the honor of taking the salute."

"I must say, Captain Smith, you're doing the town proud," rumbled Brady. "Looks like there's going to be a might fine show."

"You haven't seen anything yet, Governor." Smith seated Tara on the chair next to Brady. "You and the boy'll be all right here?" he asked.

Tara nodded. "But where are you off to?" she asked a little

desperately. She did not relish the idea of sitting on this platform next to someone she hardly knew, the center of attention, with hundreds of pairs of eyes trained on her. Nobody in Skagway was particularly interested in Governor Brady, but Smith's woman was quite another matter.

"The Governor will entertain you, I'm sure," Smith replied, saluting Brady. He winked at Tara, then sprinted down the steps of the dais, disappearing out of sight.

The little brass band played Sousa maches, and Tara sat with John, trying not to catch anybody's eye, wondering how long she would be stuck up there.

Brady leaned over to her. "A great occasion, Mrs. Kane, a great occasion." He smiled at the baby. "Cute, cute." He leered at Tara. "Do I detect his father's features?"

"His father is dead," Tara replied stiffly.

Brady laughed nervously again. "I, er, I thought that ..." he stuttered.

"I'm sure you did," Tara said.

Brady sank back in his chair.

Oh God, thought Tara, please let me get through this. From a distance, she could hear the sound of hundreds of pairs of marching feet. The parade was approaching from the top end of Broadway, and Tara craned her neck and saw a man carrying Old Glory. He was followed by a white charger, mounted on which was Jefferson Smith, sword drawn, a heroic figure tall in the saddle, riding in front of his army.

Drummers beat a blood-stirring tattoo, and the First Regiment, National Guard of Alaska tramped down the street, marching in very creditable military style considering its ranks included Smith's bouncers, bartenders and croupiers, who had been pressed into the ranks alongside genuine volunteers. The sun glinted on their bayonets, but nowhere could Tara see their deadlier weapons. None of the arms she had discovered in the arsenal was on display.

Brady was on his feet, his hand on his heart, his face twitching, taking the salute. As Smith came level with the platform, he waved his sword in a grand style which was possibly not according to the West Point manual but looked very impressive. His head was turned toward Brady but his eyes were only for Tara and, as they caught hers, he winked again.

"Magnificent, magnificent," Brady said. "A wonderful body of men. A credit to Alaska."

If you only knew, thought Tara as she watched Brady visibly expanding with patriotic pride.

Smith's militia was only part of it. He had promised Skagway the greatest show it had ever seen, and he kept his word. From somewhere he had found three Scots pipers, and they headed the next section of the parade, a series of wagons converted into floats, depicting Skagway's commerce, gold mining, the railroad, shipping, banking.

As Tara watched the contribution of Skagway's traders to the parade, she felt certain Smith had also solicited substantial donations from them. After all, he was not a man to let pass a sure opportunity of extracting money.

But it didn't matter. The spectators clapped and cheered at everyone, including a small contingent of Indians who shuffled past in native dress. They looked as if they were not quite sure what they were doing there but had been offered financial inducement to oblige.

Then came a second brass band, blaring and puffing to compete with the one by the dais. Again a cheer went up from the crowd; they were loving it all.

Anyone who wanted to could march in the parade. As long as it made the procession longer, they were welcome. So there were men on horseback who represented nobody but themselves and a group of stevedores who carried a banner proclaiming "Hooray for Jeff Smith."

The crowd gave a special cheer for the wagon loaded with dance hostesses blowing kisses and raising their skirts to the appreciative onlookers. Across the wagon was suspended a big poster which read, "Jeff Smith for Governor. Statehood for Alaska."

Brady swallowed at that but managed a sickly smile.

Tara found all the excitement infectious, and even young John seemed to be taking it in. It was loud, brash, and it made the heart beat faster. It was a great show, like a circus parade.

Then, while the tail end of the parade was still passing, Smith appeared beside her on the dais. He sat down and whispered to her, "Well, how did that look?"

"The best circus a kid could wish to see," Tara whispered back. "But I don't think the Governor was too amused by that sign."

The procession had finally passed but the crowd still stood, packed, as if they knew the program wasn't over yet. They were right. Smith's speech was to come.

He got to his feet and moved to the front of the platform. Somebody, no doubt one of the gang, shouted, "Good old Jeff," and there was a big roar.

Smith stood contemplating the crowd, while Brady looked a little put out.

"Fellow citizens of Skagway," began Smith, raising his hand for silence. "This ain't the time for speechifying, it's a time for celebrating. This great nation is at war, and we Skagway folk are going to play our part in licking the tyrants of Havana." He raised his voice.

"We're doing our duty, but we believe also that we deserve a square deal. The people of Alaska call on the Republicans in Congress to keep their faith with us and give us our own elected congressmen."

Below, the crowd stamped their feet, and guns were fired into the air.

"Now we don't want anything but our just dues," cried Smith. "What's Washington done for us? Made some lousy laws, taxed us, but what else? For years we've been the orphan. We're the Cinderella of the hemisphere. Hell, until the railroad, we only had one damn wagon road running for two miles, that's what they call opening up the Territory. That's going to change."

Tara sat fascinated. So far Smith had manipulated and schemed. Now he was playing, convincingly she had to admit, the role of statesman. She wondered if the people would ever trust him, if his speech signified that he had dropped his crazy scheme to take over the town by force. Was it supposed to show recognition and acceptance by him of her pleas? Were his future aims to be purely political, and did he intend going about them legally?

"Remember what I'm going to tell you," Smith lowered his voice slightly. The crowd had grown quiet, hanging on his every word. "This great territory, Alaska, is going to be right up there." He pointed to the Stars and Stripes fluttering in the breeze. "It's going to be one of those states. We have the greatest future in North America. We have untold wealth in this territory. Not just gold, friends. Natural resources none of us have even dreamed of yet.

"We need men in Washington who will speak for us," Smith continued. "Men of vision. Men of courage. Men who believe in Alaska and its future. Men who have the guts to take the politicians by the collar and shake them until they goddamn well move themselves. Let's send those men to Washington. The future belongs to us."

He sat down, and the crowd threw their hats into the air and cheered. Smith reached for Tara's hand and pressed it hard He reveled in the ovation the crowd was giving him, and he didn't have that hidden look she had seen before when he had manipulated people. There was nothing mocking in his expression. Tara felt certain that he had meant every word he had said.

"Great speech, Captain Smith," Brady broke in uneasily. His nervous laugh was growing increasingly aggravating to Tara. "The Party needs men like you."

"You think so, Governor?" Smith drawled. "Maybe we ought to talk about it sometime."

The end of the parade was only the beginning of the celebrations. Liquor flowed; there was singing and cheering.

The noise and excitement became too much for young John. He began to cry and Tara decided it was time to take him home. She sought out Lydia, handed her the baby, then excused herself to Brady, who looked unhappy and dour. He stood alone, whereas Smith was surrounded by well-wishers congratulating him on his patriotism. How right Smith had been, she thought wryly, when he had said people had short memories. Everybody was in a good mood, except for Brady and one other stranger who stood amid the throng, scowling. Tara saw him turn his back on Smith, then go over to the Governor and say something to him. When he had finished, Brady glanced at the man sharply. A complacent smile began to spread across his face, and he walked off with the man, his arm around his shoulder, while the other spoke confidentially into the Governor's ear.

She managed to force her way through to Smith's side. He put his hand about her waist and held her close while he talked with the crowd around him.

"Jeff," Tara said, tugging his sleeve to attract his attention. "I'll see you later. I'm going back to get changed."

"I'll send the carriage for you, so be ready when it arrives." She started to move off but Smith caught her hand. "And thank you, Tara," he added. "Thank you, my dear, for everything. You don't know how much you've helped me."

Smith did not explain further. Once again, he was hemmed in by people congratulating him.

Tara was not a woman given to nerves, but as she sat waiting for the carriage to arrive the butterflies fluttering around in her stomach made her feel distinctly unwell.

She got up from the chair on the porch and for the umpteenth time paced the short length of the cabin. She had begun her preparations for the ball as soon as she had returned from the parade. She had soaked her body in a cool bath for ages, hoping that the scented water would soothe the excited apprehension that had been building all day.

Her hair had been difficult to arrange because she had been all fingers and thumbs. By the time she got around to stepping into the black taffeta gown, she was positively fretful and would have burst into tears if Lydia had not intervened and helped her dress.

Now she looked out across the rutted street in front of the cabin,

377

her hands clammy, twisting Daniel's wedding ring on her finger. "You're being ridiculous, Tara," she admonished herself. "You're behaving like a child about to go to her first party."

She wondered how Daniel would react if he could see her now, dressed in a gown bought by another man, waiting for his carriage to take her to his ball. She couldn't help questioning whether her apprehension was due to the fact that she might be doing wrong or if it was more at the thought of showing so much cleavage in front of so many people.

Suddenly, she felt weary, so drowsy that she longed to close her eyes. The taffeta rustled like a musical accompaniment as she stretched out her legs and fell asleep.

She was not aware of the carriage drawing up, nor did she hear Bowers, whom Smith had sent to escort her, calling her name. When she awakened, he was standing over her, his eyes taking in her décolletage, and the smile he gave her suggested somewhat irreligious thoughts.

"My goodness," gasped Tara, flustered at his unexpected appearance and embarrassed by the familiarity of his eyes. "How long have you been waiting?"

"Just arrived," grinned Bowers. He was in full regimental regalia but sporting a dog collar. "Are you ready?"

"I will be in a minute."

She got up, went into the cabin, dabbed on more perfume, pinched her cheeks and licked her lips. The butterflies had taken over again. She picked up the embroidered shawl that she had wrapped John in for the parade, hastily kissed the baby on the forehead, and rushed out to the carriage.

All the way to the Princess Hotel people were celebrating. There was dancing in the streets to the discordant sounds of pianos, accordions, fiddles, bands, and raucous singing blaring out of each saloon.

"Later there's going to be fireworks," Bowers told her as the carriage jogged on. "We'll be able to see 'em clearly from the hotel."

"I hope they won't be too intoxicated to enjoy them," remarked Tara, nodding at a group of drunks who marched along, six abreast, singing patriotic songs, punctuated by intermittent shouts of "Remember the Maine!"

"Oh, they'll have sobered up and be drunk twice over by then," Bowers said.

Smith's Independence Day Ball was the nearest thing to a society event Skagway had ever seen. The Princess Hotel was ablaze with light. As the carriage drew up outside, Tara thought of the last time she had been there. How staid and hostile it had seemed that morning when she had had coffee with Tancrede in his room all those weeks ago. Tonight it seemed gay; the strains of an orchestra playing drifted out of large French windows; people were coming and going, talking, laughing.

Bowers held her hand as they mounted the steps to the entrance hall. Tara was well aware of the glances people gave her. Defiantly she held her head higher. As Bowers opened the main door, she swallowed, then smiled brilliantly as she swept into the hallway, saying to herself, "Let them stare. I'm going to enjoy every minute of this, and I don't give a damn what anyone thinks of me. At least, not tonight."

Bowers led the way to the ballroom. It was an enormous room, where hundreds of candles reflected in the crystal pendants of a dozen chandeliers. Across an expanse of parquet flooring, a small orchestra was playing. Tara was dazzled by the splendor of it all. Already hundreds of guests were milling around drinking champagne. Tara was too enchanted to notice Smith approaching, becoming aware of his presence only as he gently removed her shawl.

"My dear Tara," Smith said, kissing her hand. "You look stunning." He sighed. "I'm indeed a lucky son of a gun having the most beautiful woman in Alaska for my partner."

Tara laughed delightedly. She wanted to hear it.

"It's magical. It's going to be a wonderful evening, I can feel it," she said, her eyes dancing with excitement. "Why, I practically feel drunk already, isn't that strange?"

"Without even a drop of champagne," Smith laughed. "Now you're what I call a really good guest." He beckoned to a hovering waiter bearing a silver salver covered with glasses of champagne.

Smith raised his glass. "To the loveliest woman in the world and the belle of my ball," he toasted, and they both drank.

"Come," he went on, handing their glasses to Bowers. "It's time for us to start the dancing." He held out his arm and led her onto the floor. The other guests parted to let them through, staring after them.

The orchestra broke into a lively Strauss waltz as Smith bowed to Tara. He was an admirable partner and surprisingly light on his feet. Tara, who adored dancing, allowed herself to be swept around the floor. She felt exuberant, euphoric, marvelous. She was enjoying every minute, relishing the sheer delight of something so entirely different from anything she had been through before in the Yukon.

Gradually, other couples joined in so that the floor became a mass of whirling color.

379

"What does it feel like," he asked as he turned her this way and that, "to be the center of attention, to have every man in the room desire you and every woman envy you?"

"You're talking nonsense, Jeff," Tara said. But she was pleased.

She gazed at his face and wondered if it was the heady atmosphere that made her see laugh lines and humor where once she had seen only arrogance and mockery.

"Enjoying yourself?" he asked.

Tara nodded.

"I have never seen you look happier or more beautiful," he whispered.

The waltz stopped, and he led her over to a big table at one side of the room where bottles of champagne rested in ice buckets and glasses sparkled on the snowy white tablecloth. Even the waiters behind the bar looked elegant.

Smith handed her a glass. "Another toast," he said, holding up his, "to us."

Governor Brady came over to them. "A wonderful evening, Captain Smith," he said, "I must congratulate you. A splendid affair. Far cry from the blizzards and wolf packs, eh?"

"I'm glad you're enjoying yourself, Governor," Smith said.

"Haven't seen a spittoon all evening," joked Brady, laughing heartily at his own wit. "Soon we won't know Skagway, will we?"

He put down his empty champagne glass, then leaned over to Tara. "May I request the pleasure of the next dance, Mrs. Kane?"

Of course," Tara agreed, handing Smith her glass.

"You've made a friend for life, Captain Smith," said Brady grandly, nodding at Tara.

"It will be my pleasure," Tara murmured, and, as the band struck up, he led her onto the floor. Smith bowed slightly, and Tara caught his look, a poker player's glance.

"A remarkable man, Captain Smith," Brady said, taking hold of Tara's hand. He was heavy-footed and clumsy, and Tara hoped it would be a short dance. "Quite remarkable."

"Yes, he is," Tara agreed.

"Have you known him long?"

"As long as I've been in the Territory," she replied.

Tara realized that it was not the pleasure of her company that Brady wanted. Smith made him nervous, and he wanted to find out more about him.

"We hear he's a very successful businessman," went on Brady. "A pillar of commerce."

"I believe so," Tara said shortly.

They danced in silence for a while. Then Brady suddenly asked, "How did you two meet?"

"We had a business transaction."

He was obviously keen to know more. "And now you're settled in Skagway?" he enquired.

"I'm returning to California soon," she said.

Brady looked interested. "I didn't know Captain Smith was departing from these parts," he said. The thought seemed to please him.

"You misunderstand, Governor," Tara said. "I'm leaving. I have no idea what Mr. Smith's plans are."

She could see he did not know quite what to make of that, but the music stopped and they stood politely applauding the orchestra.

"That was delightful, Mrs. Kane," said Brady. "Dare I hope that you can spare me another one?"

"Governor," Tara replied with a charming smile, "we are all allowed to live in hope. Would you excuse me please?"

She walked back to Smith, who had been standing watching them with an amused air.

"Don't tell me," he said, as they sat down. "First he asked you how we'd met and then what your plans are."

"Not in that order."

"Did he sort of suggest that you're wasted in a hole like Skagway, that a Governor from Oregon can go places, and why don't you and he . . ."

"Of course he didn't, Jeff," giggled Tara.

"He will," Smith assured her. "Give him another whirl and he will, I promise you."

"Do you know what he called you?" Tara asked mischievously. "A pillar of commerce."

"Well, isn't that what I am?"

"I think you're an absolute rogue and the biggest scoundrel I've ever met," she smiled. Then she grew more serious. "Jeff, that speech you gave this afternoon. Did you mean what you said? You've really been thinking it over?"

Smith inclined his head.

"Remember our deal? I've kept my side of the bargain," she continued. "I sat on the saluting platform and here I am now, your partner for the evening."

"Just for this evening, Tara?"

"Jeff, please be serious. Tell me what you're planning."

381

"Later," Smith smiled. "Right now is neither the time nor the place. We're here to enjoy ourselves, so let's just do that for the moment."

The band started up again, this time playing a polka. Tara watched all the people milling around, wondering what was making her feel so happy, so carefree. Was it just the champagne?

He poured her another glass.

"If you're trying to get me drunk," Tara said.

"I wouldn't dream of doing such a thing," he protested.

"I don't believe you, Jeff Smith. I think that's exactly what you're trying to do." She picked up her glass. "To a wonderful evening."

"How about some supper?" Smith suggested, getting up and pulling back her chair.

"Marvelous. Why, I'm as hungry as a horse."

Smith had not stinted his guests. There were salvers of canapes, whole poached salmons attractively decorated in aspic, bowls of potato salad, dishes of thinly sliced cucumber, large plates of cold poultry and meat, tureens of vegetables, trays of cheeses, and a marvelously exotic collection of desserts. They returned to their table, their plates piled high.

As Smith was about to sit down a man approached. Tara recognized him immediately.

He was middle-aged, his face weather-beaten, his eyes crafty. The last time she had seen him had been that very afternoon, when he had buttonholed the Governor after the parade.

"Must have cost you a pretty penny or two," the man remarked coldly, nodding at the dance floor, "but it won't buy us, not any of us."

"I don't recall inviting you, Reid," observed Smith coolly. He turned to Tara. "My dear, my apologies. This gentleman is Frank Reid. He likes to think of himself as the city engineer."

Reid nodded at Tara curtly.

"Tell me," Smith drawled, "Where's Tanner? Where's Sperry? Don't see your friends around." He turned to Tara again. "You wouldn't know Mr. Reid's friends, my dear, but they keep themselves busy."

"They wouldn't come near one of your functions. They don't like bad smells." Reid glanced in Tara's direction. "Begging your pardon, ma'am."

Tara was uncomfortable. Reid was spoiling everything. He clearly didn't give a damn how much he insulted his host or whether he did so in front of a guest.

382

"If you just dropped in to jeer, Reid, why bother to stay?" Smith asked icily.

"I just wanted to warn you, Smith." Reid bent closer as if he didn't want anyone else to hear, "You're finished."

Smith regarded him, smiling thinly.

"You're not going to shoot down people again, I promise you. You're not getting away with anything any more. We've had enough."

"I think I have, too," Smith's eyes were like hard, cold diamonds. "If you want to talk business, any time, you know where to find me." His voice grew hard. "Right now you're boring me."

For a moment they stood poised, neither giving an inch. Reid was the one to break the tension.

"All right, Smith, you know the score. I've said my piece so you know what to expect. My respects, ma'am." He nodded at Tara and walked off, Smith looking after him for a while.

Tara sighed in relief. "What an awful man," she said, when Smith at last sat down.

"The dregs," Smith said.

"I didn't like the look of him when I saw him earlier this afternoon."

Smith didn't speak, he just toyed with his food.

"He looked so sour when all those people were congratulating you. He rather frightened me. Then he went up to Governor Brady and said something, and they went off together."

Smith glanced up at her. "Reid's a double-dealer, Tara. I found that out a long while ago. Sell his own grandmother down the river, and he would have sold me too if I'd given him the chance."

"You've known him for a while, then?"

"We used to be partners."

Tara was amazed. "What happened?" she asked.

Smith shrugged. "It's an ancient and boring story and one hardly worth repeating. Let's just say he and I no longer get on. Anyway, I don't intend for that sour bastard to louse up my evening. Eat up and then we'll dance some more."

For some time they ate in silence, Smith deep in thought. Reid's appearance had brought Tara down to earth. Had all the magic been a dream, she wondered as she forced down a mouthful of food? The veneer of Skagway's attempt to emulate fashionable society was beginning to wear thin. Everyone was getting a little louder, a little brasher. Neckties were hanging looser; one or two guests were starting to sway on their feet. A few sat slumped, glassy-eyed. Somebody stumbled and several glasses crashed to the floor. Elegant dancing was

383

being replaced by thumping feet. Genteel courtesies were disappearing. Some of the men had taken off their jackets; hair was getting ruffled; voices sounded more raucous, the orchestra weary.

It was as if Smith had the same impresssion. "Come," he said, getting up. "There's something I want to show you."

Together they walked out, past the potted plants and intoxicated guests. The Governor was standing near the door, deep in conversation with Reid. Both looked at Smith and Tara as they passed.

They walked across the lobby, Smith holding Tara's arm, the pressure on it gentle, almost relaxed, as they headed toward the staircase. "This way," he said. They mounted the steps, laid with the red carpet that was the hotel's pride.

"Where are we going?" Tara asked when they reached the top.

"I told you, I want to show you something."

"But what about the rest of your guests?" Tara asked. "They'll miss you."

Smith shrugged. "They're getting too drunk to even notice I'm not there. Anyway, I've had enough of 'em. They only came for the free food, and booze, and they've plenty of that. If they need anything, Bowers'll take care of it. Look at them," he went on, leaning over the balustrade. "Do you mind being with me instead of them?"

She stood beside him and looked down on the lobby below. For a while they watched in silence the people drifting about. Although they were only one floor higher it was as if they were on a different planet, moving apart, gradually. The noise still drifted up from the ballroom but now it had become remote.

Tara shook her head, and Smith took her hand as he led her down the corridor. She was very conscious of his touch and, despite herself, she wanted to be drawn along with him. "Where are you taking me, Jeff?" she asked.

He stopped in front of a door. "We're here," he announced.

He let go her hand, took a key out of his pocket, and unlocked the door.

"Jeff," began Tara, then hesitated.

Smith stood to one side, giving her the opportunity of returning to the ballroom. It was an astute move. If he had tightened his hold on her arm, she might have walked away. As it was, she was free to do what she wanted. It was her choice; she could either stay or leave.

He opened the door and Tara found herself in a dimly lit, plush sitting room. Candles, already lit, provided the only illumination. The carpet was thick beneath her feet. There was a large sofa upholstered in red velvet, the walls with fabric. It was very similar to the suite Tancrede had occupied.

Tara looked around. "Whose is this?"

"It comes with the ballroom," he said. "I had a suite thrown in."

She stood, uncertain. At the end of the room were large double doors.

Smith was smiling slightly. "That's the bedroom," he said and, without another word, he walked over and locked the double doors. He came back to her and held out the key. "Here," he said.

She stared at him.

"Take it. Relax. It's locked. There's the key, the only key. Satisfied?"

She felt very foolish. "Oh, don't be silly," she stammered, blushing furiously, but he shook his head.

"No, I don't want you to keep looking out of the corner of your eye at that door, wondering what's going to happen next. So have it."

"Jeff, you—" He stepped forward impatiently and thrust the small key down the front of her décolletage. The suddenness of his movement made her gasp. She felt his hand momentarily before he quickly withdrew it, leaving the cold key nestling between her breasts.

"Now sit down, take your shoes off, and relax," he ordered, going over to a cabinet.

As soon as his back was turned, she fumbled for the key, pulled it out, and stuffed it down the side of the sofa. Then she sat down, her posture the height of prim propriety.

"Try this for size," he invited, returning with two balloon brandy glasses. His teeth flashed when he saw the tense way she was sitting. "Jesus, Tara, it was only your shoes I said to take off."

There was an explosion of light outside the window, followed by the sound of people cheering. "It's the fireworks," Smith said, handing her a glass.

"Come on, we must watch them," insisted Tara, getting up and going over to the French windows which overlooked Broadway.

Down in the street Smith's militia were handing out sparklers, while overhead roman candles, rockets, catherine wheels zoomed and rained a web of shooting color in the twilight.

"Oh they're beautiful," sighed Tara as she watched, enchanted by a thousand stars exploding in the sky. "They remind me of the Northern Lights." She turned to Smith, who stood beside her. "Did I ever tell you how wonderful they were, Jeff? How they saved me? It was like some kind of miracle, a sign from heaven to guide me back to Dawson. Too beautiful to be forgotten," she added wistfully.

They watched the firework display for some time, until over-enthusiastic drunks in the street below began setting off firecrackers. The noise of people squealing, yelling, and laughing made them close the window.

Smith pulled the heavy drapes and Tara returned to the sofa, kicked her shoes off, and sat down, swinging her legs up. She looked very attractive stretched out, the sheer blackness of the gown setting off the whiteness of her shoulders, the dark fieriness of her hair, her slim fingers curled around the stem of the large glass. She sipped the brandy.

"What was it that you wanted me to see, Jeff?" she asked after a while.

He took off his jacket, sat down in the chair opposite her, and drank some brandy. "You know, they teach kids the wrong things about history," he mused, apparently ignoring her question. "Now you take Napoleon. Never mind about Waterloo. Any fellow can start wars and win battles. But this brandy . . . Now that's why he's immortal."

"Jeff," said Tara. She was watching his every move. His lazy, casual relaxation was studied, she felt. "You haven't answered my question."

"It's a little gift I've got for you."

Her green eyes were unwavering. She didn't want him to break the spell, to spoil the peace and tranquility she felt there and then.

He came over and sat on the sofa. "It's something that's yours by right, Tara. You can't turn it down." He took her hand and turned it over. He dropped a wedding ring into her palm. Her wedding ring.

She gazed down at the little band of gold resting in the palm of her hand. She read the inscription: "Daniel to Tara."

"Put it on," Smith said, "next to that one."

She looked at him, her expression a mixture of confusion and happiness. Then, slowly, she slipped the ring onto the fourth finger of her left hand. It did not slide on easily; she had to force it over the knuckle.

"Thank you, Jeff." Tara's eyes were misty. "Thank you so very much."

He had given her only what was hers, but it was the greatest gesture he could have made. She was flooded with an affection for him. She looked down at her left hand, the wedding ring back where it belonged. Now she had both of them. At last, at last, it felt right.

The warmth of the brandy on top of the champagne, the return of her wedding ring, gave Tara an inward glow. Smith had not moved closer, but his voice, his eyes as he watched her, were holding her like an embrace.

"Maybe you should ask why?" he suggested quietly.

"That doesn't matter," Tara said softly. She looked at her hand. "I've got it back, that's all that matters. What it means to me, what it represents, those are important."

Smith's eyes never left her face. "Funny thing is, I'd say a fellow who loves a woman is crazy to give her another man's wedding ring."

She glanced up at him sharply and was about to speak, but he put a finger gently on her lips.

"No, let me say it. I got to thinking about the way things are between us, and there's only one route for you and me, Tara. I want to put my cards on the table, the whole darn pack; no joker."

Tara said nothing.

"No good holding back things," he went on, putting his hand over hers. "No good trying to make you do things you don't want. And that's how I like it. That's what makes you special. Now take that little band of gold." He lifted her left hand and looked at the ring back in its rightful place. "I started figuring why was I holding onto it. To kid myself it didn't exist? To con myself there wasn't anybody else? One thing a good gambler mustn't do, he mustn't kid himself. I reckoned I was acting like somebody plumb scared of a ghost." He touched the ring. "*That* ghost. Because your husband is a ghost, Tara. Daniel's dead."

"Don't," whispered Tara, trying to pull her hand away. "Don't ever say that. He's not, he's not, he's . . ."

Her voice drifted away.

"He's dead," Smith repeated insistently. "You know it, and it's best you accept it."

"I love him," she said, choking back her tears. She looked at Smith pleadingly. "Please, Jeff."

"You can't live with a ghost," he went on, gazing into her brimming eyes. "You're flesh and blood. You can't sleep with a dream. He's dead, and you've got to come to terms with that fact, Tara."

She started to protest but Smith went on, his voice strangely soothing. "Dear God, you've been looking, searching for him for months. How long can you go on denying the truth? How long can you go on living a fantasy? How long before your heart can accept what your head already knows?"

"I love my husband," whispered Tara.

387

"He's dead," he repeated. "Dead, dead, dead."

For a moment she sat speechless, large tears coursing down her cheeks. He drew her to him, and she laid her head on his shoulder, her body trembling.

"Tara," said Smith, stroking her hair. "I want you to marry me."

He felt her tense against him. "Please don't," she mumbled, her voice muffled against his shirt, now damp from her tears.

"I love you, Tara," he persisted. "I want you to be my wife. I know you love me too."

"I'm married, Jeff," she sobbed. "No matter what you think, it can never be proved otherwise."

"Running away again, Tara?" he asked softly. "You can't go on running forever, my dear."

"I'm not running away, Jeff," she sniffed, searching for a handkerchief. Smith handed her his.

"He really is dead, Tara. You must believe me."

"Even if he is," she said, "even then I wouldn't marry you. Not even if I had his, his death certificate to prove it."

"His memory too sacred?" he asked, slightly impatiently.

"No, Jeff," she said slowly. "You asked me if I love you. Well, I don't." There was a fleeting look of pain in his eyes. "I'm sorry but you made me say it."

"I think you're lying, Tara," Smith countered. "In fact I know you are. If you didn't love me, feel something for me, then you would never have been as you are this evening. You couldn't have looked so happy, so beautiful, so in love."

"Jeff, I don't love you, I don't love you." But she could not meet his eyes. ". . . not yet, anyway," she added, lowering her head.

"Because you won't let yourself, Tara. You want to run away from me because you're scared of recognizing the truth. That's why you hang on to your fantasy. Daniel's just a convenient excuse. Your not facing the reality of his death means you're safe, because he'll always be there to fall back on, even though he's only a memory. You know you and I fit. We belong. People can love and be poison to one another but we're, we're different. You're looking fo a future, I'm building toward one. Let s join forces and io it together. For one another—for John."

"Jeff, I'm taking John back to San Francisco. Yɔ ı know I've made up my mind. Nothing will ever change that decision.'

"I'm not trying to alter that decision, Tara," Smith reasoned. "I only want what you want, and I'm laying odds it's the same as I want."

"How can it be?" she demanded.

"Because I want to come back to Frisco with you and John. We'll get married here first, and then we'll go back, the three of us, together. It'll be Mr. and Mrs. Jefferson Smith and Master Smith who'll be sailing in that stateroom."

"But what about Skagway? Alaska? Statehood? All the plans you've made?"

"They don't matter, Tara. Only you and I do."

"You'd give up everything?" she asked incredulously.

"That's how much I love you. Without you there is no future. Leastways no future that I want to live. Sure I'd get on with life, I'd probably manage OK. I'm not going to force you into accepting me. I'm not holding a gun to your head. If you say 'no' I'll stay here, but I'll go about things my way. I might land up a rather bitter man, but I'll run this territory, I'll own it. But if you agree to marry me it'll be different. I'd feel a complete man because I respect you, I listen to you, you're what you once said you wanted to be, my mentor. With you I think right, I act right, I do right."

He pulled her closer. "Why the hell do I love you so much? God knows. Maybe because you're the one woman I ever met who . . ." He paused. "Well, anyway I love you and that's for sure, and I know you and I—well, like I said, we belong. That's why it's up to you. Nobody's going to make you do anything you don't want. . . ."

He took her hand.

"Sure, there was somebody around before I came along, and that's his ring. I'm not trying to kid you, I know what his memory means to you." He was deadly serious. "I'm not trying to replace him either, Tara. I want you to marry me in my own right. I don't want you to take pity on me or look on me as some kind of substitute. You see the crazy thing is that the one reason I gave you back your wedding ring is because I love you."

He said it almost as if he were trying to explain it to himself.

"It is crazy. The way a man usually shows a woman that he want.· her is to kiss her, show her how he feels about her. Not sit talking. That's what a man does to any woman he wants to have," he said unexpectedly. "And then he has her. I can do that with any woman I want."

"Can you?" whispered Tara.

"That's what I've done with every woman I've ever wanted. Except you. You're different." He studied her. "You look so beautiful, Tara." And she did. Her face was tear-stained, her hair awry, but her eyes betrayed her passion for Smith, and there was nothing she could do to hide it.

"Why not me?"

"Because with you . . ."

Then he kissed her and she clung to him. They lingered together, closely, not speaking, for there was nothing to say for a long while. Slowly, he removed the pins from her hair. One by one each deep auburn curl cascaded to her shoulders. She gazed into his clear gray eyes, and they told her that he was going to make love to her, and she knew she wanted him to. He kissed her lips, and she put her arms around him and leaned back against the sofa. She lay in his embrace and their mouths met. Tara closed her eyes, not protesting as he unhooked her gown, as he undid her bodice, or when his fingertips gently traced the contours of her naked breasts. She kissed him, pressing her body against his, feeling the warmth of his bare back beneath her hands, her fingers, her wedding ring.

Smith loved her, and he proved it by the way he made love to her. As they lay on the sofa in the dim light, for both of them it was the fulfillment of something they had wanted. They sought one another's mouths, their lips pressing together, their tongues meeting, his hands on her body, hers stroking his. Tara wondered if she had ever been so desired, if a man had ever wanted her so much and proved it so beautifully.

They lay in one another's arms, not speaking, after the passion had faded. She knew that later she would feel guilty, but now she did not care. She was with him, and he held her and embraced her and cherished her with his body.

He smiled down at her and gently brushed away the tumbling hair from her face. "Tara," he whispered and kissed her again. "I love you. I love you so very much."

She looked up at him and smiled. She felt luxurious, sensuous, female. "I think I love you too, Jeff," she replied softly. "I really do." She stretched out so that their bodies made an elongated line, her face against his chest, their hips meeting, their arms intertwined. "I'm so happy, Jeff," she whispered, kissing his arm.

"I'm not going to ask you now," he said softly. "We've said all that we need to say tonight."

She was grateful to him for not insisting on an answer. Then she drifted into sleep.

She was awakened by Smith's lips on hers.

"Jeff," she murmured, "I must get home."

"Not yet, my dear. Please, not yet."

"I must. I must get back to John."

Smith did not argue further. She lay watching him as he got up and pulled the curtains so that the room was bathed with the early morning sun.

He went back to the sofa and knelt down beside her, curling a tress of her hair in his fingers, looking deep into her eyes. "Stay a little longer," he urged quietly, bending over and kissing her once more. "Don't leave me yet, Tara."

"I won't, not yet," she whispered, running her fingers down his face, along his shoulder, his arm, taking his hand and kissing it, then putting it to her cheek.

Afterward, they walked back to the cabin in silence, Smith holding Tara close to him all the way. The town was still asleep; they met no one. Broadway was littered with the aftermath of the night's celebrations, the bunting waving lazily in a light breeze. There were the occasional sounds of dogs barking and seagulls mewing around the harbor.

They passed the saluting platform, Tara hardly able to believe that this time yesterday the parade had not yet begun, that this time yesterday what had passed she had not even imagined lay ahead. She looked into Smith's eyes as he gazed down at her. Do I love you, she asked herself, or is it that you've made me think I do?

Outside the cabin he stopped.

"Tara," said Smith, taking her hands, "don't tell me what you've decided now. Take a few days. Spend the time with John and think over my proposal."

He bent down and kissed her lightly on the lips.

"And always remember, my dear, no matter what your answer is, I'll understand. There'll be no recriminations, no argument, no harassment. Whatever you say goes. I just pray, oh God how I pray that you'll say yes."

Then he walked off, Tara watching him go, a part of her wanting to run after him. But she remained where she was and, true to character, Smith never once looked back.

CHAPTER TWENTY-EIGHT

Tara knew that in spite of everything she could not marry Smith. She loved him. She had let him make love to her. She had rejoiced in the way he had made her feel a vibrant, sensual woman, reciprocating his desire with passion. She trusted him, too. Over the past few months he had been generous, kind-hearted, and honest with her. She had grown to enjoy his companionship, his style; his humor was infectious.

She also knew what she owed to him. He had mocked and humiliated her in the past, but without him she would never have survived. Even the gun that had saved her life had been his thought. And she had learned the most important thing from him, almost unwillingly. If the Mounties had taught her the practicalities of survival, from Smith she had picked up self-confidence, coolness. He had given her something very important, a belief in herself and her own capabilities.

Yet she could not marry him. What would happen if, one day, Daniel did return? If she were married to Smith that would make her a bigamist, a woman who, without proof, had lost faith in her husband and married another man. That was unthinkable.

She and John would have to leave for home very soon. It was the right course. It was the only course.

As she made her way along Broadway, she rehearsed how she would say it. She told herself over and over again that there was no reason to be nervous about being honest with Smith. After all, that's what he had asked her to be. Cards on the table, he had said, and she had agreed with him. No recriminations, no arguments, he had promised.

But with each step her apprehension grew. As she reached the alley that led to the Oyster Parlor, her heart was pounding so violently that she felt faint. She took a deep breath and willed herself to go on. She was just about to open the door when Mort, Bowers, and the deadly Yeah Mow rushed out, nearly sending her flying.

"Sorry," apologized Bowers, steadying Tara. "We got trouble." Without further explanation he ran off with the others toward Broadway. Tara looked after them, only then realizing that they had all been wearing guns. She had never seen them in such a hurry; Bowers had even forgotten his clerical dignity.

Tara ran into the Oyster Parlor.

"What's going on?" she asked the bartender, who was standing uncertainly by the door.

"The boss." He appeared to be listening for something.

"What about him?" Tara demanded 'mpatiently. "Isn't he upstairs?"

Joe shook his head. "There's some trouble," he said. "He went out."

"What sort of trouble?" Tara pressed.

He shrugged. "Something at the docks," he said. "Reid called hi.n out."

"I'll be back," Tara said.

She started half walking, half running tov ard the waterfront.

She passed Guido, the crippled Italian shoeblack. He had come out to the Klondike to make his fortune, but his legs had been crushed by a rock fall before he had even washed out a pan of gravel. Now he lived off the quarters people paid when he polished their boots. Smith always gave him a silver dollar for a shoeshine, and Guido never forgot it.

"He went that way," he called to Tara, pointing. "Armed with many guns."

A terrible fear swept through her. It was not Smith's style to display a gun openly.

As she rushed on, two men raced past her going in the same direction. Outside Kalem's, the outfitters, they yelled at the old proprietor, "Hurry up. They're after Smith."

Tara quickened her pace. Ahead of her, she saw a rapidly growing crowd gathering by a warehouse.

Tara pushed through the throng. Some of Smith's gang stood blocking the sidewalk, staring at the crowd, their hands hovering near their guns. Beyond them were two men.

As she squeezed her way to the front, Tara saw Yeah Mow give an imperceptible nod. Two other gunman stepped aside and let her slip through. She stopped dead in her tracks, her heart racing, her breath coming in short, rasping gasps. All around everyone was silent.

Jefferson Smith and Frank Reid stood poised. Smith was holding a Winchester rifle like an elongated handgun, the barrel pointing at Reid, his finger lightly resting on the trigger. Reid stood a few feet away. He wore a gun belt, and the butt of his pistol was outside the flap of his jacket. His arm hung limp, his hand loose, his fingers twitching near the gun butt.

"Jeff! Don't! Don't!" Tara cried out. Smith's hooded eyes remained fixed on Reid.

The crowd started pressing closer. Then she heard Mort warn them, "First man to move gets daylight in him."

Reid, erect, eyes unwavering, took a step toward Smith.

"It's the end of the road, Soapy," he shouted. "We've had enough of you and your men. You've done it once too often. I know what you've got planned for this town, you bastard."

"Why don't you get lost, Reid," drawled Smith. "None of chis is any of your cotton-pickin' business."

Slowly, purposefully, Reid took another step forward. "You got twelve hours to leave, Smith," he snarled, "you and your rat pack. Get out of Skagway, get out of the Territory."

Smith laughed.

"And take your cardsharps and your fancy women with you," spat Reid.

Tara felt her stomach tighten.

"You got a lot of nerve all of a sudden, Frank," goaded Smith. "Found your guts at last?"

Reid, white-faced, spat at Smith's feet.

"Damn you, Reid," Smith bellowed, "you're a walking cess pit. I should have shot you down when I first smelled you."

The rifle was absolutely steady. Reid and Smith were only a foot or two apart, their eyes locked. Then, quite deliberately, Reid grabbed the barrel of Smith's rifle with his left hand, and tried to force it down. In his right hand he held his sixgun.

"You goddamn fool, don't make me kill you," warned Smith, ignoring the gun just inches away from his chest.

Horror-stricken, Tara saw Reid's finger tighten on his trigger. Then the hammer clicked, the chamber spun, but there was no shot. The bullet was a dud.

"Sorry about that," Smith drawled, his eyes not blinking. He jerked up the barrel of his rifle and fired in one movement.

Reid rocked, his face a grimace of agony. Blood was already spreading across his stomach. He was swaying, but he still held the sixgun. He raised it and pulled the trigger once more, before he collapsed. Glass tinkled as the bullet shattered a windowpane behind Smith.

Smith stood looking down at Reid. His face was expressionless. He was about to turn when a voice called, out, "Smith!"

From the crowd, his back to Tara, stepped a man.

"What do you want, mister?" Smith cried, facing him.

"You . . ." the man said in a low voice. He wore a gunbelt, and his right hand hovered over the holster.

Smith nodded. "That figures."

Out of the corner of her eye, Tara saw Mort move forward, but Smith waved him back.

"Anybody interferes, and they're dead," called out Smith. "This is between me and him."

Tara stared at Smith's face. She wanted to cry out to him, but her voice just croaked.

The gunman went for his .45 just as Smith raised his Winchester again.

But the gunman fired first.

Smith staggered but managed to pull his trigger. The gunman reared like a stricken creature, then fell, face downward.

Smith dropped the Winchester and slowly sank to his knees. The gunman's bullet had gone through his chest.

Tara screamed and ran forward, the crowd jostling behind her, pressing closer. She had no eyes for Tancrede, the railroad boss, standing to one side, like a privileged spectator who had been specially invited. All she wanted was to be near Smith. She dashed over to where he lay, three feet from Reid, who rested in his own pool of blood. Nobody bothered about the dead gunman.

"Jeff! Jeff!" she sobbed as she knelt down beside him. Smith groaned, his eyes shut; there was blood everywhere. Then Tara felt herself roughly pushed aside and Bowers and Mort were bending over him. Yeah Mow faced the mob of spectators, a gun in his hand, his lips drawn back in a snarl.

"Don't anyone move. Keep back," he ordered. "Go near him, and you're pig fodder."

Bowers and Mort picked Smith up and started carrying him through the murmuring crowd. As they walked, his head lolled and his arms hung limply. Above the blackness of his vest a red stain was growing.

Tara caught up with them and seized Smith's clammy, freezing hand. All around them rumors were spreading: "Smith's dead." "Soapy's been shot." "Smith's finished." The mob were jostling one another to get a good glimpse of his pale, drawn face as he was carried past. He was still breathing but very shallowly.

"You've got to live, you've got to live," Tara muttered as they headed down State Street, unaware of how much she wanted him to survive.

She never let go his hand during that terrible journey through the strangely still streets to the Oyster Parlor. All the way they were escorted by Yeah Mow and others from Smith's militia. They surrounded the grim procession, their guns drawn or rifles resting in the crooks of their arms, eyes raking the gaping bystanders, daring them to come forward. Tara saw none of them, not even Cahill and Wilkins, hovering nearby.

Somebody had already summoned a doctor, and by the time they arrived he was standing by the bar with his little black bag.

Gently, Mort and Bowers carried Smith upstairs and put him on the couch in his office. The doctor bent over him and Tara looked on anxiously as he cut away Smith's bloodstained vest and shirt.

The stalwarts crowded around, Bowers, Mort, Yeah Mow, and other men whose faces Tara knew but whose names she had never learned.

"He's alive," announced the doctor, straightening up.

"Thank God," breathed Tara.

"But he hasn't got long."

"Can't you get the bullet out?" Bowers asked.

"No point," replied the doctor, snapping shut his Gladstone bag. Then he noticed Tara's ashen face and added, a little more kindly, "Nothing I can do. He's shot to hell."

He left, and somebody covered Smith with a blanket. Then they all stood around, uncertain, gazing down at Smith as if they expected him to take charge again and issue orders.

Tara gradually became aware of a droning noise like a swarm of angry bees closing in. There was the sound of crashing glass downstairs. Almost immediatedly the door flew open and Joe the bartender burst in.

"We got to get out," he yelled. "There's a mob down there. They're after us."

"Shut up," Bowers commanded.

"Jesus, man, don't you understand? The whole town's going wild. They've heard the boss is dead. They're grabbing guns and looking for us. We've got to get out before they string us all up."

"Well, he ain't dead," Mort said. "You tell the bastards that. He's going to be alive and kicking, and if there's any hanging to be done, you know who'll do it."

"You go out and tell 'em," ordered Bowers.

Yeah Mow, smiling thinly, checked the magazine of his gun.

"Come on," said Mort. "Let's go."

They all ran out, leaving Tara and Bowers alone with Smith. Bowers went over to the brandy and poured her a drink. Tara knelt down beside Smith, searching his drawn, white face for some flicker of life.

"Here," Bowers said, holding out a glass. "You need this."

Tara shook her head; then Smith spoke, "Hell, Tara, never turn down a good brandy."

His eyes were glazed but open, and he was looking at her. His face was the color of parchment, his voice hardly audible, but he managed to smile.

"What a dumb thing to do," he said and tried to shake his head but the effort caused him too much pain.

"Boss," cut in Bowers, going over to him. "Maybe we ought to get you out of here."

From the street they could still hear the crowd. It was an ugly sound, just like it had been in Dawson when the lynching party arrived outside Mrs. Miles's house. Then there were several shots, and the angry buzz faded. They were all still afraid of Smith's wrath.

"Charley," he muttered. "Just leave us."

Bowers hesitated. Tara looked up, her green eyes pleading to him.

"I'll be around," he said and went out, closing the door softly in his wake.

Smith smiled at her. "Sorry to have kept you waiting," he said, and for a moment she thought he was delirious. Then it all came back. "I thought I'd get that business finished quicker. What's the time?"

"There's all the time in the world," Tara said gently, stroking his damp forehead.

"Sure," he said. "And we've got lots to do haven't we, you and I. If . . ." He looked at her longingly. "You know what I want to know. You don't have to tell me if you don't want to. But it would be nice if you could."

His face contorted as a spasm of pain shot through him, but he gritted his teeth.

"I love you, Jeff," choked Tara, forcing back her tears. It was the truth.

"You'll marry me?" he whispered.

"Of course."

"You sure now?" he pressed.

"Would I say so if I didn't mean it?"

He sighed. There was a look of great relief on his face. "Well, Mrs. Smith," he said, "aren't you going to kiss the bridegroom?"

He was so weak he could not hold her, but his mouth sought hers urgently. She closed her eyes and pressed her lips to his.

When she lifted her head, his eyes remained shut. For one terrible moment she thought he had died, but then he coughed. It grieved Tara to see the terrible pain it caused him, and a thin trickle of blood meandered out of the corner of his mouth.

"I never wanted anything more in the world than you," he

murmured, slowly reopening his eyes. "Tara, why hasn't someone dug this slug out of me? What the hell are they waiting for?"

"The doctor will do it," she assured him.

"Damn sawbones should be here," he complained. "What happened to Mr. Public-Spirited Citizen?"

"You killed him, Jeff," said Tara. In truth she didn't know what had happened to Reid or the other gunman, and she didn't care.

"Good," he croaked. "I never should have bothered."

"Why did you?" she asked in a low voice.

"They called me out. No man does that to me. You wouldn't want a husband who . . ."

"Oh Jeff," moaned Tara, squeezing his hand tight.

He shivered. "You'll stick with me, won't you? Always?"

"Of course I will. I love you, Jeff. In your own right. I really do."

"Tara," he whispered. "Hold my hand."

Then she knew he was gradually losing all feeling in his limbs. She was grasping his hand tightly, and yet he didn't even know.

"There," she said, trying hard to smile.

"There's lots to do," he said with a surprising flash of energy. "We got to, we got to . . ."

But it was like a flickering candle.

"Little John," he said. The candle was slowly growing dimmer. "Our boy . . ."

"Our future, Jeff," Tara added.

He gazed at her wistfully. "Tara, you're so very beautiful," he whispered. "I love you. I . . . I want to . . ." he tried once more. "See you . . . only you . . ."

His face was still turned toward her, his eyes were on her, but they could no longer see.

Jefferson Smith was dead.

She bent down and held him to her for a long while. Then she kissed his cold, lifeless lips, her tears mixing with his blood. She sat up and gazed down at his body. There was a patch of blood on the blanket where she had pressed against the wound.

Gently she closed his unseeing eyes. "Goodbye, my dear," she whispered. "Goodbye dear, true friend."

In death, Smith's face was serene. There was even a smile somewhere.

The door opened quietly, and Bowers walked in. For a moment he stood silent, looking down at Smith's body.

"Guess he was right," he said at last. "He always said they'd never hang him." He coughed. "What are you going to do now?"

"I don't know," Tara replied dully.

"You'll have to get out of here. We all have to. They're full of courage, those worthy citizens, now he's gone. They'll string us all up if they get the chance. You too."

"Me?" she asked, dazed.

"You were his woman. Funny thing is the boss never talked about you. Except once." He looked at Smith's body again. "He said you were the only woman he'd ever respected, ever trusted." He shrugged. "And there was only one man he had ever envied in his whole life."

Tara had no need to ask who that was.

"Yes sir. That's what he said, and he made me promise that if anything ever happened to him, I'd make sure that you were OK. Now that's the last thing I can do for him."

He went over to the desk and helped himself to one of Smith's cheroots. "Right now you have to stay off the streets. Don't let 'em see you. I'll book passage for you to Frisco. You and the kid."

Tara nodded.

Bowers blew out a smoke ring. Tara winced. She found his behavior grotesque with Smith lying dead on the sofa.

"You'll come to the funeral?" he went on.

"Of course," she mumbled.

"We'll bury him quietly so that it doesn't attract too much attention. But he would have liked you to be there."

"Oh for God's sake, Reverend," she begged.

"I'll arrange it," he assured her. "You can leave it all to me."

Tara said nothing; she felt numb.

"They won't be looking for me," continued Bowers. "Being a man of the cloth, I'm safe. Somebody's looking after me. Guess it must be the devil."

Bowers insisted on escorting Tara home, taking her out through the secret exit. Downstairs, all the windows of the Oyster Parlor had been smashed. In the middle of Broadway, they were burning an effigy of Smith. These were the very people who had so willingly joined in Smith's Independence Day celebrations. They were the ones who had crowded around him after the parade, slapping him on the back, congratulating him, telling him he was their man.

Bowers grabbed her hand, guiding her through back streets and alleys to the cabin.

Gangs of Reid's followers were roaming the streets, brandishing copies of the *Skagway Intelligenger*, which had hastily published a special edition announcing what the whole town already knew, that the king was dead. Reid was still alive, but just. It was only a question of time before he died too. The dead gunman's identity was a mystery.

That night all hell was let loose as bloodthirsty, rampaging bands of citizens gathered for the kill. Smith's men fled for their lives, hiding in the woods and hills around Skagway, followed by murderous posses.

Toward midnight the Oyster Parlor was set on fire. In the cabin, bereft, Tara watched the glow in the sky, silhouetting the town's skyline.

The virtuous, law-abiding people had taken over Skagway. They called their drunkenness celebration, their cold-blooded brutality, retribution. The men who prided themselves that they were cleaning up the town and had at last driven out its evil spirit meted out cruel violence as they roamed the streets in bloodthirsty mobs. Private scores were savagely settled in the guise of punishing lawbreakers. Embittered sourdoughs and broke gamblers sought out those they blamed for bilking them. The streets of Skagway had never been more lawless.

Dazed and heartbroken, Tara sat alone in the dark cabin, holding John, and mourned. Lydia had disappeared, running off when she saw the columns of smoke rising over the town.

For Tara there was no sleep. Her fear and grief were too great to allow her anything more than a fitful doze, from which she continually roused herself with sudden shock. The baby was fretful, sensing the menace in the air, whimpering. She tried to give him a bottle, but he rejected it. He was upset and confused.

Although the cabin was gloomy, she did not light the lamps. For her, time stood still. The shock and melancholy of the past hours had sapped her strength. She sat staring into space, her mind a blank, her face pale and drawn, dark hollows circling her lifeless eyes. Then she heard the sound of horses outside and the creak of a wagon, followed by a hurried knocking on the door.

She opened it cautiously and saw Bowers standing there, but a different Bowers. The dog collar had gone, and so had the phony pious manner. Under his jacket he had on a checked shirt, and he wore heavy boots. He was armed.

"You got to get away," he said. "They're coming for you, I got to get you out."

"Who?" Tara blinked at him. She could see in the twilight behind him a wagon, hitched to two horses.

"Stop asking questions," he growled. "Grab the kid, quickly. They're going to burn you out."

He did not wait for her to say anything, but picked up John from his cot, wrapped him in blankets, and put him in her arms.

"No time to take anything. They'll be here soon."

"My bag." cried Tara.

"God almighty," he snarled impatiently, but he picked up the bag and pushed her out, shutting the door. "Quick," he ordered and helped her into the wagon. Then he climbed on and took the reins. The wagon rumbled off into the gloom, Tara shivering and clutching the baby to her.

Then she noticed a coffin on the floor of the cart. Her voice froze in her throat. She knew without asking that lying in that wooden box was Jefferson Smith.

The wagon creaked and bumped along a path away from town toward the hilly ground and the forest. She recalled the last wagon ride she had had from the cabin—in that swank four-wheel carriage with the smartly dressed driver, on her way to that glittering ball, to that wonderful night, to his arms.

They had been rumbling along for some twenty minutes when Bowers reined in the horses and pointed into the darkness. They were on high ground, overlooking the sprawl of Skagway, and she could see her cabin.

She could also see something else—scores of burning torches, dozens of horsemen, shadowy figures, gradually closing in on it. She was too far away to hear anything. Then suddenly a glow appeared, and the cabin flared up and became an inferno.

Without a word Bowers picked up the reins, and the wagon moved onward again, into wooded territory. Tara's eyes were transfixed by the blazing cabin that had been her home. She felt sick. She could imagine what would have happened if they had found her and the baby inside.

She could not remember, afterward, how long they traveled in the wagon, but finally Bowers pulled up. She was taken into a cave, cold, clammy. She cuddled the baby, holding him closer still, while Bowers lit a fire.

He crouched over it, warming his hands. The flames began to thaw Tara too.

"Nothing's left," said Bowers at last. "They've looted everything, burned it, the goddamn scavengers." He snorted. "Law-and-order men! Well, they got their law and order now."

Her mind was on the coffin, in the cart outside, but she asked quietly, "What about the others? Yeah Mow?"

"He's dead," shrugged Bowers. "They strung him up before he could get out of town. Mort's hightailing it to Dyea."

"How did you get away?"

He smiled for the first time. "I put my trust in the good Lord, Sister Tara. And I ran like hell."

He looked around the cave. "I know it's not the Ritz, but believe me, this is the best place right now for the likes of you and me."

Tara nodded. "What happens now?"

"Well, I got him outside." There was no need to explain more, and he knew it. "We'll take him to the graveyard at dawn and bury him. Couple of the boys will be there." He looked at her sharply. "We owe it to the boss," he added.

"Yes," she said simply.

"And after that, we'll get you and the kid away."

"And you?"

He stroked his stubbled chin. "Don't worry about me, Sister Tara. I guess the Lord will provide for a devoted servant." He said it mockingly, and she understood better than ever how it was that he and Smith were such close companions in crime.

They sat in silence for a long time. Bowers kept the fire blazing, and Tara stared into the flames, and her thoughts were her own.

Toward dawn she looked across at Bowers. "I can't believe what's happened," she murmured, a lump in her throat. "I can't understand why he let himself be provoked, why nobody stopped him."

He rubbed his eyes. He looked like a man who hadn't slept for forty-eight hours. "We tried," he said dully. "I begged him to let us deal with it. He said no. He said"—and suddenly he was staring straight into Tara's eyes—"he said it was something he had to do himself. He said he owed it, it was the right way, the only way, he said. Christ knows what got into him." He shook his head. "Any of us could have taken care of it. We wanted to. He looked like a guy who was out to prove something. But why?"

I could tell you, thought Tara. I could tell you a lot about the boss. But neither said any more.

It was half light when they set off from the cave, Tara huddled in the back of the wagon, the baby in her arms, staring at the wooden casket. And as they bumped along, she was sobbing silently. If Bowers, sitting with his back to her, was aware of her sorrow, he never said so.

Skagway's graveyard was a couple of miles out of town, at the start of the trail northward. A mountain stream flowed past it, and the little graves were surrounded by tall pine trees. Nobody had planned this cemetery. Way back, someone had been buried there, and next time a man died he was put there too. So, by default, a cemetery had been born. There were not many graves; far more men died along the trails, where they ended their days in unmarked mounds.

The drizzle that had begun when they left the cave had ceased by the time Bowers helped Tara off the wagon. He nodded to two men who were leaning on shovels, both of them chewing tobacco. They walked around to the back of the wagon and began dragging off the coffin.

Bowers guided Tara to the hole that already yawned in the muddy ground.

"Where's the priest?" she asked, looking around.

"The Baptist wouldn't listen, the Methodist refused, the Roman was out of town, and the Presbyterian said he wasn't sure. I couldn't find a Rabbi, so I guess it'll be up to us sinners." Bowers peered at Tara. "Like you and me."

The two men carried the casket to the grave and lowered it into the hole. Then they started unceremoniously shoveling in the earth.

"It's been good knowing you, Boss," Bowers murmured. "Keep a game going for me. The boys send their best, but you know how it is. Too many necktie parties going on, so they asked me to say it for 'em."

He stopped and glanced at Tara. She was staring into the grave, the tears drying on her face. She was not crying just for the man who had loved her; she was crying for the child she had lost, for the man she had not found, for all of them.

The wind rustled through the pines, and Tara felt unutterably sad.

Bowers stood beside her, and the men stopped shoveling for a moment. Then he threw in Smith's dice and a deck of cards.

"We'll never know who he might meet," he muttered. Then he nodded to the two men to continue shoveling. "Could be a great poker game. The boss with the Father, the Son, and the Holy Ghost. Amen. I know who'd win."

"Can you say a prayer for him?" Tara whispered. "Please."

Bowers shook his head. "Don't want to offend you, but the boss would die laughing. Me saying a prayer for him? No. You just think one."

So this is the end of the man who had been king, she thought, watching the plain coffin finally disappearing under the muddy earth. This furtive, hasty little excuse of a funeral, hidden away, early in the morning so that no one would know. How he would have resented it.

Jeff Smith would have arranged his own burial magnificently: an honor guard, a muffled drum, a brass band to play Chopin's Funeral March, probably even some saloon girls all dressed up in black and sobbing appropriately. He would have ensured that he was planted in the greatest of style.

And afterward there would have been champagne and speeches, and he would have looked down on it all from his new saloon in another world and grinned sardonically.

She held the baby close as she looked, for the last time, on Smith's resting place. Then she turned and walked back to the wagon. She climbed in and waited while Bowers paid off the two men. Then he got in and picked up the reins. Slowly the wagon moved off; in true Smith style, Tara never once looked back.

"You got a berth tomorrow. On the *Columbia*," Bowers told her as they jogged along. "She's a good ship, new, a steamer. I got you and the boy a cabin. She sails for Frisco on the tide."

"Tomorrow?" So quickly, so suddenly. The end of the Klondike? The end of her quest? She had thought that when the time came she would be pleased, but now she was flooded by a million doubts, a million regrets.

"The sooner you're out of this, the better," Bowers said. "It's all fixed. I'll give you the ticket when I collect you."

Tara said nothing.

"What the hell is there to stay for any more?" asked Bowers, glancing at her.

"Nothing," she mumbled.

Of course this was the only way. She had to think of the future; it wouldn't help either of them to live in the past. She had to think of John. But could she ever replace what she was leaving behind? Wouldn't so much of her always remain here, in this strange, savage, bitter land? With the two men who had mattered most in her life?

She gazed at the distant mountains, the rolling forests, and at that moment they looked beautiful. The memory of the pain, the anguish, the agony, the horror, the hardships, the misery, the cruelty of the Territory melted away because this country had given her so much more.

This icy land, which had torn so much out of her life, had been generous in many ways. She had John. She had regained her self-respect. She had found love again. And perhaps, one day, Daniel would come back. Perhaps, one day, they would be together again.

In her heart, heavy as it was, there remained hope.

That was for the future. The immediate was brought home by Bowers. "You got to hide away until the ship sails," he told her. "Don't be seen around the boss's old haunts."

He took them to a shack among some fir trees, and there Tara stayed out of sight. It was a lonely spot, way off the beaten track, and out of the path of the marauding packs still looking for members of the Soapy Smith gang.

There were some provisions, milk for the baby, and once the stove was lit the little shabby habitation became warm enough for Tara to stop shivering.

"You'll be OK here," Bowers assured her. "Just don't wander about. I'll get you aboard the boat, never worry."

"You haven't told me one thing," said Tara.

"And what's that?" he asked.

"Why you're doing all this for me—and for him." She nodded at the boy, sleeping in his blankets.

He shrugged. "You know me, Sister Tara. I always obey orders." He allowed himself a wry grin.

She knew he was risking his life to stay behind and protect her. He could have got out of town with Mort, ahead of the mob fury; as long as he was in Skagway, someone might spot him. Then there would be little justice for Smith's right-hand man.

He seemed to read her mind. "Oh, don't fret," he said. "The guy who gets the better of Charley Bowers hasn't sucked his mother's milk yet." He chuckled. "The Lord willing," he added in mock piety.

He left her, promising he would be back in good time for her to reach the ship.

It was only after he had gone that Tara gave way to sorrow. But there was no one there to see it and only she knew whom she was crying for.

A couple of times the timbers of the log shack creaked. She raised her tear-stained face to the door as if she expected to see Smith standing there, smiling at her nonchalantly, puffing his constant cheroot, slowly walking over, taking her in his arms.

But it was only the wind, and the room remained bare and friendless, and the terrible empty sense of having lost the man she loved filled her with a sadness she had never known.

CHAPTER TWENTY-NINE

Bowers had changed again when he came for Tara. His appearance was citified; to the eyes of the townsfolk he was a dude to his toecaps. He had a big shawl to cover Tara's head.

"If anyone stops us, you're my lady wife," he said. "Mr. and Mrs.

Jenkinson, and their little boy. I work for the White Pass Railway Company, and you and the baby have come out to join me."

In the event, the journey through Skagway passed without incident. The town had calmed down after its orgy of violence. No one took any notice of the couple and their baby driving down the street.

Bowers pulled up at the quay. The *Columbia* already had steam up.

"You'd better get on," said Bowers gruffly. He handed her the ticket.

"Charley," began Tara, but the words died on her lips.

"This is for you too," he grunted, "from Jeff."

He had pulled out a sealed envelope, and he gave it to her.

He stood looking at her awkwardly. "Well, guess this is it, Sister Tara."

She nodded, too choked to speak.

Then he turned and rapidly walked away like a man not trusting himself to say anything.

Holding John tightly in her arms and clutching the ticket and the envelope, Tara slowly walked up the gangway.

The *Columbia* was a smart, well-appointed ship. Tara found, to her surprise, that Bowers had booked her a first-class passage. She was shown to a neat and tidy cabin on the top passenger deck. Already a cot for John had been set up. Bowers had taken much trouble for his boss.

"Oh Jeff, Jeff," sighed Tara but she held back her tears.

She went back on deck, John in her arms. A young boy was selling *The Skagway Intelligencer* and Tara bought a copy. For her it was the final edition, the final souvenir of the town, the Klondike. At the rail she gazed for the last time at Skagway, beyond it the White Pass. On the quayside stood Bowers. She waved to him and held the baby up to wave too.

As each line was taken in, another link with Alaska was broken and her heart seemed to ache a little more. The engines grew louder, and around her other passengers waved to the well-wishers on the dockside. Bowers had disappeared.

"Goodbye Skagway, goodbye Alaska, goodbye," Tara whispered. As the ship gently eased away from its mooring, her sense of loss was like a physical pain.

She stayed on the deck for a long time, watching Skagway recede and with it, gradually, the Yukon. She stood as the *Columbia* steamed through the majestic panorama of the Lynn Canal. She could see, far away, foaming waterfalls cascading down, huge masses of crystal twisted into fantastic shapes, endless stretches of woods.

It had been a land of magic; a living, exciting, challenging world she would never forget. She had crossed it, she had survived it, and it would always be part of her. But it was fading, the great icy kingdom, the all-pervading solitude. When finally the *Columbia* passed Cape Fox, the last tip of British Columbia, Tara knew the past had gone.

Then she remembered the letter Bowers had handed her. She went below to her cabin, where she had left it on the little night table next to her bunk.

She sat down, with John on her lap and, slowly, she opened the envelope. There was a note:

My dearest Tara:
When you open this I'll be played out. I don't know when I'll be dead but I am putting this into good hands in case it ever happens. You won't get it unless I've finally thrown in my cards. I hope that will never be, because there's so much I want to do with you. So you'll never read this, if I'm lucky.
I love you.

Jeff.

There was something else in the envelope. She held in her hand a banker's draft addressed to the Bank of California, Market Square, San Francisco: a certified draft payable to Mrs. Tara Kane for the sum of one hundred thousand dollars in gold, signed, with a flourish, Jefferson Randolph Smith.

For a long time Tara stared at the check. One hundred thousand dollars. Then she put John's tiny hands on it.

"It's yours, my love. With love from your godfather," she said, bending down and brushing his forehead with her lips.

"Thank you, Jeff. Thank you so very much dear, kind, wonderful man," she whispered.

After she had put John down, Tara sat on her bunk and opened the newspaper. The front page was dominated by a photograph of Reid, lying dead, surrounded by several worthy-looking Skagway citizens. Under it was an article headed:

SMITH'S KILLER NAMED. GUNMAN WAS ON RAILROAD PAYROLL
Skagway, 10th July
The man who shot down Jefferson Smith was a newly hired railroad employee, local company officials have confirmed.

According to them, he was a down on his luck gold miner

407

whose prospecting fortunes had failed, and had been hired only twenty-four hours before to ride shotgun on high-value consignments.

But Sir Thomas Tancrede, railroad boss, told the *Intelligencer* that the man at the time of the shoot-out "was not on company business."

"While we are not unhappy that the community have been rid of Mr. Soapy Smith and his ilk, we did not hire a gunman to kill him. The man was simply a recent employee of ours," he declared.

Asked why the killer should have taken on Mr. Smith, Sir Thomas Tancrede said he had no idea, "but there must be a lot of people who had their own reasons for wanting to see Smith dead," he added.

The gunman, after firing the fatal shot, died immediately from Smith's bullet. He never spoke, but the railroad have named him as Daniel Kane, 27, of San Francisco. Kane came to the Klondike about a year ago.

"It can't be," Tara pleaded, "it can't be true."

She read the piece over and over again, the words slowly sinking in. But she could not believe that she had seen Daniel kill Smith without knowing. That she had been less than ten feet away from him and not recognized Daniel. That she had stood by without sensing, knowing what was going on. That she had gone off with Smith and left her own husband dying in the street alone, abandoned. And that while Daniel lay dying, she had agreed to become another man's wife.

She had to go back. She had to be sure. Then something she had said long ago to Linda Miles came back to her: There could be no turning back.

Perhaps that was how fate had intended it to be all along. In less than a year her life had turned full circle, and there was a price to be paid. Already she had been deprived of the two men she loved—would ever love.

Stunned and desolate, Tara wrapped herself in her cloak, kissed the baby, and although it was past midnight went up on deck. She stared across the black sea. Before her stretched a rippling astral carpet, the silvery moon undulating in a liquid abyss. It was entrancing, beautiful, hypnotic, calling.

And it reminded Tara of another natural phenomenon—the Aurora Borealis. That had been a sign from heaven in the frozen wilderness. This was also a promise.

"Dear God," she sobbed, looking up at the sky. "You have taken so much from me, but you've given me the greatest gift of all. I have John, a future to live for, and that is one thing for sure. Who knows what lies ahead but, with your help, I'll get through." Always one day at a time.